Same Sun Here

Same Sun Here

SILAS HOUSE
AND
NEELA VASWANI

CANDLEWICK PRESS

Copyright © 2011 by Silas House and Neela Vaswani

Illustrations copyright © 2011 by Hilary Schenker

Photographs on pages 30, 58, and 231 courtesy of Silas House
Photographs on page 213 © Terraxplorer/iStockphoto;
© Steffen Foerster/iStockphoto; © Michael Courtney/iStockphoto
Photograph on page 214 © Mlenny/iStockphoto
Illustration on page 215 © Chen Fu Soh/iStockphoto
Photograph on page 288 courtesy of Lisa Parker

First edition 2012

Library of Congress Cataloging-in-Publication Data
House, Silas, date.
Same sun here / Silas House and Neela Vaswani. — 1st ed.
p.   cm.
Summary: A twelve-year-old Indian immigrant in New York City and a Kentucky coal miner's son become pen pals, and eventually best friends, through a series of revealing letters exploring such topics as environmental activism, immigration, and racism.
ISBN 978-0-7636-5684-3
[1. Pen pals—Fiction. 2. East Indian Americans—Fiction.
3. Letters—Fiction.]   I. Vaswani, Neela, date. II. Title.
PZ7.H81558Sam 2011
[Fic]—dc22   2010048223

11 12 13 14 15 16 BVG 10 9 8 7 6 5 4 3 2 1

Printed in Berryville, VA, U.S.A.

This book was typeset in Cheltenham.
The illustrations were done in ink and pencil.

Candlewick Press
99 Dover Street
Somerville, Massachusetts 02144

visit us at www.candlewick.com

For Donna Conley
and in memory of Judy Bonds
S. H.

For children who carry another home in their hearts
and for courageous adults learning to read and write
N. V.

August 2, 2008

Dear River,

    I cannot tell from your name if you are a boy or a girl so I will just write to you like you are a human being.

    You are the first American I know whose name means something, so I think maybe you are not from this country. My brother says you are. He says all people in Kentucky are Americans—not like in New York City, where most people are from everywhere in the world.

    My brother is seventeen years old. He has a big smile and strong legs because he is a bike messenger. All the girls love him, which makes him very conceited. Personally, I don't think the girls would love him anymore if they had to pick his smelly socks up off the floor, like I do.

    When I first came here, I didn't like NY, but my brother helped me find appreciation by telling me interesting things. For example, did you know there's a curse on the Brooklyn Bridge? When my brother looks at something, he sees how it works. He is like that about things like skyscrapers and subways. Next year, he will be a student at CUNY. He wants to make a great invention so he can go to MIT for free. He may have smelly feet, but he is still my favorite human being. I say human being because I have a favorite dog (his name is Cuba) and a favorite parakeet (her name is Xie-Xie).

You know what goes with rivers? Fish. My name is Meena and that means "fish." Everyone in my family calls me Mee-Mee. I am twelve years old. I like to run up and down the stairs of our building, and I can go all five flights without stopping. I like to feed pigeons, even though it's against the law, and I like to read books from the Seward Park Library, which is eight blocks from here. This week, I borrowed <u>A Tree Grows in Brooklyn</u>, a novel by Betty Smith. I am on page 92, and it is sad and very exciting.

I think you're like me and don't have a computer, since your name was on the snail mail list. I could go to the library and send you an e-mail from my brother's Yahoo, but the line is always long and you only get a half hour and I type very slow like a turtle. Kiku (that is what we call my brother, but his real name is Karan) has a computer, but he always keeps it with him in his backpack. Anyway, I am used to writing letters, because my grandmother doesn't have a phone. And I am reading in my book about a girl named Francie who lived in 1912 when there were no computers. I have decided that I want to be like her.

I wonder what you look like. I am short and skinny. This is a good thing for squeezing on the subway. But I would rather be like Kiku's secret girlfriend, Ana Maria, who is so pretty she stops traffic. I do think my hair is nice. It is long and black like Ana Maria's, but hers is curly and mine is straight.

I guess I should tell you more about myself. I was born in India, in a town called Mussoorie, in the youngest and highest mountains in the world. Mussoorie is the most beautiful place I have ever seen. Everywhere you look, there is mountain and sky, and some days we are lost in the clouds. The trees are always full of birds with clear voices and monkeys with long tails and bad tempers.

When I was nine years old, Dadi (my grandmother) brought me to New Delhi (the capital of India) on the train. It took eight hours to get there. Then we went to the airport and I flew to America by myself. That took twenty-two hours, with a stopover in Germany. I felt cold and sick in my stomach the whole entire time. I think if human beings were meant to fly around in the sky, we would have been born with wings.

Mum and Daddy and Kiku have been in America nine years. They got here two years before 9/11. They left Mussoorie when I was three years old. It took them a long time to save enough money to bring me over, and I did not recognize them at the airport. It was strange to look into all the faces and not know if any of the people were my mother or father.

I came here on the H-4 visa. That means I can't work but I can go to school. Daddy says I should always tell Americans about my visa so they don't think I'm illegal. This year, my parents will apply for naturalization. They just got their I-551 Alien Registration Cards in the mail, so in about a year, maybe, maybe, they will be citizens. You should see the amount of papers and phone calls it takes to become an American. Mum says it is like having another job. I think it's funny that we have Alien Cards — as if we come from outer space! I promise, I don't have any antennae on my head. I am 100% Homo sapiens.

Daddy says soon we can bring Dadi over to this side. I do not think she will come. I do not think she could wake up in the mornings if the mountains were not there. In New York, the buildings are like mountains in some ways, but they are only alive because of the people living in them. Real mountains are alive all over.

Have you ever been to New York City? It is hot and smelly in the summertime. Our street smells like dog pee and garbage. Everything bakes on the pavement, and there are so many tourists you can't take a step without someone asking you for directions.

I love to walk around and look at everything and everyone. I love to ride the subway, especially the 7 train because it pops above ground in Queens. We live in Chinatown, on the corner of Orchard and Hester. The F train on Delancey is very nearby. Every Friday afternoon, I take the laundry to the Suds-o-Rama in my neighbor Mrs. Lau's little red cart. She gives me quarters for the machine, and in trade I do her laundry with ours. She is seventy-two years old and has hard times getting up and down the stairs.

My mum takes care of two little children, one boy, one girl, on the Upper West Side. She is their nanny. Our family doesn't have a nanny or a maid, so I do our laundry. I hate dragging the big bag up and down the stairs, but if I didn't do it, none of us would have clean clothes. This is what I tell myself every Friday. I do the laundry on Friday afternoons before Mum comes home so that we have time for fun on the weekend when she does not have to go away.

Daddy works at a big restaurant in New Jersey. It is thirty miles away from here, but in NY it takes two hours to go thirty miles because of all the traffic. Daddy rides a bus home one weekend a month, and even then he is tired but he tries to pretend that he isn't and he takes us out someplace nice to have a good time. Mum always cries when he packs. And when it is time for him to go, he has to pull her fingers away from his arm and rush out the door.

Even though we live on the corner, it's quiet on the fifth floor because we are high above the street. We live in a one-bedroom apartment with rent control. We have five windows, and two of them have a view onto Orchard Street. The other three windows face shaftways where there are piles of stinky garbage. It's dark in the apartment except in the bedroom, where the sun reaches. Since it is summer, the sun goes across the bed from 1:00 to 3:00 p.m. Mum says Orchard Street is depressing. She says India is better for her and Daddy, but here is better for me and Kiku.

When Daddy comes home, I sleep on the couch and Kiku sleeps on the cot. When Daddy is away, Mum and I share the bed and Kiku sleeps on the couch. I want to get a job and help like Kiku does, but Mum says not till I am older. I want to make a lot of money so I can always keep my family together, and so I can get them a dishwasher and an air conditioner.

Right now I am sitting on the fire escape, where I can see the street and all the cars and the tops of people's heads and a little square of blue sky between the buildings. It is so hot today that the delis on Delancey have brought their flowers inside. Mrs. Lau, who has the NY1 channel, says there is a smog alert.

If I lean over the railing, I can see the pagoda trees. There are four on our side of the street. I know they are pagoda trees because the middle one has a tiny sign nailed to the trunk that says, PAGODA TREE.

This morning all of these trees let go of their flowers. Pagoda flowers look white on the tree, but when they fall on the pavement, they look yellowy green. Just a few hours ago, I helped Mrs. Lau down the stairs, and we swept up the yellow petals in front of our building. *Swish swish* went our brooms, up and down the street.

Cuba sat on the stoop and watched. He is old now, and when I walk him, I don't have to use a leash. He stays close to me, and if he gets ahead, he stops and waits at the corner. Cuba is black except for the white star on his chest. He gets very hot in the sun in his thick fur. Today, he lay on the steps, panting, with his tongue hanging to the pavement and his body going fast, up and down, up and down.

When the ice-cream man drove by, Mrs. Lau flagged

him down by waving her handkerchief, and she bought me a raspberry ice. The man also gave us a little bowl of water for Cuba, and when I put it in front of him, he wagged his tail to say thank you. He has the prettiest brown eyes and very good manners. I gave him the last bit of my ice because he looked at me like he wanted to taste it. I guess maybe he hypnotized me. You know how dogs can do that? Kiku calls it "canine mind control."

After sweeping, we sat on the stoop and watched all the people walking by, and Mrs. Lau told stories. One story she told was about how Cuba got his name. Guess how! OK, since this is a letter, I'll just tell you. She named him after the country her best lover came from!!!! She said he's been dead for thirty years but she still misses him. Isn't that funny and kind of sweet?

Mrs. Lau has been in America twice as long as she was ever in Hong Kong. She has lived in her apartment for fifty-five years. She says NY Chinatown is home. In six years, I will have been in America for the same number of years as India. I still miss the mountains every day.

By the way, I used to speak English more like a British person, because that is how we do it in India. But when I came to the States, Kiku taught me how to talk like an American.

I wonder how you got your name.

Here is a picture I drew of Mrs. Lau and Cuba on the stoop:

I don't usually talk this much unless I've had a Coca-Cola. Usually I am quiet. But you're easy to talk to, River. My hand really hurts, and I bet, if you're still reading, that your eyes are hurting. My brother is looking over my shoulder now and saying I wrote too much and you probably won't write me back because you will think I am a crazy person. But he is a big dummy and smelly, too, which is not surprising because he is wearing his OBAMA FOR PRESIDENT T-shirt for the *third* day in a row. (He is completely obsessed with the election and goes around quoting Obama all the time, like a lunatic.)

I hope you do not think I am a crazy person. It is very nice to meet you, River. I hope you are having lots of good fun in Kentucky, and I hope you will write and tell me about yourself.

Your (hopefully) pen pal,
Meena Joshi

P.S. My brother says there was a famous movie star who died a long time ago with your name. Is this true?

P.P.S. We live five blocks away from the East River in New York City. Do you live near a river, too? Also, what kind of music do you like?

10 August 2008

Dear Meena,

I am real pleased to meet you. I am going to just get right at it and answer your questions and tell you everything I can think of, as I have been wanting to write you ever since receiving your letter, which I have read four times now.

Well, I am a boy. My mother named me River because she loved growing up on the Cumberland River and because her and my father's first date was at this restaurant down on the Powell River. We have all kinds of rivers and creeks here. Did you know that Kentucky has more waterways than any other state except Alaska? I always thought that was real interesting. I like knowing things like that, although nobody else I know really cares.

I have never met anybody from New York City before. I've always heard that people from up there are real rude and will not hold the door for you, and you'll get mugged if you walk down the street. Is this true? My mamaw says it is probably a stereotype, which I looked up in the dictionary and it means "an oversimplified opinion." She also said to remember the Golden Rule, which she says a lot. She is real big on the Golden Rule, which is from the Bible, I guess. I don't have time to look it up right now. Do you believe in the Bible? Since you are an Indian, I don't really know.

Mom used to make me go to church with her every Sunday, but she doesn't go anymore, because she's sick. It wasn't too bad, I guess, but I didn't much like going to Sunday school, where it always smelled like chalk and they only had grape Kool-Aid, which I despise. Mamaw quit going to church a long time ago because the preacher said something about women's rights that made her mad, and she never did go back. But every Sunday she reads to us from the Bible and she prays all the time, loud.

My mother and I live with Mamaw now. We used to have our own good house up on Free Creek, but now we live over here right outside the town of Black Banks, in the house my daddy grew up in. Daddy used to be a coal miner who went waaaaay back in the mountain to work, but the underground miners are all losing their jobs, so he had to go down to Biloxi, Mississippi, to find work. He is having to live down there while they rebuild Biloxi from where Hurricane Katrina ruined everything. My mother used to work in the school lunchroom, but now she has the blues all the time. She also gets sick headaches and has to take to bed. Sometimes I hold a wet washrag to her forehead and tell her all about my day, but usually I am with Mamaw most of the time.

You said your brother was your favorite human. Well, mine is Mamaw. Almost every day we climb the path up the mountain and she tells me the names of all the trees, or we go along very quiet and watch the ground for treasures. We have a nature collection that has things in it like feathers from blue jays and redbirds, chips of quartz, buckeyes, acorns, hickory nuts, and lots more. My other favorite thing to do with her is when we go fishing together in Lost Creek, which is full of bluegill (my father and I used to go fishing all the time, before he left). Mamaw and I clean them together and then she dips them in milk, and then meal and flour, and fries them. They're delicious. Mamaw is the best cook in the world. This evening she is making my favorite meal: pork chops, biscuit and gravy, fried potatoes, and fried apples. I can't wait. What's your favorite meal? I guess my second favorite meal is fish, hush puppies, and fried potatoes.

The reason I'm not on the e-mail list is because I thought it'd be cooler to write letters to somebody, since I can write e-mails to anybody. Lots of my friends just play Nintendo or get on the Internet all the time, but I have never been much for that. I only like to get online if I'm looking up something, not to play games or check e-mail. I don't know why. I think it's boring.

I'm weird I guess. I mean, none of my friends really wants to spend that much time with their grandmothers. Or at least they don't admit it. Mamaw says it is all right to be weird and that if the end of the world came I'd know how to survive, and the rest of the people my age would only sit in front of their dead computers and not know what to do. I believe Mamaw likes being on the computer better than I do. She is on there all the time researching stuff, because she is what is called an activist.

Anyway, that's why when Ms. Stidham put out the sign-up sheet for pen pals that I only put down my mailing address and not my e-mail address (I have one, but I just don't check it much). Mamaw was real proud of me because of this. She says that everyone used to write long letters all the time and it is a lost art form. I don't see what's so arty about it, but I like to do it. Sometimes I think I'd like to be a newspaper reporter.

I can't tell any of my friends at school these things because they'd make fun of me too bad. I am real good at basketball, so that's all I talk about with them. Let's say right now that we can tell each other our secrets and we won't make fun of each other. Don't take this the wrong way, but you sound weird, too. I am glad of it, because I can be my own true self with you. Maybe it's because of your looooong letter. Nobody ever wrote me that much, ever. I'm glad it was long, though. And maybe because our names go together so good.

Why did you pick me to write to?

I've never read <u>A Tree Grows in Brooklyn</u>, but I looked at it in the library and it's pretty thick. It looks kind of girly. Is it? When I was little I was obsessed with the Spiderwick Chronicles and Beverly Cleary, especially <u>Dear Mr. Henshaw</u> and <u>Strider</u>. But my favorite author ever is S. E. Hinton, especially <u>The Outsiders</u>. That book has characters in it who are their own true selves, only with each other, too, and I guess it's my favorite of all time. S. E. Hinton (who is a GIRL if you can believe it!) was only four years older than me when she wrote it. That blows my mind. I don't get to read as much as I used to because of basketball practice. If you're wondering why I underlined the titles it's because you're supposed to, to be grammatically correct. Ms. Stidham is real strict about stuff like that. She says that since people all over the world think we're stupid here in Kentucky, we have to make sure we have good grammar skills. She says that we can have accents and talk any way we want to as long as we're speaking correctly. So I try to have real good grammar. She's the only teacher I know who makes us all want to learn and doesn't tell lame jokes.

I would die if I had to do the laundry. That's like the worst possible thing I can think of. What are you some kind of saint or something? LOL.

I liked your drawing of Mrs. Lau and the dog. Did you REALLY draw that? It's REALLY, REALLY good. You should think about becoming an artist. You have good handwriting, too. I don't see how you wrote all of that loooooooong letter by hand. I would have been worn out. Once I had to write "I will not talk during arithmetic class" 500 times for my teacher, and I thought I was going to fall over dead before I got finished. I put two pencils together, one on top of the other one, so that I could write it twice at one time. Have you ever tried doing that? It works pretty good, but better if you're doing it on college-lined paper, because the lines are closer together. Just a little trick in case you ever get in trouble for talking in school.

I better go. Time for basketball practice.

Take it easy, Cheesy (ha!),
River Dean Justice

August 16, 2008

Dear River,

Hello from New York City!! Thank you for saying you liked my drawing of Mrs. Lau and Cuba. I think my handwriting is messy, so I am glad you think it's neat.

It was nice of you to say those things, but I am wondering, why did you call me weird and cheesy? Also, I'm not "some kind of saint." You wrote LOL after that but I couldn't tell if you meant it nice or mean. I don't mind doing the laundry, even on a Friday. I don't think you would mind either if you had lived far away from your mom and dad and brother for seven years. I am glad to finally be with them. If you want to know the truth, I think Americans have it easy. I was raised to do whatever is best for everyone in my family — even if it is something that is not fun or relaxing for me. Mum would say I shouldn't say rude things about Americans to an American. But I guess I already said it, so it is too late.

You asked how come I picked your name and address, so I will tell you. Kiku always says, "Tell the short version of the story or I'm not going to listen." He thinks he is Mr. Cool and he is so not. Anyway, I like long stories. I hope that is OK with you.

I think this has been a lucky summer. First, I got into the Arts and Humanities Summer Program by writing an essay about Mrs. Lau and how we are friends. Second, Ms. Bledsoe, my teacher at the Summer Program, is really nice. Every week we go someplace new, and it is all free. This week we went to Ellis Island. It was so interesting, all the different people and photographs. My favorite picture was of a little boy who got sent back to Italy alone because he had tuberculosis. I liked the picture because I could see what he was feeling by looking at his face. Everything at Ellis Island reminded me of our family, except that we came on planes not boats.

Last month we went to the Van Cortlandt House, where Dutch people lived a long time ago; the Brooklyn Botanic Garden, where the red hibiscus is blooming; and the Tenement Museum, where we saw what life was like in Chinatown in the 1880s. Back then it was a Jewish, Italian, German, and Irish neighborhood. We also wrote a group letter to Mayor Bloomberg. I love to write. Whenever I put my pen on paper, I cannot stop. When I grow up, I want to be a poet.

I also love fruits and vegetables, and actually that is how I came to be writing to you.

Ms. Bledsoe took the Summer Group to the supermarket last week. Everybody said it was a lame field trip, but I was excited. Ms. Bledsoe says city kids don't think about where things come from, especially food. She's from North Carolina and grew up on a farm. She talked about how food is shipped into the city and how big trucks use a lot of gas and that young men and women fight wars over things like gas. She told us to be mindful of what we waste and use. I like that word: mindful. It makes me feel like my brain is a big bowl brimming over.

So we went to a D'Agostino (that's a grocery store) on Essex Street and stood in the vegetable section. Some of the lettuce was getting watered from little sprinklers and we got wet. Ms. Bledsoe picked up an apple and said that in NY, apples get picked off the trees in October, so for us to have apples in August means they have traveled a great distance.

We looked at the labels on the apples. Some were from Israel. Some from Washington State. Ms. Bledsoe said we should picture those places on the map, to see how far the apples had come. While she was talking I saw a pile of okra. I thought maybe it had come from India, like me. It was in a wooden box that said KENTUCKY on the side, and there was a picture of mountains. I looked at the okra and the mountains and I wanted to go to Kentucky. It looked just like home.

When we got back to class, Ms. Bledsoe handed out a list of names and addresses. She said the assignment was to pick a pen pal and write a letter. Everyone said this was stupid and babyish, but I thought it sounded like fun. All the other kids wanted to do e-mails, but I wanted to write a real letter and put a pretty stamp on it, so I got a different list. There were lots of names and addresses on the list, kids from all over. Malaysia, Scotland, Hawaii, Trinidad, Moscow. Everyone, even Ms. Bledsoe, thought I would pick someone from India. But all the addresses were in New Delhi, and I didn't like it there the one day I saw it. When I saw your name and that you live in Kentucky, I wanted to write to you.

Do you grow okra? If you do, I will send you my grandmother's recipe for भिंडी = OKRA *bhindi.* That's how you say okra in Hindi.

Hmmm. I guess I told the realllllly long version of the story. Sorry about that.

I have to go help Mum make dinner now, but I will write you more very soon. I am wanting to talk to you about basketball and those nice walks you take with your mamaw.

I hope you are having a nice day.

Your pen pal,
Meena Joshi

P.S. Please write a longer letter next time.

P.P.S. Sorry if that was bossy.

23 August 2008

Dear Meena,

Sorry my last letter wasn't longer. I was running late for basketball practice and just wanted to get something in the mail to you. But I still don't think I can write as much as you.

You asked what I look like. I am redheaded, with freckles all across my nose and shoulders. Mamaw says the freckles are because our people are originally from Scotland and Ireland. So I guess when you really think about it, we are all from some other place, way off across the ocean. Mamaw is half Cherokee, so I have her big nose. People give me a hard time about it and call me Toucan Sam sometimes, but I don't care. I kind of like my nose. Mamaw says I will grow into it and it will be the best thing about me. I wish I was taller so I could be a better basketball player. Lately I have been doing this leg-stretching exercise my buddy Mark told me about, where you squat down and put one leg at a time out behind you as far as you can. It's supposed to make you taller. I've only been doing it a week and already, according to my measuring tape, I have grown 1/16 of an inch. It's pretty amazing.

It's weird that you are originally from the mountains, because that's where I live now. I looked up where you were born online, and it's cool because the mountains there look so much like mine, with pine trees and everything. I always expected India to only have big palm trees, for some reason. You said your mamaw wouldn't come to America because she would miss the mountains too much, so maybe she could move here instead of New York City. At least that way she'd be way closer to you than she is now, way over in India, and I bet she'd like the mountains here. My uncle sells houses and could find her a place. Let me know if you need help with this.

We have an Indian who lives here, Dr. Patel. My mamaw goes to him because she has sugar diabetes, and they are always laughing together. He says that she reminds him of his mother, and you should hear the way he says "Mama Justice" (that's what he calls her). It's funny with his accent, although Mamaw says it's not polite to laugh at him over that and that he must be real smart to be able to even learn our language and to be a doctor besides. We have seen him and his wife at the Piggly Wiggly before, and she has a red dot on her forehead. Do you? I would like to know how those things work. Are they glued on there, or is it a Magic Marker, or what? I don't understand, and Mamaw always elbows me when I stare at her.

My father is nothing like Mamaw, though. He is always making fun of anybody who is different. He used to say the N-word all the time (especially when we were watching basketball), but now he is friends with all kinds of black people down there in Biloxi. He works with them. So I wonder if he still says that word. I hope not. It makes me feel tight inside, like I am smothering.

You asked if I have been to New York City. HA!!! I've never been anywhere except to Dollywood, which is a big amusement park not too far away, with this awesome roller coaster called the Thunderhead. You should ride it sometime. When somebody is real sick they get sent to the hospital in Knoxville, and that's where Mom used to go to shop for my school clothes on Tax Free Day, so I have been there a few times. It's the only city I really know, but it's too loud and there are too many cars. The houses are right on top of each other. I don't believe I could stand it without my woods.

You asked me about music. (We have been studying poetry at school and how it doesn't have to rhyme, so I think I'll write this next part like a poem.)

I mostly like music that my parents
were always playing back when we all lived
together on Free Creek. Sometimes, in the
evenings, Daddy would put on his
favorite album, which was by Tom Petty,
and he'd play this song called "Wildflowers."
Daddy would put me up on his hip and
Mom would lean in real close and we were like
a circle going round and round the room.
This one time I remember Mom putting
her head against Daddy's and singing all
the words with her eyes closed. Sometimes I think
that was the last time we were all together,
but I don't know if I just have that mixed up
in my mind or not. When I am missing
my parents real bad I put on that CD

and listen to it and feel sadder,

even during the real fast and happy songs.

Actually, one reason I did that was because my English teacher gave us homework to write a poem about a memory, and so after I typed that I realized it was a memory and I could kill two birds with one stone by writing to you about it but also making the poem for English class. Do you think it's any good? Ms. Stidham says that the main thing is to make every line of poetry a mystery so that the reader wants to go on and read the next line. I thought that was pretty cool, when she said that, because I always thought the most important thing was to make it rhyme, but she said, no, and that nowadays poems that rhyme are kind of lame. We all laughed because it was funny to hear a teacher say something is lame. Don't you think so? The only poetry I have ever really read is Sharon Creech stuff, like in <u>Love That Dog</u>. And I love this poem by Joyce Kilmer, but the only part I know by heart is "I think that I shall never see a poem lovely as a tree." Mamaw recites the whole poem sometimes when we are out walking in the hills. She says it real loud, the way preachers will boom out a big prayer sometimes right in the middle of church.

Anyway, I did try to put in as much mystery in my poem as I could, but I still don't know what to call it. I've been reading it over and over but I can't think of a title. I think I'll just call it "My Memory Poem." Or maybe "Wildflowers" or maybe "A Memory." I don't know.

Oh, there is one more thing you need to know to meet me. I also have a dog, Rufus, who is the best dog that ever was. Everybody says so. I have had him since I was four years old (I am 12 now), and he is the best friend anybody could ever ask for. He will run around and play with me if I'm in the mood for that, or he will sit real quiet with me and look out at the mountains, too, if that's what I'm in the mood for. He always goes along with me and Mamaw when we go walking in the cool of the day. That's what Mamaw calls it, the cool of the day. When we go fishing, Rufus just lies down on the creek bank with his chin on top of his paws—until we start to reel in a fish. Then he gets so excited that he runs back and forth along the water's edge with his tail wagging and his whole butt shaking, he's so wound up.

Rufus smiles all the time. Have you ever seen a smiling dog? I don't know what kind he is. "You old mutt," Daddy always says, and gives him a good pat on the side. Mamaw thinks he has beagle, blue heeler, Jack Russell, and maybe even some pit bull. I've put a picture of him in here. It's not a very good one because he moves around so much that it's hard to take a picture of him. But I got him to lie still by rubbing his belly.

About that okra: Mamaw grows a big garden and okra is one of her favorite things. She says it's beautiful to look at and delicious to eat. When it's ready, she slices it up and soaks it in buttermilk, then rolls it in meal and flour and fries it in the skillet. It's delicious, especially with fried green tomatoes. One time Daddy was eating some of Mamaw's okra, and he said, "This is so good you have to pat your foot to eat it," and we all laughed like it was way funnier than it really was. Have you ever had a fried green tomato? It is the best thing in the world, guaranteed.

I guess I better go and get my chores done. I have to mow the yard this evening. I can't believe I wrote so much, but that's what happens when I get to typing. My mother taught me to type when I was only eight because she said that a person can't do anything nowadays if they don't know their way around a computer. And I can type almost as good as I can play basketball. I'm not meaning to brag, it's just that those are the only two things I can really do good at all. I suck at lots of things, especially mechanical things. Mamaw is all the time having to put the chain back on my bicycle, because I never can figure out how. I'm terrible at cooking, too. I can't even make a peanut-butter sandwich right. I always tear the bread when I'm trying to spread the peanut butter.

What are you good at?

I sure hope you'll write me back. Tell me more about New York City. I can't imagine what it is like to live there with all those taxi cabs and people in suits and going to plays all the time and eating at the Rainbow Room. I don't believe I'd like it, but it sounds like an exciting place to visit.

Sincerely yours,
River Dean Justice

P.S. The movie star your brother is thinking of is River Phoenix, who died two or three years before I was born. My mother always loved him, but I'm not really named for him as much as I am for the rivers of this place.

P.P.S. Sorry this letter is typed on paper that has already been used on one side, but Ms. Stidham taught us all about the environment last year and she says that it's better to reuse before you recycle, so that's what I'm doing here. Just ignore the writing on the back; it's just stuff Mamaw had typed out about some kind of mining she's getting informed about. She is always saying that she's getting informed about something.

August 27, 2008

Dear River,

Thank you for your letter!!! It was as good as reading a book. I put Rufus's photograph under my library card in my box of Special Things. I keep the box hidden behind the sack of rice in the kitchen closet. Nobody, not even Kiku, knows about this hiding place. It is also where I keep my watch set to India time so I always know when Dadi is sleeping.

I have been thinking of what you said—that we can tell each other secrets and be our own true selves. That sounds very nice to me.

I think it is cool that you play basketball. There is a basketball court near here, and I like to watch Kiku and his friends play. Kiku taught me H-O-R-S-E, and sometimes he picks me up so I am almost as tall as the basket and I toss the ball into the net. I guess that is cheating in real basketball, but Kiku says for me it is OK. What is it like to play a real game? It must feel good when everyone cheers for you.

I would like to try eating okra the way your mamaw makes it. It sounds delicious. Dadi and I used to watch the okra leaves in her garden turn to follow the sun across the sky, from east to west. It was like a kind of magic. I am so happy to know that you live in mountains full of okra. And no, I have never eaten a fried green tomato before.

I wonder if we can mail things like tomatoes to each other?

I like that your poem is about how things used to be in your family. You should keep writing lots and lots of beautiful poems until you have enough to fill a book. And I think it's super funny that your teacher said "lame"!

On the subway, there is something called Poetry in Motion. Poems are printed up above the seats so that when you are sitting there on your way to the next station, you have something to think about. I read a poem on the subway that rhymed called "I Know Why the Caged Bird Sings." I never knew before that the title of a poem could be a whole long sentence, did you? Actually, maybe you could do that for your poem! Maybe you could call it "We Were Like a Circle" or "What We Used to Be."

This month there is a poem printed in the subway

called "Quarrel." It's like something you'd overhear walking down the street. I memorized it because it's short and
because I was on the F train for a long time. It doesn't
rhyme, so maybe you will like it:

> Bob and I
> In different rooms
> Talking to ourselves
> Carrying on
> Last night's
> Hard conversation
> Convinced
> The other one
> The life companion
> Wasn't listening

Sometimes Mum and Daddy act like that.

After I read that poem, I started listening in on
people's conversations, and all of a sudden, it was like
everybody was talking in poem. Here's something I over-
heard this morning while I was walking to the library.
A lady in denim shorts and red high heels, carrying a

package of toilet paper she'd just bought at the deli, said it into her cell phone.

> If you had been there
> It would have been
> The best bus ride ever.

It's nice to have someone to talk about poetry with. Thanks!

Are freckles bumpy? I have always wondered. I think red hair is beautiful. My best friend in Mussoorie, Anuradha, has red hair and gray eyes. She is light skinned, like a white person, but she does not have freckles. Kiku says my skin is the color of tea in a cup. He says that in America, being dark and foreign can get people in trouble. He says that is clear if you look around the world and read the New York Times. I didn't know what he meant until last month when we were at the library waiting in line at the photocopy machine. A crazy man called us terrorists. Then Kiku called the man an _____ and the security guard made us leave the library. I had never heard Kiku say a bad word before. He was so mad he punched a garbage can. I wish Kiku had explained that we are not terrorists. I am afraid the security guard at the library thinks I make bombs. I walk by him very quickly now. I never told anyone about this because Kiku said not to. He said it would make Mum cry.

Kiku says there are only two ways to be American:

1. Being born one
2. Getting papers from the government

He says once you are an American, even if someone calls you a terrorist, you can get a lawyer for free, and you can vote for Barack Obama.

I have never heard that people in Kentucky are stupid. If I ever hear someone saying that I will tell them they are wrong. I wonder why feeding pigeons is against the law but saying mean things about people isn't. That doesn't make any sense to me.

I think New Yorkers are very nice. On the subway, people give their seats to the elderly or children or pregnant ladies. Strangers carry strollers and heavy suitcases up the stairs for one another. People talk to each other, just because. When I first came here, I thought everyone was scary because they walked so fast and said a lot of bad words. But now I walk fast, too, and sometimes I say, "What the hell?" I have never been mugged and neither has Mrs. Lau, who has lived in Chinatown for fifty-five years. I told her what your mamaw said about stereotypes, and she said it was true. She said, "There's good and bad people everywhere." I wrote that down in my journal.

Maybe I'll try it out now like a poem:

There's good
And bad
People
Everywhere

That was fun. Kiku says tourists who come here get drunk and shop and sightsee, but they do not understand the city. They think it is a playground, not a real place to live. He says it is because in the movies, New Yorkers always have a lot of money or are shooting each other. One thing I like about New York is that everyone is different. So nobody is weird because everybody's weird. Maybe that doesn't make any sense. But I am not going to cross it out.

I have never been in a cab, but my daddy's friend Sushil-Uncle drives one. We walk and take the subway and sometimes the bus. Even Mayor Bloomberg takes the subway to get to work. I think it would be fun to raise my hand for a taxi and see it stop. But it is expensive.

Do you have a brother or sister?

I have not answered all your questions, but I have to go now and wash the dishes before Mum gets home. There are a lot in the sink and Kiku never does them.

August 28, 2008

It is one day later. I think I will write this letter like a journal. I have just taken Cuba for a walk. First I had to clean the sofa, because Kiku got bicycle grease on it. He doesn't notice that it is always on his legs.

Your grandmother sounds very interesting. We learned about activists last year on Martin Luther King

Day. I wrote a paper about how he was like Gandhiji, who fought the British. Can you tell me what is your mamaw fighting for? I hope she will win.

Is it fun to mow the lawn?

How many windows are in your house?

Do you have your own room?

Last night a big storm rolled in off the river. When I heard the thunder, I went out the window and stood on the fire escape so I could see the sky. It was grey and OMINOUS. I looked down in the street and saw everyone walking fast. Nobody had an umbrella because it had been sunny all day. The wind got strong and cold, and a garbage can on the corner blew over and rolled in the street and a taxi almost crashed into it. Then it started to rain so hard that people ran and flattened themselves against the sides of buildings. I could hear the gutters filling and the wind howling in the shaftways. I love when storms come and remind everyone that Mother Nature is stronger than anything. It is easy in New York to forget that.

The rain sounded different all over, hitting the garbage bags on the curb, the tops of air conditioners, the big cloth awning above the bodega, the windows, and the rusty fire escape. Then the lightning came. I was completely soaked and Mum leaned out and scolded me and told me to come inside. When I came in she gave me a towel for my hair, and I heard Cuba barking next door and remembered that Mrs. Lau had her windows open, so I went over there. I always wear the key to Mrs. Lau's apartment around my neck.

Cuba was shaking, and his ears were flat against his head because thunderstorms scare him. All the parakeets were puffed up and squawking, and Mrs. Lau was trying to shut her window but it was stuck. I wish the landlord would come and replace her windows. She has been asking him for two years. They are not safe and they leak.

When I went back to our apartment, Kiku and Mum had lined up three chairs in front of the bedroom window. They had their feet on the sill and they were getting wet and laughing and passing a bowl of popcorn back and forth. They had left the middle chair for me. "*Arrey,* come, come, Mee-Mee!" Mum said, and we sat there and held on to each other and screamed like crazy every time the thunder came. It sounded like the storm was right on top of us. The curtains blew straight out and Mum rolled up the peacock bedspread so it wouldn't get wet. We sat there and watched the storm like it was a movie, laughing and screaming and having so much fun. But you know, even though I was happy, I missed Daddy. He should have been having fun with us. And I missed Dadi. That is just what me and her always did when a big storm came in off the mountain. We'd stand together in the doorway and wonder at such a strong thing in the world. "God is great," Dadi always said, especially during storms. Now there is no one to close the windows for her. There is no one for her to watch storms with. I am here and she is all alone. Just like Daddy, poor Daddy, who has to eat his meals standing up in the restaurant. He says the best thing about coming home is getting to sit down and eat all together as a family.

At one point during the storm, Kiku looked over at me and said, "I hope Ana Maria's doing OK." Then his face got pinched and scared because the big dummy had forgotten that Ana Maria is a secret!!!! He's SO in love with her that he HAS to talk about her all the time!!! Anyway, Mum frowned, then raised her eyebrows like she does when she is both interested and suspicious. She said, "Who is this Ana Maria?"

I thought Kiku was going to fall down dead. He opened and closed his mouth like a fish. I felt so sorry for him that I made up a lie. I said, "She's a girl at my school who is scared of lightning. Kiku thinks it's funny so he's being a jerk."

Mum tsked and sighed and said, "Oh, Kiku. You be nice to that Ana Maria."

Kiku looked at me and made his eyes wide and laughed his head off. He said, "If you say so, Mum."

Whew. It was a close calling.

By the way, the reason why Ana Maria is a big secret is because Mum wants Kiku to marry an Indian girl. She says if he marries an American girl, she will die of GRIEF and SHAME. She also says I'm not allowed to EVER go on a date EVER and that she will pick out a nice boy for me when it's time to get married. Kiku and I already have a plan that I will look ugly and act like a wild animal whenever I meet these boys Mum wants me to marry. And when I am seventeen, I will have a secret boyfriend FOR SURE.

When I was in India and it was just me and Dadi, we had a world map from <u>National Geographic</u>. We would unfold it and count all the mountains and rivers and countries and cities in between us and Mum and Daddy and Kiku. I think about that and I wonder if now Dadi counts alone. It is so sad to be far away from each other. We write Dadi letters, and we call Daddy on the phone, but it is not the same. Sometimes I get so sad that I have to stop in the middle of the sidewalk and stand still. It's like my legs won't move. All the people keep walking and all the cars keep driving and after a few minutes I know that I have to keep going. I know there is nothing to do but keep going like everybody else in the city. I think that, and then I am able to move again. But some days I worry so much I feel like my head will break into a zillion pieces.

I don't know why I just told you all that. Sorry.

After the storm, Mum and myself wiped down the sills and floor and put the fans in the windows to drag in the cool air from the outside. The air was clean, the buildings were dripping, and the pavement was steaming and smelled like stones. I love the smell of summer pavement after rain. It is funny because Francie in my book also loves that smell. I want to try drinking coffee because she likes it. I think we have a lot in common.

By the way, I think <u>A Tree Grows in Brooklyn</u> is not girly. I knew a girl in Mussoorie who would not wear her glasses, so she always got bad grades. She said she would rather be pretty than see properly. I think that is girly. But <u>A Tree Grows in Brooklyn</u> is an amazing book for anyone. I am not sure, though. I have never had a friend who is a boy, except for Kiku.

One more by the way . . . I CAN believe that S. E. Hinton is a girl and that she wrote a book. Girls can do anything.

August 29, 2008

It is another day later and I am sitting on the fire escape. The sun is setting and the tops of the buildings look pink and gold. I can hear the couple on the fourth floor fighting. Kiku says they should get a divorce and stop keeping us awake at night.

You ask a lot of questions, so I think you will be a very good newspaper reporter some day. I have read your letter so many times that I have it memorized. It is good that the Summer Program has ended, because I have lots of time to write to you.

The red dot you asked about is called a *bindi*. Mum had a laugh that you thought it was Magic Marker. She said to tell you the bindi marks a place of wisdom on the body. It is a decoration, like jewelry. I've seen Christian people who wear a cross around their neck. A bindi is the same kind of thing. Mum wears a small one made of felt. It is only as big as the tip of a pencil, and it works like a sticker. It is red because she is married. I wear one during the festival season in October and November, if we go to temple or a party.

There are some famous white people who like to wear bindis, too, like Madonna and Gwen Stefani. I think it is kind of weird that they do that. Kiku says they are both Italian.

I have never been asked what I am good at, so I had to think about that question for a long time. I think I am good at reading and noticing things. I am also good at making a bundle of firewood on my back as I walk through the forest. But I cannot do that in New York City. Also, I have a very good sense of smell.

It would take a zillion pages to list all the things I am NOT good at.

At the library this morning, I looked at the book by your S. E. Hinton called <u>The Outsiders</u>. It was missing pages, so I didn't take it out. I have put in a request for a copy from another library. It took me three months to get <u>A Tree Grows in Brooklyn</u> because all the copies in the city were missing or on hold. I think it is a very popular book. I have already finished reading it, and I am now halfway through it again. It has some hard words but they are beautiful. My favorite new word is SUCCULENT. Since reading this book, everyone I pass on the street seems full of stories and dreams and a secret sadness.

My favorite meal is *chawal* (rice), *kala dal* (black lentils), *roti* (bread), *raita* (yoghurt), spicy mango pickle, and *sitaphal* (a kind of fruit). Dadi and I ate this meal all the time. Actually, I do not know if it is still my favorite, because I cannot eat it with Dadi and part of what made it taste good was being with her. I think Dadi would like where you live. If she comes to America, I will tell her about your uncle who sells houses. She does not speak English, so I would live with her and be her interpreter. Then we could all be neighbors.

It is very exciting that your mountains look just like mine. I googled Black Banks at the library and read that is in the Appalachian Mountains. Mum always says, "People are people." I guess mountains are mountains. I never knew that before. In Hindi, the word for pine tree is this: चीड़

I don't think I believe in the Bible because I am Hindu. But in our bedroom, Mum has an *aarthi/puja* space, where she keeps a picture of the Virgin Mary right next to Lord Krishna. Also, Mum always says, "Do unto others," and I think that is from the Bible. In Mussoorie, I went to St. George's School, where there were many Christian teachers. There are lots of missionaries in Mussoorie because the British used to go there when they felt hot. Kiku says Christians think that everyone should change to be like them or we will all go to hell. You are a Christian and it does not seem like you think I should be one, too. Do you?

Sometimes Kiku says mean things because he is a teenage boy with a lot of hormones. I wasn't going to tell you this, but I had to ask him what "the N-word" means. He told me, and then he said a white person who uses the N-word hates Indian people, too. I am telling you this so I am not keeping secrets from you, but I hope you are not upset.

I asked Mrs. Lau what kind of dog Cuba is and she said, "He's a New Yorker." She said he followed her home from work twelve years ago. She thinks he is one of those fight dogs, but he was too nice to fight so he ran away. This was a new story for me. If I had not met you, maybe I would never have asked Mrs. Lau that question. I am so glad to have met you.

I hope your mother doesn't have a headache today. Has she been to Dr. Patel? By the way, I think it's not nice that you think the way Dr. Patel speaks is funny. And I think your mamaw elbows you because it is rude to stare at someone just because they look different from you.

You said yourself it was bad when your daddy didn't like people different from him, right?

I bet Mrs. Patel is homesick like me. I don't like it when people make fun of the way I talk. It doesn't seem like I have an accent, because I am writing, not speaking, to you. But I DO have an accent, and if you made fun of me for it, I would not want to be your friend anymore and Kiku would probably beat you up.

Next week, the day after Labor Day, school starts. When I first came to New York, it was March, so I could not go to school because of the city rules that say you have to wait till September. That year, Kiku taught me from his books and made up examinations for me and put smiley faces on them. And then for three years, I went to PS 110, but we didn't do much except read out loud from textbooks. Ms. Bledsoe at the Summer Program got me transferred to PS 20. It is just ten blocks from here. I start there next week. I do not know anyone, so I am a little nervous. I don't know if I will make any friends.

Mrs. Lau says you shouldn't have more friends than you have fingers. She says real friends are hard to find. I think she is right. My best friend, Anuradha, has not written me a letter since I moved to New York. I think she has a new best friend and has forgotten all about me. Mrs. Lau says if this is true then Anuradha was never my best friend in the first place, so I shouldn't sit around feeling sad about it.

Next weekend, Daddy comes home. I cannot wait to see him.

I hope you and Rufus are smiling. Please write back soon and tell me more about your real true self.

Your pen pal,
Meena Joshi

P.S. I have been thinking of what you said about computers. Tomorrow I will practice typing at the library.

P.P.S. Here is how Dadi makes okra:
Heat oil in a pan and throw in a pinch of cumin seeds. Fry till the seeds stop sizzling, then add 1 sliced onion, 6 cloves of garlic, and fry till onion turns pale brown. Next add okra. It will be kind of sticky at first but don't worry, that goes away as you mix. Add a pinch of coriander

powder and a 1/2 pinch of mango powder. Fry it all for a little while, then add 2 cubed tomatoes. Cook for another 2–3 minutes. Eat with rice or *chapatti* and . . . YUM.

P.P.P.S. I have started doing those leg stretches. I think it's working.

P.P.P.P.S. Last thing, I promise. I have never been to an amusement park. I am afraid I would throw up on a roller coaster, but the Thunderhead sounds like so much fun it would be worth it.

11 September 2008

Dear Meena,

I am writing to you today with real sad news. I don't know how to say it all, so I will just say it and hope that it doesn't come out like a big jumbled mess. Here's what happened:

Yesterday, the bus dropped me off at the end of our driveway, just like always. We have a real long driveway and it takes a while to walk it, but it is lined on both sides by big woods full of old, old trees that remind me of big stone columns like you'd see on an ancient temple. Lost Creek is there, too, which is where we always go fishing. Lost Creek is mostly shallow with big gray rocks, but every once in a while there is a deep fishing hole. Because of the rocks and the rushing water, you can hear Lost Creek from a long way off, so it's like a music in the woods. I usually walk through the woods instead of taking the driveway because it's a different world there. It's cooler, and the birds are louder, and there are all kinds of things to see. Sometimes I take my time and run my hand over all the moss. I get down real low and look at the ferns. This one time last summer I was moving real slow and quiet like that, and I looked up and there was a little fawn standing ten feet away, in the middle of Lost Creek, watching me. We stared at each other a full minute and I felt like it was reading my mind. Then it just eased away and disappeared into the woods.

Anyway, I was in the woods, doing my thing, and then I noticed that the birds had all hushed. This was real weird because it's always crazy loud in there, with so many birds hollering and singing. So this made me listen harder, and then I could hear a machine running somewhere, even over the rushing of the creek. So I ran through the woods toward the sound, because we're far enough outside of Black Banks to not hear any traffic usually. I could tell it was a big machine, like the kind you see working on the highway when they are making a new lane.

Finally, I came to where the big drop-off is, which is this line of cliffs that are about fifty feet high. You can see them from Black Banks and they're what the town is named for, because when you're in town you can look up and see them like a big set of black teeth on the side of the mountain. Before I got out to the edge where I could see, I stood in the woods, trying to catch my breath. Have you ever run so fast that it feels like something in your side has come undone? That little place was hurting me real bad, so I held my hand over it and breathed hard.

I'm not real crazy about heights, so I kind of eased out as close to the edge as I could. As soon as I got out of the trees I could see it. There were three ginormous bull-dozers and a HUGE dump truck working on the mountain over to my left. The 'dozers were pushing down ROWS AND ROWS of trees. I couldn't believe it. I know we have to cut down trees to build our houses and stuff like that, but they were <u>PUSHING</u> them down into a big mess and piling them up. Then the back of the dump truck raised up so that all these tires rolled out on top of the trees. Then the driver got out and poured gas all over the tires and trees and struck a match and—*POOF!*—they all caught fire, like somebody snapping their fingers.

I sat there a long time, wondering what in the world they were doing, and they just kept on pushing down more trees. Then I looked down at Black Banks. Looking down on the town from up there, you'd think that every-thing was perfect below. All the little houses in their neat rows, and the Black Banks River catching some sun on its waves, and the cars going about their business. I could see seven or eight church steeples and my school down there right at the foot of Town Mountain. Everything just right, while a mountain that close to town was getting treated this way.

When I got home Mamaw was worried to death, because I was never that late. When I told her what I had seen, she froze and said for me to tell her every single thing and not to leave out anything, so I did. Then she got on the phone right away and called somebody. She went in the laundry room to talk to them so I couldn't hear her. I went over to the door and tried to listen in as good as I could, but the washer was running, so it was hard. But I did hear her say the words "mountaintop removal" over and over and over. And when she came back out, she told me that that's what I had seen.

"I've been working with this group on fighting mountaintop removal for about a year now," Mamaw said. She had set down across from me and was talking to me like I was grown. She has always treated me like I'm older than I am, and she says this is why I make good grades.

"I knew that it was happening more and more, but I never dreamed it would get as close as Town Mountain."

Mamaw said that Town Mountain was public land and the coal company had leased it, and now they could pretty much do whatever they wanted to do to it. She said that mountaintop removal is just what it sounds like: they take the whole top off of a mountain to get to a thin little seam of coal! I took my mother's camera and got a picture of it and am going to paste it in here:

Can you believe that used to be a mountaintop, that had birds and deer and foxes and a million trees on it? Do they do this to your mountains in India?

Then whatever dirt and burned up trees or whatever else they have left over, they push down between two mountains and make a valley fill, and this causes all kinds of bad floods. Mamaw said that if a place has coal and poor people, then the coal companies will take it out any way they can and don't care what happens to the people. She told me so much stuff that I never will remember it all. It was just too much to take in. The thing I will never forget is that she said we might as well prepare, because eventually they'll get closer to the house, since that land is right up against her property.

I don't want to think about it anymore, Meena. And I can't talk to anybody about it except for you and Mamaw. My friend Mark called me this evening, wanting to know if I could come stay all night with him, and I started telling him about it and then he got real quiet and said, "What are you talking about, man? Do you want to come over and play Nintendo, or not?" Like I was mental or something.

All right, so I have to get my mind off of it. I'll do it by answering the questions you had in your last letter. I'll try to make my answers brief, since this letter is going on waaaay too long.

1. Freckles are not bumpy.

2. I'm an only child.

3. I wouldn't say it's fun to mow the yard. But I kind of like it, too, because I can think the whole time I'm mowing. The thing I hate to do is weed-eat, which takes forever and is so annoying you can't think about anything while you're doing it.

4. We have three bedrooms, one bathroom, a kitchen, a laundry room, and a living room. So that's seven rooms. And a total of ten windows (the laundry room doesn't have one, but the living room has three). That's a weird question, by the way. Nobody has ever asked me how many windows I have in my house.

5. Yes, I have my own room. It used to be Mamaw's guest room, and when I first moved in it had pink curtains and a big fluffy bedspread, but we finally got rid of that and now the bed has my Simpsons comforter on it and blinds instead of curtains.

6. Yes, I am a Christian but I don't think you're going to hell. You're way too nice.

Now I'll reply to some things in your letter that weren't really questions but need responding to.

1. I'm sorry somebody called you and Kiku terrorists. To tell you the truth, though, I might have thought the same thing before I met you, because I never knew anybody different from me before. I hope that doesn't hurt your feelings, but it's the truth. But even if I had THOUGHT that, I would have never been as rude as that moron who called you all that.

2. I think it's really cool that your mayor takes the subway. The only time we ever see our mayor is in the homecoming parade, when he rides in the backseat of a convertible Cadillac and waves to everybody. He has jowls, which tremble when he waves.

3. It's easy to remember that Mother Nature is in charge when you live in Eastern Kentucky, like me. If we stand out at the cliffs where the big black teeth are on the side of the mountain, we can see storms coming from a long way off, and

smell them, too, long before they get here.

4. I think "Cuba" is the best name for a dog, ever. Besides Rufus.

5. Thanks for telling me that the red dot is a bindi. I like learning something new.

6. You talk a lot about Obama. I know Mamaw is voting for him, but I don't think a lot of foks here are. I know Mamaw gets into arguments at the Piggly Wiggly about him. (Do you all have Piggly Wigglys? It's a grocery store, in case you're wondering.)

7. I see what you're saying about staring at the Patels, but I didn't do it to be rude. I just think they're interesting to look at. I don't understand how that's bad of me.

8. You said that people made fun of you because of your accent. Well, just like I mentioned above, people do this to other Americans, too. Where I'm from we talk real different from everybody else in the country, so people are always making fun of us, especially on TV and in the movies. Mamaw says that the only people it's

still OK to make fun of out in the open are hill-billies and crazy people. One time Mamaw was in Cincinnati visiting her brother, and some woman called Mamaw a stupid hillbilly, just because of the way she talked. Mamaw told her off, which is what you should do when people make fun of your accent.

I guess that's all. I'm going to try to go to sleep now. It's real late and I'll never be able to get up and go to school tomorrow. I'm going to read a chapter of <u>Old Yeller</u> (that's what I'm reading now and it's real good) and then go to bed.

Since you are in New York, I wonder if you are thinking about 9-11, too. It happened seven years ago today. I remember my parents sitting in front of the TV all day and night, crying. We had a moment of silence at school today.

Oh, one more thing. I don't want to make you mad or anything, but I need to tell you something. In your letter you said that something was "a close calling." I think what you meant to say is "a close CALL." I didn't know if I should mention it or not, but then I thought, a good friend is somebody who will tell you when you are doing something that might be embarrassing. Like if you had a booger on your face or a big trail of toilet paper stuck to your shoe after leaving the bathroom, I'd tell you. So I guess I should tell you that you are saying something wrong.

12 September 2008 (one day later)

Dear Meena,

I was going to go ahead and mail your letter but then today happened, which I HAVE to tell you about.

Today in school, my science teacher, Mrs. Heap, was talking about "cohesion" and giving us instructions on this exercise we had to do in class where we got into groups and tried to see how many drops of water we could get onto one penny. Right while she was telling about this, I figured out that she'd probably know even more about mountaintop removal, since she is a science teacher, so I raised my hand.

She ignored me for a little while, but then finally she put her hands on her hips and looked aggravated and said, "Yes, River? What is SO important?"

I asked her if she could explain mountaintop removal to us.

"We're not talking about that right now, River. If you were paying attention, you'd know that." I never have liked that woman. She always sits and eats Skittles right in front of us, even though she knows we're not allowed to have any kind of candy at school. I think that says a lot about her. Plus, she wears way too much perfume, and sometimes it gives people headaches.

So then I said it was so important that maybe we OUGHT to be talking about it.

"Well, fortunately you don't dictate what gets talked about in here, mister," Mrs. Heap said, and laughed a little bit, looking at her daughter, who is also in my class and is the biggest snob in the entire school. She tells everybody she is rich, but Mamaw says that sometimes people just try to act rich and are actually in debt up to their eyeballs, and this must be the case with the Heaps, since they are both teachers and teachers don't make squat.

Mrs. Heap smiled in this real fake way and took a step toward me. "Why are you so curious about it, anyway?"

"Because they're doing it to Town Mountain, and a lot of other mountains, and my mamaw says that if something doesn't change, then every mountain we've got is going to be flattened. If the coal companies have their way."

"Let me remind you, Mr. Justice, that lots of people in this county make their living by working in the coal industry," she said. "So your mamaw ought to mind her own business."

Well, that made me real mad. I felt my face go red. So then I told her some of what Mamaw had told me last night. I said that lots of people, like my very own daddy, had lost their jobs because MTR (mountaintop removal) uses more machines than it does people. And then I told her that my mamaw had said that this WAS our business and if Americans hadn't spoken up for what they believed in we'd still have slavery and women wouldn't be able to vote and besides that we'd probably still be a colony of England instead of our own country. Right about there Mrs. Heap started telling me to hush and kept coming closer and closer, slapping her pointer across her palm, but I couldn't hush. I felt like I had to say it all out, to set her straight. I had to take up for Mamaw. So I just kept talking. The last thing I said was "Mamaw said that the only way to be a good American is to speak up for what you believe in."

So Mrs. Heap sent me to the office for disrupting class. I had to wait forever in the front office because the principal, Mr. Wright, was in the lunchroom breaking up a fight. He finally came in and looked down at me and said, "Let's go, son," and swung his arm through the air like a traffic cop directing me into his office. He thinks he's really cool but I think he's a big turd. He wears his pants too tight and the back part of his tie is always hanging lower than the front, and he is always fooling with his hair and checking himself out in windows or mirrors or anything that will show him his reflection.

He asked me all about the problem and I told him

exactly what had happened, and he just said I couldn't interrupt the teacher like that and I needed to stay in after-school detention. I got real mad. I couldn't help it. "But I didn't do anything wrong," I said.

He stood up and leaned over his desk and pointed his finger in my face and spoke in a tight little voice. "You better watch it there, buddy," he said, and widened his eyes at me. Then he said he was calling my mother.

So I had to sit for a half hour and wait again. I had to sit there while he signed papers and read letters without ever saying a word to me or even looking at me. Once I asked him if I could go get my copy of <u>Old Yeller</u> out of my locker so I wouldn't have to sit there and stare at my shoes, but he just said no without looking at me. I had to miss history class, which I really love. We were supposed to learn about the Boston Tea Party today.

But after a while, here came Mamaw (I knew Mom wouldn't come; she hasn't left the house in ages). I was so glad to see her, but she didn't hug me or anything the way she usually did. She just shot me a funny look like "What have you done?" and sat down and put her big old pocketbook up on her knees and asked Mr. Wright what was the problem.

"River here interrupted class by refusing to stop questioning the teacher today," Mr. Wright said. He had his elbows up on the chair arms and was touching all ten of his fingertips together the whole time he talked. For the first time, I noticed he had sleep in the corners of his eyes. It was brown.

"Well, that's not like him. He usually has awful good manners," Mamaw said, looking at me like I ought to give her some kind of clue as to what was happening. "What were you questioning her about, River?"

"I was trying to get her to tell us about mountaintop removal, and she wouldn't."

Mamaw told the principal that seemed like a perfectly good question to ask a science teacher.

"Mountaintop removal is a controversial topic in these parts, as you well know," Mr. Wright said. "And it's not appropriate for teachers to be talking about with students."

"If it's controversial then that's exactly WHY she

should be talking about it with them," Mamaw said.

Mr. Wright said "perhaps" I ought to wait out front, but Mamaw said no, she didn't protect her children or grandchildren from the truth. "Tell me exactly what happened, River."

So once again I had to tell it, and by the time I got to the part where Mrs. Heap told me that Mamaw ought to mind her own business, I could tell that Mamaw's blood was boiling. So then she turned to Mr. Wright and said she wanted to speak to Mrs. Heap with him. He sighed and started to make up some kind of excuse, but Mamaw said, "I want to see this woman RIGHT NOW!" So he picked up the phone and called her to the office, and that's when Mamaw turned to me and said that maybe it <u>was</u> a good idea for me to wait out front so she could talk properly to Mrs. Heap.

When it was all over, Mrs. Heap was the first one out of the door. She shot past me, her arms swinging as she walked away huffing and puffing. Mr. Wright said I could go back to class and there would be no after-school detention. Mamaw winked at me and said she'd see me later. So I went on back to class, but I couldn't concentrate on anything at all. During my chorus class Mrs. Heap came in and whispered something in the ear of my teacher, Mrs. Greer, and then they both looked right at me. They are real good friends, so Mrs. Heap was probably in there telling her to give me a hard time.

And when I got home, the bulldozers were even louder. After supper (salmon patties and soup beans, which I love), we walked back out to the high cliffs, and you wouldn't believe how much damage they've done in one day. It made me want to throw up. We stood there with the sun setting so red and orange that it seemed like the whole world was on fire, and for a long time Mamaw didn't say anything. Something about it reminded me of when your grandmother said "God is great" during that big thunderstorm, because it was like Mamaw's silence was saying that very same thing while we looked out at the good mountains and the one that was being destroyed.

I can't even talk about it anymore. I'm sorry that I've written such a depressing letter, but I had to tell you all of that.

13 September 2008 (Saturday)

Dear Meena,

I was going to mail your letter this morning, but
then one good thing happened and I wanted to tell you
about it, so that I wouldn't have to send a letter full of
bad stuff.

This morning I went in and sat with Mom awhile.
She was in agony with a headache and couldn't even talk
to me. I rubbed her temples for a while and then read
a whole chapter of <u>Old Yeller</u> out loud to her, and that
made her feel better. She kissed me on the cheek and told
me to go play.

But I went to the grocery store with Mamaw instead.
And sure enough, soon as we got to the Piggly Wiggly,
there was Dr. Patel and his wife. Dr. Patel started laughing and threw out his arms for a hug and said, "Mama
Justice!" and Mamaw hugged him and they talked and
went on, and his wife leaned over just a bit and smiled
at me. "Hello, young man," she said. Meeting you gave
me the courage to talk to her, so I said hello. And then
I asked her what her name is. It's Chandra. (What does

that mean?) She told me I should call her that, and not Mrs. Patel.

Then I told her I have a pen pal from the mountains of India who now lives in New York City, and she seemed real pleased by that. She asked which mountains but I'm sorry I couldn't remember, so I just said, "The ones that look like these," and she laughed a little and said she was from Ahmedabad. I had to ask her to repeat it a couple times, and finally she said, "Here," and held out her palm and wrote it there with a blue ink pen, so I could see. I told her I wanted to be sure to tell you where she was from, and so she wrote it on my palm, too, holding on to my fingers with her other hand. Her skin was very warm and she smiled the whole time she wrote it. She was leaning down close to my face, so I got to stare at her bindi real close. You were right, too, because hers is made of felt, just like your mom's.

Mamaw was finally finished laughing with Dr. Patel, and so Chandra put out her hand to shake mine. "I am very pleased to meet you, River Justice," she said. "I'm always glad to make a new friend." She has really brown eyes that stare right into you. I liked her a lot.

I wanted to let you know that now I have TWO Indian friends, all because of ONE (you).

I'm looking forward to your next letter.

Sincerely,
River Dean Justice

October 17, 2008

Dear River,

I am sorry such trouble has come to you. I think if the top of Town Mountain is cut off, you and the rest of the people of Black Banks will be homesick forever. It is so sad about the trees. I have been thinking of them as they must have been when they were alive: birds singing from little nests, ants running up bark, squirrels sleeping in the shade of leaves, worms clinging to long, deep roots. It is terrible those creatures have lost their homes. It is terrible the trees have been burned and wasted. I don't understand why those men in bulldozers didn't at least save the wood.

I did not know that such things as mountaintop removal happened in America. I asked Ms. Bledsoe to teach our class about it. (Remember how Ms. Bledsoe was my Summer Program teacher? Now she's my regular teacher!) Even though she is an English teacher, I think she will do it, because she is someone who cares when bad things happen—not just to herself but also to people she has never ever met. She had not heard of mountaintop removal before, so I showed her the photographs you sent. She said, "My God," and went online and started reading. I have noticed that whenever she is upset she bites her lips and blinks a lot. She was doing that when I left to go to history.

I could see and hear and smell everything in your letter, as if I were right there with you. That made some parts extra nice and some parts extra scary. You are a very good writer. You are also realllllllllly brave. I have never been to the principal's office. If I did go, I would be in trouble in two places—at school and home, both. Nobody would stand up for me like your mamaw stood up for you. At home, they would just yell and say I have to get good grades and do whatever the teacher says and be a good girl, no matter what. Even Kiku would say this, although he himself is always breaking rules in little ways. He will not admit it, but he thinks boys do not have to behave as good as girls.

I found an old cookie tin yesterday that someone had left out by the trash. I cleaned it and am using it to keep your letters safe. In New York City, when you don't want something, you leave it on the sidewalk so someone else can find it. Mrs. Lau got a lot of her furniture that way. A long time ago she found a ficus tree in a little ceramic pot sitting on the sidewalk next to the trash. The ficus is very big now, on its third pot, and it stretches almost to Mrs. Lau's ceiling. Cuba used to lift his leg and pee on it, looking very proud of himself, but he got such scoldings that he finally stopped. It seemed like it was a real pleasure for him, but I guess you can't have a dog peeing indoors. How is Rufus, by the way? Please tell him I say hello.

I am worried the bulldozers will come even closer to your house with ten windows. I hope you will be careful in the woods and on the cliff where you feel nervous. Where I come from, even little children of two years run on the mountain paths without feeling scared. Dadi says when you are born on the edge of a cliff, that is where you always walk best. When she and I were in Delhi, walking on flat pavement made our knees ache, but I have become used to it here in New York.

Thank you for saying you might have thought me and Kiku were terrorists, too. That sounds funny but what I mean is that I am glad we tell each other the real whole truth, and I am glad we can change each other's mind.

I feel like I am learning a lot from you about Americans and what they're really like. I would have been afraid to go to Kentucky before I met you. Kiku says that everyone in the South wants to hang us by our necks from trees. But since meeting you, I have told him he's wrong. He doesn't believe me, of course, because he thinks he's never wrong.

I will say "close call" from now on. It didn't make me mad that you told me the right way to say that. And I would definitely tell you if you had a booger hanging out of your nose.

You asked if things like your mountaintop removal also happen in Garhwal. They do. My family lost its farm because of a big dam that took twenty years to build. The farm was small, but it had been in our family so long that no one remembers the name of the ancestor who first turned its soil.

Even though the government came and moved all the people from our village, they didn't flood the area right away. So we used to go back and visit the land and harvest the crops. The vegetables grew without us, especially the turnips. I only remember a few things about the farm. I remember Dadi and me picking beans in our bare feet and the cool dirt between our toes. I remember falling asleep under a banana tree and getting bitten by a spider. And once, Dadi and I were walking to the river and we saw big crowds of purple flowers on the hillside. I asked Dadi their name, and she said, "They are wild-flowers. They would not want a name."

I guess there are some things that are not meant to be tamed. Like mountains and wildflowers and my dadi.

When the dam came, Dadi had to move to Mussoorie, where Mummy-Daddy were teaching. I was not yet born, but Kiku remembers leaving the farm. He said everyone in our village cried. They shut the doors to their houses and left in a big group, herding the goats and buffalo. When they got to the Naya Road, some people went left and some people went right and then they were sepa-rated forever.

There is a big lake there now, and tourists come and rent boats that bob up and down in the water. They pose for pictures right above the spot where our village used to be. What's weird is that the power from the dam goes to people in Delhi, which is five hundred miles away.

Meanwhile, the lights in Mussoorie go out all the time. Often this would happen while Dadi and I were eating dinner. We would feel our way through a meal in the dark and keep talking and eating as if nothing had happened. Later we would light a candle and set it on the table, and I would do my homework and Dadi would practice her letters or knit. I love candles and the way they make a room peaceful when they flicker.

Did you know that the English word "jungle" is the same as the Hindi word for forest? There is something nice about two different languages sharing a word, don't you think? जंगल = JUNGLE

I told Mum about the trees you had seen, and she said that a long time ago, in the 1970s, when she was little, Dadi and many other village *ghasayi* (grass-cutting) women fought for the trees. They were led by a woman named Gaura Devi, who was Dadi's childhood friend and who started the Chipko movement.

Mum said Gaura was the smartest person she ever met and was the one who taught her that the trees are our brothers and sisters. (Oh, and "chipko" means to hug.) What happened is that when the contractors came to cut the forest, the women and their children held hands and stood in circles around the trunks of trees. They hugged pine and oak and devdar and saved them with their own bodies. They sang songs and shouted, "First cut us, then the trees!"

The women did this after working all day, taking care of their families and animals, cutting grass and gathering wood and planting crops. The contractors were too ashamed to hurt women and children, so they left. Later some men came from the city and heard about the women, and they talked to the government and a law was passed that stopped the businesses from taking trees.

Most people have forgotten that the village women started the change, though. Most people have even forgotten Gaura Devi. Mum says this is how it is all over the world. She says often a woman does the work but a man gets the credit. She says the Chipko women were also for-gotten because most of them did not know how to read and write, so people did not believe in their intelligence.

My dadi learned to read and write when she was fifty-two years old, and she is the smartest person I know.

It is funny how the government that stopped the bad tree cutting is the same government that created the bad dam. If a government can do one good thing, why can't it do good things all the time?

Writing this to you has made me remember a song Dadi used to sing. I will translate it for you:

Come, rise, my brothers and sisters,
Save this mountain
Come plant new trees, new forests,
Decorate the earth

I have just sung it aloud. I feel as if Dadi is close, and I also feel hollow inside, as if I am hungry but no food will help.

Today is Karva Chauth, which means Mum is fasting for Daddy to be healthy and safe. I should go and make dinner. The city lights are bright, and it takes a while for the moon to rise above the buildings here. Mum will be eating late. She can only stop her fast once she has seen the moon. This is the first year she will do Karva Chauth. She says it is not something Garhwali women follow, but this year she will do it because her husband is far away.

I have written a lot about home but I have not yet told you what is happening in Chinatown. You and your mountains remind me so much of Dadi. Some days I feel like I am living in two places at once. Garhwal in my mind and New York in my body. I do not yet know where my heart is. Good night for now, River.

October 20, 2008

I also don't like when people wear too much perfume. I always know when the college girls on the fourth floor have come home, because I smell their tangerine scent coming in through the window. They own their apartment, but Kiku says they did not buy it themselves. Their daddies are rich, and that is why they have loud parties and put out cigarettes in the hallway.

We do not have the Piggly Wiggly in New York City. I was taking the subway with Kiku when I read your letter for the first time. Piggly Wiggly is such a funny name, I laughed out loud and couldn't stop. A few people on the subway looked at me and either smiled or frowned, depending on their mood. Mostly, though, everyone just kept doing their own thing. You could stand on your head in the middle of a New York subway and no one would ask what you were doing. Piggly Wiggly. Piggly Wiggly. It is fun to say.

School is going pretty OK. I like English class with Ms. Bledsoe the best. I also like history and science and maths. I do not like homeroom because everyone talks, so it is hard to concentrate on reading. In science, I am lab partners with a girl named Valentina. She is from the Dominican Republic. She showed it to me on the classroom map. It is an island near Florida. She speaks Spanish and English and is always singing. When I tell her she sounds beautiful, she says, "Oh, forget about it," and smacks me on the arm. She was in the school play last year and is auditioning this year. I had a lot of fun helping her "run lines" the other day.

This year, they are doing a show called <u>A Chorus Line</u>. It's a New York City story about a bunch of actors auditioning for a play. Valentina says the Broadway version is realllllly dirty, so the drama teacher cut a bunch of songs and changed the words to others.

Valentina is trying out for the part of Maggie because she is what is called a soprano. If she gets the part, she will have a solo. Her big competition is Marvel Jenkins, who scares me because she is sooooo confident. Even when she makes a mistake, Marvel manages to look strong. Like the other day in science, we were comparing buoyancy in plain and salt water, and Marvel dropped a beaker and it broke. Glass went everywhere. I would have been very embarrassed if this had happened to me. In fact, I am always careful with the beakers because I do not want to drop one and have everyone stare. Marvel was texting when she dropped the beaker, so she should have gotten in BIG TROUBLE. But she just slapped her own cheeks and rolled her eyes and said in a cartoon voice, "Oh, no, Marvel, look what you did!" It was really funny and everyone started laughing—even the teacher. I don't know how Marvel changed something naughty into something funny. I wish I could do that.

I am too shy to sing and dance in front of people, but Valentina saw me drawing in my notebook and said I could paint backdrops for the play. I am going to ask Kiku about it. I think I would like to be in the Drama Club. All the drama kids sit together at lunch, and I have heard that people kiss backstage. Apparently Jeffrey Mazano and Amanda Fritz got caught doing that last year. I don't want to kiss anyone (blech) but it is interesting to hear about.

Today, as I was coming back from school, I saw the exterminator leaving the building. When I went up to Mrs. Lau's, she said the exterminator had not come to her apartment or to ours or to the Woos', on the second floor. She said the building manager must have said not to spray the rent-controlled apartments. They are hoping we will be overrun with bugs and will move out, so they can sell our apartments for a half million dollars each. That is also why they do not fix Mrs. Lau's broken windows or the crack in our ceiling that leaks.

I still have not gotten <u>The Outsiders</u> from the library. All the copies are lost or missing. But I have put in a request for <u>Old Yeller</u>. I have finished <u>A Tree Grows in Brooklyn</u> for the third time. It taught me a lot, and I cried all over its pages because it was so real. When I returned the book to the library, I thought about how maybe someone else will cry over it, too. I like that library books have secret lives. All those hands that have held them. All those eyes that have read them.

I keep forgetting to tell you that Mrs. Lau uses something called Tiger Balm when she has a headache. It is a minty kind of oil, and when you rub it on your skin, you feel warm and tingly and the pain goes away. If you do not have this in Black Banks, I will ask Mrs. Lau if I can put some in a bottle and send it for your mother. Mrs. Lau also puts Tiger Balm on her hands, which have arthritis from sewing in a factory for thirty-three years. The factory used to be on the next block, but it closed down after Mrs. Lau retired, and now there are fancy shops there and a high-rise luxury building.

I was very glad to read about you making friends with Mrs. Patel. Her first name, Chandra, means moon. I knew from her last name that she was Gujarati. Indian last names tell you things about a person, like what part of the country they are from or what their religion is. Now that you and Mrs. Patel are friends, I am thinking you will not make fun of the way I talk. And if you ever go someplace where you are the only person like yourself, you'll see how it feels to be stared at, and maybe then you will better understand what I was saying.

Today I am writing from Mrs. Lau's apartment. Cuba is lying across my feet and the parakeets are angry. Mrs. Lau is at the senior citizen center on Gold Street. On Monday nights, they have ballroom dancing. Now that Mrs. Lau is retired and in her "golden years" (this is what she calls them), she goes out and enjoys life. She eats dinner at the senior citizen center two nights a week. It is only $1.25 for a plate of food, either chicken and vegetable, beef and vegetable, or baked fish. Mrs. Lau likes that they have disposable plates. She used to go to the senior center on Essex Street, but they used real plates and didn't clean them properly.

The sun sets so early these days. This week, the ivy on the building across the way has changed from green to red. The delis on Delancey are selling pumpkins and gourds, and the big oak on 12th is full of acorns. The mannequin in the new boutique next door is wearing a wool hat and a scarf and a big red sweater. Right now, at Mrs. Lau's apartment, there are six pigeons looking in the window at me. They are wanting Mrs. Lau because she feeds them seed every morning and night. Whenever there is not seed on the fire escape, the pigeons wonder what is wrong, and they look in the window to see if Mrs. Lau is home. If they don't see her in the living room, they fly to the bedroom window and look for her there. If she is not in the bedroom, they fly back to the living room and wait.

When the parakeets see the pigeons, they get reallllly mad. They scream and flap around their cages. I think it upsets them to see birds that are free. Parakeets are also very jealous animals. They don't like for Mrs. Lau to love anyone but them. They pull on poor Cuba's tail with their beaks if he stands too close to their cages. He wants so badly to be friends. He wags politely and tilts his head and cups his ears forward when they squawk. But only Xie-Xie will be his friend. She is a white parakeet with a yellow crest, and when she is out of her cage, she sits on

Cuba's rump and cleans herself. Sometimes she even lets Cuba lick her. She looks a little bit sick about it but also like she knows he does that because he is a dog. When Cuba comes back from a walk, she flaps prettily to show him she is glad, and she makes a crackling sound in the back of her throat. She doesn't make that sound for anybody but Cuba. Mrs. Lau says if a dog and a parakeet can love each other, then so can anybody. I think she is right.

October 22, 2008

I don't know if it is OK to tell you this since you are a boy. Mum and Dad and Kiku would say it is not OK. But I would like to tell you since we agreed to be our real true selves with each other. Well, here goes. Yesterday it was very hot, as if it were the middle of summer. I had on a pair of culottes that came up to my knees. A boy in my maths class said my legs were nasty and hairy and asked me if they had razors in India. Everybody laughed, and I pretended I didn't care and kept on working. Reepa, an Indian girl who was born in New York, was sitting near me in class and she laughed, too. Later I saw her in the bathroom, and while I was washing my hands she stood next to me and said that her cousins in Bengal also didn't shave their legs, but no one noticed because they kept them covered. I didn't say anything. It made me mad that she laughed at me in front of everyone but tried to be nice in private.

When I got home, I was upset and told Kiku what had happened, and I asked if I could borrow his razor. At first he said no, but all of a sudden he changed his mind. We only have a shower, not a bathtub, so he filled the bucket we use to catch leaks with warm water, put the lid down on the toilet, and told me to sit there with my legs in the bucket. He showed me how to apply the shaving cream and how to shake the razor in the water to get the hairs off. Then he left and shut the bathroom door, but he stayed just outside and talked to me about a fight he'd had with Ana Maria. It really helped me to hear his voice. . . . Oh, my gosh, River. Shaving was kind of scary. I thought I would cut myself and bleed to death. I know boys have to shave their faces, but faces are small and legs are long. It took forever to do one leg, and then I still had the other to go! When I was finished, Kiku came in and checked my work. He said, "You missed some hairs on your knees. Girls always do that." So I shaved them off and wondered if he has seen Ana Maria's knees up close. I think he has.

My legs felt so weird. The air stung my skin and I felt like a different person somehow.

When Mum came home, we showed her my legs and she said that was the last time she'd leave Kiku in charge. She said I was too young and that Daddy would be mad at her. Then she gave me some cocoa lotion that burned, and said the hair will grow back thick and coarse and I will have to shave my legs for the rest of my life. But I don't care. I like how it looks and no one can laugh at me now, and when I am very old, I will let it go hairy and wild again.

Right now I am sitting on the floor, wrapped up in a red-and-purple blanket Dadi knit. It was hot yesterday but today it is freezing. I can see out the window onto Orchard Street. The crispness of the air changes the streetlights. They look brighter and sharper than they do in the summer. I love when it gets cold. Do you? It makes me want to curl up with a book and a hot cup of tea.

I have been saving the best for last. Daddy was home this past weekend. He took the bus in and we met him at the Port Authority and went bowling. There is a bowling alley right at the bus station. Isn't that funny? Their fountain soda tastes great. Better than soda from a can. Anyway, Kiku won, like he always does, and I got one lucky strike and a lot of gutter balls. It makes us all laugh how Mum kneels at the end of the lane and pushes the bowling ball with both hands. She got three strikes doing that, and we laughed till we cried. Bowling is something we never did in India. Kiku tried it one night with his friends here, then showed us.

After bowling, we stayed up late. I read to Daddy from my journal so he would know what we've been doing and wouldn't feel left out. Mum gave him the muffler she has been knitting. It is blue and the stitches run in long tight chains. I love the way it looks. I have never seen people knit here the way we knit in Mussoorie. Up at Landour Bazaar, the women walk, or sit in a circle, and make sweaters and gossip about whoever is not there that day. Their fingers move faster than their tongues, and they never look down at their work and they never make a mistake. Well, Mum gave Daddy the muffler and said she had thought of him with every stitch. It was not cold that night but Daddy wrapped the muffler around his neck anyway. It went around twice, and he said, "I am a lucky man." It was sweet.

Have I told you before that Daddy works at a catering hall? I can't remember. It is a good job that Sushil-Uncle got him. If you work in a restaurant, some nights are slow and you get bad tips. But if you work in a catering hall, you are always guaranteed to make $150 a night, and whatever else you make in tips. Daddy eats for free at the catering place five days a week, and he shares a room in a hotel with three of the busboys, who are all from South America.

Daddy loves to watch people and tell stories. At the

catering hall, he sees lots of weddings and sweet sixteens and anniversaries and corporate meetings and confirmations and bar and bat mitzvahs. He has told us about all of these things. It is crazy how much money people will spend on a party that lasts only one night.

Here are the two best stories Daddy told about his work:

#1 One night a sweet sixteen happened at Old Miller Ridge (that is the name of the catering hall). The birthday girl wore a pink dress and a diamond crown. There was a DJ at the party and everybody ate lobster, even the children. The teenagers at the party were rude to the waiters and waitresses, and the girl's father kept talking about how much money he had. (Daddy said the man never even talked to his daughter. He was too busy showing off.) At one point, the man stood on a table and ripped a $100 bill in half! Daddy said he did that to show he had so much money he could afford to waste it. And all of the teenagers applauded. Well, right when the party ended, someone got sick from drinking beer and threw up in the hallway. Daddy was very irritated and went to get a mop, and when he opened the cleaning closet, he saw the girl's father in there. The man was kneeling on the floor in the dark, and guess what he was doing . . . he was putting that ripped $100 bill back together with Scotch tape!

Oh, we laughed so hard at that story! Daddy acted out all the parts. You should have seen him leaping on the table.

Here is the other work story he told:

#2 It was a nice wedding with yellow flowers and salsa music. The bride was a pretty girl with a lot of energy. She danced for hours and talked to everyone. She was from Mexico, and only her mommy and daddy had come to the wedding. The rest of her family was still in Mexico. Her husband was American, and Daddy said you could see he loved the girl, and so did his family, because they all kept hugging her. In the middle of the party, the girl came bursting through the kitchen doors. Her dress was white and full and made lots of swishing sounds. She came into the kitchen to tell everyone how good the food was and to say thank you, and then she started talking a mile a minute in Spanish to the cooks, and it turned out her cousin was from a village close to Javier's (Javier is the head chef at the Miller Ridge). She sat down on a grapefruit crate, with her dress spread all around her. Next to her was a big bucket of potatoes and a peeler, and all of a sudden the girl picked up the peeler and started to work. She sat there for fifteen minutes in her beautiful white wedding dress and peeled potatoes and swapped jokes with the young dishwashing boys, who had all fallen in love with her. She would have kept on working and talking, except that her mother came looking for her, so she had to go. At the very end of the night, the bride and groom came into the kitchen with the leftover wedding cake and champagne and told everyone to enjoy it. Daddy said the cake tasted like butterscotch and the champagne gave him a headache and he couldn't stop laughing because the dishwashing boys kept fighting over which of them the bride had liked best.

I asked Daddy why the girl had peeled potatoes, and he said he thought the boys in the kitchen reminded her of her family in Mexico, so she wanted to be with them for a little while.

It seems like there are so many homesick people in the world. It seems like so many of us live far away from where we were born. Is it like that in Black Banks, too?

On Sunday Daddy had to go back to New Jersey. I am sorry to have written so much in this letter. I have been trying to tell stories to make you feel better. I hope it has worked. You can talk to me anytime, about anything.

I am still sitting on the bedroom floor, but now the moon is shining bright through the window. It is just two days past full, with a little chip off the top. It is hard to see the page, so I think I am writing crooked, but I don't want to turn on the lamp and wake Mum. I hope you can read this. Write to me soon.

Your friend,
Meena

P.S. I translated this for you so you could meet Dadi:

Corn is hung from the ceiling. *Loki* and pumpkin are done. Cauliflower, garlic, and *mooli* are coming up. Tomorrow I will plant potato. Anjali is still talking about the *chai-wallah* who asked if she liked his mustache. When I walk near the school across from the

मकई छत से लटकी है। लौकी और कद्दू खेते हैं। फूलगोभी, लहसुन और मूली बढ़ती है। कल मैं आलू जमा लूँगी। अंजली अब भी चायवालेकी याद करती है। उसने पूछा था क्या मेरी मूंछे पसंद है? चर्च से भर जो स्कूल है, वहाँ मैं बच्चों का पाठ सुनती हूँ। वे हिन्दी में साल के महीने नहीं सिखाते है। अभ्यास भूलनहीं करो। ठंडी तो नहीं है? अच्छीतरहसे भोजन करती हो? किस क्रम है? पिछले हफ्ते मुझे बुखार था, लेकिन कसूरीमेथ की गोलियाँ ने ली और बुखार चले गया।

इस साल, साँप बुरे है। लकड़ियाँ नदी के दूर नहीं जाती है। फिरभी अनेक नकि कर गई। कुछ हमेशा होता है। बहादुर ने नाला की एक गुज्जर का लड़का नकिंयोंके साथ था। एक बड़े गरुड़ने नकिके बच्चोंको धब्बलिया और चट्टानकी ओर भगा लिया। भागती नकि चट्टान से गिर गई और मर गई। गुज्जर लड़केने देखा की गरुड़ा ने नकिंको अपने पंजेमें पकड़ लिया और धीमी गतिसे ऊंचा पढ़ाड़ुकी ओर उड़ गया। महसूस न हो क्योंकि गरुड़कों भी खाना है। गरुड़ बहुत होशियार था।

शरद मेला शुरु हो गया है। बहुत नाच और गाने और ढोल। गाँव की लड़कियोंने दशहरा के लिए अपने अच्छे पोशाक और गहने पहिने थे। कोयली की बूढ़ी उषा और उसकी पोतियों के सथा मैंने परेड़ देखा। याद है उसका पोता जो हमेशा ठिठकी करता था? वह मिशिगन नामक शहर मे अमेरिका में रहते है। उषा ने कहा कि वहाँ एक बड़ा झील है जो समुद्र के रुप मे है। लेकिन यह झील नांध से नहीं बना है। मैं तुम्हारी किताबों के पत्र और अक्षर पढ़ रही हूं। पढ़ना मुश्किल है, लेकिन यह बूढ़ी औरत क्या कर सकती है। आज मैं नाश्ते के लिए, तुम्हारी पसंदी मूला का परांठा बना दिया। पेड़ के नीचे बैठी खाने के लिए और चिड़ियों को देखा। मैं हर सांस से प्रार्थना करती हूं कि भगवान तुम्हे सुरक्षित रखे।

दादी

church, I hear the children chanting lessons. They do not teach the months of the year in Hindi anymore. Make sure to practice and not forget. Are you keeping warm? Eating well? Is Kiku? I had a little fever last week but took the musk deer pills and it went away.

This year the snakes are bad. No one is grazing their goats by the river. Still, one was lost. No matter how you plan, something always happens. Bahadur came for a visit and said the Gujjar boy was grazing his goats high up and a huge eagle came and swooped and a baby goat got scared and ran away from its mother. The eagle chased the baby off a cliff, and it fell on the rocks and died. The Gujjar boy saw the eagle flying with the baby goat in its claws. It was beating its wings deep and slow, going towards the high peaks. I know you are feeling sorry for the baby and its mama, but remember that the eagle must also eat. I think it was very smart about getting its dinner.

The autumn festival has started. Much dancing and singing and drumming. The village girls came in their best dresses for Dussera. I saw old Usha and her grand-daughters from Kolti. She is still as strong as a bull and stubborn as a mule. We stood with each other and watched the parade. You remember her grandson who always had the hiccups? He is also in America, in a place called Michigan. Usha says they have a lake there as big as an ocean, but it is natural, not from a dam. I am practicing my letters and reading the schoolbooks you left. My spelling is bad, but what can an old woman do. Today I made your favorite *mooli paratha* for breakfast and sat out under the trees to eat and watch the monkeys. I think of you with every breath and pray that God is keeping you safe.

Grandmother

4 November 2008

Dear Meena,

    We are out of school for Election Day, but I had to get up early anyway because Mamaw wanted me to go with her to the voting booth this morning. She says that it's important for me to understand how lucky we are to be able to vote. She votes at the fire station, and even though it was cold and gray and drizzly, there was a long

                      long

                long

            long

         long

           long

              long

            long

        long

        long

        long

        long line of people waiting to vote. Mamaw says she can't remember ever seeing so many people turn out. It's because people feel so strongly about this election, with lots of them for McCain and Palin and some of them real big on Obama. I wasn't allowed to go inside with Mamaw when she voted, so I stood there and studied everybody, and I thought it was really cool that people would stand in the rain to make their voice be heard. It made me want to be old enough to vote.

When she came out, Mamaw nodded and smiled to the rest of the people in line, but then this man I'd never seen before—he had a big bushy beard and his mouth was real little and real red—hollered and said, "I bet you enjoyed pulling that lever, didn't you, tree hugger?"

"You bet your ass I did," Mamaw said. I had never, ever heard her cuss before. Some of the people in line laughed, but most of them just kept their eyes on the ground. I felt like I should defend Mamaw, but I didn't know what to do. So I just gave him the dirtiest look I could muster up. He laughed at me, which caused his little red mouth to spread out and show his yellow teeth. I was so mad I couldn't stand it, but when we got in the car Mamaw told me to let it go. "He's just stupid, honey. Ignorant people don't know any better, but stupid people WANT to be stupid. So just forget it."

I am really glad your dad got to come home. It sounds like you all had a real good time together. Mine won't be home until Thanksgiving, but I talked to him on the phone last night. Our conversation didn't go so great because I was telling him how the mine is getting bigger and bigger and how worried I am over it and all that and he said that I should just accept that one person can't change things.

I don't believe this. Last year in history we read about a student in China who stood in front of a tank when the government didn't want to listen to any young people's complaints. After that, people started to pay more attention to how people in China had lost their freedom.

But when I said that, Dad just said, "Yeah, and he's never been seen since, either, has he?" So, see, he completely missed the point. Because I think the point is that if that boy hadn't stood up for what he believed in, then people wouldn't have paid as much attention. And also that tank driver refused to run over him, although they were killing people left and right. So that says something about him, too. Have you ever heard this story?

This happened ages ago, like in the '80s sometime, if I am remembering right.

When I told Mamaw what Dad said, she just shook her head and she tried to bite her tongue and not say anything, but you know her, she couldn't stand it, so she up and said that sometimes she didn't know where he got some of his beliefs, because they sure weren't from her.

The mountaintop removal is getting worse over on Town Mountain. Mamaw goes over to the cliffs every day and makes sure the 'dozers are not getting over on our land. The coal companies are real bad to just take whatever they want, she says. It worries me because even though Mamaw is a true firecracker of a person, she is still old, and sometimes her head swims because she has the sugar diabetes. So I worry about her being up on the cliffs.

I have to stay after school every day because I have basketball practice. I do love basketball. It is one thing that Daddy taught me that has been of use to me. Sometimes, when I get real frustrated, there is nothing that feels as good as running down that basketball court and jumping up to swoosh that ball right through the hoop. It's like flying, sometimes. Seems like when I let that ball leave my fingertips, it's like my troubles are floating away with it, too. Not always. But a lot of the time.

Used to be I liked most of the boys on the team, too, but lately it seems like the only one I can really talk to is my buddy Mark. I've been knowing Mark Combs since the first grade, and we have always been good friends. (He's my best friend here, but you are my best friend period.) He likes to read, too. He's a real brain, although you wouldn't know it to talk to him because he only talks about playing Wii and basketball, but when you go over to his house he has shelf after shelf full of books. He loves all those Narnia books and he's crazy over Harry Potter and he's dying for me to read <u>The Hunger Games,</u> which is his favorite book, but right now he's hooked on the Twilight books. He says he only reads them so he'll have something to talk to the girls about, so he can get them to go out with him, but I think it's because he really loves them.

Mark's mom picks us up every day after practice and then they drop me off. Mom can't come get me because her headaches are getting worse. And Mamaw has started working at this office downtown where they are organizing stuff to fight mountaintop removal.

I always have Mark's mom drop me off at the end of the driveway (which always bothers her because she feels like she should drive me all the way up to the house) so I can walk through the woods along Lost Creek. Well, yesterday as I was walking through there I saw that the creek was muddied up really bad, the way it gets after a big storm, when all the leaves and branches and sand along the banks have been washed in. But it hadn't rained. And as the creek ran on I saw that it wasn't just muddy, but there was some kind of orange gunk in it, too. Our creek has always been as clean as a whistle, so clean that I used to drop down onto my knee and scoop up a handful of it on a really hot day. I told Mamaw and she called some people to come test it.

A couple evenings ago Mamaw and I were out taking our walk in the cool of the day. Rufus was trotting alongside us. Usually he likes to take off occasionally, then come back to check on us, but this time he stayed with us the whole time, like he was afraid to leave us alone. Every once in a while he would look up at me and smile, his tongue lolling out. He's the best dog. It was so warm that some crickets were even still hollering, and it almost sounded like springtime in the woods. The best thing about Mamaw is that she doesn't talk your head off about stupid stuff. She only talks when she has something to say. A lot of grown-ups will always ask how things are going when they don't really care, but she actually wants to hear what you're saying. Anyway, I really like that sometimes Mamaw and I can just be quiet with each other. And that's what we were doing. Looking at the night sky. Listening to that little bunch of crickets that were still hanging on into the fall of the year. I love the way Mamaw walks, easy and slow, but determined, like she has somewhere important to go.

All at once, out of nowhere, Mamaw turned her face to me and said, "It may be that I have to get into some trouble over these mountains, River."

I didn't know what to say, but I quit walking.

"I mean, it might end up that I get arrested or something. But sometimes the law arrests you to make a point. If I were to get arrested, you remember that I <u>intended</u> to, OK?" She dragged out the word "intended."

I just nodded. I still didn't really get it. Still don't.

"And people might say bad things about me at school. But you just tell them that I'm standing up for what I believe in. If something legal is unjust, sometimes people have to do something illegal to get attention. It's called civil disobedience. Have you all studied Rosa Parks yet?"

I asked her if she meant the woman who refused to sit in the back of the bus, and she said yes, and that was an example of civil disobedience.

I told her if anybody ever said anything bad about her at school I'd bust their mouth, but she didn't like that one bit. She talked real fast and loud. She said that was no way to act, and that kind of attitude was what got countries into wars they didn't belong in and caused many a good soldier to die.

Then we listened to the crickets some more, quiet while we looked out at the darkening world.

Some really cool things in your letter:

1. That the Hindi word for forest is "jungle."
2. That those women fought for the trees.

3. That old folks can get food for a dollar and a quarter a plate! Everybody always says that food in the city is REAL, REAL high, but I guess not.
4. That the parakeet sits on the dog's rump.
5. That there is a bowling alley at the bus stop. Our bus stop is the parking lot of the Burger King. I only know this because Dad had to ride the Greyhound home from Biloxi one time because his car was broke down.
6. That the bride peeled potatoes. Mamaw told me that when my parents got married my mother wouldn't let anyone spend money on flowers from the florist because she thought that was a waste of money. So instead she and Mamaw and Dad went up into the mountains and cut ivy and wildflowers and honeysuckle and decorated the whole church that way. So that girl peeling potatoes reminds me of that somehow. This was back when Mom laughed and danced in the living room and wore lipstick and looked at herself in the mirror. Back before her headaches and

before Dad lost his job in the mines and had to go off to the Gulf to find work.

What I did not like about your letter:

1. That man who tore up the hundred-dollar bill in front of people and then taped it back together. I can see why you all laughed at that story, but it made me mad! (Mamaw says there are lots of people around here who live in big fancy houses and drive big fancy cars even though they can't afford them, and that's why the country's in a real mess and the taxpayers are having to bail everybody out. She says that's part of the problem with MTR, because it exists because people are greedy and want something instantly.) I can't stand people who brag and go on in front of people. What a big phony. And . . .

2. I appreciate you telling me everything, but to be honest I have no interest in ever hearing anything else about you shaving your legs or hair

of any kind, period. Sorry, but I'm always honest with my friends and, well, that part about you shaving and all that kind of freaked me out.

OK. Moving on.

Have you noticed that I really like to make lists? It's a weird obsession of mine. When I was little I would make lists of all my books and DVDs and video games. I have notebooks full of lists I used to make. I told you, I'm a weirdo.

I really liked the letter from your grandmother. It made me real sad, though. I thought about if I had to live way across the ocean from Mamaw and how bad I would miss her. I hope that you all get to see each other real soon.

I also forgot to tell you that there is a big mountaintop removal mine over by Mark's house, too. I didn't know it, but today I was trying to talk to him about it again, and trying to describe why it is wrong, and he said they were running that kind of mine on the mountain above his house and that it's noisy and dusty, but his parents told him that was just where they lived so to get used to it.

But he says his mother won't drink the water out of their pipes now.

Basketball practice has been wearing me out lately. It's hard at first, when you're not used to practicing that long everyday, but I'll get back in shape soon and it won't bother me a bit. Coach says that if I keep up the way I've been playing in scrimmages, he's going to start me this year. I've never been a starter before, so this is a big deal. I'm still doing my stretching exercises and I've grown $1/8$ more of an inch. I am now 5 feet and 7 $3/4$ inches.

I guess I better go. Mamaw is hollering for me to come watch Obama give his acceptance speech.

Sincerely,
River Dean Justice

P.S. Have you ever heard anything by the White Stripes? Mark made me listen to them the other day on his iPod and I am really liking them now. I usually don't like hard rock but they are really good. I bet your brother has some of their stuff.

P.P.S. My favorite band ever is the Beatles, though.

November 21, 2008

Dear River,

When I got back from school today, there were all kinds of things lined up in front of our building—furniture and boxes and lamps and Kiku's bicycle with a sign stuck to the handlebars: PLEASE TAKE. It's lucky I came home when I did because a man was just about to wheel the bike away. I told him he couldn't have it, and I dragged it all the way up five flights of stairs by myself. I had to take my backpack off and rest on the landings. It was really hard but I did it.

What happened is that the building manager told the super to take everyone's stuff out of storage in the basement and put it on the sidewalk as if it were trash. He said if any of the renters want to store their things, they will

have to pay fifty dollars a month. That is six hundred dollars a year. We cannot afford that. Mrs. Lau says this has never happened before, storage has always been free, this is just another way to scare rent-controlled tenants.

Her son's high chair from when he was a baby was taken off the street before we could get it. It was something her husband made by hand many years ago. Mrs. Lau is very upset and says one day we will all be pushing shopping carts on Canal Street and begging for food.

When Kiku got home, he hammered some big nails into the wall behind the couch and lifted his bike up there so it would be out of the way. For saving his bike, he made me a peanut-butter sandwich cut into the shape of a heart. It was tasty.

There is something I have to tell you. I haven't told you before only because it is not just my secret but my family's secret and Mrs. Lau and her family's, too.

We are living in our apartment illegally. Only Mrs. Lau's son is allowed to live here, because it is his father's name on the lease. But Mrs. Lau's son lives in Brooklyn. And we live here in his apartment. Mrs. Lau doesn't charge us one penny more than the rent-controlled amount. She does not make any profit. She says it is enough for her to have people next door who will help an old lady when she needs it and walk her dog.

We were going to move out to Queens and get a legal

apartment, but then Mummy and Daddy had to spend all our savings on a plane ticket to bring me to America.

It is very hard to keep a secret like this. It makes me feel like a liar and a cheat, and we are always sneaking around and always afraid of being caught. Mummy-Daddy, Kiku, and Mrs. Lau say if there were another way, we would do it. They say we are not hurting anyone, and as soon as we can change the situation, we will.

I was so scared when I saw Kiku's bike out there today. No one can know that we live here. Once every three months, there is an inspection in our building, and on that day, we take all our photographs down and put up pictures of Mrs. Lau's son and his family. We roll up the peacock bedspread and lay down a Chinese brocade sheet. We hide our spices and borrow some of Mrs. Lau's to stack above the stove. We pack up all our clothes and put them in the trunk of Sushil-Uncle's cab, and when he drives off we go to the White Lotus Chinese restaurant and drink a lot of tea until Mrs. Lau calls Kiku on his cell phone and tells him it is safe to come back. Sometimes I dream at night about people breaking down our door and throwing us out the window into the street. I always wake up before any of us hit the pavement, and I always wake up crying.

Once, this summer, the building manager saw me sitting on the stoop with Mrs. Lau and he asked who I was. She said I was the little girl who helped her with laundry and groceries. When he asked me where I live, I got nervous and said, "Next door." Mrs. Lau said I didn't speak much English and had gotten confused and that I live on Delancey. He asked about her son and she said he was doing business in Hong Kong for two months. Mrs. Lau said she thought he believed her, but I don't know; he kept staring at me. It will be all my fault if we lose our apartments. I should have been able to lie for my family.

I hope you still want to be my best friend. I wanted to tell you the truth all along. But I wasn't sure it was something you wanted to hear. It seems like there are some things you don't want to hear. For example, I am sorry I freaked you out about shaving my legs. I would think it was very interesting if you told me about shaving your face. Since I don't shave my face, it would be my chance to find out more about it. Anyway, I won't tell you about that stuff anymore, since it makes you have the nervous breakdown. But I just have to say that you reacted the way Mummy-Daddy would react. Like, because I'm a girl and you're a boy, we can't talk about certain things. Well, I think that's stupid and babyish. Also, if I'm being my true self with you . . . well . . . I'm a girl, so you may have to hear some girlie things. And I don't understand why boys are always talking about their gas and their poop and all kinds of gross things. But if a girl says something about her body, a boy gets freaked out. Maybe it's just certain boys who are that way.

We both love mountains, so I figure you'll know what I mean when I say that mountains have different moods. You know? The city feels like it has moods to me, too. Sometimes the whole city feels happy or sad or tired or silly or angry. Lately it feels nervous. Sushil-Uncle says people are not taking cabs these days. Mum says three of the other nannies she sits with at Central Park have gotten fired. And I heard a man on the news say that the only people who do well in hard times are undertakers.

How is your daddy doing with his job?

I did not get a letter from Dadi last week. Kiku says sometimes mail is slow or gets lost but I feel worried. I am wearing my watch set to India time today. It makes me feel closer to Dadi, and when I need to know what time it is here, I just subtract ten and a half hours. Sometimes I try to send Dadi messages in my mind. I think that's called telepathy. I don't know if you believe in stuff like that, but I feel like if I concentrate very hard, Dadi can hear me. Do you think that's possible?

What your mamaw said about not busting anyone's mouth, we call that *ahimsa* in India. It means nonviolence and it was how Gandhiji got rid of the British. One time I tried ahimsa when Kiku sat on me to make me promise not to tell Mum he had been out with Ana Maria. I didn't bite him or push him or scream. I stayed still with my eyes closed and said very quietly, "You're hurting me, please get off." I didn't move at all. I let him sit on me and yell. After a few minutes, he stopped shouting. He stood up and said he was sorry and gave me a hug. It was really weird how it worked.

Maybe your mamaw has to get arrested so Mark can have clean water and Town Mountain can stay a mountain. It sounds scary but maybe something good would come of it. Gandhiji got arrested many times, and he

INTENDED to, like your mamaw. If he hadn't done that, India would not be a free country today.

If you come to New York City, I will take you to see the statue of Gandhiji in Union Square. Whenever I look at it, I think about how Mum says Gandhiji was a great man with a very lonely wife. She says, "Think of all the people she had to share him with! The whole country, the whole world. There was nothing left for her and the children." We have to share Daddy with the catering hall. But he is working there for us, so it is different, I think. I don't know. Maybe it isn't. Maybe Gandhiji did what he did for his wife and children, too.

Oh, I forgot to tell you that Valentina got the part of Maggie, and Marvel Jenkins is Diana, with a solo. Every day after school, I have been painting a New York skyline "backdrop" for the "closing number" of <u>A Chorus Line</u>—a song called "One." I have learned all kinds of new words in theater language, such as "lower the fly" and "in the wings," and I know where "downstage left" is, because I am always making little x's with masking tape there so the actors know where to stand. I really like Drama Club. I like the lights and the big red curtain and the way everyone works together. I like how one minute people are laughing and then all of a sudden they are crying, and it isn't crazy, it is just the way they feel. Most of all, I like the singing and dancing. I think Aamir Khan should do a Bollywood version of <u>A Chorus Line.</u> It would be very good.

You know how I said Marvel Jenkins is so strong she scares me? I've been watching her during rehearsal and I've noticed that she always takes her shoes off and that she sits down when she talks to boys. I think she feels bad about being tall the same way I feel bad about being short. I didn't think there was anything in the world Marvel Jenkins felt bad about. Now that I know there is, I don't feel scared of her anymore.

Lucky you with no school on Election Day! I'm glad you stared down that mean man who shouted at your mamaw. A lot of schools in New York stayed open on Election Day, like mine. We even had a test in history. Our teacher told us there are only five states where all schools are closed, and Kentucky is one of them.

My school, PS 20, was one of the voting stations in our neighborhood, so our gym classes were canceled and the whole gym was taken over by people standing in a loooooong line so they could vote. I peeked in and saw the machines with the big levers and the secret blue curtains. I saw a lady in a waitress uniform standing in front of a cop standing in front of a man in a business suit standing in front of a girl wearing hot-pink Rollerblades (every time the line moved, she rolled forward). Some people were serious and some people seemed giddy. It felt like something special and important was going on.

That night, Mum and Kiku and I watched the TV at Mrs. Lau's. We all squeezed on the couch, and Cuba stretched out at our feet. Kiku wore his OBAMA T-shirt and booed every time McCain won a state. He really wishes he were already a citizen and already eighteen, so he could vote.

I felt so nervous watching all the numbers and commentary and the US map filling in with blues and reds. It was weird to see New York blue and Kentucky red, like you and I should be enemies or something. And then, when it was announced that Obama had won, I could feel it all through the air. It was sizzly, like thunderstorm air. Kiku jumped up and pumped his fists and shouted, "YES!"

Actually, it seemed like everyone in the city started screaming at once. We could hear people yelling in the building, and out on the street, everyone was honking their horns. The lady who lives below us shouted, "HALLELUJAH!" and started banging pots and pans together, and when I went out on the fire escape, there were lots of people running up and down chanting, "O-BA-MA," and strangers hugging and slapping five. I wrote Dadi a letter to let her know. She and most everyone in Mussoorie will also be happy. Kiku says there are Republicans in the city, but I didn't see or hear anybody saying mean things about Obama on our block.

Mum cried during Obama's speech. She said he was a decent man and she said it was the first time she had ever heard a United States president mention Hindus. She smacked the couch and said, "It is a good country. It is a good place to be."

Kiku stretched his arms above his head and said, "Mee-Mee, this night is something we will always remember."

I asked Kiku about the White Stripes, and he played that "Blue Orchid" song for me. It made me jump up and down. Every morning before school, Kiku plays AC/DC while he gets dressed and puts gel in his hair. He head-bangs all over the place and makes me and Mum laugh. Sometimes he plays M.I.A. She is my favorite. Have you heard her? I like the Beatles, too. Especially that song with all the violins and lonely people. Which one is your favorite? Kiku told me to tell you that if you like the White Stripes, you should check out the Clash. He says they're really old school.

It is sooooo cold here that it hurts to smile. The wind feels like hammers against my teeth. All the leaves on the pagoda trees have turned yellow and dropped to the sidewalk. I am getting excited for Thanksgiving. It is my favorite American holiday because I love cranberry sauce. Daddy has to work that whole weekend so he won't be coming home and that makes me sad. But Mrs. Lau and Cuba and Xie-Xie will come over and eat with us.

In class today, Ms. Bledsoe told us to write up a list of ten things we are thankful for. I wrote fourteen and could have kept on going but the bell rang. Here is my list, copied from my notebook:

I am thankful for my hands and eyes.

I am thankful for Dadi and the way she loves me.

I am thankful for mangoes.

I am thankful I can do a cartwheel.

I am thankful for my brother and my parents, who always make me laugh.

I am thankful they have jobs.

I am thankful Mrs. Lau's arthritis doesn't hurt today.

I am thankful for mountains and trees and rain.

I am thankful there was no pop quiz in science.

I am thankful for my best friend, River Dean Justice.

I am thankful for Mussoorie and New York.

I am thankful Cuba has silky ears that feel nice to pet.

I am thankful for the book I am reading, <u>Roll of Thunder, Hear My Cry</u>.

I am thankful for the F train that brings Mum home every night.

Yesterday I went with Mum and Kiku to the free citizenship class at the library. Mum brushed my hair and braided it and tied a red ribbon around the end. Kiku put on some of the cologne that Ana Maria got him for his birthday (he told Mum his boss had given it to him). Mum put on her favorite *salwar kameez*. It's yellow with green flowers stitched all over, and whenever I look at it, I smell spring in Garhwal.

The citizenship class was very interesting. It was held in the basement of the library where Mrs. Lau goes to learn English. They have a lot of books down there and tons of computers and everyone is nice. The lady teaching the class is named Mai. She said that ever since Obama won the election, the citizenship class has been full. Mai is American and Chinese. Her hair is very shiny and her skin looks like milk. Kiku kept saying things to try and make her laugh, but she cared more about teaching than boys. She had everyone in class say their name and where they were from. Myself and Mum and Kiku were the only Indians. Mostly people were Chinese and South American. There was one man from the Ukraine who was wearing a grey suit that didn't have a single wrinkle in it. The teacher talked about how we shouldn't get too nervous about the test because that would make it harder to think. She said her parents had been naturalized thirty years ago and that the United States was a great country, one to be proud of.

I don't have to take the test because I am under

the age of eighteen. So once Mummy-Daddy are citizens, I can be one, too. It's called "derivative citizenship" (there are a lot of big words that go along with becoming an American). But I am still going to study for the test, because I want to know how to be a good citizen. Mummy-Daddy have to get their fingerprints done in two weeks, which is another part of the process.

After the class, Mai answered questions. Kiku asked one about how to join the Army so they will pay for your college. I do not want Kiku to be a soldier, but he says it might be the only way to get to MIT.

There was one thing I learned that I didn't like. I didn't know that to be an American citizen you have to "give up prior allegiances to other countries." Kiku defined that for me—it means that once you're an American, you can't be loyal to the country you come from. I don't know why I can't be loyal to India and America at the same time. Kiku says it's more complicated than that, but I don't know, it seems like that's what the words are saying. I am also worried that if the government finds out about our apartment, they will not let us be citizens. There is something on the paper Mai gave us about "no perjury," which Kiku says means lying.

We saw Mai leaving the library. She has an iPod. I told Kiku I wanted one, too, and he pinched me really hard. When Mum went to the bathroom, he said that Mummy-Daddy can't afford to get us those and if I said I wanted one, it would make them feel bad. I hadn't thought of that before. I hope I didn't hurt Mum's feelings.

I should go finish my homework but I want to tell you about one more thing. Something weird happened Monday night, and I can't stop thinking about it. Mrs. Lau was at the senior center and I was sitting on her couch with Cuba, watching the news. I pressed mute for the commercials, like I always do, and heard the sound of a woman crying. I couldn't tell where she was because the sound was coming down the shaftway where three different buildings connect. I have never heard anyone cry like that before. It sounded like she was dying. Every time there was a commercial and I pressed MUTE, I heard her. She never stopped. It went on for a half hour. I kept looking at the clock. I was just about to call 911 and tell them someone was hurt when Mrs. Lau came home. I ran over and told her what was going on, and she took off her coat and held it in her arms and listened to the woman. Then she shook her head and said, "Someone she love betray her. Her heart feel like squashed tomato." She sat on the couch and scratched Cuba's belly and talked to him in Cantonese.

Isn't that a funny thing to say? She seemed so sure of what was wrong with the woman. I hope Mrs. Lau has not ever cried like that. I hope Mum hasn't either. I am still afraid that woman died, but Mrs. Lau says she is positive that she is alive and walking around with a squashed-tomato heart.

I hope you are making good scrimmage and I hope you will start up soon.

Happy early Thanksgiving to you and your family.

Sincerely yours,
Meena

7 December 2008

Dear Meena,

Here are all the bad things that have happened since I wrote you last:

Last week, my mother had such a terrible migraine that she had a fit. She was rolling around in the bed, screaming with pain, and when Mamaw went in to try to help her she jumped up and knocked Mamaw down by accident (she hit her head HARD on the end table but she's OK). By then I had ran in there. She was in so much pain that she knocked everything off the dresser and the chest, then she went to the window and TORE the curtains off the hooks. She ran to the closet and started ripping all of her clothes off the hangers, and finally she fell right down in a heap and put her hands to either side of her head. She pulled out a big hunk of her hair, then screamed from the pain of doing that, too. That's when Mamaw made me get out.

I went into the living room and sat down on the couch, and this is hard for me to admit—so you better not tell ANYbody, not even your brother—but I sat down there and cried. I couldn't help it, I was so afraid. Now, you know that I trust you with my life, or I would not tell this. I thought she was going to die, or that she had cracked up and would never be the same. I'm still not sure if she will be.

Before long Mamaw came out CARRYING my mother. I couldn't believe it. It made me think of you, hauling that bicycle up all those stairs. Mom has lost a lot of weight, though. I hadn't seen her in the full light of day in what seems like forever. She looked so little in Mamaw's arms. This made me want to cry even more, but something in me knew that I had to be strong now, too, so I got up and opened the door for Mamaw, then the car door. Then we drove her to the hospital. On the way there Mom rolled all around the backseat, screaming and crying. "I can't stand it!" she kept saying, over and over.

Mamaw reached over and put her hand on top of mine and said, "It'll be all right. Not soon, but eventually." Then she tightened her fingers around my hand and said, "Don't fret, buddy."

But I am still fretting, because Mom has been in the hospital ever since. And I heard Mamaw on the phone, telling Dad that it could have been an aneurysm. I looked that up on the Internet and that's real bad. I'm awful worried.

The other bad thing is that I got into a fistfight at basketball practice, and now I'm kicked off the team for the first game of the season, which is against our arch-enemy, Blankenship Middle School. That really, really sucks. But I didn't have any other choice but to fight Sam Brock, who is on the team, too. He got mad because we were playing Shirts and Skins in practice, scrimmaging against each other, and my team was beating the fire out of his. We were twelve points ahead when he fouled me. He accused me of charging him, though, and one thing led to another and he got so mad that his whole body turned red and he was shouting so loud that the whole rest of the gym went quiet and finally he called me a tree-hugging faggot.

His father works for the coal company that is mining Town Mountain, and Sam has had it out for me ever since I brought up the mining in science class that day.

Mamaw was fit to be tied when she heard what he called me. "You mean they let him use that word and didn't suspend HIM from playing?" I don't believe I've ever seen her so mad. I was the one who got suspended because I threw the first punch, I told her. "But he said that awful word," Mamaw said.

I told her I had once heard the principal use that word himself, when he told the coach that he better not let "that other team of faggots" beat us. He laughed like it was hilarious, but Coach just looked at him. As soon as I told Mamaw this, I regretted it, because I was afraid she'd go down to the school again. I know you are supposed to always stand up for what you believe in, but she can't be running down to the school every single time somebody does something wrong. Because she'd STAY down there if I told her every little thing.

That was when Mamaw just sat down on the couch and put her hands over her face. "Lord have mercy," she said. "What kind of world are we living in?" I thought she might be about to cry herself, her voice was so choked up. But she didn't. "So full of hate," she said, and sat there a long while, shaking her head, like she wouldn't accept it, like it couldn't be that way.

There is one thing about it, though: Sam is all bark

and no bite. He got in one good hit, which busted my mouth. But I busted his mouth AND his nose AND gave him a black eye.

Mamaw grounded me for hitting him, though. After she had sat there and grieved awhile, she got up and had her mad-at-me tone. "And what about YOU, young man? What did I tell you, not more than a few weeks ago, about hitting people?" She put her hands on her hips. Her eyes looked like blue marbles, hard and shiny. "I've always been real proud of you, River, but you shouldn't have hit that boy. Hitting someone is the last thing you should do."

I asked her what I was supposed to do, then?

She was quiet for a long time, thinking, and for a minute I thought she'd reconsider and agree with me. But then she said, "The best thing would have been to have told him he was a stupid, ignorant boy, and then walked away. Sometimes you have to stand up for what you believe in, and then walk away."

"But sometimes you have to stand up for what you believe in and fight back," I said. Mamaw looked at me for a minute, almost like she didn't even see me before her, and then she turned around and went into the kitchen and started peeling potatoes.

About your secret (which I will never tell another soul, never): what is rent control, exactly? I don't believe we have anything like that here. I looked it up on the Internet, and the best I can tell is that it means people who have rent-controlled apartments only have them if their family members were living there when rent control started. Right? And that only her family can live there legally. Right? I'm not sure I understand.

It only feels wrong because you all have to lie. But Mamaw says that sometimes the government and other people are so crooked that you have to tell a little white lie for the greater good. Maybe that's what this is?

And listen, Meena: I would want to be your best friend no matter what. You are the best person I know. But I'm sorry, I still don't like to talk about shaving your legs and all that. This is something we will have to agree to disagree on. (That's a saying my father used to say all the time when he would be on the phone, talking to contractors who hadn't paid him yet.) It's not about you being a girl and me being a boy. It's just that I think any-thing to do with hair is gross, man.

Sometimes you write things in your letters that I thought nobody had ever thought before, except for me. But then there it is in your letter. Like when you said that the city and the mountains have different moods. I don't know about cities, but I do know about mountains, and I know for a fact that they have different moods.

Today, as soon as I got up, Rufus and I went walk-ing in the woods and went all the way out to the cliffs so I could look at the mountains and see what they were doing over at the mine. Rufus would stay right beside my leg so that I could reach down and cap my hand around his head while we walked, then he would zoom off into the woods like he was tracking a rabbit or possum. Then he'd slink back out of the brush and walk alongside me quietly for a while, then zoom off again. He's funny that way.

I tried my best to not look at the mine. Since it is Sunday, they weren't working, so it was quiet. I could hear everything, I felt like. Even though it was cold today, there were lots of cardinals calling to each other in the trees. Their song is "Birdie, birdie, birdie!" which I think is real interesting, for a bird to say that. Maybe that's why they are called birds in the first place, because of that song? I don't know.

Anyway, there were the birds and the cold wind, and I know this sounds crazy, but it was like I could hear the mountains breathing. They were all spread out below me, back behind town, and all around, too. It seemed to me they were resting today, which is what you are supposed to do on the Sabbath. Even though we don't go to church anymore, I know that you are supposed to remember the Sabbath and keep it holy. Daddy is real upset that Mamaw doesn't take me to church anymore, but she says the woods are as holy as any church and that I'm in them plenty. Mamaw reads the Bible more than anybody I know.

Anyway, the mood of the mountains today was resting and peaceful and sleepy. Maybe it's the only day of the week that they're not listening to Town Mountain being torn down. On those days I bet they are nervous wrecks.

I believe in telepathy. I bet we could have telepathy. I am going to think something real hard, right now. It is

6:34 in the evening on December 7. Maybe when you get this letter you will remember hearing a message from me at this time. Let me know.

Sometimes I think I have telepathy with the mountains.

I would love to see that statue of Gandhi. We learned about him in world civ.

I have not heard M.I.A. You said that was a "she." What kind of girl is named something like M.I.A.? Is it pronounced Mia? Weird, how it has the periods between the letters, like it stands for Missing In Action. My favorite Beatles song is "Here Comes the Sun," but that's a secret. I only listen to it when I'm alone. I'll look up the Clash on YouTube the next time I get online.

That's cool about the citizenship class you went to. I can't imagine seeing all those people from different countries together in one room. Here everybody is American, except for Dr. Patel and his wife. Most people are white, too, but there are a few black people and some Cherokees.

I haven't even told you about Thanksgiving. The main thing about it is that Dad didn't get to come home. He said he had to work, and that if he didn't come home for Thanksgiving he'd get to come home for an extra two days at Christmas. I thought he'd come home early because Mom is in the hospital, but he said on the telephone that he couldn't be of any help to her while she was in there, so he might as well work. I wish he had come home to see her. Used to be when she got a headache, he would make her stretch out on the couch and put her head in his lap. He'd rub her head until she said it felt better, then he'd lean down and kiss her on each closed eye, and after that she'd be well. She said he had a magic touch. And now he won't even come see her when she's in the hospital.

He is supposed to be here in two weeks. I am looking forward to seeing him, but for some reason I am dreading it, too. I don't know why, and it makes me feel bad to say that. But it's the truth.

I've been meaning to ask you, how come you always write out GANDHIJI instead of just GANDHI? In our world civ book is is spelled Gandhi.

I liked your thankful list. I would do one but I'm in a weird mood. I've been kind of sad ever since Mom got put in the hospital. But one thing I am thankful for is knowing you. I'll write you sooner next time. Please forgive me for taking so long. Write me as soon as you can.

Sincerely yours,
River Dean Justice

P.S. The other thing is that they found some kind of chemicals in Lost Creek, so Mamaw has called the government about it. But they haven't come out to check it yet. It makes me sick when I think about good little Lost Creek being polluted like that. I just hope that someday it'll be clean again. Mamaw says we can't fish there anymore because the bluegill are probably poison now. I hate to think about this.

December 5, 2008

Dear River,

~~I hope you are having a nice day. The weather here has been very cold.~~

It is hard to write this. But Ms. Bledsoe said I should get my feelings out.

Dadi has died.

I have said it out loud three times but this is the first time I've written it. Every night since we found out I have dreamed of me and Dadi walking past Jabberkhet, up to Flag Hill. We sit under the banj trees and lean into each other and we don't say anything. We watch the fog drift. I can hear her breathing and I can smell the *amla* in her hair. Once, in the dream, she laughed. She sounded like a little bird. When I woke up, I could still hear her laugh in my ears and I felt happy. But then I remembered.

She died on 20 November but we didn't find out till 23 November when my cousin Anjali called Daddy at work. She'd gone to see Dadi and found her lying on the floor with a fever. Dadi had been grinding corn, which is very hard work. She didn't recognize Anjali, kept calling her Mee-Mee. Oh, River. She was looking for me.

She was always there when I needed her. She always took care of me, even when my own parents and brother left and went to America. It was Dadi who loved me and fed me and made sure I was not alone. But I wasn't there for her when she needed me. I am feeling so bad.

Anjali took her to Landour Hospital, but she needed medicines they didn't have, so Anjali hired a car for Dehradun. It is a very long drive to the city. Anjali said Dadi kept her face pressed against the window all the way down to the valley. She was looking at the mountains. She was saying good-bye. At the hosptial, Dadi went unconscious. Anjali held her on her lap because she didn't want to put her on the floor. Anjali is skinny like me. They sat like that for seven hours and Dadi died in Anjali's lap, and only then did the doctor come. He said Dadi had an infection that had gone into her heart. She was 58 years old.

I keep thinking about Gopi, our neighbor's cow. She is pretty, with a long white tail, and she is very spoiled. Every day she waits for Dadi at the corner of Char Dukkan and they walk together to Sister's Bazaar. She will not understand why Dadi doesn't come. She will be standing there, swishing her tail and waiting for Dadi. She will have to walk home alone.

We were not able to go to the funeral. It is too much money for the plane, and we would not reach there in time because it is such a long journey. Poor Daddy is having a lot of trouble. We have not seen him yet, but when I talked to him on the phone, he could not stop crying. I have never heard him cry before. It scared me. Dadi is his mother. I cannot remember if I told you that before. Mum knew Dadi the whole of her life, too. She was their next-door neighbor, and Dadi was the one who encouraged Mum to be a teacher. She always said, "Teachers are the seed." The thing that makes it harder for Mummy-Dadddy-Kiku is that they have not seen Dadi in nine years.

I used to want to be a poet but now I want to be a teacher. That is what Dadi wanted to do more than anything in the world. She learned reading and writing, but it made her sad that she couldn't do it as well as she cut grass or cooked or climbed a mountain. She said she would never be able to do it without thinking, the way

I did. One time when I got a bad grade at school, Dadi told me how much it hurt that she was not able to go to school as a child. All her brothers were allowed to go but because she was a girl, her father said she didn't need to learn. She went with her mother into the forest and worked. She used to try to read her brother's books, but she could not understand them.

Once when Dadi was pregnant with my uncle, a man cheated her out of 300 rupees. The man took her money and gave her a piece of paper. He said it was a prescription that would make her baby strong. But when she brought the paper to the pharmacy, they said it wasn't real. All the paper said was, "This woman is stupid." Dadi had kept the paper all those years and she showed it to me. She said she was cheated because she could not read or write. She said she did not want something like that to happen to me. I have never gotten a bad grade since she told me that.

I am angry. For many days I was sad. But now I am angry. I am angry at Anjali for only visiting Dadi once a week. I am angry at Landour Hospital for not having medicine. I am angry at Mummy-Daddy for moving to New

York. I am angry at New York for being a place people want to come to. I am angry that Dadi died in a city waiting for a doctor. I am angry at myself. I knew something was wrong when she didn't write a letter that week. She must have been sick then. I should have asked to borrow Mrs. Lau's phone. I should have called Anjali then.

There is something terrible trapped inside me. I think if I open my mouth to say anything, even "Hello," that terrible thing will come out. So I have not been talking. Nobody has. We are all sad and quiet. Mum called in sick to work for two days and Kiku stayed home from school to be with her. She hasn't eaten anything but grapes and crackers. When I came home from school the other day, she was in bed, staring into space, holding a cup of tea. The tea was completely cold. She must have been sitting like that for a long time.

I feel like a different person. I guess anger and sadness are things that settle in your bones and become a part of you. I am still wearing my watch set to India time. I will never take it off.

December 8, 2008

It is three days later. This afternoon, when Mum came home from work, she called Daddy. On Mondays, Daddy's shift doesn't start till late, so he and Mum have a chat. I made Mum a cup of tea and she sat in the bed under the covers, and she and Daddy told stories back and forth about Dadi and what she was like when they were young. Kiku wasn't home yet and I got so sad listening to Mum's side of the conversation. I wanted to hide. But there is no place to be alone in this city. It is not like home where you can walk out into the trees. I know you will say this is weird, but I will tell you about it anyway. I went into the closet by the front door and sat on the floor. I don't know how long I sat in there, but when Kiku came home, he opened the closet door and found me. He looked down at me and sucked in his breath like he'd been punched in the stomach. Then he shook his head and took my coat off the hanger and held it out for me to put my arms through. He said, "Come on. I'll show you something."

We walked east on Delancey past the men selling Christmas trees and the Golden Chariot Bakery and the boutique that sells winter booties for dogs. It was so cold we could see our breath in the air. When we got to the F train entrance, Kiku put me through on his MetroCard. I followed him to the Downtown side. It was about 6:00 p.m., rush hour, so it was really crowded.

I stopped walking, near the benches, because there was a woman playing the trumpet. But Kiku said, "Keep going," and took my hand and pulled me farther down the platform. We had to squeeze around people and we kept getting separated and finally Kiku picked me up and carried me, because it was easier that way. Normally I would be embarrassed but today I didn't care. I put my head on his shoulder and closed my eyes and listened to the trumpet. I don't know what song it was, but it matched the feeling in my heart.

Kiku kept walking until we were at the very end of the platform next to the little red traffic light and the mouth of the dark tunnel. Then he put me down. I had never been to the end of the platform before. It always looked so far away and scary.

We could still hear the trumpet. We watched a rat running on the tracks. We looked across the platform at the people waiting on the Uptown side. The trumpet kept playing. After a while, we saw the two big headlights of the subway far down the tunnel, like yellow eyes in the darkness. Everyone on the platform who was sitting stood up. Everyone who was standing moved closer to the track. The sad trumpet kept playing. Kiku put his hand on my shoulder and said, "Just watch me and do what I do, OK?" I felt like something really crazy was about to happen.

The lights of the train got closer and brighter and then the tracks began to rattle and all of a sudden we could hear the train, and the sound got louder and louder and it swallowed the song of the trumpet, and then the train came roaring into the station and I could feel the wind of it, so hot and smelling of old nickels and quarters, and I looked at Kiku and he looked at me and then he opened his mouth really wide and squeezed his eyes shut and started screaming. I couldn't hear him. I couldn't hear anything but the subway. But I could see that he was screaming as hard as he could. The veins in his forehead popped out and there were tears coming from his eyes.

So I started screaming, too. As hard as I could. I couldn't hear myself but I could feel that terrible thing inside me coming out. I kept screaming and screaming and the train flew by, the cars blinking so fast, and all I heard was the subway and its roar.

We screamed until the subway slowed down and got quiet and stopped. Then the doors opened and all the people inside rushed out and all the people outside rushed in and the doors closed back up and the train pulled away. Me and Kiku stayed where we were and screamed at the next four trains that came into the station. Not a single person heard us. It felt good and we both lost our voices. Poor Mum thinks we have caught a cold. She has such dark circles under her eyes. I am going to make her some of Dadi's *pakoras* tomorrow. I hope she will eat them.

So Kiku has figured out a way to be alone in the city. All you have to do is stand at the end of the subway platform and scream as the train comes into the station. I think some of my anger is gone. I keep thinking about it hanging in the air above the F train platform. I hope it doesn't go inside anyone else. Before I got in bed tonight,

I gave Kiku a big hug. He is just like Dadi in his kindness. But he does it in his own Kiku way.

Today in history, Mr. Orff was talking about the New Deal and how if FDR had waited even one more day to start it, many more people would have starved to death and suffered. He said, "Don't forget that every moment counts." When he said that, I thought about Dadi. I wish I could have just one more moment with her. I miss her hands. I miss the gap between her two front teeth. I miss the way her knees creak in the morning. I miss everything about her.

You have not written in so long that I think you do not want to be friends with someone who commits perjury. Maybe you are not writing because something is wrong in your life. I hope not. And I hope you hug your mamaw extra tight tonight.

Bye,
Meena

11 December 2008

Dear Meena,

I am so so so so so so so so so so sorry. There is nothing else to say. But I'll try.

I cannot imagine Mamaw dying. It seems like the whole world would shut down, so I know how hard this must be. I will be praying for you. Some people I know say that I am a sinner since I never go to church anymore, but who are they to judge me? Don't tell anybody, but I still talk to God all the time. I pray every night, mostly that Daddy will come home from the Gulf Coast and that Mom will stop having such terrible headaches and that Mamaw will be OK.

Sorry about that last part. At first, I wrote it without thinking and then started to delete it because I thought it might upset you worse, what with your own mamaw passing away and all. But then I thought, no, I know Meena, and she would want me to write what is on my mind.

But now the more I write, the more I feel like I might be making it all worse instead of making it better. So I'll just close by saying that I'm sorry, again. I felt like Dadi was somebody I knew, too, so I was sad for that reason. But I guess the main reason I am sad is because I hate to think of you being sad, and hurting.

There are only two other things I want to say:

1. I am glad you want to be a teacher. But you can be a poet, too. My teacher Ms. Stidham is the best English teacher in the world, but she is also a poet. She doesn't like to talk about it at school, but one of her poems got published in a magazine, and another teacher at school, Mrs. Sherman, was so proud of her that she had the secretary announce it over the PA system. Ms. Stidham's cheeks got blood red, and when we all clapped too long she didn't even get mad like usual, but just laughed and kept putting her hands out as if to tell us to stop, but we didn't, and I think she might have cried a little, too. We begged and begged for her to read her poem to us but she wouldn't. So you don't have to choose one or the other. You can be both, like Ms. Stidham.

2. I liked the part of your letter about Kiku carrying you and then you two screaming in the subway. He seems like a real good brother. I wish I had one. And I bet the screaming will help you to not feel so mad anymore.

Mamaw says that sometimes it's real good to get mad, that it's just what a person needs to do. But you can only stay mad so long without it making you feel bad. That's what I think, at least.

I hope you know that I am thinking of you and hoping that things get better. Oh, and right now I am loving the Clash. I've listened to all of their songs on YouTube. My favorite is "Should I Stay or Should I Go." I couldn't help but to dance to it, so I got up and danced all over my bedroom, bouncing on the bed and jumping all over the place. When the song went off, I was sweating and breathing hard. It felt good, like I had gotten some frustration out in a good way.

Sincerely,
River

December 10, 2008

Dear River,

I was so happy to see your letter in the mailbox. It's been lonely without you. I thought you didn't want to be friends anymore. I think our two letters must have crossed in the mail.

How are you doing? You must be so worried. Is your Mum still in hospital? Is she going to be OK? That was all really scary to read. I will not tell anybody that you cried. I would have cried, too.

It is very good that you and your mamaw were there for your mother when she needed you. I loved what you said about the mountains. That was so beautiful and true.

In ten days it will be one month since Dadi died. I think about her all the time. I try to remember everything I can about her. I am afraid I will forget. Mum is eating again but she has not laughed in a while. Kiku is finding it hard to concentrate on his homework.

It made me sad to read about your parents and how they used to be. Maybe they will be like that again someday. Sometimes I think Mummy-Daddy don't fight anymore only because they hardly ever see each other.

I can't believe you gave Sam Brock a black eye. Your fistfight sounded just like a movie!!!! I hope you will be back playing soon. I agree with your mamaw that it's not good to hit people, even stupid boys like Sam Brock. But I agree with what you said, too. Sometimes it is very hard to know what to do.

I had never heard that word "faggot" before I came to New York. I asked Valentina what it meant and she said, "A boy who wants to make out with other boys." I said, "Like gay?" And she said, "Yeah, but a mean word for it."

There's a boy in Drama Club named Carlos. He is in the ninth grade and knows about everything. Marvel Jenkins says he doesn't live with his parents because two years ago, he told them he was gay. They beat him up and made him sleep on the floor of a church, and Carlos called the cops on them and they all went to court. Now Carlos stays with his aunt on Essex Street and they go to midnight movies all the time and on weekends they don't change out of their pajamas if they don't feel like it.

Carlos knows the words to every single movie that was ever made. He's playing the part of Gregory Gardner in <u>A Chorus Line</u>, and he's also doing hair and makeup for the girls. He's better at it than Ms. Bledsoe. Anyway, someone wrote that mean word on Carlos's locker. I didn't see this happen because I was absent that day, but Marvel Jenkins saw and she told everyone. It was in between classes and there were lots of kids and teachers in the hallway, and Carlos took out a black Magic Marker from his backpack and he drew a flower and a rainbow on his locker. Then he wrote in big letters underneath the word "faggot": AND PROUD OF IT. He got detention for defacing school property, but he said, "I refuse to honor my detention unless the other individual who wrote on my locker confesses to his crime like a real man."

Well, the principal said that was fair. Nobody confessed, so Carlos didn't get detention. All that stuff is still on his locker. I went and looked at it the other day. He's really good at drawing flowers.

Maybe you could do something like that if Sam

Brock calls you that word again. If you take the bad word and make it good, then you won't have to hit him and you could just play basketball like you want to.

Do you think you would like making out with a boy or a girl? I asked Kiku that and he said, "Duh. I have a girl-friend, stupid." But his friend David has a boyfriend and they call each other sweetie and wear each other's jeans. That sounds nice to me.

Everybody at school is getting excited about Christmas. Sometimes I feel left out at Christmas because I don't know the songs and we don't have a tree. Do you have a tree? I bet you and your mamaw make it beautiful. I saw the big one at Rockefeller Center on Mrs. Lau's TV. She said they should just plant one there and decorate it every December and stop killing a new tree each year. I think that is a very good idea.

Daddy will be working through Christmas. Because he is not Christian, the catering hall asked him to. But he will come home for New Year's. I am dreading the New Year. I don't want it to turn 2009. It will be the first year we will live in a world without Dadi.

We have been working hard in Drama Club. The play

goes up in five weeks. We are going to have rehearsals even over Christmas break. I am still painting the backdrops, and I am learning how to do the light cues. I like that everyone in Drama Club has at least two jobs. You learn more that way.

We had three inches of snow yesterday. You can always tell how much it has snowed by looking at the tops of the parking meters. It came down like confetti and made me miss Dadi so bad I thought I would vomit. She loved snow and called it God's blessing. I wonder all the time where Dadi is now. I know she would say she is in things like snow and sunshine. She would say that nothing ever dies, it is just remade. But I still miss her.

I sat on the fire escape in my coat and hat and gloves and watched the snow for a long time. It went past my ears like whispers and it turned the sky pink. I saw a woman in the building across the way watching the snow, too. She was standing in her window, and when I waved at her, she waved back.

The city salts the pavement after it snows, which makes it very painful for Cuba to walk. The salt cuts up his paws and makes him bleed. I looked at those booties for dogs but they cost $20. When I told Kiku, he said he would "do a mad engineer rendition of a bootie." Sometimes he talks crazy. Well, he cut up old socks, layered them with duct tape, and then rubber-banded them around Cuba's paws. Homemade booties. He is very inventive, my brother. And Cuba looks so funny! Watching him, Mrs. Lau and I can't stop laughing. With the booties on, Cuba can't walk properly. He lifts his paws up high and tries to bite the booties off, and then he sits down and refuses to budge and looks very, very sad. But I think he is starting to like them. I think he has realized that when he has them on, his paws don't get hurt by the salt. Today he even licked my ear as I put the booties on him.

This is what Cuba looks like in his mad-engineered booties:

Does Rufus come inside when it's cold?

I do not know much about rent control, so I asked

Mrs. Lau. She said hers was started in 1971. So long as she or her children live nonstop in the apartment, they can keep paying the fixed rate. Mrs. Lau says the law was invented to help tenants, so landlords couldn't keep charging more and making life impossible. But these days, landlords want all the rent-controlled people to leave, so they can sell their apartments for a lot of money. Sometimes they do very bad things to make people leave. For example, there is a woman named Jennifer who lives on the second floor. Her mother had their apartment with rent control, and when she died Jennifer got the lease.

Jennifer has a baby. Last week, Mrs. Lau was talking to her on the stoop and she found out that because the landlord hasn't repaired Jennifer's apartment in 25 years, it is falling apart. There is mold everywhere from the leaks, and you can see the pipes in the walls and ceiling. Jennifer said Child Services got an anonymous call, and when they came and saw her apartment, they said she could not raise her daughter there—it was too dirty and dangerous. She said she knows it was the landlord who made the anonymous call. But he won't fix anything and Jennifer doesn't have the money for repairs.

So now she either has to put her baby in foster care or move. Mrs. Lau says they will have to leave New York and go to New Jersey, but the girl doesn't know how to live anyplace else. She doesn't even know how to drive a car because she has always taken the subway and bus. She was born here, and so was her mother and her grandmother.

The address you mail letters to is actually Mrs. Lau's post office box. That is something else I do. I get the mail every day. We do not have mail sent to the apartment because then people would know we live here. That is also why we don't have TV or a landline or Internet—besides the fact that it is expensive—so there is no record of us with any companies. I don't know what kind of lies we are telling, if they are white or green or red. But they are hard to tell and I wish we didn't have to.

I don't remember hearing a message from you on December 7 at 6:34 p.m. Unless what you said was HI. I will try to send you a message now. There. I just did. December 10, 9:07 p.m. Did you hear me? I think we could have telepathy, too. That would be really fun. And it would save money on stamps.

I hope you will not be jealous but I have a new pen pal. It is Daddy. I am helping him study for the citizenship exam. We read the readings on the same day, and then I make up little quizzes and mail them to him. He sends them back to me and I grade them. Kiku got me a red pen and I am practicing to be a teacher.

In a weird way, it is hard to do the readings. I feel like I shouldn't be a citizen of a country that wasn't Dadi's. Sometimes I want to run away and go back home. Maybe if I go to Mussoorie, Dadi will be there, singing a song, watching a thunderstorm. Maybe I just need to go home and then she will come back. Maybe she is waiting for me.

M.I.A. stands for Missing In Action. It is cool that you knew that. I had to ask Kiku what it meant. M.I.A. is Tamil but grew up in Sri Lanka, and her daddy was a revolutionary who hid from the army. So she grew up without him. She is like us, away from her daddy. I don't know if you would like her music. She curses and she talks a lot about being a girl. I bet she is someone who would write a song about shaving her legs. Kiku calls her "sassy." He and Mum and I listen to her albums all the time. But we don't play them in front of Daddy. He only likes Bollywood songs from the '70s and the Rolling Stones.

I do not know "Here Comes the Sun." I will ask Kiku if he has it. If you like it I know I will, too.

I forgot to answer one of your questions from a while ago. You asked about Gandhiji. In Hindi, "ji" is something you put at the end of someone's name to show that you respect them. जी = JI Gandhiji is to be respected, so we always say "ji" at the end of his name. You do it for people who are older than you, too. Like if I had met your mamaw in India, I would call her Mamawji. MAMAWजी

It is a sad night here. I can hear Mrs. Lau's television through the wall. I better go fold the laundry. Having Kiku's bike inside has made everything very cramped. Right now the bike is in the middle of the living room, covered in all of our underpants and socks. It saves money on the dryer to hang things up. I can see Mum studying at the kitchen table. She has decided to go to nursing school when she becomes a citizen. There is a lot she has to learn first, though.

I have been trying to be cheerful in this letter. I hope it has worked. I hope you are doing OK. I will send you another telepathic message tomorrow. Maybe if I stand on the roof you will hear me better. I hope that your mother is home and that she doesn't have a headache. I hope your daddy arrives soon and in a good mood. Merry early Christmas. Keep your chin up. Ms. Bledsoe has been saying that to me. Keep your chin up. I like it.

Namaskar, mera dost,
Meena

P.S. I never heard that word "Sabbath" before. It's very pretty. Thank you for telling me about it. I think it would be a good name for a parakeet. I will tell Mrs. Lau.

P.P.S. Today the sun was out, and as I walked to school I wondered if it was sunny in Kentucky, too. And then I thought to myself that it's the same sun here as it is there, and that made me feel like you're not so far away after all.

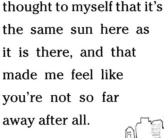

15 December 2008

Dear Meena,

There were lots of good things in your last letter, but I think you're a total nymphomaniac for asking me if I'd like to make out with a boy or a girl. I don't want to even THINK about that, man!

Let's make a deal right now, that we won't talk about things like this anymore, because it's just weird. I am writing a contract below and you can sign it and mail it back to me, OK? All right.

I, Meena Joshi, do solemnly swear that I will never again write to my friend River Dean Justice about
   1. anything to do with hair
   2. making out of any kind
Signed, _____
(your signature)
Date _____

Bye,
River Dean Justice

December 17, 2008

NYMPHOMANIAC!?!?!?! I'm a nymphomaniac for asking if you'd rather make out with a girl or a boy?!?!?!?!?!?!?!?!?!?!?!?!?

1. I had to look that word up in the dictionary.
2. Who says gross things like that?
3. It's not true. I AM NOT A NYMPHOMANIAC.
4. I am not going to sign your stupid contract. If I were a lawyer, I would sue you for "defamation of character."

You are JUST like Mummy-Daddy. You get mad about the craziest things. If you don't want to tell me who you'd rather kiss, you should just say so. You don't have to insult me to get out of answering.

By the way, I'd still be your friend no matter how you answer.

Let's see how YOU like it when I call YOU names:

You're a great big squawking, mean, cowardly chicken-boy.

I can't believe I had to waste a stamp on this letter. I'm not writing to you again until you apologize for freaking out on me.

This letter is from:

Your Friend Who Shaves Her Hairy Legs

(Hahahahahahahahahahaha. I bet you're really freaking out now.)

19 December 2008

Dear Meena,

  We have been in a fight for three letters now, and that is too long for friends to be mad at each other. I have decided to say I'm sorry for calling you that name. It wasn't right of me, and I'm sorry. I have been worried about it, and sometimes when I try to go to sleep at night I lay there for a long time, wondering if you are still mad at me.

  Mamaw got mad the other day because somebody called Sarah Palin a bad name. She said that even if you don't agree with somebody that you shouldn't call them names and that when you start calling names you've lost control of the conversation. So that made me think about what I had said to you and made me realize that I'm real sorry.

  If you are sorry, too, please write me back so we can be friends again.

  Yours truly,
  River

December 22, 2008

Dear River,

Thank you for your apology. I am glad we can put these bad times behind us.

I don't think I should be sorry for being myself and asking you a question I was curious about. So I am not going to say I'm sorry for that. What I am going to say is that I am very sorry to have upset you. I did not mean to do that. I hope I never upset you again.

Mrs. Lau says that boys mature slower than girls. She says that maybe you are not ready to talk about things like what I asked you about. She says I should respect that it upsets you and just not talk about it anymore. So that is what I will do.

I want you to know that you're my friend no matter what. OK?

Yours truly,
Meena

Google News Item

December 22, 2008, 4:56 p.m.

Boulders Dislodged from Mine Site Crash into School; Building Destroyed, At Least Five Children Hurt

(Black Banks, KY) A bank of rocks—left over from a mountain blasted by thousands of pounds of explosives at a coal mining site—crashed into a Kentucky middle school, leaving behind irreparable damage and injuring five children who were in the gymnasium during basketball practice.

"It's a miracle the boys weren't killed," said Carl Blanton, a parent of one of the injured basketball players at Daniel Boone Middle School. "If school hadn't been out, there would have been dozens of dead children here."

Most of the boys' injuries resulted from them trying to escape the approaching boulders, which were slowed down only by the thick walls of the gymnasium. However, the jolt of the boulders caused ceiling trusses to fall into the gymnasium and onto five of the boys.

The largest of the boulders managed to break through an exterior door and struck Mark Combs, who remains in stable condition after his left leg was crushed by the three-ton boulder.

The massive rocks—more than a dozen—rolled down a 1,500-foot-high embankment at a mountaintop removal mining site. Mountaintop removal is a controversial form of coal mining that has recently come under fire from citizens groups in the Appalachian Mountains. In this practice, the entire contour of the mountain is changed forever and waste—or overburden—is stored in nearby "valley fills," impoundments containing rocks, dirt, and felled trees.

Opponents of the mining practice say it was just a matter of time before someone was injured by the mining site, which stands atop Town Mountain, whose final slopes serve as the backyard to the school.

The Environmental Protection Agency is on-site and assisting in the cleanup. The school's principal, Harold Wright, who refused an interview for this story, would only say that the buildings are beyond repair and will have to be razed and rebuilt. In the meantime, when students return from their Christmas break, they will attend school at a local church and will take lunch in double-wide trailers that are being supplied by FEMA.

The fate of the basketball team, which was on track for the state championship, is more uncertain. A local elementary school's gymnasium is available for practice, but with so many team members out for the rest of the season, the coach is unsure about restructuring his team.

"I can't even think about that right now," says Coach Ted Simpson. "These boys are like my own sons, and all I can think of right now is them getting better."

Local grassroots activists have been fighting the mining practice for years and have been galvanized by the recent opening of the mine so close to the school. Nellie Justice is among the most vocal of those opponents. "We've been saying for years that something like this would happen," Justice says. "They think we've fought hard before, but they've not seen anything yet. This means war."

Justice's grandson, River Dean Justice, is one of the members of the team but was not harmed in the accident.

From: <kikurocks@yahoo.com>
Date: Dec 23, 2008 at 3:18 PM
Subject: Very worried
To: kybasketballboy94@mountain.net

We heard about your school and the boys on the basketball team getting hurt. I know you are alive but I am very, very, very, very worried. Please don't take a long time to write me back. Last night I dreamed you were all bloody and had no teeth. I hope you are OK.

Your friend,
Meena

P.S. This is Kiku's e-mail but you can write me back here.

From: <kybasketballboy94@mountain.net>
Date: Dec 23, 2008 at 6:45 PM
Subject: Re: Very worried
To: kikurocks@yahoo.com

Meena,

It was so good to see your e-mail. Thank you for worrying about me. I am all right but it was awful scary. I'll tell you about it as soon as I can. They say that the boulder that came through weighed THREE TONS. You remember me talking about my best friend here, Mark? They say now that his leg is torn up so bad he'll never play basketball again. I've been real upset for him. I better go for now, but I wanted to let you know that I'm OK and will write soon.

If something like this ever happens again, you can call me at 606-553-4852. We should have given each other our phone numbers way back, but I just never thought of it. Sorry. I guess sooner or later we would have to break our rule about No E-mail.

R

25 December 2008

Dear Meena,

It is Christmas morning and the house is real quiet since everybody is still in bed, so I thought I'd write you. We open our presents on Christmas Eve, so all that is left to do today is open the stockings. Then later this afternoon we would usually have Christmas dinner, but not this year since we are going to the hospital to visit the boys who are still in there.

I guess there is not much use in telling you all about it, because the whole country knows about it now. People let the big businesses get away with anything until the news gets involved. Mamaw says it's only because a school is part of the story—and it also makes for a good Christmastime story because it's sort of a miracle that we weren't all killed. She says that they'll forget all about us until the next time something like this happens. Mamaw says that mountain people get rediscovered every once in a while, but usually only when something bad happens.

When my parents were little, there was a big mud slide caused by the coal company that killed 125 people.

But people have forgotten about that, too, although everybody was all mad about it at the time. Mamaw says that people don't really care about people here because they think we're a bunch of stupid hillbillies who are looking for a handout. She said you'd understand that better than anybody, because people think that immigrants are all looking for a handout, too. She said that the stereotype is that Indians are smart, though, and either REAL poor or REAL rich. Mamaw says that the bad part is that people "reduce" us—hillbillies AND Indians—down to some kind of little "generalization." These are her words. They sort of make sense to me, though.

Anyway, I'll try to make this quick as possible.

We have to practice basketball even during Christmas break, which sucks, but Coach is pretty cool, and I really do think he makes us work so hard just because he cares about us. So we were at basketball practice and we'd been there about an hour. Had a pretty hard workout. Skins verses Shirts. Then all at once it felt like there was an earthquake. We have them here sometimes. The biggest one I've ever felt was a 6.5 on the Richter scale. This felt way stronger than that. We knew that they were blasting up on the mountain because we'd felt little tremors all day long, like it was running right under the hardwood of the gym floor. But this was a thousand times stronger than that. I truly thought the floor would stand up in front of us. It was like we all froze, not knowing what to do.

Then we heard the first big rock slam into the side of the gym. My first thought was that a car had run into the wall. It hit so hard the wall buckled. I could see it, in slow motion, as the crack ran on up the ceiling and caused some of the humongous lights and rafters to fall. One of them fell right on Paul Jenkins. Right across his chest. I thought for sure he was dead, but turns out it just broke his ribs.

Then the big boulder came right through the side door. It took out the door and parts of the wall around it and rolled right across the floor toward Mark. He just stood there. I hollered, "RUN!!!" as loud as I could. Later I found out that I had hollered so loud it hurt my throat. It's still a little sore. Just when I said that, Mark jumped back but not completely in time, because the rock just smashed his leg. He passed out as soon as his leg was flattened.

I started to run to him, but a big rafter fell right between us and I thought for sure he was a goner. Coach, too, because I had seen him running toward Mark, screaming and waving his arms.

Then I figured out that I should run, too, because it seemed like the whole ceiling was caving in. I could hear the other boys behind me, hollering, but it was like they were way down in a well somewhere, they sounded so far away. So we ran out the door on the other side, and I looked up and it seemed like every bit of Town Mountain was rolling down to crush the school. All these big rocks, and lots and lots of real small ones, and a big wall of dirt.

That's when Coach came running out with Mark in his arms. I swear, Meena, there were two big rocks that came so close to him that I bet he felt the wind off of them. And then everything got real quiet. The strangest, deepest quiet I have ever known. Coach popped up and started counting everybody. He was like somebody wild. "Who am I missing?" he said, breathing hard, talking so fast spit was flying from his lips. "Who? Who's not here?" He kept saying, more to himself than us, but then I told him we were all here. Four other boys were hurt pretty bad. But Mark was the worst. His leg looked like a piece of ragged meat and his face was going blue. There was blood everywhere. I saw it spreading out in a big pool around his leg. He was moaning, with his eyes rolled back in his head, and one of his hands wouldn't stop shaking. I couldn't stop looking at his hand because it was freaking me out the way it kept shaking. And that's the last thing I remember for a while.

Next thing I knew there were all kinds of sirens. Then we were at the hospital and I passed out. They said I was in shock. But I got OK. They gave me a Coke and a Little Debbie, which made me feel better.

I couldn't believe it, but my mom came to the hospital. I hadn't seen her out and about in ages. But there she was. I know this sounds crazy, but I had forgotten how she moved. I was so glad to see her up and walking on her own, to not be lying down in bed with a washcloth on her forehead, that my first thought was that this was all worth it. I felt bad later, thinking that, especially because Mark may never walk again and they might even have to amputate his leg, although that's not in the papers yet.

Mom ran in with Mamaw close behind. Mom ran over and wrapped me up in her arms and then tears were just

S
T
R
E
A
M
I
N
G

down her face like little waterfalls. But I didn't cry. I was so happy to see her, but I was numb, too. I don't know how to explain it. But I thought, this is how a rock feels all the time.

I guess people would say rocks don't feel. But not feeling is a kind of feeling, too. Does that make any sense?

Then Dad came running in, and I've never seen him so scared. He was as pale as a ghost, and once he saw that I was all right, he actually had to run in the little bathroom there in the emergency room and throw up. Being scared messes with people in different ways, I reckon.

Some of the boys are still in the hospital and all the news crews are camped out down there. I mean everybody. NBC, ABC, CBS, CNN, FOX, MSNBC, every one of them. Mamaw has been on ALL of them. Have you seen her? You'd know it was her, instantly, especially since her last name is Justice, just like mine. Nellie Justice. I guess you don't really know her name since I always call her Mamaw. But that's her. Dad said she was "giving them hell."

Mamaw and this bunch of people she works with called Kentuckians for the Commonwealth are planning a big march on the state capital. There are movie stars and singers and writers coming to march, too. But mostly just regular people. And even coal miners. You won't believe it but my mom and dad are going, too. Mamaw has everybody all fired up. She has been on the phone nonstop since it happened.

Since all the rocks fell, it's easier to see how much of Town Mountain they've taken. Used to be you really couldn't see all the damage from down in the valley, but now it is just **GONE**. It makes me sick.

I have thought of you many times through all of this and wondered what you were seeing on the news about it. I know it is a big news story but wonder how much you've seen. Let me know.

They wanted to put me on the news but my parents said no. They have been showing the picture of the whole basketball team, so you might have seen me that way. It is weird to be on the news like that. Every time we turned on the TV for a couple days there I was in that group picture. Then they show the gym with all the rocks piled up against it. On one channel they have made up special music for when they talk about us, and they have this big movie title that glides onto the screen that says, "Christmas Miracle in Kentucky." Mom says this is ridiculous, for news to have theme music. She has been better since all of this happened. I don't know why. But anyway, now we just don't even turn the television on.

How are YOU, Meena? I am so sick of talking about all of this that I would much rather hear what's going on with you. I still think about your dadi and feel bad for you. I hope you are not too sad, still. I hate to think of you being sad.

It started snowing yesterday and I thought of what you said about your grandmother being in the snow and the sunshine.

To answer your question: No, Rufus doesn't come in when it's cold. He's a country dog and would freak out if we brought him in the house. One time he ran in the house because he was scared of a thunderstorm that was coming (he heard it before we did), but then he got even more scared to be walking on the linoleum, so he ran back out and ran under the porch and wouldn't stop shivering for the rest of the night.

In all the excitement I guess I haven't really told you about Dad coming home. He had only been home a couple days when the rockfall happened, so I haven't been with him the way I would have regularly. But the first couple days were real good. When he came in I realized how much I had missed him, and I hugged him so hard I hurt his neck. "Whoa there, now, little man," he said. "You're going to break me in two." I had forgotten that he called me little man sometimes.

When he went in to see Mom, he kissed both of her eyes and whispered, "Oh, how I have missed those pretty, pretty green eyes." But later on that night when I was supposed to be asleep (but was finishing the new <u>Spider-Man</u> instead), I heard them arguing. Their words were muffled through the wall, but I could tell by the way the words bounced around that they were fighting. She was in the hospital until about a week before the rockfall and wasn't doing much better, really, until the rockfall. She hasn't had a headache since.

There was one more question I needed to answer: I only listen to "Here Comes the Sun" when I'm alone, because it makes me sad, even though it's a happy song. I don't know why it makes me sad. It just does.

I know, I'm weird. But I can be weird with you. Remember, we can be our true selves with each other.

I'm looking forward to hearing from you soon. Write me as soon as you can.

Yours truly,
River Dean Justice

P.S. What I said on Dec. 7 WAS "Hi." So you did hear me. And on December 10 at 9:07 I believe I heard you say, "I am here, River Dean Justice! It's me, Meena." At least that's what I thought I heard. And later that evening I thought you said to me, in my head, "Did you hear what I said earlier?" So I think we do have telepathy. Let me know if these are the messages you sent me.

January 7, 2009

Dear River,

Happy New Year. Everyone is so glad you are OK. Mum did a special aarthi for you and I have been sending lots of telepathic messages. Are you still needing Little Debbies to feel better? What kind of medicine is that?

I am writing tiny so I can fit on the back of this flyer. I have just finished hanging twenty of them up around school. I drew the picture and Carlos did the lettering. The show "goes up" next week.

How is your friend Mark? I hope he still has both his legs. I hope he is not in pain.

We did see your mamaw on TV. I knew it was her from her last name and from what she was saying and because, I don't know, I just knew. In the group photo, I think you are the smiling boy with freckles at the end of the front row. Am I right? When the photo came on TV, I jumped up and pointed, and said, "That's River! I know that's him!" Mrs. Lau yelled at me for getting fingerprints all over the screen.

It was so scary to find out from TV. I was watching the news with Mrs. Lau and Cuba and then all of a sudden there was Town Mountain looking like something had taken a big bite out of it. It was terrible to see the trees knocked over and your school squashed flat. When the news lady said boys from the basketball team were hurt, I got so scared I couldn't breathe. I can't believe this has happened to you.

We watched the story on TV for three days. Mrs. Lau cursed in Chinese whenever that man who owns the coal company came on. She said he was greedy and had a liar's chin. For the past week, there hasn't been anything on about your school. Now all the stories are about Obama's inauguration and the subway fare hike.

Since Jennifer and her baby got kicked out of the building, Mrs. Lau has been picking up Jennifer's newspaper from the vestibule. She cut out all the articles on Town Mountain, and Mum let me put the picture of your basketball team on the fridge. I started saying, "Hi, River," every time I opened the fridge. Then Kiku started doing it, too, to make fun of me, and now everyone does it, even

Mummy-Daddy. Not like it's funny, just like it's something that's part of opening the fridge around here.

I have read your letter five times to myself and once out loud in Ms. Bledsoe's class (don't worry, just the part where you described the rocks coming down). There are seven other kids from the Summer Program in class, but nobody but me is still writing to their pen pal. They were all surprised that we are best friends but we haven't ever met. Ms. Bledsoe said that's what happens when you find a "kindred spirit."

Where are you going to school now?

I am sorry about all the bad things that happened. But it is good that your mum got out of bed and your daddy came home and that people are listening to your mamaw and helping her fight. It's like everything you've been praying for has come true.

I feel like we have been through some very hard times together. I am almost out of page. Sorry this is so tiny. I will write more soon. Be safe, River Dean Justice. I am thinking of you and Town Mountain.

Your kindred spirit,

Meena

15 January 2009

Dear Meena,

This will be short because I have so much homework to make up. Ms. Stidham is making us write another
poem, so I am going to practice by making this letter like
a poem. So here goes.

Here are the answers to your letter:
Little Debbies are not medicine.
They're little cakes. We are going to school
in the Lost Creek Church of God now. It's weird
to be going to school there. We are
in the basement, which is damp and cold all
the time, and smells like Summer Bible School.
I liked how your teacher said we were "kindred
spirits." I looked that up on m-w
.com and it says that means we are related
spirits, like family who is not blood
family. I told Mamaw this and she said,
"Sometimes that's the best family of all."

There, that seems like a good place to end the poem. I actually kind of like writing them. It's fun to count up the syllables and think about where the best place is to make the line break so that there is a mystery. I guess I better run for now, but write to me when you can, please.

What is an "aarthi"? You said your mum did one. I'm guessing it's like a prayer. ?????????????????????

Later, Tater,
River

January 20, 2009 (Sometimes I forget and still write 2008. Do you?)

Dear River,

Surprise! I've been learning to type!!! It just took a second to make all those exclamation points.

I don't think I would have ever learned to type if it weren't for you and our letters.

I am at the library. The man at the computer next to me keeps sneezing, and everyone around him keeps saying, "Bless you." It is kind of funny. I never used to say "Bless you" when someone sneezed at home. That is something I started doing since I came to New York.

Happy Inauguration Day. We watched it on TV at school. Did you? Ms. Bledsoe was so happy she cried. She talked to the class about what it means to have a president who looks like her and so many other people in the country and world, and she talked about how times have changed. Her great-great-grandparents were slaves in North Carolina. She said she wished they were alive to see this day.

Kiku said that if he and Ana Maria have a baby

someday, maybe it could be president. He said he would like to have a half-Mexican, half-Indian leader. I like Obama because he is very smart and because it seems like he tries hard to be fair to everyone. Also, I think he has nice hands and teeth.

My favorite parts of watching the inauguration were the music, the pictures of Washington, D.C., and when President Obama said his middle name. "Hussein" is also an Indian name, and it made me feel very proud and like I belonged to what was happening, in some way.

I am at the library because there is no heat in our apartment. There is also no water, and yesterday a dead mouse fell through Mrs. Lau's ceiling and onto her kitchen table. Cuba stretched his nose over the edge of the table and sniffed the mouse for a long time. It is so cold we have all been sleeping in our coats and hats and scarves, and when Mum gets home we turn on the oven and leave the door open and huddle around it to warm up.

Mrs. Lau says the water and heat aren't really broken. She says it's the landlord trying to make us all so uncomfortable that we will leave the building so he can sell our apartments for a lot of money. Mrs. Lau says this is illegal but it is what happens all over Chinatown. She says if it were rich white people living in our building, the landlord would fix things and take good care of everyone.

I have been listening to "Here Comes the Sun." It is a really nice song. I love the way he sings "It's all right." Kiku gave me a little picture of the Beatles from a magazine, and I taped it inside my locker right next to my picture of Beyoncé.

A Chorus Line is over. It went really well. I'll tell you about it now:

When the show started, the first thing you saw was the backdrop I drew and painted. It took me until the day before the show to finish. It's a New York City scene of the Empire State Building and the Manhattan Bridge and the Statue of Liberty. At the bottom of the backdrop is a street full of buses and cabs and the entrance to the F train and lots of people walking on the sidewalk. I drew lots of random faces and also people I know, like Mrs. Lau and Cuba, Kiku on his delivery bike, Mum and Dad in the back of Sushil-Uncle's cab. All along the sidewalk, I drew every kind of person there is in New York: black, white, Thai, Mexican, Pakistani, Jewish. I spent a long time trying to get their faces right. I stink at drawing noses but I'm pretty good at eyes and mouths. I have not told anybody this, not even Kiku, but in the middle of the block, I drew a little pagoda tree with a monkey sitting in it, and underneath the tree I drew Dadi in her white sari holding her grass sickle and schoolbooks. She is the best drawing I have ever done. She looks just like herself. It made me feel a little better to put her in the show and to put her in New York.

Daddy could not see the show because he had to go back to New Jersey. Mum was supposed to come to closing night but Mrs. Rankin had an emergency at work, so Mum had to stay late babysitting. Sometimes it makes me mad that those two little children see more of Mum than I do. I was really sad about Mum missing the show, and Kiku and Mrs. Lau tried to make me feel better.

They both got dressed up. Mrs. Lau wore a long red skirt and a black turtleneck and a jade comb in her hair, and Kiku put on Daddy's suit (he called Daddy first to make sure it was OK). We ate an early dinner and Mrs. Lau called Kiku "good-looker" and they argued about politics. Mrs. Lau doesn't like Obama as much as Kiku does, and that makes him really mad. Afterward, when we were cleaning up, Kiku sat on the couch and watched TV. I said, "Hey, good-looker, do you think you're too pretty to wash dishes?" And he said, "I'm too pretty to wash. But not too pretty to dry." He took off Daddy's jacket and rolled up his shirtsleeves and we stood together in the kitchen, me washing, Kiku drying, Mrs. Lau putting everything away.

The show was so good. I wish you could have seen it. Beforehand, we did voice warm-ups, and Ms. Bledsoe made a speech about togetherness and gave us each a red carnation. I saw her in the wings crying during "What I Did for Love." As for me, I only messed up one light cue, at the very end, and Kiku said no one noticed.

Some things did go really wrong, though, like one of the trombonists got a nosebleed in the middle of "At the Ballet." And Alice Tong stuffed socks in her leotard so it would look like she had boobs, and one fell out while she was dancing. Also, Peter Schiff had an asthma attack just before his solo number.

It is so amazing how all this stuff goes into making a play and how all these crazy things happen backstage, but to the people in the audience, it looks perfect and easy. It's like there are two worlds in Drama Club. The world onstage and the world backstage. It reminds me of how I feel all the time. Like there is America right in front of me, but backstage, in my mind, are Mussoorie and Dadi and the mountains.

At the end of the show, the audience gave us all a standing ovation. Everyone who worked backstage, like me, also came out and got to take a bow. I could see Kiku and Mrs. Lau smiling and clapping in the third row. I wished Mummy-Daddy and Dadi and you could see me. Afterward, Mrs. Lau said maybe it was good that Mum hadn't been there, because she would have been upset about the girls in leotards. Kiku said, "That was my favorite part." Totally Gross. But then he said he was proud of me, and when we got home, he told Mum about everything and said it was the best play he'd ever seen.

I am really glad I joined the Drama Club. It makes me feel like I belong at PS 20. I can hardly wait for next year's play. We are going to be doing <u>Oklahoma.</u>

It's the time of year in New York when lots of Christmas trees are dragged to the trash. There's tinsel flying everywhere in the street. There aren't many trees out at the curb in Chinatown, but where I go to school, which is a little bit north of here, there are. In six days, the streets of Chinatown will be filled with confetti and firecrackers for Chinese New Year—the Year of the Ox. Mrs. Lau knows the boy who will be dancing in the head of the dragon. She used to work at the factory with his grandmother.

Things with the apartment have gotten bad. There is a big CONDEMNED sign on Jennifer's door, and Mrs. Lau is worried that we will be found out soon. We wait at the top of the stairs and listen before walking down so that we won't see anyone in the building. We used to say hi to people, and Mrs. Lau would tell them we helped her with cooking, cleaning, and laundry and to expect us to be coming and going all the time. But now it seems better to disappear. At least for a little while. None of us has been sleeping much.

A few days before New Year's, Mum woke me up in the middle of the night and said, "Help me cut my hair."

The light was bright and I was sleepy and confused. I sat up in bed and watched her as she stood in the middle of the room and cut off her hair. She said she had to do something to change things, to feel different, or she'd die of grief. Her hair fell all over the floor in big black ropes. It used to hang past her waist. Now it is as short as a boy's. What's weird is that as soon as her hair was cut, she looked in the mirror and said she felt better. And she's been happier ever since. I think she looks quite pretty with short hair. And I like seeing her ears. They are small and sweet.

Daddy came home a few days later. He got upset when he saw Mum. He loved her long hair. He said she looked American, not Indian. She said, "It will grow back; don't worry," but he went in the bedroom and shut the door. The next day, they had a big row because Daddy gave Mum money for the electricity bill and she said she didn't need it, she'd already paid the bill. Daddy started shouting and, well, since I'm on the computer, I'll type it out for you like a play:

DADDY (shouting): You already paid it?

MUM (whispering): Be quiet—they'll hear you downstairs.

DADDY (quiet now but still very mad): So these days you pay the bills and tell me what to do? Who is the man and who is the woman?

MUM: I *have* to be the man while you're away.

DADDY: And now that I am here, there are two men?

Here Mum started to cry and went over to Mrs. Lau's to get away from Daddy. I sat with him on the couch. He had the citizenship study book open on his lap, but he wasn't reading. He said, "Nobody needs Daddy anymore. Everyone is fine. Making their decisions and paying the bills." I told him that wasn't true and that Mum had only cut her hair because she was so sad and she needed to make a change. He looked surprised but then nodded. By the way, I forgot to say all of that actually happened in Hindi.

I know just how Daddy feels. Sometimes when Mummy-Daddy-Kiku talk about something that happened before I lived with them in New York, it hurts my feelings. I feel left out and small, even though I know they don't mean to make me feel that way. Like over New Year's, they talked about their second year in New York and how they had gone to Times Square and gotten confused about the subway. . . . They laughed so much as they told the story, and I could see it had been a really good time. I thought of me and Dadi at home in Mussoorie while the three of them were laughing in New York. It hurt. Kiku noticed I was sad and he made a face at Mum and they changed the topic. But it still hurt.

Mum always says it was money and immigration laws that kept us apart all those years. But I don't know. Sometimes it feels like they just abandoned me. Like they wanted to leave me, like they wanted to go off and live a happy life without me and Dadi. Maybe that sounds crazy but I don't think they missed me as much as I missed them.

I better get off the computer. I have been typing to you for 17 minutes and 20 seconds. Since the library has free computers, there's a time limit: 20 minutes for each person. It makes it easier to share. Write soon and tell me what is happening with you and Town Mountain. I am getting the telepathic messages from you but I still get worried. OK. Time to press PRINT.

Bye for now,
Meena

P.S. Yes, an aarthi is a kind of prayer with lamps and oil and burning wicks and bells and singing and gods and goddesses. It is very beautiful to watch. Mum does this two times a day.

13 February 2009

Dear Meena,

I am so sorry that it has taken me so long to write you back. Even though I've been thinking of you every single day, I haven't been able to write, mostly because I haven't been able to think straight here lately.

I have been over at the hospital a lot, with Mark.

They had to cut off his left leg.

All the way above the knee.

Every time the sheet is off him I get a little sick to my stomach when I see his half leg there. I don't mean this in a bad way. I think I just get sick because I feel so bad for him. I think of him and the way he was always running and jumping. If you think about a thing like that too much it'll drive you crazy. So I can't even imagine how Mark is feeling. But the weird thing is that he's just as happy as can be all the time. He has bad days sometimes, but for the most part he is upbeat.

I was at the hospital the other day and he was telling all these jokes and laughing big and loud and I was thinking how I hoped I'd be like that if I were in his situation

(I started to write "if I were in his shoes," then that seemed weird since he only has one shoe now).

Anyway, I must have zoned out, thinking about that, because all at once Mark was slapping his hands together and hollering, "Earth to River! Hey, man, are you still there?" And so I realized that I was staring off into space. Mark knew what I was thinking, though. "The way I look at it, them rocks could've killed us, man," he said. "So I feel lucky."

They say Mark will be in the hospital for at least two more months.

Yes, in the group picture I am the boy at the end of the front row. With the freckles. It's kind of cool to know that you see me every time you go to your refrigerator. It's weird to think I am in somebody's kitchen in New York City. There were two or three photographers who came here yesterday. One of them was from New York. I asked him if he knew you, and he laughed real big and said, "Well, New York's a pretty big town there, partner." I hate it when people call somebody "partner." It's stupid. And it embarrassed me in front of the whole class. I knew that New York was a big town, but I thought there might be some weird coincidence where he'd know you. You know what I mean? But I didn't say that to him. He also said, "I'd sure as heck remember a name like that," when I said your name. It made me feel like he had insulted you. Anyway, out of all the photographers, one of them was the nicest and he was from <u>People</u> magazine. They took a picture of me and all the other boys gathered around Mark's bed. I am sitting up on the bed right beside him. I think they said it would be out in a couple of weeks, so look for it. Do you all have newsstands out on the streets like they always show in the movies of New York?

We were out of school for snow on the day of the inauguration (since we have real curvy mountain roads and are not used to that much snow, we get out of school even if it only snows a half inch), so I watched it at the hospital, with Mark.

Usually the hospital is a big noisy place with nurses hollering to one another or joking with the patients, people running this way and that. But when the inauguration started, everything got very quiet. Lots of people were gathering in the big waiting room down the hall to watch it, and Mark said he wanted to watch with everybody else, so I wheeled him down there in his wheelchair. His mom went with us. The waiting room was so packed with people that she and I had to stand behind Mark's chair and watch. Nobody said a word the entire time, but when Obama was sworn in, I heard someone let out a little weeping sound and I looked around and there was Dr. Patel. I hadn't even known he was there. He had tears in his eyes. So then I looked at every single person and MOST of them had tears in their eyes. Mark's mom kept her hand over her mouth like she was amazed. This little old woman sitting in a plastic waiting room chair beside me dotted a wad of Kleenex to her eyes. It was the strangest thing.

So then I thought about what it meant, to be watching something so historic. The first black person to become president. If he could overcome the odds, then so could a hillbilly, or an Indian, or anybody. And it made me feel like anything was possible. People are always saying how you can be anything you want in America, but I had never really believed it, or even thought that much about it. But when Obama was sworn in, I DID believe it. And I think that's why everyone had those tears in their eyes, because they knew that, too. I'll never forget that moment.

But then, later that night, I was in the waiting room getting a bag of Funyuns and a Sierra Mist and this big beardy man was in there talking bad about Obama to this little nasty-looking woman who just nodded to everything he said. He said the country was going to hell, and he called Obama the N-word. When he said the word, I felt like somebody had punched me in the belly. There were lots of people in there, including some people I had seen with tears in their eyes earlier, but nobody said anything. I didn't know what to say, so I just stood there with my pop and my Funyuns and I gave him the dirtiest look I could. It took him a minute to realize I was staring at him on purpose, but then he went, "Take a picture, boy." I didn't know what to say, so I just stomped off.

I feel really terrible about that. When I got back to Mark's room I kept thinking how I should have said something, how I should have told him that he shouldn't have said that word. But I didn't know how. I felt like a big coward, like the biggest chicken in history. Since then I have thought of lots of good comebacks (like "Who'd want a picture of somebody as stupid as you?" or "I wouldn't want to break my camera" or "I don't take pictures of racists"), but at the time I just froze up.

So I feel awful bad about it and wish I could do it over.

I wish I could've seen <u>A Chorus Line.</u> It sounds like a lot of fun. Our school never does any good plays. I wish you had taken me a picture of your drawing of Dadi with her grass sickle and schoolbooks. That sounds awesome. Next time you design a set, draw me into it so that I can say I have been on a stage in New York City. I keep thinking about Ms. Bledsoe crying in the wings when "What I Did for Love" played. I don't know why I can't get her out of my mind, but I keep wondering why she was crying. I looked up the lyrics online, and to tell you the truth, I think it is a pretty good love song. I bet she loved somebody and they left her and now she'll never get over it and die a lonely old woman who sits by the window crying every night because she can't move on (actually, this reminds me of the woman you heard crying, the one Mrs. Lau said has a heart like a squashed tomato). I like to make up stories for people sometimes.

Sometimes the made-up story is way more interesting than the real one.

Since you are so good at designing sets and all, maybe you should think about getting a job working on Broadway. I can write plays and you can design the sets and do the lights and help everybody memorize their lines. We could be partners.

It's weird that your parents have been fighting, because mine have been getting along better than ever. Dad stayed with us as long as he could stay away from the job down on the Gulf, but he finally had to go back. Before he left he spent the whole evening playing basket-ball with me, the way he used to. And we went to the Dairy Dart and ate foot-long chili buns and large orders of onion rings and root beer floats. Mamaw never takes me to the Dairy Dart. She doesn't believe in hot dogs and cheeseburgers.

The day before Dad had to go back to the Gulf, I was coming out of the woods and I heard my mother laughing. I hadn't heard her laugh in so long that I thought I had forgotten what it sounded like, but as soon as I heard it, I knew that laugh belonged to her. Her laugh is like a kind of music. And when I came around the porch Dad was kissing her on the forehead. She hasn't had any more headaches yet and has been going down to the little office building to help Mamaw make posters and get ready for the big rally.

I've been helping make signs for the rally. Here's what some of them say:

SAVE THE ENDANGERED HILLBILLY

NOT AN ACT OF GOD—AN ACT OF GREED

NOT ONE MORE MOUNTAIN,
NOT ONE MORE SCHOOL,
NOT ONE MORE CHILD

Last night Mamaw had a bunch of people come up to the community center and teach everybody how to get arrested without getting hurt. She says that some of the people in the rally might end up getting taken to jail. They also learned how to do what they call "non-violent protest." Some of them are talking about chaining themselves to the front porch or the front doors of the capitol building.

On our way home I told Mamaw I didn't want her to get arrested. I'd be worried to death about her if she got taken to jail. She pulled the car over to the side of the road, and we weren't even halfway up the mountain to home.

"Now, listen here, River Dean Justice," she said. She propped her elbow up on the steering wheel because she was turned all the way around in her seat to face me. "The law isn't protecting the people, son. They're not making the coal company go by the law because it has all kinds of money. So we're going to go up there and get their attention."

All night long I thought about what she said. And I believe she's right. So, late that night I got on the phone and called all the boys who had been there when the rocks came in on us (they are all out of the hospital now; Mark was the only one who got hurt really bad). So we all decided that we are going to the capitol, too. Ever since it happened, I've been wanting to do something to help Mark. There's not been anything I've been able to do except sit in the hospital and watch TV with him. But now I can do something for him. So we're all going to march. We're going to march for Mark. And for Town Mountain.

More later,
My Own True Self,
River Dean Justice

February 18, 2009

Dear River,

Today I am a teenager. Thirteen years old. Hello 12, Hello 13, Hello Love (that's a song from <u>A Chorus Line</u>). Mum brought a bakery cake home after work that said NINA in blue frosting. I thought maybe they had given Mum the wrong cake, but she said the bakery hadn't heard the name Meena before, so they misspelled it. Kiku stuck his pinkie in the frosting and made NINA into MEENA and then put some frosting on the tip of my nose. He is such a goof. I am almost out of room, so I will write you another postcard.

PART II. We called Daddy and put him on speaker-phone and everyone sang "Happy Birthday." We sang quietly in case the landlord was lurking in the stairwell. Mum gave me socks and some of Mrs. Rankin's old books. <u>David Copperfield</u>, <u>The Wind in the Willows</u>, and a biography of a scientist named Marie Curie. Best news: Mummy-Daddy's citizenship exam date is May 14. In three months, maybe we will be citizens. Hello to the postal people, if you are reading this. Meena

22 February 2009

Dear Meena,

    I have never gone to the store and bought a birthday card before, but we were at the Dollar General yesterday and I had just gotten your postcard saying it was your birthday, so, well, I thought it'd be a good time to buy a birthday card for the first time. I am not much for writing in longhand, so that is your birthday present, to see my handwriting in more than just my signature, which is

all you usually see. Not much of a present, huh? Since it really is not much, I'm also enclosing a buckyeye, which I found in the creek. That's why ~~why~~ (sorry, I'm not used to writing by hand so much) it's so smooth. You probably never heard of a buckeye before. They grow on trees. Some people here carry them in their pockets for good luck. I thought you'd like it better than if I went and tried to pick out some kind of stupid gift. Anyway, I hope you are knowing that you're my best friend and that I'm real happy you're alive, and I hope to know you for many more birthdays. So I hope you have a good one.

Happy Birthday (one more time)!!!
River

P.S. If I had known in advance, I would have sent the card BEFORE your birthday, so just in case you need to know, mine is June 8.

February 25, 2009

Dear River,

I am writing to you from under the bed. It is 1:00 a.m. and I have rubber-banded a flashlight to the springs beneath the mattress so I can see.

Mum and I had a big scary row tonight.

She came home from work in a bad mood. I can always tell her mood from the way she takes her shoes off at the door. If she slaps them down on the ground, she's frustrated. If she lays them down gently, she's happy.

Well, tonight, she slapped her shoes down hard and then she started banging pots and pans around in the kitchen like she was REALLY mad at them.

She cooked *aloo gobi* (potato and cauliflower) and *dhahi vada* (yoghurt and donut things that are too hard to explain). The whole time she was making dinner, she was acting forgetful, like her mind was flying around somewhere else. She forgot to salt the potatoes, she forgot to start the rice, but the worst thing was when she let the *phulka* (bread) burn, which set off the smoke detector.

Mrs. Lau had told us to never let that happen because it would draw attention to us.

Kiku took the broom handle and knocked the batteries out of the smoke detector, and I flapped the bedroom door open and shut to make the air move around. Mum whispered some curses and huffed around. She was covered in flour and looked a little crazy. And in the middle of all this, Kiku's phone rang with Beyoncé's "Put a Ring on It," which is Valentina's ringtone. He handed me the phone.

Valentina was excited and talking fast and squeaky. She said a bunch of Drama Club kids were going to a 6:30 movie with Carlos's aunt as a chaperone. I had to call her back in ten minutes to say if I could go so she could buy me a ticket before they all sold out.

So Mum was in a bad mood but I had to ask right away if I could go see <u>Coraline</u>. I guess you can already see where this is going. . . .

I almost didn't ask. I almost called Valentina back and said, "Sorry, I can't go out on a school night." But then I thought about how you said that sometimes I should do what I want to do.

I got Kiku to meet me in the bathroom, and I asked him for some money. He gave me enough for a ticket and popcorn. He said, "Good luck, Mee-Mee," and patted me on the head like he felt sorry for me.

Then I went back to the kitchen and asked Mum.

She slipped almost immediately into her "No" face and said, "Who are these people from Drama Club?"

I said, "Valentina, Carlos, Jeremy, Tasheka, Peter, and Carlos's aunt Bianca, who is a grown-up. She's a guidance counselor, so she's very responsible. And I don't need any money for a ticket because I have some of my own."

Mum didn't even look at me. She sighed and stirred the aloo and said, "Boys, too? I don't know these people. I don't want you sitting in dark places with them. You're too young to see films without your family."

I guess I should have stayed quiet, but all of a sudden I wanted to see the movie so badly I couldn't breathe. I pictured all my friends laughing and eating popcorn and having a great time without me. I felt like all my bones were frozen in place and I was completely alone in the world. So I guess I kind of freaked out.

ME: Maybe you'd know them if you weren't always with other people's children.

I sounded mean and desperate even to myself, but I couldn't stop the words from coming out of my mouth.

Mum slammed down the *tava* (a flat kind of pan).

MUM: Meena, if your father heard you speaking this way, he would spank you.

ME: Well, he's not here, so I have to ask you—even though you NEVER let me do anything. And I'm just going to marry whoever you make me marry, so what's the big deal with boys being there?

MUM: Meena. Don't forget yourself. You are my Indian daughter, not my American daughter.

ME: Breaking news, Mum. YOU BROUGHT US TO AMERICA.

MUM: You're not going to see a film on a school night. And stop shouting or we'll get thrown into the street.

ME: You're the one who set off the smoke alarm, so if we get thrown out, it will be YOUR fault.

MUM (now crying): I am your mother, Meena. I am not your enemy. I had a very long day and I don't want to see you behaving so badly. Please go to the bedroom and leave me alone.

(By the way, all this time she was talking in Hindi and I was talking in English.)

ME: That's what you really want, isn't it? For me to leave you alone. For me to disappear. Mothers don't leave their daughter for six years! Mothers don't abandon their child and move across the world and bring only their son with them JUST BECAUSE HE'S A BOY. Mothers don't do that, but guess what! That's what you did. That's what you did to me.

I was crying so hard I didn't even know what was going on when Kiku picked me up and dropped me on the bed. He stood in front of me and said, "Mee-Mee, you better stay here and be quiet for a while. I'll call Valentina."

As he was closing the door, I saw Mum lying on the kitchen floor. She was holding her head in her hands and kind of rocking from side to side like her stomach hurt. Oh, River. I felt so bad. But at the same time, I also felt like what I said was true. She did leave me. And I always have to say and do what she wants because SHE works so hard, because SHE made sacrifices, because SHE may die of grief and shame. But what about me? What about when I feel sad and angry? What about what I want?

And then I sat alone in the room for a while. I thought about climbing down the fire escape and running away. I still had the money from Kiku in my pocket. But then I thought about Mum on the kitchen floor and I just couldn't do it. So I lay down on the bed and cried until I fell asleep.

When I woke up, it was completely dark outside and Mum was sitting next to me. She had lit her aarthi candles, so the room was glowing and her face was, too. I felt like our fight was a dream, but then Mum put her hands on my shoulders and said, "Mee-Mee, I didn't want to leave you in Mussoorie. We had to do that because you were just a baby. We thought we would make a lot of money and have you with us in a month or two. We thought you would never remember us leaving when you grew up. It was not what we wanted. It was just what happened."

It was strange to hear Mum explain herself to me like I was a grown-up. Her hands were shaking and she looked so worried and tired and sad.

I felt terrible. I sat up and hugged her and we didn't let go. I said I was sorry for talking so meanly to her.

She said, "Let's forget about sadness and go to sleep. I'll take you to see the movie this weekend and you can bring any friend you want."

So I got back into bed. Mum turned on her side and fell right to sleep, and I watched the shadows on the wall until the candles burned out. I wondered if I was Mum's American daughter or Indian daughter. I wondered if I was turning into a mean person who makes her mother cry. And then I got up and crawled under the bed to write to you.

Thanks for being my friend. Since I have you to talk to, I don't feel so lonely anymore. I don't know what I'd do without you.

Good night,
Meena

P.S. I almost forgot . . . thank you so much for the birthday card. It's beautiful. I love the buckeye and I carry it every day in my pocket. Actually, I accidentally left it in the pocket of my jeans the other day and it went through the washing machine. But since it's a lucky buckeye, nothing happened to it.

February 28, 2009

Dear Meena,

I was really sorry to read about your mom and you fighting. It made me feel bad for both of you. I thought both of you had good points (and in the end she was really nice to come in and make up with you like that), but I have to tell you that you were pretty rough on her. If I had said some of that stuff to my parents or to Mamaw, they would've busted my hind end. I guess I should tell you that "busting a hind end" is not as bad as it sounds. Mrs. Tipton, our new math teacher, who is not from here, says that people in Appalachia exaggerate everything. It's just the way we are. I mentioned it to Ms. Stidham, and she said it's because we are "a storytelling culture." Anyway, to bust someone's hind end just means that you get a slap on the butt. So it's not as bad as it sounds.

ANYWAY . . . I have gotten way off the subject (as usual). So back to the subject:

Like I was saying, you were pretty tough on her, and so I felt sorry for her. But on the other hand, it's good that you've started to stand up for yourself a little bit more and to tell people how you feel about things. Mamaw always says that life is too short to be unhappy and that a lot of times people are unhappy just because they failed to speak up for themselves.

I see your point about them leaving you for seven years. That'd bother me, too. Dad is gone off to Biloxi to find work, but that's different because at least Mom stayed here to be with me and it is not halfway around the world, like India is from America, and all that. When she explained it I still didn't really get why they left you behind, but I believed her (didn't you?) when she said that she didn't want it to be that way. It must be one of those things that we'll understand when we get older. Half the time when I say I don't understand something, a grown-up tells me that I will understand when I get older.

Did you get to go see <u>Coraline,</u> then? I've been wanting to go because I loved the book, but I've been so busy I've not been able to. A kid I know saw it and said it freaked him out and the 3-D made him a little bit sick. He loved the book, too, and was mad that they changed it in the movie so that Coraline lives in America instead of England.

I have a secret and you can't tell anybody—I love that Beyoncé song you were talking about, that "Single Ladies" song, or whatever it's called. Have you seen the video? The cheerleaders at school have been doing a dance routine to it, so every day when school is out we see them practicing it on the yard outside the church and we hear the song and some of the boys start acting stupid and acting like they can do that dance. DON'T TELL ANYBODY I LIKE A BEYONCÉ SONG, OK? But it makes me want to dance.

I thought it was pretty genius of you to rubber-band a flashlight to the springs under the bed.

The march in Frankfort is tomorrow, so I better get in bed. We have to get up at like 5:30 so we can be there plenty early. It takes us about two hours to get there. I'll write you all about it as soon as I can.

Yours truly,
River

P.S. That's cool that nothing happened to the buckeye in the washer.

March 3, 2009

Dear River,

I'm writing you a quick note from history. We were assigned some readings about "empires," but I finished them already, so I decided to use the extra time to write to you.

I think it's called "Single Ladies (Put a Ring on It)." Don't worry, I won't tell anyone you like the song. It's a good song and it's SUPER FUN to dance to. Kiku let me play the video from YouTube. He was studying for a chemistry exam, but he let me play it over and over again until I had all the moves down and could do it right along with Beyoncé and those two other girls. I don't do it as good as they do, but it's still fun. You should try learning it. Carlos is a boy and he knows all the steps. Why shouldn't you?

I didn't see <u>Coraline</u> yet. Mum had to go into work over the weekend. But she says we will go next weekend for sure.

I liked what you said about wanting to do things

over. I feel like that a lot. I wish I hadn't yelled at Mum, for one thing.

OMG. This girl Marla who sits near the door just started laughing so hard that she snorted like a pig! When the teacher asked her what could possibly be funny about the empire handout, Marla said, "Napoleon had the tiniest hands and feet!"

Your big march at the capitol sounds very exciting. I hope you save Black Banks and all the mountains. I think you will. I can't wait to hear all about it.

Peace out,
Meena

2 March 2009

Here's what happened:

Everybody we knew all piled in together on a bus we had rented from a church. It was an old school bus that had been painted white, and instead of saying CROW COUNTY SCHOOLS down the side like a normal bus, it said JOHN 3:16 on one side and HONK IF YOU LOVE JESUS on the other side. People were honking their horns, and truck drivers would sound their big loud horns at us all the way up the interstate, and at first it was funny but then it got old real quick. On the way up, one of the community organizers (that's what Mamaw is, too, a community organizer) led everybody in songs. We sang all the way to Frankfort, which is a two-hour drive from Black Banks. We sang "Will the Circle Be Unbroken" and "Which Side Are You On?" and "Hard Times." Those are real old songs that people in the mountains sing all the time, so I'm not sure if you've heard them or not, but I've been hearing them all my life. It's like if you're from here, you're sort of born knowing those words, like they're part of your body or something. The organizer had changed some of the words to fit our situation, so for example, like in "Circle," instead of it being the real line, like

There's a better home a-waitin'
In the sky, Lord, in the sky

it was changed to

Take my hand we'll work together
We won't let these mountains die

One of the people on the bus had a fiddle and another had a banjo and another had an Autoharp (here's a picture of one I got from the Internet, because nobody hardly knows what they are and they are mostly an instrument people here play) and they played some of

the songs right there in their seats. That woman played the fiddle on "Hard Times," and the way she played it was like you could hear all of her sadness pouring out right through the strings. She closed her eyes when she played, and I don't even know how to describe her face. It was like a rock, somehow, how hard and firm and solid it was. Her face made the song even better.

I guess there were about 60 of us on the bus, and I knew just about everybody on there. All the boys from the team were on there with us, and they didn't sing along, but they were ready for the march. They were into it.

Mom and I sat right behind Dr. Patel and Chandra, and on the way up there, Chandra turned around and talked to me most of the time. She asked me all kinds of questions and had me tell her the whole story of when the rocks caved in, and when I told her about thinking Mark was probably dead and how scary it was, her face sort of fell in on itself and her eyebrows went together and then I realized she was crying. Her tears fell in two lines down her face and then she had to turn away. I thought I had said something to hurt her feelings, because Dr. Patel was patting on her and saying, "Shh, shh, it's all right," and then he talked in Hindi to her (I'm guessing it was Hindi; I don't really know, but since that is the language you speak, I'm figuring that's what they speak, too? Sorry if this is stupid of me . . . I don't know if everybody in India speaks the same language or not) and that calmed her down.

After a little while she turned around in her seat and said, "Forgive me, River. I'm sorry I got upset. Your story just reminded me of something bad that happened to my brother, in Mumbai." (Later I googled "Moom-bi"— because I didn't know how to spell it—and the search engine came up and said, "Did you mean Mumbai, India?" so I guess that's how you spell it.) When I typed in "Mumbai," one of the first things that came up was "Mumbai attacks," and so I read about all these bombings that happened there last year. Do you know about these? It might not even be what happened to her brother, but somehow I felt like it was. I don't know why.

We were all caught up in singing when we got close to the capitol, but then everybody hushed—the hush worked its way back through the bus from the front to the back—because Mamaw was standing by the door with her hand over her mouth. When everybody got silent she pointed out the window and said, "Oh, my Lord." We looked out and we couldn't believe it.

There is a big wide street that goes for a straight mile in front of the capitol, which sits up on a hill. We were on the bridge at the end of the street and the entire mile of road in front of us was taken up by people. The police had shut down the street because there were so many. They are saying now that at least ten thousand people were there. I had never seen so many people in one place in my life. All of them carrying signs. They were from all over the state and all over the country, even. Mamaw said that they were there to help us in the fight.

So we marched.

My sign said:

MY BEST FRIEND LOST HIS LEG TO MTR

I asked Mark if it was OK to put that on a sign, and he laughed his loud crazy laugh and said, "Hell, yes!" and his mother slapped at him and acted shocked over him saying that, but then she laughed and said, "Yes, River, yes.

Carry that sign for all of us." So I did. I was also carrying a mason jar full of water I had gotten out of the creek. The water was solid orange. It looked like watered-down carrot juice sloshing around in there.

I can't explain to you properly how it felt to be with all those people, walking up that street. Mamaw and the other community organizers told us we could be most effective if we would be absolutely silent until we got to the capitol steps. So we were. All of us just walking along, and it seemed to me that every single person's face looked like the fiddler's had. It took me a long time to figure out what that look was, but then I knew it was defiance. I learned this word in history class, back when we were talking about that boy who stood in front of the tanks in China. And that was the way I felt, defiant. And that was the way everybody looked like they felt, too.

It was cold as knives. There had been a big snow a week before that hadn't really melted all the way, especially where it had been pushed into little hills on the sidewalks. In one yard we passed, all the snow had melted except for a snowman that stood there, completely solid, like he had fallen from the sky into that brown, wet yard.

It was so cold that every time I breathed I could feel the cold air way way way down in my lungs. My nose felt like an ice cube. But we were bundled up good with layers of clothes, so the only thing that got really cold was my face. In some weird way it felt good, too, though.

All along the street there were state troopers standing with their hands on their hips, not looking any of us in the eye. They didn't say anything, but they kept their faces completely square and had guns right on their belts, like we were dangerous criminals or something.

Not all of us could fit, so some people had to spill over on the lawn on the sides of the capitol steps, but when we had all finished walking up the street, Mamaw stood at the very top step and yelled into a bullhorn, "Whose mountains?" and the whole crowd hollered back, "Our mountains!" and then Mamaw said, "Whose streams?" and the crowd said, "Our streams!" and then Mamaw said, "Whose future?" and every single one of us said, as loud as we could, "Our future!" We kept saying it over and over until it sounded like a song, and I believe that everybody in the town must have heard us. I bet people heard it through their walls and wondered what had happened. I imagined them going to their windows and looking out to see what the ruckus was all about. I thought that some of them probably stepped out onto their porches to look toward our sound coming from the capitol steps, standing on the porch in their sock feet, hugging themselves against the cold.

And then, all at once, Governor Evans came out the front door of the capitol with two state policemen on either side. Mamaw said he had never come out to talk to our side before, that this was a real first. She says he is a good man but not good enough. I think this means that he wants to do the right thing but isn't brave enough to stand up to the coal companies. Mamaw says this is the problem with a lot of politicians. "They want to do right, but they're too scared to," she says.

The governor stood there and answered questions in the cold. He hadn't worn his coat, and I think this was on purpose, so he'd have an excuse to not stand there too long, since it was so cold.

He didn't give any real answers to anything. When someone would say why didn't he put a stop to MTR, he'd say something that sounded rehearsed, like he was reading it off little note cards. "We are looking at different options for making sure that the coal industry stays productive while also protecting our citizens." He just kept finding a way to avoid the questions.

Then Mamaw turned to him and said, "Why is it that we, as Americans, are having to come here to ask that our children be protected? That our water be protected? Those are the two main things that we should always be looking out for." And a big roar rose up from the crowd, everybody hollering and clapping.

The governor said that he didn't think our water was polluted, that he'd drink out of any stream in Eastern Kentucky.

When he said that, everybody started booing, and then all at once the whole first line of people (Mamaw, and my mom, and Dr. Patel and Chandra, all the boys from my basketball team, and lots of others) were bobbing their signs up and down and chanting, "Save our water! Save our water!" over and over. Everybody's anger spread out over all of us, and then I saw that some of the state troopers were moving in, one on each side, and the governor was moving toward the door, looking every which way while some of the policemen at his sides talked into their walkie-talkies. It felt like everything was about to blow up, like it was all about to go wrong, so I stepped toward the governor. I don't know why, but I just felt like it was the right thing to do. A state trooper stepped toward me, his eyes right on me, and I couldn't believe it but he put his hand on the handle of his pistol. When he did that, the governor put his hand out across the cop's chest and I took another step forward, seeing that the governor's eyes were on me, too.

All through the crowd I could hear people shushing one another. "Shh, shh," the sound ran back through all the people, like a slow, strong wind through summer leaves.

I guess it wasn't much more than a couple seconds, but it seemed like I stood there looking right at the governor a long while, and finally I held out the jar of nasty water I had been carrying the whole time, and I said, "Drink it, then."

Everybody had gotten so quiet that even people far away could hear my voice, bouncing off all that marble of the capitol building.

The governor laughed a little bit in the back of his throat and said, "What, son?"

And I said, "This came out of our creek. Our creek was as clean as a whistle until the mine moved in next door. Now it looks like this."

He patted me on the head like I was a dog. So I forced the jar right into his hands and I said, "You said you'd drink out of any creek we had, so drink it," I said. Then I didn't want to sound disrespectful, so I added, "Sir." There were so many cameras flashing in front of me that I had to blink to see.

It felt like something was about to happen, like everybody was holding their breath. I didn't know if I was doing the right thing or not, but it felt like the only thing to do.

But he just laughed again and said, "Aw, son, I don't believe I will." And then once again every single person started booing and bobbing their signs up and down in the air, so that the signs made a kind of booing sound all their own. The governor went back inside the capitol building, waving with both hands and smiling, as if he thought everyone was applauding instead of booing him.

He wouldn't come back out.

Mamaw rushed over to me and held me real close to her, and then she squatted down and looked me in the eye. Her lips were trembling, and not from the cold. "That was a real brave thing, River. Now none of us will have to get arrested, which will save everybody a whole lot of money."

"Why not?" I said. I was a little disappointed, to tell you the truth. I had been scared of getting arrested, but now it seemed like we had failed somehow by NOT getting arrested.

"Because what you did will get us more attention than the getting arrested. You did things the most peaceful way of all, by just standing up and asking a question. And every photographer here took a picture of it."

It was a long day. We stood out in the cold and listened to lots of people speak against MTR, and then some people sang songs and led us in chants, and some people went in and talked to the legislators. People kept coming by and shaking my hand and telling me I had done a brave thing.

By the time we got back on the bus, I was freezing

and so tired that I fell asleep even before we got back on the interstate. At some point I woke up and my head was in Chandra's lap and she was singing a pretty little song. I may have just dreamed it, though. I don't know. Then later I was aware of Mom and Mamaw walking me into the house and putting me into my bed. I had never been so tired in my whole life.

First thing this morning I got up and went right to writing you, because I felt like you were with me the whole time, and I wanted to put it all down on paper while it was fresh in my mind, hoping you could see it, too.

Yours,
River Dean Justice

March 22, 2009

Dear River,

I have a gigantic maths test tomorrow but I just had to stop by the library and type to you. Thank you so much for your beautiful letter. I felt like I had been to the rally WITH you. You're a really good friend to Mark and a really good friend to the mountains and you're the bravest boy EVER. I'm proud to know you.

I hope Mrs. Patel's brother is OK.

When I picked up your letter from the post office box just now, I saw an interesting old man. I have seen him walking around the neighborhood, but this is the first time I have seen him at the post office. He is Chinese, and he walks with a cane and is so bent over that he is always looking at his shoes. Well, I watched him open up his post office box. It took him a long time to twirl the dial and he had to lean on his cane with one hand before pulling the little door open. Then he looked into the mailbox. There was nothing in there but he stuck his hand inside and moved it around just to be sure. I felt sad for him and wondered who he was waiting to hear from. It made me think how you and I are lucky to have each other. Maybe we can start writing to that old man, too, so he will have some letters in his mailbox.

I want to tell you about Kiku's birthday present to me. I had to wait a whole month for it because the weather was too cold. But it was worth it! Kiku installed two sturdy foot pegs on the back of his bike so I can stand there and keep my hands on his shoulders and ride around the city with him. It's kind of scary, which is I guess what makes it fun. Anyway, yesterday afternoon, Kiku rode me all the way across town to the Hudson River. He weaved in and out of traffic, and when we went past buses I had to close my eyes so I wouldn't scream. When we got to the edge of the city, to the river, where there is a long park with no cars, we got off the bike and walked along the water. Kiku showed me all kinds of secrets, like where the Italian men go to fish with scraps of butcher meat. And where the old piers have sunk under water and left little bits of rotten pole for the seagulls stand on. And how to rent a kayak. And the willow trees where homeless people sleep. It was very warm, strangely so—65 degrees Farenheit. Kiku said it was because of global warming. There were so many people out, enjoying the day after the long winter.

Under one tree was guess who . . . Ana Maria! Kiku's secret girlfriend. She was standing next to a cart full of mangoes. He said, "Girl, you look good today," and she said, "You should have seen me yesterday," and then they kissed right in front of me! Ana Maria gave me a hug and said, "I was sorry to hear about your grandmother." She called me Mee-Mee because that is how she hears Kiku talk about me. I really liked that. It made her feel like family.

She explained to me how after school and on weekends, in the spring and summer, she sells mangoes on sticks with her uncle. She took a knife from her belt and peeled the mango in a few seconds with big strokes. Then she stuck the mango on a stick and slashed at it, all around, then sprinkled salt, lemon, and red

chili pepper over it. She had cut the mango in such a way that I could bite large pieces of it off the pit very easily. And my hands didn't get slimy, because I was holding the stick. She said this is the Mexican way to eat mangoes. I love it. It is the best thing ever. When you come to New York, we will have to eat some together.

After we ate mangoes, I sat on Kiku's bike, and Ana Maria put her iPod in my ears and played M.I.A., and she held one handlebar and Kiku held the other and they ran up and down the esplanade by the river and said it was my very own birthday roller coaster ride. It was so much fun. Then Ana Maria called Kiku *mi amor* and kissed him again and said she had to keep wheeling her mango cart up and down the river. I think she gets so many customers because she is so pretty. People just like to be near her. She's also really smart. She's the one who helped Kiku with his college essay. He never listens to anybody but he listens to her.

When I asked Kiku what "mi amor" means, he got embarrassed and said, "Nothing, stupid." Tomorrow I am going to ask Carlos what it means. He speaks Spanish, too.

So I thought all that was my present, but it turned out

there was more. I got up on the bike behind Kiku and he rode me all the way up to the George Washington Bridge. We rode a loooong, loooooong time, six whole miles, up to 237th Street. We stayed along the river where there aren't any cars, just people biking, jogging, Rollerblading, walking their dogs. Usually Kiku is protective of me and doesn't let me do anything that he does. I knew the fact that he was treating me like a friend, not a little sister, was part of his present. I couldn't stop laughing, standing behind him on the bike. I probably looked like a crazy person, but I didn't care. The river stretched out silver to our left. The wind was so strong that Kiku's tears flew back at me. They felt sharp as needles on my cheeks. It was fun to see the bridge getting closer and closer and then to be right under it.

When we got off the bike my legs felt funny, almost like I couldn't walk, because I'd been balancing for so long. I followed Kiku down a dirt footpath that led even farther under the bridge, and there, right in front of us, was a red lighthouse! I'd never seen a lighthouse before. It was the best surprise ever. There was a plaque in front of the lighthouse and we read all about it.

It was built in 1890, which is very old for America, and there is a children's book about it called <u>The Little Red Lighthouse and the Great Gray Bridge</u>, which was written in 1942. The plaque said that in 1951, the city was going to tear down the lighthouse, but a lot of people got very upset (mostly people who loved the book about the lighthouse) and they fought the city and won. So the lighthouse stayed. That all made me think of your mamaw and you and Black Banks. It's nice to think of a bunch of people getting together to do something good for something they love.

Me and Kiku sat by the water, on big cool rocks, next to the red lighthouse, the bridge spanning above us. The river made a long swirly circle around the jetty, and there were lots of boats going by. Across the way were little hills, almost like Garhwal mountains, but much smaller.

Kiku said to me, "I thought this was a place you and Dadi would have gone to together." I felt sad missing Dadi, but I was also happy to be there with Kiku. The river was louder than everything—except the occasional truck on the bridge thumping heavy and loud. No ambulances or garbage trucks or honking cabs. No subway. We could hear the sound of cars on the West Side Highway, but somehow it was so far away and mixed with the river's voice that the cars sounded like trees swaying in a forest. I had not seen hills or sat on a big rock in many years. The city, the skyline, looked blue and distant. It made me feel like we are all very small and unimportant. It is just when you are inside something that you forget that. But when you are outside of it and looking from far away, you can see. Kiku says that's called "perspective."

Kiku said across the river, over the bridge, was New Jersey—a whole other state. He said he'd ridden his bike over it once and then gone twenty miles into New Jersey to meet Daddy at his restaurant. It's a secret that even Mum doesn't know. She would be really mad if she knew Kiku had ridden so far on his bike. He said he skipped school one day when he was worried about Mum and went to see Daddy to ask him what to do. Then he told me about the houses in New Jersey, how everyone has a lawn and lots of trees and it's peaceful.

My parents work so hard. I want to get a good job and get them a house in New Jersey. I said that to Kiku and he said, "We'll work hard, too, and then we'll take care of them." We shook hands on it and I felt very grown-up. I was thirteen years old, sitting under the GW Bridge, in New York City, with my brother, who trusted me with his secrets. Sometimes Kiku can be mean, but mostly he is sweeter than a big bag of gummy bears.

When we started riding home, it was getting dark. I felt bad for Kiku having to take us all the way home, but he said I was light. The city looked twinkly, lit up against the dark. It got cold. My hands felt stiff on Kiku's back. The warm spring day had disappeared.

By the time we got home it was 9 o'clock and Mum

was mad. She pressed her lips together like she does when she is about to say no. She said that Mrs. Lau had come by and told her two more people in the building had been evicted that morning. Mum ran her hands through her short hair. She looked worn-out and bitter. She said, "We should pack a suitcase in case we have to leave here quickly." Kiku said, "Mum, it's late and Mee-Mee's tired." Mum sighed and put her hands on either side of my face. She stared at me and started to say something but then stopped. I said, "It's OK. Let's pack tonight."

I put a few outfits in the suitcase and my box of Special Things and the three books Mum gave me for my birthday and all of your letters and all of Dadi's letters and a paperweight from Mrs. Lau and the lucky buckeye. Kiku put in some of his stuff and Mum added hers and Daddy's and also some food and water in plastic bottles. The bag is still right by the front door, just in case.

I better get off the computer now. There's a line of people waiting for it.

Meena

27 March 2009

Dear Meena,

Can you believe they put that picture of me holding that jar of dirty water out to the governor on the cover of Time magazine???!!!!????

Mom and Mamaw bought about twenty copies and then Time sent us a big box full of them, so I am including one here for you. Mamaw says this is the most exposure mountaintop removal has ever gotten and that now that people know about it, they will get mad about it. She says that Americans usually do the right thing if they know about it, that it just takes a long time to get their attention, especially if something bad is happening to poor people.

When we go to town, everybody feels like it's perfectly fine to pat on me or get real close to my face and talk about being proud of me. But if it helps to save the mountains I don't care.

The other day we were in Piggly Wiggly and old Mrs. Heap was in there shopping. She wouldn't even speak, just acted like she didn't know us when Mamaw and

I walked by her, me pushing the buggy. I could tell that she said something, but didn't know what. I just heard her mumble. But Mamaw has ears and eyes and everything like a hawk, so she heard her as plain as day. Later Mamaw told me Mrs. Heap said, "Tree huggers," in this real hateful voice, like she was spitting. Mamaw just spun around on her heel and went back over to Mrs. Heap and said, "I'm praying for you, honey. Because you're a fool." And it was like she had cussed Mrs. Heap or slapped her face, the way Mrs. Heap acted all shocked and offended.

The opposite of this is that Ms. Stidham told me she was real proud of me, though. She asked me to stay after class one day and I thought I might be in trouble for something, but then she looked at me like I was a grown-up and she said, "River, I want you to know that I'm proud to know you." I didn't know what to say, so I didn't say a word, although I guess I should've said thanks or something. Then she held out a little purple paperback book. "Here," she said, and shoved it into my hands. "This book is about doing the right thing, too. It's my favorite."

I looked down at the cover. <u>To Kill a Mockingbird</u>.

"I want you to have it," she said, and I swear it

was like there were little tears in her eyes. But then she straightened herself up and said, "Go on, then," and turned me by the shoulders and walked me to the door. I finally managed to say thank you.

She just told me to go on, before I was late to my next class, but when I looked back she was standing at the door, watching me walk away.

After the rockfall, you know that our basketball team has had a real hard time getting it all together again because we lost two of our best players. But I think it made us stronger, too, and here is proof.

We played Lexington Middle School the other day and we

BEAT

THEIR

SOCKS

OFF!!!!

We have never beaten them before, ever. I hadn't played in a game that good in forever and ever, and it reminded me why I love basketball so much. Because it's like flying when you are going down the court bouncing that ball, zooming in and out of bodies, the sweat running down your forehead and into your eyes, and the crowd chanting from the bleachers, "River! River!" and the cheerleaders shaking their pom-poms and doing the splits, and the announcer's voice a blur on the loudspeaker, and then I am sailing through the air, taking a big run and jump as I do a bank shot and that *WHOOOSH* as the ball slices through the net. And then I realized that I had put in the winning shot and the whole crowd was on its feet, everyone clapping and people hugging and so happy because we had been the underdogs for so long, always getting beaten by the big city school, and finally we were the little country school and we were the winners. While everybody else was celebrating it seemed like the whole crowd—all the noise and movement and everything—zoomed away and all my attention went to Mark, who was sitting there on the sidelines with his crutches propped up on the seat next to him. He hasn't gotten his artificial leg yet because they are still making it especially for him. But he didn't look sad that he wasn't out there with us. He just looked happy for us. All the other guys were trying to lift me on their shoulders, but instead I said, "No, let's go to Mark," and we did. We all went over there and huddled around him and did a big group hug.

I was glad that we didn't lift him up on our shoulders. It wouldn't have seemed right, since he lost his leg. Instead, we went down to him, and that felt right. That felt better.

I know that some people think that sports are stupid and get too much attention. They probably do get too much attention. I mean, nobody ever has a pep rally for the people in the academic team or the band, and that's not right. But sometimes sports are a real good thing, because they can remind you that if you work hard for something you can succeed. And being a basketball player is hard. You have to be a hard worker to be an athlete, and practice every day, and be determined. So it's like being a musician or writer that way. And I know that winning is not everything. That's not what I'm saying. Even though it felt real good to not be the losers to Lexington Middle School for once, it felt even better to know that we had played a good, fair game, and we had worked hard to do the best we could.

And guess what—even Sam Brock, that big turd I got into a fight with a few months back, came over and told me I had done a good job. I thought that was pretty big of him.

By the way, I think that Kiku's present was pretty much the coolest thing I've ever heard of. He makes me wish I had a brother.

Your best friend,
River

April 10, 2009

Dear River,

Spring! It's here! It's here! Today the mannequin in the boutique window is wearing a sundress and sandals. I stood on my tiptoes on Hester Street and peered into a window box and saw some flowers blooming. I know the yellow ones are daffodils and the purple ones are crocus. Do you have those flowers in Kentucky?

At the library garden, there are lots of white flowers that look like upside-down teacups and a few with pink bushy blossoms. At night, walking past the library garden, you can hear crickets chirping. The air is warm and it seems like there are little bits of electricity in everyone's eyes.

I feel like I will grow a little bit now that spring has come. Kiku is still growing, which seems unfair because he is already tall—six feet tall! We know he is still growing because the other day he was walking down the hall and he hit his head on the pots hanging from the ceiling! That has never happened before. I don't know if I've told you this, but our kitchen is also our hallway—they are the same place. We only have one closet in the apartment, so we hang all the pots from the ceiling and keep all our plates and glasses on shelves that Daddy nailed into the wall. It is good we are not big people, because if we were, we would have to turn sideways on the way to the bedroom.

Thank you for the copy of <u>Time</u> magazine. It's crazy that you're on a magazine cover, like a famous person, like a MOVIE STAR!!!!!!!!! What does that feel like?

If you move to Hollywood, I hope Mum will let me come visit you.

It seems as if everyone is really paying attention to the Appalachian Mountains now. I was really happy that your team won the basketball game, too, and that you did the big last basket and that Mark was there to watch the game. I hope he gets his artificial leg soon. Kiku says those are very expensive.

Today my history teacher gave a lesson on serfdom. He started out by saying that luck is as simple as where and when you're born and who you're born to. In the old days, if you were born a serf, you stayed a serf. Every single country in the world has had serfs or slaves:

England, Egypt, Russia, Iran, Japan, India, Spain, Ghana, China, France. Mr. Orff said it's because there are some people in the world who want to control other people, who want to be comfortable and rich and protected, and they don't care who they hurt to get that way. It seems so unfair that some people work hard but don't have anything to show for it.

Someone asked if America has serfs nowadays, and Mr. Orff said the closest thing is illegal immigrants who have to pay money to the people who smuggle them into the country. Mr. Orff said that a lot of American employers take advantage of illegal immigrants because they will work for less money than citizens. I kept thinking about Mum and Daddy and all the people Daddy works with at the catering hall. I usually talk a lot in history, but when the discussion went to illegal immigrants, my hands sweated and I felt like a knife had come through the air and cut me apart from the rest of the class. But no one but me knew it had happened.

After school I went to the library with Mrs. Lau because Mum and Kiku were both working late. Remember when I told you about Mai, who teaches the citizenship class at the library? She also teaches Mrs. Lau's free ESL (English as a Second Language) class. She is so nice. Today she gave a writing assignment, and I sat next to Mrs. Lau and helped her with it. Now I will type up the story Mrs. Lau wrote, so you can read it, too:

One day I sat on subway next to a lady wearing pants sewn in my factory. I recognize the pants from the seams. I ask the lady if her pants were comfortable, and she said, "Yes." I ask the lady where she bought the pants and she said, "At Macy's, for thirty-five dollars." I never knew how much our pants cost. Thirty-four dollars is how much money I made in two days of work. I sat on the subway and thought about all the people I worked with at the factory and all the pants we made and how many people there were in the world wearing them.

Isn't that a good story? Now whenever I look at someone's clothes, I wonder who made them. I always like shirts that say MADE IN INDIA on the tag, like the manhole covers in New York. It is amazing to me that those big round pieces of metal on NY streets came all the way from India, just like our family.

I asked Mai if working in a factory was like serfdom,

but she said she didn't know. Then I asked Mai about that line Mummy-Daddy will have to say to become citizens. I have memorized the line because the words are so grand, almost like a prayer: *I hereby declare, on oath, that I absolutely and entirely renounce and abjure all allegiance and fidelity to any foreign prince, potentate, state, or sovereignty of whom or which I have heretofore been a subject or citizen.* I can say it all in one breath. I did it like that for Mai and she laughed. She said it was not anything to worry about. She said we could still go back to India whenever we wanted. She said there are so many Americans—legal, illegal, citizens, not citizens—who love America and, also, the country they or their ancestors come from. I asked her if she felt that way about China and she said, "That's what it means to be an American. To be free to love who and what you want, and to keep a lot in your heart at once."

When Mrs. Lau and I got home, the landlord was waiting in front of her door. It's a good thing I didn't go to our apartment first, and it's a good thing I had my schoolbag with me. Mrs. Lau said, "This girl is walking my dog. I'm too old to go up and down the stairs," and she leashed Cuba and he and I left.

We walked around and around Chinatown. It felt like hours. Poor Cuba was panting and walking slower and slower, so we went to the library. I wrapped his leash around my leg and sat on a bench and did my homework, and he lay down and watched the pigeons and barked at a boy on a skateboard.

I had some pretzels in my bag, so I ate those for dinner and fed some to Cuba. He took the food so gently from my hand. I could feel his whiskers and soft tongue and little front teeth on my fingers. After a long time, we went back to Mrs. Lau's apartment. The landlord was gone. Mrs. Lau said he had been very rude to her and that he had demanded to know where her son was. He also refused to look at the leak in her ceiling where the dead mouse had fallen through, and when she showed him her cracked windows where the wind and rain comes in, he said, "They look fine to me."

Then Mrs. Lau said we should clean. She said, "Spring-cleaning make everybody happy." We took a bucket and filled it with water and soap, and then we swiped Mrs. Lau's windows with newspaper. I didn't believe her when she said newspapers are better than rags for cleaning windows, but she was right. We got the windows to sparkle.

Then we flipped over Mrs. Lau's mattress, and I stood out on her fire escape and shook out her two rugs. It felt like we were making a new world, just the way we wanted it to be. The best part was when we let all the parakeets out of their cages. They flew around the apartment. All seven of them, flapping and squawking and dancing from foot to foot on the furniture. Sometimes Mrs. Lau clapped and they rose up all at once with a great whirring of wings. One parakeet even pooped on the sofa while he was flying! Cuba ran around the apartment wagging his tail at all the birds, and Mrs. Lau sat on the couch and laughed and laughed. Sometimes Cuba bowed down and stretched out his front paws like he wanted to play, and then Xie-Xie flew to his back and he would start to circle, trying to catch her. His toenails sounded like fast little drumbeats on the wood floor.

While the parakeets were flying around, we cleaned

their cages. We got rid of all their poop and changed their water and put down new clean newspaper. It was kind of sad catching them and putting them back in their cages, although they didn't seem to mind.

Well, the library is closing in ten minutes and my time on this computer is up. So good-bye for now, River Dean Justice. Please give Rufus a pat for me.

Cheerio, from your best friend,
Meena

30 April 2009

Dear Meena,

    I AM COMING TO NEW YORK CITY!!!!!!!

    Because of what I did at the capitol and me getting on the cover of the magazine and all that, Mamaw's group has chosen me to represent them for this big environmental thing at the United Nations. So I get a three-day stay in New York City, all paid for, AND they are going to put me on the <u>Today</u> show, which I have been watching every school morning of my life for ages. I hope it is Meredith Vieira who interviews me, as she seems like the nicest one of the whole bunch and I used to watch her on <u>Who Wants to Be a Millionaire</u> when I was real, real little. I feel kind of bad, to tell you the truth, because I didn't do anything to deserve a paid trip to New York City or being on the cover of a magazine or anything else. There are so many people who are fighting hard and standing up for what they believe in that they should get the attention instead of me. Like Mamaw. She has worked like a dog to get people to pay attention to all of this, and she's not on the cover of <u>Time</u>. But she says she is proud of me. That's better than any money or anything else, I reckon. And she is coming with me, too, so you will get to meet her. I told her about your mamaw passing away, and her eyes got wet and she said she couldn't wait to "hug your neck." That doesn't mean she's going to hug your neck, really. That's just what people in the South say when they mean they want to give you a big hug.

My dad and I went fishing today, over on Free Creek, where we used to live. They haven't started any mines over there yet, so the creek is still clean and clear and full of bluegill and shad this time of year. We hadn't been fishing together in a real long time, and it was about as pretty a day as anyone could ask for, with the sunlight so bright in the new leaves that they seemed to be glowing.

I like the way that when we are fishing we can go a long time without saying anything, then all at once have a big, deep conversation. We had been there about an hour and I had already caught three bluegill when Dad all at once sat down beside me on the big flat rock shaped like a turtle, where I always loved to sit when I was little.

"River," he said, "you remember how I used to talk bad about people because of what color they were, or if they were different somehow?"

"Yeah," I said, not taking my eye off my fishing line.

"Well, I was wrong about that, little man," Dad said. "About all of that. Working down there with all different kinds of people made me realize that we're all more alike than we think we are. I want you to know that."

I told him I did know that. I didn't tell him that I knew that because of you, because you are my best friend and that our friendship is better because we are different but also because we are so much alike, too.

He was quiet for a time, and I felt like he was studying me. Finally he put his arm across my back and pulled me toward him, and his voice was sort of low and trembly. "I just wouldn't want you to think that any of that talk I did before, calling people names and all, was right," he said. "I've been wanting to clear that up with you."

I nodded again. It didn't seem like there was any need for me to say anything. Then we just went back to listening to the creek flowing over the rocks, which is just about the best sound in the world if you ask me.

I have bad news, too (what would my letters be without that? LOL): Mark and his family are moving to Louisville. His mother is too afraid of rockfalls now, and they have that big MTR site up close to their house. It got to where none of them could sleep at night for worrying. Maybe I'll get to see him every once in a while. It'll be an excuse for me to go to Louisville sometime.

Here are the things in your last letter that I wanted to respond to (you know I am always looking for a reason to make a list):

1. I googled "daffodils" and they look just like the flowers we call Easter flowers. I also googled "crocus" but I've never seen any of those, although the Internet says they grow here, too.
2. I looked inside my shirt just now and it says, MADE IN VIETNAM.
3. I loved picturing all those birds flying around in the apartment. You should draw a picture of that (IN COLOR) and send it to me.
4. You must have been scared to death when the landlord came. Were you?

I can't believe we are all going to be in New York together. ☺ ☺ ☺ ☺

Yours very truly,
River Dean Justice

May 14, 2009

Dear River,

You're coming to New York!?!?! Is it really real? It feels like a dream. I can't wait to hug your mamaw's neck. Mrs. Lau is very excited about watching you on the <u>Today</u> show. She says, if you get a chance, to please tell Mr. Lauer that she says hello and that she likes his old hairstyle better than his new one.

We have been friends for almost a year and we have gone through so much together. And now you're coming here! It's crazy, isn't it?

I have some good news, too . . . Mummy-Daddy passed the citizenship interview and exam. We are all really happy. There is just one more step to go—the swearing-in ceremony.

It was really nice to read about your fishing trip with your daddy. I am happy that he said all those things to you and that you got to spend time with him and have fun together.

It's so hot today that I could smell the fruit ripening when I walked by the deli on Essex Street. Hot cherries, hot grapes, sold on the sidewalk. It smelled like fresh-baked pie.

Last week, there was no electricity in our apartment or Mrs. Lau's. The landlord turned it off and wouldn't return Mrs. Lau's calls. The electricity went out in India all the time, but it didn't happen on purpose, to punish people. Mum got very upset because she couldn't use her hair dryer, and Kiku was mad he couldn't charge his cell phone. But it wasn't really a big deal for us to not have electricity. It was very hard for Mrs. Lau, though. She gets lonely without the TV, and she has trouble seeing at night and Mum was afraid she would knock over the candles and start a fire. So I stayed with her and helped. Two nights Kiku and Mum came over, too, and slept on her floor in a big pile of blankets. It was kind of fun.

The electricity came back on yesterday, but a few hours later the water was shut off. I can't believe someone would treat an old woman this way. Mrs. Lau is such a good person. She says she is going to contact a lawyer. Mai told her that a new law was passed in February that allows NYC tenants to sue a landlord or managing company for harassment. Mai said the law was passed because of what is happening to so many people in Chinatown and the Lower East Side.

Daddy left for New Jersey and work this morning after he and Mum had the interview and exam. I am missing him already. So is Mum, but since she cut her hair and started studying to be a nurse, she is stronger. She still cries a little when Daddy leaves, but she doesn't cry like she'll never stop.

My favorite time with Daddy happened really early today when Mum and Kiku were still asleep. It was about 4:00 a.m. and I woke up and heard Daddy. He was drinking tea at the table and studying for the citizenship exam with a flashlight. I sat down and started quizzing him. He got everything right. I said I was a little hungry, and he put two pieces of bread in the toaster and we watched the red coils shade the white bread brown. Then Daddy took a sharp knife from the drawer and cut one piece of toast into a shape. "Texas," he said to me, and I laughed. Texas is my favorite state because it is shaped like India. So then Daddy cut two pieces of toast into Texas. He cut each Texas into four curved pieces and then moved all eight pieces around on the plate, mixing them up. He made a toast puzzle! We fit the pieces together, matching curve to curve, until the pieces became two Texas(es). Then we slathered the Texas(es) in butter and ate, sliding each piece away till there was nothing left but the white of the plate.

Isn't that cool? Daddy said one of the dishwashers at the catering hall taught him to do that with toast. It's something his grandmother did for him in Peru, and he does it now with his daughters. Maybe we can keep telling people and get the whole country to make toast puzzles.

I noticed something about Daddy this morning. He has little smudges of brown in the white parts of his eye, like the color from his eyes has leaked out. It's really pretty and interesting. Something about writing to you makes me notice things better. It's like I want to remember everything really well so I can tell you about it later.

I am so happy you will be in New York City soon. I can't wait to meet you. Some days it feels to me like you are made of words. But soon I'll be shaking your hand in person.

I can tell you three things that will help you not get lost in the city. I will make a list for you since you like lists so much:

1. 20 New York City street blocks equal one mile. 4 New York City avenue blocks equal one mile.
2. All the even-numbered streets in the city run east, and the odd run west.
3. All the odd-numbered avenues run south, and the even run north.

If you remember all that, you can't get lost. And you can always ask someone on the street for help. Don't forget that New Yorkers are very nice people.

Here Comes the Sun,
Meena

P.S. Here are some sample US citizenship exam questions. I figure you've never seen these before, since you were born American:

1. Name one war fought by the United States in the 1900s.
2. What did Susan B. Anthony do?
3. What is one thing Benjamin Franklin is famous for?
4. There were thirteen original states. Name three.
5. What is one responsibility that is only for United States citizens?
6. What does the judicial branch do?
7. Name your US representative.
8. Who makes federal laws?
9. What does the Constitution do?
10. What is the supreme law of the land?
11. Name three rights of freedom guaranteed by the Bill of Rights.
12. Who has the power to declare war?
13. Which president freed the slaves?
14. In what year was the Constitution written?
15. What are the first ten amendments to the Constitution called?
16. Name one purpose of the United Nations.
17. Where does Congress meet?

18. Whose rights are guaranteed by the Constitution and the Bill of Rights?
19. What is the introduction to the Constitution called?
20. Name one benefit of being a citizen of the United States.
21. What is the most important right granted to US citizens?
22. What do we call a change to the Constitution?
23. How many changes or amendments are there to the Constitution?
24. Who makes the laws in the United States?
25. What are the duties of Congress?
26. Who elects the Congress?
27. How many senators are there in Congress?
28. Name the two senators from your state.
29. What is the capital of your state?
30. Who is the current governor of your state?
31. Who becomes president of the United States if the president and the vice president should die in office?
32. What are the 49th and 50th states of the US?

33. How many terms can the president serve?
34. Who was Martin Luther King, Jr.?
35. Who is the head of your local government?
36. According to the Constitution, a person must meet certain requirements in order to be eligible to become president. Name one of these requirements.
37. What is the chief executive of a state government called?
38. Who wrote "The Star-Spangled Banner"?
39. Where does freedom of speech come from?
40. What is a minimum voting age in the United States?
41. Which president is called the "father of our country"?
42. What Immigration and Naturalization Service form is used to apply to become a naturalized citizen?
43. Who helped the Pilgrims in America?
44. What is the name of the ship that brought the Pilgrims to America?

45. What kind of government does the United States have?

46. How many times can a senator be reelected?

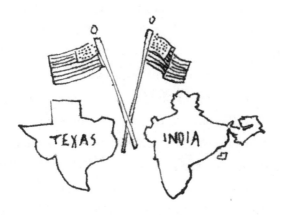

19 May 2009

Dear Meena,

    I tried cutting Kentucky into different pieces of my morning toast, but I just made a big mess and Mamaw got on to me. I should've done it BEFORE I put the blackberry jam all over it. I'm stupid sometimes. Plus, Kentucky is shaped too weird to be cut out easily.

    Have I ever told you that you are a real good hand at drawing? Well, you are. You're, like, the best artist I know. You said in one of your letters that you weren't good at anything, but you are good at SO MANY things. Especially writing and drawing.

    COUNTDOWN: In ONE MONTH I will be in New York City!!!!!!!!!!!!!!!!!!

    I got to thinking (and worrying): your mom doesn't like for you to be around boys much, so is she going to be cool with you hanging out with me when I'm in New York? I sure hope so. Tell her Mamaw is going to be with us all the time, and she's welcome to come with us, too. The more the merrier, I always say.

Today we had a little warm spell and it seemed like we could see the little green buds heating up on the tree branches and showing themselves in the bright light that washed itself out over the mountains.

Daddy had come home for a few days, just to visit us and to look for work back here at home, so we decided to all load up and go over to Cumberland Gap, which is a big national park about an hour from here. I have been going there all my life, and it is one of my favorite places in the world.

Have you ever learned about Daniel Boone in your American history class? He was an explorer who opened up the west by building a trail through the Appalachian Mountains called the Wilderness Road (which goes right through my county and is only about a mile from our house). The main gap through the mountains was Cumberland Gap, and since it was lined up with another gap called the Narrows, this became the easiest way for people to go west, and millions of people passed through that gap back in the 1700s and 1800s.

Now the park is mostly just woods that are being

protected from ever being cut down or mined or hurt in any way. There is a nice visitor's center there with a little museum, and all kinds of good creeks and over-looks (from one you can see three states), and a cave that takes two hours to go through, and picnic areas, and an old Civil War fort. But the best thing is all the trails. My favorite place of all is the actual gap that the pioneers passed through. I love that trail because it's so quiet, and you can't hear anything but birdcall and the sound of Gap Creek falling out of the mountain. The best thing of all is that Mamaw, Daddy, Mom, and I walked along the trail and let each other be quiet. Usually there are all kinds of tourists there who are making a big racket and not pay-ing the place the proper respect, but today we were the only people there. So we walked along in silence and just looked at the world, which is coming awake with spring-time. Sometimes we'd get separated a little bit, and every-one would do their own thing. At one point I was down by the creek skipping rocks, and Mamaw was up on the mountainside looking around on the ground for signs of herbs and plants that might be coming up, and Mom and

Daddy were sitting on a little bench holding hands and whispering to each other. I love to see them like that. I sat there and listened to the creek, and then I could hear something else that started out so low I couldn't really make it out, but then I knew: Mamaw was singing as she walked the mountain. This is what she sang:

I sing because I'm happy
I sing because I'm free
His eye is on the sparrow
And I know he watches me
His eye is on the sparrow
And I know he watches
I know he watches me

I listened to her, and the birds, and the creek, and I looked at the creek, and the trees, and the sky, and I thought this was how the world must have been before people had to worry about bulldozers taking everything away.

I was so caught up in all this that I didn't even notice

that my parents had come down to sit beside the creek with me. There they were, on either side of me. I could tell by the way they acted that they had something important to tell me even before they said anything. So here's what they said (I'm going to write it out like a play, like you do sometimes):

MOM: River, we have something important to tell you.

DADDY: We getting us a new house, buddy.

MOM: We've been saving and saving, ever since your daddy has been working off in Mississippi, and we've finally saved up enough to buy us a little place.

I was glad we'd have a house of our own, but I also didn't want to leave Mamaw's. I was perfectly happy right there—and told them so.

DADDY: We need our own place, though, buddy. We're going to try to buy a place as close to your mamaw as we can.

MOM: The best part is that your daddy is going to be able to come home, River.

DADDY: Yep. I have one more week to work down in Biloxi, and then I'm coming back.

MOM: He got a job in Knoxville, working construction.

DADDY: And now I can be around all the time, instead of just once every few months. That sound good to you?

I nodded, and I meant it. But then I said how he was still going to have to drive two hours round-trip every day, and Mom said that was better than living all the way in Biloxi and only getting to come home once in a while.

MOM: And, River, you need to know why I was sick for so long, too. Because it was the fault of the coal company.

I said I knew that, too, but she went on anyway.

MOM: They broke our whole family up. Your daddy had

worked for them all those years, and then they just up and laid him off because the jobs were going to MTR sites instead of underground, like your daddy did. And then we lost our house on account of it. I was so worried over everything that I had those headaches all the time. And then your daddy had to go off, plumb to Mississippi. So I just gave up, and I ought not have. When the rockfall happened . . . when I almost lost you, that woke me up. That made me see that I had to live again. So I did.

The whole time Mom said all this she capped her hand around my neck and ran her thumb back and forth on the skin between my hair and the collar of my shirt. She hadn't touched me that way in a long time.

Then we sat there a long while, being quiet and still and feeling the mountains on either side of us. And, Meena, it was the strangest thing, because I thought that not only could I feel the mountains, but I could feel the presence of all those people who had passed through the gap years and years ago, just looking for a better life. I guess they were all immigrants in their own way, just like you and your family. We all are, I reckon.

After a while Mamaw came down from the mountain clutching a little handful of spring beauties. She said, "Look, the first flowers of the year," and then she tucked them behind my mother's ear, in her hair, and put her hand on the side of Mom's face for a second. Then we all four walked out of the gap together and drove home with the windows down, smelling the spring.

Yours,
River Dean Justice

P.S. I tried to answer the immigration questions and I only got like ten right. Those are REALLY hard questions. So your parents must be really smart.

P.P.S. Enclosed is a postcard I got you while we were at the gap today, to show you what it's like. I hope you get to go there someday.

Greetings from
HISTORIC CUMBERLAND GAP

June 4, 2009

Dear River,

    Time is thick as glue. The past few days have felt like years.

    Everything went crazy 72 hours ago. When I came home from school, Mrs. Lau and Cuba and all the birds in their cages were on the street in front of the building. The birds were screaming and Cuba's tail was drooping and Mrs. Lau said, "Mee-Mee, I've lived here for fifty-six years. How can they take my home away?" And that is what has happened. All the rent-controlled people in the building are out. We are homeless.

    I sat down on the stoop next to Mrs. Lau and tried not to look at her as she cried. She said everyone had gone to the senior citizen center, but she wanted to wait for us. Her hands were all crippled up and she looked very, very old.

    When Kiku came home from school and saw us, his face didn't budge. It was like he had been expecting this. He ducked under the yellow police tape across the front door and disappeared inside the building. He came back with our suitcase, the pressure cooker, and his bicycle. We each took two birdcages and walked to the senior citizen center. When we got there, Kiku called Mum at work. Then he called Daddy, but the people at the catering hall said Daddy couldn't come to the phone because he was working an important party. Then Kiku called Ana Maria.

Mrs. Lau's son came from Brooklyn with a big U-Haul, and they went back to her apartment to get her stuff. She gave me her son's cell phone number, and when I tried to give her the apartment key from around my neck, she started to cry and said to keep it. Cuba kept licking her hands, and when I bent down to pet him, he put his paws on my shoulders like a hug. When they left the senior citizen center, he looked back and wagged his tail at me. I felt like my heart had fallen out and a big metal pan had been put in its place.

When Mum came she was very calm and quiet. Kiku told her he couldn't get through to Daddy on the phone and that he was going to get him on his bike. Mum said, "No." Kiku said, "It's not far. I've done it before." Mum said, "You've done what?" Kiku said, "I've biked to Jersey to see Daddy." Then Mum slapped him across the face.

His cheek turned bright pink. She said, "You and your father are keeping secrets?" She was so upset she was shaking. I thought Kiku was going to run away, but he just said, "I'm sorry, Mum," and then Mum looked at Kiku's cheek and her lips went all wiggly and she hugged him and said, "Get Daddy."

And right at that moment, Ana Maria walked in. There was a man with her, her uncle, who shook Kiku's hand. Kiku cleared his throat and said, "Mum, this is my girlfriend, Ana Maria, and her uncle, Rafael. You and Mee-Mee are going to stay at their apartment tonight, and I'll get Daddy and meet you there." He sounded like a man all of a sudden. Mum was completely shocked. She didn't say anything.

Poor Kiku. All of his secrets are out now.

Kiku got on his bicycle and rode away and Mum and I went to Ana Maria's apartment. Her family lives on the top floor of a building on Essex Street. It is rent-controlled and has been in their family for forty years. There is a big luxury apartment building under construction across the street. The jackhammers and cranes are really loud, every day, from 8:00 a.m. to 5:00 p.m.

Ana Maria's family gave us dinner and made us a soft bed on the floor and told Mum what a good boy Kiku is. They were so nice and Mum was nice, too, but I could tell she was uncomfortable. She tried to do the dishes but Ana Maria's mum wouldn't let her. And she tried to give Ana Maria's daddy some money but he wouldn't take it. It was like the Ramirezes' being nice made Mum ashamed. She stayed awake all night and sat out on the fire escape wrapped up in her shawl. I watched her because I couldn't sleep either.

At 7 in the morning, Kiku and Daddy arrived. They had gotten a ride from a nice cook at the catering hall who has a 1971 El Camino. He put Kiku's bike in the back of his car and drove them into the city. Mum and I were still awake, waiting for them.

That all happened three days ago and ever since then Kiku has been calling rental places in Chinatown to try to find us a place to live. Everything is so expensive. When school ends in two weeks and Kiku graduates, we will leave Ana Maria's apartment. We may have to move to New Jersey. I won't see Ms. Bledsoe and Carlos and Valentina or paint the backdrop for <u>Oklahoma</u> next year.

I won't walk Cuba or clean Xie-Xie's cage and I won't get to hang out with Mrs. Lau. I won't go to the Seward Park Library anymore. I wonder if the trees will miss me.

In three hours we will go uptown to the INS offices, where Mummy-Daddy will do the swearing-in ceremony to become American citizens. I have been drawing tiny American flags on my notebook paper and taping them around toothpicks all morning so that Ana Maria can stick the toothpicks through apples and strawberries for the party afterward. It feels strange to think we will soon be citizens but we do not have a place to live.

I have started reading <u>David Copperfield</u> for the second time. He goes through lots of troubles but ends up happy. I think it will be the same for us. Ever since I started writing this letter to you, I have felt sure of it. There is something about writing that always makes me feel like everything is going to be OK.

Kiku and I called Mrs. Lau just now, and she said she is having a good time bossing her son around and that her daughter-in-law is making her favorite kind of chicken for dinner. They have a backyard, so Cuba and the parakeets sit outside in the sunshine for most of the day. Mrs.

Lau said she had talked to Mai on the phone and they are going next week to see a lawyer at the Chinatown Tenants Center. She said she is so homesick for Chinatown she could die, but then she said she won't give those rotten sons of _____ the satisfaction of seeing her dead. She said, "We'll get back home, Mee-Mee. You be a good girl, now, and don't worry."

It's kind of fun staying with Ana Maria. Today she braided my hair in a new way. It looks like a ladder, starting at my forehead instead of at the back of my neck. She also showed me how to do eyeliner. It's hard not to poke yourself, but it makes your eyes jump out of your face. Just like outlining a tree in black paint on a backdrop makes it easier to see from the audience. Ana Maria also loaned me this really cool tank top. She has the best clothes. She says you don't have to be rich to look good, you just have to have a sense of style and be creative. I can see why Kiku loves her. And I think Mum is starting to see, too. Even though Ana Maria isn't Indian, she is like us.

There is something else I like about staying with Ana Maria and her family. Someone in the building plays the trumpet every night. I think it's a woman, because it's a light and quiet footstep walking up the stairs. First I hear that, then I hear the door to the roof opening. Then the ceiling creaks and I hear the footsteps walking right above my head. Then I hear the trumpet. Scales for about an hour, then a song. One long song that sounds so beautiful it hurts. The song swoops around the air like a bird. Someone standing on the roof, playing to the city, to the sky . . . Oh, River, the way it sounds twining through the shaftway. It's like life, full of joy and mourning. Everything changing, this way then that way. I sat in front of the window last night and listened. I saw a man in the next building leaning out his window, watching the traffic on Essex Street. He was listening to the trumpet, too.

When it got dark, I couldn't see anything except my own face reflected in the glass. Listening to that trumpet, I felt like I don't know what's coming next, but whatever it is, it will just make me more me. It's kind of weird because when I was sad about Dadi, on the subway platform, I heard a trumpet, too. Maybe it's a sign of some kind.

I thought I would be upset about losing all our stuff, our pots and pans and sheets and clothes. But I'm not. I feel like I have everything that really matters—Mummy-Daddy-Kiku. And there is always the library for books. Daddy says no matter where we go, there will be a library, because almost every town in America has one. Isn't that amazing?

I don't know if Mrs. Lau still has the PO box, so I don't know where to tell you to send letters. I'll go to the library every day and check for an e-mail from you.

Remember how I told you about the statue of Gandhiji in Union Square? I will meet you there on Sunday, June 14, at 3:00 p.m. We don't have a camera, but here is a little portrait of me so you will recognize me when you see me. I practiced drawing it last night when I was looking at myself in the window. I am using the pencils Dadi gave me. I have sharpened them so many times they are almost too small to hold.

When you get here, I will be an American citizen, just like you. We will eat mangoes with chili pepper and sit on a park bench and watch the people go by. I'll give you your birthday present and teach you how to buy a MetroCard so you can give me a tour of the UN. And I will show you my watch set to India time.

Right now, in America, it is 8:00 p.m. and I am sending you telepathic thoughts.

Everything is going to be OK. It is, it is.

See you soon, River Dean Justice.

Your friend,
Meena

ACKNOWLEDGMENTS

Ardent thanks to the places where Meena's letters were written: Sisters Bazaar, Mussoorie, India; Swamp Annie's, Choteau, Montana; Gap Year College at IIIT, Hyderabad, India; The Flop, New York City; Knox College, Illinois; Spalding University's MFA in Writing Program; two porches in eastern Kentucky; SIDH, Kempty, India; New York–Presbyterian, 10 Central. And ardent thanks to the people who fed Meena's half of the book: Hilary Schenker and her inspired hands and eyes; Joy Harris; Terry Sheehan and the New York Public Library's Seward Park Center for Reading and Writing (especially Senetta, Teresa, June, and Vasyl); the Chinatown Tenants Union (NYC); Naomi Shihab Nye; Sabrina Brooks; Ranjana Varghese; Karuna Morarji; Vinish Gupta; Mridu Mahajan; Jitendra Sharma and family; Sonu Vishnoi; Kapil Gupta and Tara Maria. For good eats on 10 Central: Sabs Shakley, Edelen McWilliams, Sam Zalutsky and Ed Boland, Matt and Lisa Lowenbraun, Liz Gordon, Kelly Van Zile and Andrew Grusetskie. Ashok Vaswani for his Hindi translation and penmanship. Much gratitude to the fine folks of Candlewick Press for making and supporting beautiful books, and to collaborator extraordinaire, Silas House, for writing the other half of this one. To my mother and father, as always. And to beloved Ann and Jim Gordon. To my grandmother, Sita Manganmalani, who was raised in Mussoorie, and to her mother, whose name has been lost. And to Holter, first and last reader, and my favorite human being for eighteen years and counting. —Neela Vaswani

❧ ❧ ❧ ❧ ❧

My daughters, Cheyenne and Liv, have taught me just about everything. Liv was our very first reader, and an especially helpful one since she was the same age as River and Meena when she read the manuscript. Jason Howard has patiently and lovingly lived alongside these characters for a couple years now, and I can't thank him enough—for everything. I thank Berea College and Spalding University for their support. I have too many heroes fighting injustice to list, but chief among them are Wendell Berry, Chad Berry, Teri Blanton, Mari-Lyn Evans, Ashley Judd, Jessie Lynne Keltner, Kate Larken, George Ella Lyon, Bev May, Daniel Martin Moore, Megan Naseman, Deborah Payne, Erik Reece, Anne Shelby, Lora Smith, Ben Sollee, Patty Wallace . . . so many others, particularly the many students I know who are refusing apathy and making a difference in the world. To learn more about mountaintop removal, please visit http://ilovemountains. org. I am thankful to Karen Lotz, Nicole Raymond, and everyone at wonderful Candlewick for all their good, hard work. Neela Vaswani has broadened my view of the world and the human heart, and I am indebted to her. To all of my family (created and blood): my love and affection. To everyone who has read this book, thank you for spending time with us. Now, go do good. —Silas House

LITTLE, BROWN AND COMPANY

New York Boston

Dumpling Days

A novel by

Grace Lin

Little, Brown and Company

Hachette Book Group
237 Park Avenue, New York, NY 10017
Visit our website at www.lb-kids.com

Little, Brown and Company is a division of Hachette Book Group, Inc.
The Little, Brown name and logo are trademarks of Hachette Book Group, Inc.

The publisher is not responsible for websites (or their content)
that are not owned by the publisher.

First Edition: January 2012

The characters and events portrayed in this book are fictitious. Any similarity to real persons, living or dead, is coincidental and not intended by the author.

Library of Congress Cataloging-in-Publication Data
Lin, Grace.
  Dumpling days / by Grace Lin.—1st ed.
    p. cm.
  Summary: When Pacy, her two sisters, and their parents go to Taiwan to celebrate Grandma's sixtieth birthday, the girls learn a great deal about their heritage.
  ISBN 978-0-316-12590-1
  [1. Taiwan—Fiction. 2. Family life—Taiwan—Fiction. 3. Taiwanese Americans—Fiction.] I. Title.
PZ7.L644Du 2012
[Fic]—dc22

                                                    2010048036

                                        10 9 8 7 6 5 4 3 2 1

                                                        RRD-C

                                    Printed in the United States of America

TO LISSY, WHO many years ago said
I SHOULD write about our first family trip
to Taiwan...and I answered no.

MUCH gratitude to Mom, Dad, Alvina,
Bethany, Libby, Saho, Neil, and
Christine for making this book possible.

Special thanks to Ann Glass of
Darlington Lower School for her daughter's
inspirational travel stories and to
Felix Chen for his Taiwan memories.

my family on the way to Taiwan

map of Taiwan
(not to scale)

"PINK, PINK, PINK," I SAID OVER KI-KI TO MOM. LISSY, Ki-Ki, and I were sitting next to each other on an airplane, and we were wearing the same hot-pink overall dresses, the color of the neon donut sign in the food court back in the airport. "Why did it have to be pink?"

neon donut sign

"That was the only color they had that was in all three of your sizes," Mom told me. "And I wanted to make sure you matched so it would be easy to keep an eye on you."

"I can keep an eye on myself," I said as I pulled at the brilliant-colored denim. The matching jumpers made it easy for everyone on the airplane to keep an eye on us, and it was embarrassing. Lissy thought so, too.

"I hope no one I know sees me," Lissy had said, horrified.

"I can't believe you're making me wear the same dress as a six-year-old."

"Seven!" Ki-Ki had said. "I'm seven!"

But Mom hadn't listened to even our loudest protests, and now we were on the plane in matching dresses. Whenever people passed us, they smiled and I didn't blame them. We looked ridiculous, like plastic birds in a flock of flying ducks.

"This is an important trip," Dad said. "Traveling is always important — it opens your mind. You take something with you, you leave something behind,

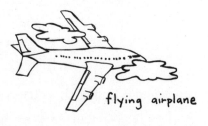
flying airplane

and you are forever changed. That is a good trip."

"Yeah, but why does it have to be a trip to Taiwan?" I asked. Dad always spouted in dramatic ways about things, sometimes to be funny but other times because he really meant it. When he meant it, we usually ignored him. "Why couldn't it be a trip to Hawaii? Or California? At least then we could've seen Melody!"

Melody was my best friend, and last year she had moved to California. I wished so much we were going to visit her. But, instead, we were going to Taiwan. Taiwan was far away. It was so far that I wasn't even sure where it was. Mom and Dad called it their homeland. But to me and my sisters, our small town of New Hartford, New York — with its big trees and sprawling

2

lawns, the one shopping mall, and the red brick school with the tall, waving American flag — was our homeland.

our house in New Hartford

I was also grumpy because I had to sit in the exact middle of the row. Mom and Dad sat on either end, Lissy sat next to Dad, and Ki-Ki next to Mom. I was stuck between Lissy and Ki-Ki, and I didn't get to see anything that was going on. "What do you want to see?" Dad said when I complained. "There's nothing to see. You would be just as bored sitting on the end as you would be sitting in the middle."

"And I can't believe we're going to be gone for the whole summer," I said. It seemed so unfair. All my friends at school got to go to fun places for the summer, like the beach or amusement parks. Melody lived near the Universal Studios theme park. *They have a ride there*, she had written me. *It's even better than 3-D. They call it 4-D!*

"It's not the whole summer," Mom said. "It's just one month. Twenty-eight days."

"It's not like you have anything better to do," Lissy said.

"You don't, either!" I said. But she was kind of right. Even though I had other friends, ever since Melody had moved away, my school vacations seemed to drag on like waiting in line at the supermarket. But I still knew I'd rather be at home than go to Taiwan.

"I have lots of things to do," Lissy said with a superior look. "Why can't we leave earlier, like when Dad leaves?"

"I have to leave earlier because I have to work," Dad said before I could say anything to Lissy. "You are the lucky ones! I wish I could stay the whole time."

"Besides, we aren't staying that much longer," Mom said. "Just twelve days more. We want to be there for Grandma's birthday. She's going to be sixty, so it's important."

"Why?" Ki-Ki asked. Ki-Ki was always asking why. Ever since her teacher had told her that there was no such thing as a stupid question, Ki-Ki never stopped asking any. She used to even ask things like "Why is why, why?" Her questions weren't as silly anymore, but she still asked a lot of them.

"Well, remember how there is a Chinese twelve-year cycle — every year is named after a different animal, and it repeats every twelve years?" Mom said. "Grandma is going to be sixty, and that means she has lived through all twelve Chinese animal years five times. That is very lucky."

"Pacy and Ki-Ki, you've never been to Taiwan before. And

Lissy, you were probably too young to remember," Dad said. "We need to go to Taiwan so you will get to know your roots."

"Roots?" Ki-Ki said, swinging her legs to show Dad the bottoms of her feet. "I don't have roots!"

Lissy and I rolled our eyes. Ki-Ki still liked acting like a baby sometimes. Mom said it was because she was the youngest.

"Silly," Mom said. "You know what he means. We want you to see the place where we came from, before we came to the United States."

"You should know Taiwan. It's…" Dad said, his face dimming as he tried to think of the right word in English. His face fell, and he said it in Chinese instead. "It's…Taiwan is…*bao dao.*"

Bao dao? I didn't know a lot of Chinese, but that word seemed familiar. It sounded like the Chinese word for . . .

jiaozi
(dumplings)

"Pork buns!" I said. "Fried dumplings? Taiwan is wrapped meat?"

"No," Mom said, and laughed. "You are thinking of *baozi* and *jiaozi*! I guess *bao dao* does sound a little like the words for pork buns and dumplings. But *bao dao* is completely different. It means 'treasure island.' People call Taiwan an island of treasure."

"Treasure?" Ki-Ki asked. "Is there buried gold there?"

"Well, no, not gold," Dad said. "Treasure like forests and water and rich earth to grow food."

Taiwan suddenly sounded like the woods in our backyard at home. Ki-Ki thought so, too.

"Taiwan sounds like camping!" she said. "Is that the treasure?"

I looked at Dad eagerly. Camping was interesting. We had never gone camping. Dad didn't like it. He always said, "What's so good about camping? Who wants to sleep on the ground?" Maybe he would like it if we were camping in Taiwan?

"No! Taiwan is not camping!" Dad said, and we could all tell he was having a hard time thinking of how to explain it. I was disappointed about the camping. "Taiwan is cities and cars and culture and restaurants. In Taiwan, there are beds and good food. A lot of good food!"

"So, food is the treasure of Taiwan?" I asked. I was still thinking about the dumplings.

"Yes!" Dad said, and he and Mom laughed as if I had said something very funny. "Yes, it is! Food probably is one of the treasures of Taiwan. We will definitely eat a lot when we are there."

I heard Lissy give a little sigh. I felt like sighing, too. I'd have to last twenty-eight days in Taiwan until I could come back home. That was so long. Already, it felt like forever.

"Don't worry," Mom said, watching us with a grin. "It will be fun."

"Are you sure?" It wasn't that I thought Mom was lying; it was just that sometimes her kind of fun wasn't the same as mine.

"Yes." Mom smiled. "You'll see."

Chapter 2

On the airplane

airplane window

BEING ON THE AIRPLANE MADE ME FEEL AS IF I WERE stuck in a plastic bottle. It was hard to tell if we had been flying for one hour or ten. At first, we played with the TVs. We all had our own — each was in the back of the seat in front of us, and we could watch any movie we wanted. At home, Mom let us watch only three TV shows a week. We'd each pick one and watch it together, which wasn't always fun. Lissy had just started choosing some silly hospital show with lots of kissing, and Ki-Ki liked a baby cartoon that we (even Ki-Ki herself) were all too old for. So I was excited to be able to watch whatever I wanted.

TV on the back of the airplane seat

But after a while, even that

became dull. I tried to read my books, but my head felt all stuffed up and I couldn't concentrate. Dad was right when he said there was nothing to see. The airplane ride was so long and so boring. It seemed as if the only thing I could do was sleep. Which I did, until Lissy elbowed me awake.

"They're bringing the dinner!" she said. A flight attendant was wheeling a cart and handing out prepacked meals to everyone. I turned the knob that held up my tray table on the seat in front of me. *Clack!* It fell open with a clatter, but no one paid any attention. Everyone was too busy getting the food.

Lissy passed down to me a tray full of covered containers all shiny and smooth. The largest container was wrapped with foil, which I carefully began to peel off. Getting airplane food was fun; it was like opening presents! Though not the most delicious-looking presents. Pale, flattened noodles and unknown meat chunks were drowning in the orange-brown overflow of curry sauce. A mix of sliced cucumbers, corn, and dark purple beans filled one of the small containers. The other container had faded melon cubes, the same color as unripe grapefruit. The dessert was in a wrapper with big white, fancy letters that said CHOCOLATE-CHIP SHORTBREAD, even though it was really just a chocolate-chip cookie.

On the side were a napkin; a fork, a knife, and a spoon (all

airplane food

plastic); and a pair of chopsticks. Lissy pushed the chopsticks toward me.

"Since we're going to Taiwan," she said to me, "you'd better learn how to use chopsticks."

"I've eaten with chopsticks lots of times!" I told her. "I know how to use them!"

"No, you don't," Lissy said. "You hold them all wrong."

Did I? No one had ever taught me how to use chopsticks. I had just taken them and eaten with them the best I could. It had worked fine — I had always been able to get food to my mouth.

"Look," Lissy said. "You're supposed to hold them like this. Hold the top one like a pencil. They aren't supposed to cross over like that."

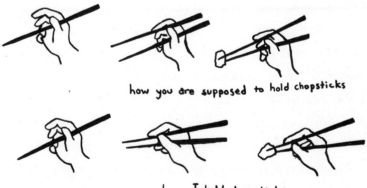

how you are supposed to hold chopsticks

how I hold chopsticks

I tried holding the chopsticks the way Lissy showed me. They felt awkward between my fingers, but I aimed them toward the container of cucumbers and corn and grabbed.

Plop! The slices fell from my chopsticks back into the tray like raindrops. I tried again. *Plop! Plop!* The cucumbers slipped off the chopsticks again.

"See!" Lissy said triumphantly. "You can't use chopsticks! I told you you're going to have to learn!"

"Speaking of learning," Mom said, leaning over, "I found out about a special cultural program they have in Taiwan. It's made just for kids like you — kids from America. We've signed you up for classes."

I stopped trying to pick up cucumbers. Classes sounded like school. Lissy thought so, too, because she made a noise that sounded like she was gargling mouthwash.

"Classes!" Lissy said. "But it's summer. It's vacation!"

"We want to make sure you don't get bored," Dad said.

Lissy, Ki-Ki, and I looked at one another. We all knew never to say we were bored when Dad was around. If we ever complained about having nothing to do, he always said something like "Let me give you some math problems."

"In Taiwan," Mom said, "a lot of kids study in the summer, too. But, anyway, don't worry. We just signed you up for fun classes."

This was another time that I didn't trust Mom's idea of fun.

"What kind of classes?" I asked.

"All different," Mom said. "Lissy has calligraphy, Pacy has painting birds and flowers, and Ki-Ki has paper cutting."

10

"I can cut paper!" Ki-Ki said. "I don't need a class for that."

"This is special paper cutting," Mom said. "You'll learn how to cut pictures out of paper."

"Isn't calligraphy Chinese words?" Lissy interrupted. "How can I paint Chinese words when I don't even know Chinese?"

"Yeah!" I said. "None of us speak Chinese! How can we take a class in Taiwan?"

"Remember, it's a special program. The teachers will be able to speak English," Mom said. "We were very lucky to find this. Remember that Taiwanese-American convention we went to with Melody's family a couple of years ago? It's run by a group like that. They want to make sure Taiwanese-American kids know about their culture. There is even a special boat tour, but that is for teenagers."

"I'm a teenager! Fourteen is a teenager!" Lissy said. "Why don't I go on that instead?"

"It's for older teenagers," Mom said. "High school."

"I'm almost in high school!" she said. "I could go!"

Lissy was still talking, but I had stopped listening. Lissy was always being boring about how old she was, like we would forget that she was the eldest. But besides that, hearing about the painting class had me worried.

I wasn't worried about actually painting. I was good at art. I wrote and illustrated a book that won four hundred dollars before, and I was going to write and illustrate books when I grew up. I had decided that a couple of years ago. I knew I would be able to paint fine.

But I remembered that Taiwanese-American convention Mom mentioned. Even though I had gone with Melody, I hadn't liked it. It had been horrible. The kids there were Taiwanese-American, and so was I, but they weren't like me at all. In New Hartford, now that Melody had moved, I was the only Asian girl in my class. I tried to be just like everyone else, and I always spoke English, even at home. But at that Taiwanese-American convention, all the girls there could speak Chinese and Taiwanese, and they called me a Twinkie. They said I had lost my culture. "You're yellow on the outside, but white on the inside!" one girl had said to me. "You're a Chinese person who's been Americanized."

And it was true. I was Americanized. In New Hartford, *Americanized* meant being like everyone else and having friends. But at that convention, it meant being humiliated and disliked. Was it going to be like that in Taiwan, too? Would everyone there make fun of me and call me a Twinkie? *Plop!* Another cucumber slipped from my chopsticks onto the tray, and I felt as if it were just like my heart falling.

Chapter 3

Uncle Flower

bouquet
of lilies

I WAS SO SLEEPY WHEN WE FINALLY GOT OFF THE PLANE. We had to wait in a long, long line for something called customs, which was really just a man in a uniform who stamped passports. When we exited, there were crowds of people waiting in front of us. It was like we were walking onto a stage with an audience. But before I could feel scared, we heard a yell and two people ran toward us, waving excitedly, like birds with flapping wings.

"Jin!" Mom said as they ran over to us. Auntie Jin hugged us with a big grin that seemed to stretch across her round face, like a jack-o'-lantern at Halloween. Her husband

Auntie Jin running
toward us

laughed, handed me and Lissy a bouquet of flowers, and took a suitcase from Dad.

Somehow, Auntie Jin herded us out of the airport and into a bus. It was hot! I felt like an ice-cream cone melting as soon as we exited. Luckily, the bus was air-conditioned. Mom and Dad and Auntie Jin and her husband kept talking and laughing in what I guessed was Taiwanese the whole time, though it could've been Chinese—I wasn't sure. Lissy, Ki-Ki, and I sat across from them and looked at the flowers. They were white and pink like stars with raspberry-colored freckles. Their smell seemed to sweeten the air.

"Are they real?" Ki-Ki asked.

"Of course they're real," Lissy said. "Feel the petals. They're lilies."

"Do you think they spray perfume on their flowers here?" I asked. "They smell so strong."

"Maybe," Lissy said, trying to look wise.

"What's our uncle's name?" Ki-Ki asked. "The one who gave us the flowers?"

I shrugged. Lissy looked confused as well. "It's...it's...I know it...."

"You don't know!" I said to her.

"Yes, I do!" Lissy said.

"What is it, then?" I asked.

"It's...it's Uncle Flower," Lissy said.

"No, it's not!" I said.

14

"Yes, it is!" Lissy said, and we all laughed.

"What are you laughing about over there?" Dad asked.

"Nothing," we said as we looked at one another. None of us wanted to ask what Uncle's name was while he was in front of us — then he would know we didn't know it. And that might make us look rude.

"Are you hungry?" Auntie Jin asked us. "Once we get to Grandma's, we can go eat."

"Yes, yes," Uncle Flower said. "First thing you do when you come to Taiwan is eat. Eating is a hobby here in Taiwan."

We grinned at that. Auntie Jin's and Uncle Flower's English was like Mom's and Dad's. It was a little hard to understand what they were saying at first, but once we got used to the way they said the words it wasn't too bad. Besides, they were talking about food, and that was always easy to understand. I was hungry. I had ended up not eating much of the airplane food.

"Okay," I said. "What are we going to eat?"

"Anything," Auntie Jin said. "We're in Taipei, the capital city! It has everything. What do you want to eat?"

"Pizza?" Ki-Ki asked.

"Ki-Ki! Don't pick pizza!" Lissy said. "We're in Taiwan — you have to pick a Chinese food!"

"You don't have to," Uncle Flower said. "There are all kinds of food here in Taipei. We have McDonald's — all that American food, if you want. But Taiwan has the best Japanese and Chinese food — sushi, ramen..."

"Dumplings?" I asked. I remembered how I had mixed up Taiwan being *bao dao* to *jiaozi*, which was a kind of Chinese dumpling. And it was also my favorite Chinese food to eat.

"Dumplings!" Uncle Flower said. "Taiwan has the best dumplings in the world!"

Uncle Flower, Auntie Jin, Mom, and Dad began to speak in Taiwanese to one another really fast. We knew they were all talking about food, and their words sounded like clicking chopsticks. All that talk was making me hungry. I wondered what the best dumplings in the world tasted like.

The bus stopped, and we all got off. So this was Taiwan. I looked at the gray buildings towering overhead and the

Taipei, Taiwan

people and taxis and motor scooters rushing by all around us. So far, all I could tell of Taiwan was that it was very busy. As Dad, Auntie Jin, and Uncle lifted our luggage from the bus, I nudged Mom.

"What's Uncle's name?" I asked her.

"Uncle?" Mom said. "It's Li-Li. He's Uncle Li-Li."

"Lily!" Ki-Ki and I laughed, and Lissy shouted, "I told you he was Uncle Flower!"

dumpling in
spoon

DAD AND UNCLE FLOWER LUGGED OUR SUITCASES UP
the stairs behind us while we walked into a roomful of aunt-
ies and uncles waiting with hugs. Grandma's and Grandpa's
faces wrinkled with smiles as they squeezed each of us at
the same time. Although we hadn't seen Grandma and
Grandpa in a long time, they still looked the same to me. But
we looked different to them. "So tall now!" Grandma said to
me, and "Young lady," Grandpa said to Lissy.

There were new cousins, too. One by one, they were introduced to us. Some were just babies, but there were two who
were about our age. I couldn't remember everyone's Chinese
names right, so I just made up names that sounded close to
them. Everyone laughed when I called the sharp-faced boy with
the laughing eyes Shogun instead of Xiaoquan and changed
his sister's name, Chulian, to Julian. But they didn't really seem

to mind, and they still answered when I spoke to them. Shogun was Lissy's age, and Julian was in between my age and Ki-Ki's.

"Speak in English!" Aunt Bea urged them, but they just smiled at us bashfully. "They learn English in school," she told us. "But now they're shy!" She turned to them again. "You can do it!"

Julian looked back and forth like there was a fly in the room. "Hello!" she said finally, and then looked at Shogun for help. He gave a mischievous smile.

"Okay!" he said loudly, and then started to laugh.

"That's it?" Aunt Bea said. Shogun and Julian nodded and laughed harder, and Lissy, Ki-Ki, and I joined in, too. I didn't know if we would be able to talk to the cousins, but I knew I liked them.

"Can you say something in Chinese back?" Auntie Jin asked us. Lissy and Ki-Ki shook their heads hard. We never spoke Chinese in New Hartford, not in school or at home. We didn't know any Chinese words. Well, no, that wasn't true. I did know one Chinese word.

"Jiaozi?" I said.

"Dumplings!" Auntie Jin whooped, and everyone laughed. "I guess that means we should go and eat!"

Everyone laughed again, and the adults began talking about the where and how of dumplings. Finally, something was agreed on, and we followed Grandma, Grandpa, Auntie Jin, and Uncle Flower down the stairs.

19

Uncle Flower stopped two taxis for us, and we got in.

"Grandma doesn't have a car?" Lissy asked.

"No," Mom said. "You don't need a car in Taipei. It's like New York City. There are so many taxis."

And I realized it did seem a lot like New York City, at least what I could remember of New York City. I had been there only a couple of times with Mom and Dad. But all the bright yellow taxis and the tall buildings and the people walking here were just like it. Except I couldn't read any of the signs. They were all in Chinese.

"Look!" Ki-Ki said to me. "Watch the light!" She was pointing at the crossing light, a flashing sign that told people when it was safe to walk.

But this light had a little green figure walking, like a cartoon. Above him was the countdown of how many seconds left there were to walk across the street. As the number got lower and lower, the figure started walking faster and faster until it was running! When the number got to zero, he turned red and stood still, and our taxi zoomed forward. We laughed. I had never seen a man actually *move* on a walk light before.

When we got to the restaurant, Uncle Flower laughed.

"Usually there is a long, long line," he said. "But we are very early."

"What time is it?" Lissy asked.

"Four o'clock," Mom said. "Are you tired? It is four in the morning at home."

I was tired, but I was also hungry. As we waited for the hostess to seat us, I looked into the kitchen, where the chefs were making dumplings. It was like a fast and frantic dance, the chefs' fingers flying as dumpling after dumpling were made. Six chefs chopped and mixed vegetables and meat. Also in the kitchen were a chef who made the dough, a chef who cut the dough into small pieces, another who rolled out dumpling skins, and a fourth who filled the skins with the meat mixture. And during all of that, more chefs lifted bamboo trays of cooking dumplings out of giant steamers, and hot misty clouds filled the air.

how they make soup dumplings (I don't know where the soup comes from!)

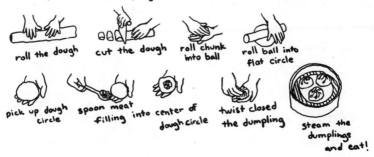

roll the dough   cut the dough   roll chunk into ball   roll ball into flat circle

pick up dough circle   spoon meat filling into center of dough circle   twist closed the dumpling   steam the dumplings and eat!

"They make the dumplings so fast," I said.

"Eh?" Grandma asked. Grandma and Grandpa could speak English okay, but sometimes they had a hard time understanding it. Usually we had to repeat things to them.

"The chefs," I said, speaking slower, "they make the dumplings fast."

"Yes." Grandma nodded. "In China, there is a famous dumpling chef. She can make one million dumplings in seven hours and twenty minutes."

"That's fast!" Lissy said.

"But is it faster than you can eat them?" Dad said. "We'll have to see."

The hostess brought us to a table, and almost as soon as Grandpa was finished ordering, the waiter came out with the dumplings, which were like little pinched bags in a bamboo basket.

Mom put one on a white spoon and handed it to me. I was glad I didn't have to use chopsticks.

"Careful when you eat these," Auntie Jin said. "They're special."

I'd had dumplings lots of times. How special could these be? But as I took a bite, I almost stopped in amazement.

"There's soup in these dumplings!" I said.

All the adults at the table laughed.

"I told you they were special!"

xiaolongbao
(soup dumplings)

Auntie Jin said. "They are called *xiaolongbao*. They have soup inside of them. They're good, aren't they?"

I took another bite. The hot soup filled my mouth, and the mixture of soup and meat and dumpling skin seemed to melt

22

into a warm, rich flavor. They *were* good. Very, very good. I began to realize why Uncle Flower said Taiwan had the best dumplings in the world.

They were so good that I didn't even notice that I had soup dribbling down my chin. I quickly wiped it away.

"They say if you can eat these dumplings without making a mess, you are a 'real Chinese' person," Uncle Flower said.

"It's because these dumplings are made so that one side has thinner skin than the other," said Auntie Jin. "And you are supposed to break the dumpling on the thinner side to sip the soup out so you don't make as much of a mess. But they say only a 'real Chinese' person can tell which side has the thinner skin."

A real Chinese person? I bet that meant not a Twinkie like me. But I carefully put another dumpling on my spoon and looked at it closely. To me, the delicate, shiny skin looked the same on all sides. Did this side look a bit paler? Maybe this was the thinner side. I took a bite...and more soup dribbled down my chin. Even the dumpling could tell I was just visiting.

But I could still eat them. I could eat a lot of them and fast. Lissy and Ki-Ki could, too. Grandpa had to place two more orders for us.

"We *can* eat the dumplings as fast as the chefs can make them," I told Dad. "I bet I could eat a million dumplings!"

"If you ate a million dumplings, you would be a dumpling

23

yourself," Dad said. "You'd be a dumpling stuffed with dumplings!"

Then the waiter came with our dessert. In a round bamboo steamer were nine buns shaped and colored like delicate pink-and-white peaches. They had been so carefully made and decorated that they looked like they had just been picked from a tree. I reached for one.

"These are special peach buns," Auntie Jin told us. "Did you know the peach symbolizes longevity? We are going to have these at Grandma's birthday party, too — to celebrate her long life. You eat these peach buns when you are celebrating something you want to have for a long time."

I took a bite. The peach bun was warm and soft with a creamy, sweet red-bean paste filling. It was good but kind of unexpected. I had thought it was going to taste cool and juicy — like a real peach.

peach buns

"Like all of us being together now, eating these peach buns," Auntie Jin continued, "means that we will be together for a long time."

"And happy," Mom said. "Eating these peach buns while we are happy means we will be happy for a long time."

"Does it mean we'll be eating dumplings for a long time?" I asked. "Does it mean we can have dumplings tomorrow?"

"Tomorrow? And then the next day, too?" Dad teased. "You know, if you have dumplings all the time, you'll get tired of them."

"No, I won't," I insisted. "I could eat dumplings for a long time."

"Well, no matter what," Dad said, "I do know that eating these peach buns after being stuffed with dumplings means we'll be full for a long, long time."

Chapter 5

Visiting Ghosts

fire in barrel

"GET UP!" MOM SAID, SHAKING BOTH KI-KI AND ME. Ki-Ki made a whining noise and kept sleeping. "It's the afternoon!"

With my eyes half-closed, I followed Mom and Lissy out of the room, leaving Ki-Ki alone on the bed. Mom was right. It *was* the afternoon. We had slept all through the night and the morning, and now it was already the middle of the day. The bright sunlight flooded the hallway. I had to rub my eyes as I walked blindly. When I could see again, I saw the kitchen was full of people.

"Finally awake!" Auntie Jin said, smiling at us.

"Ahh, jet lag," Grandma said, nodding knowingly.

"Jet lag?" I asked. I still felt in a daze.

"It's when your body is all mixed up," Mom said. "When it's morning here, it's night at home, so your body is confused and you are tired at the wrong time. That's jet lag."

"Oh," I said. My body wasn't the only thing confused. Maybe my brain was jet-lagged, too.

"Anyway, good thing you are finally awake!" Dad said. "We're going out to lunch!"

"We are?" I said. I tried to shake myself to feel more awake. I didn't want to miss any good food. "Can we have dumplings again?"

"You and dumplings," Dad said, laughing. "Well, you can if you want to. We're going for dim sum."

I looked at Lissy. Dad said *dim sum* like we should already know what that was. But I didn't, and, even though she was pretending she did, I could tell by Lissy's face that she didn't, either. Neither one of us wanted to ask in front of everyone and look dumb. I wished Ki-Ki were there. This would have been a perfect time for her to ask questions, like she always did.

But even without Ki-Ki, we would find out soon. Everyone seemed to be in a rush to go, speaking in Taiwanese so quickly that it sounded like a fast-forwarded movie. I was a little surprised when Uncle Flower, Aunt Bea, Grandma, Grandpa, and the cousins got up and left. They must have been really hungry.

"They're going to the restaurant first, to get us a table," Dad told us. "You usually have to wait. This way, we don't waste any time waiting for you to get ready."

"But you still have to hurry," Mom told me. "Go get ready. And wake up Ki-Ki!"

I ran to change out of my pajamas, and by the time I had brushed my teeth and hair, Ki-Ki was almost ready, too. Mom was brushing her hair and helping her put on her shoes at the same time.

As we stepped outside, my tongue fell out of my mouth. It was really hot! The air was thick and sticky, and I felt like a dumpling being cooked in a steamer. I was glad when we got into a taxi. I didn't want to walk, and the taxi was air-conditioned.

taxi

Hundreds of signs in Chinese blurred by during the ride. Red, blue, and green Chinese characters seemed to decorate every surface of the buildings we passed. It was strange not to be able to read anything — it was as if everything were in a code that I felt like I should be able to figure out but couldn't. That kind of made my head hurt. As we drove by another tall building, I saw a metal barrel with black smoke in front of it. Brilliant orange flames burst upward like a flickering flower.

"Fire!" I said, pointing. "Something's on fire!"

Mom, Dad, and Auntie Jin looked and spoke in Taiwanese.

"What?" I asked. "What?"

"It's probably for the Hungry Ghost Festival," Auntie Jin said. "It's almost Ghost Month."

"What's Ghost Month?" Lissy asked.

"Well, it is a little bit like Halloween in the United States,"

Mom said. "It's kind of a Chinese holiday where people honor spirits or ghosts."

"Do you trick-or-treat?" Ki-Ki asked.

"No." Dad laughed. "It's not quite the same. In fact, it's the ghosts who get all the treats during Ghost Month."

"What do you mean?" I asked.

"Well, you know how, in Chinese culture, it's very important to honor one's ancestors?" Dad said. "During the year, families often make offerings to their dead relatives — they make food or burn special 'ghost money' paper for them to have in the spirit world."

"Ghost money?" I said.

"Not just money," Auntie Jin added. "Now people make all sorts of things out of paper — clothes, shoes, computers, even cars. Anything you can think of, they can make it out of special paper for you to burn for the dead. That way, the ghosts can live in luxury, too!"

"So what's Ghost Month, then?" Lissy asked. I was kind of surprised she was interested. She never acted interested in anything, at least not since she became a "teenager."

"Ghost Month is the month that the gates between our world — the living world — and the ghost world are opened," Dad said. "It's the time when all the spirits can come visit their families."

"So what was the burning fire back there for?" I asked.

"When the gates are open, all the spirits can come into the

29

living world," Dad said. "And there are always spirits who have no family to visit—spirits who have been forgotten or lost. We call them hungry ghosts. They wander, poor and starving, because they had no family to feed them or send them money during the rest of the year. So during Ghost Month, people make big plates of food and burn offerings just for them. That burning fire was people giving ghost money to the hungry ghosts."

"Why?" Ki-Ki asked.

"Because people feel sorry for them," Mom said. "And also a little afraid. A starving person is usually a desperate person, so a starving ghost is probably desperate, too. People don't want starving ghosts to make any trouble, so that's why they always make the offerings outside, away from their homes."

"And feed them so well!" Auntie Jin said, laughing. "At some temples, there are hundreds of plates of food, all different kinds."

"Why?" Ki-Ki asked again.

"Maybe because people don't know exactly what food the ghosts like," Dad said. "Spirits can be picky eaters, just like people. Like Great-Uncle Zhuzhan."

HONORING GREAT-UNCLE ZHUZHAN

The Lunar New Year after Great-Uncle Zhuzhan died, we had a grand feast. Our family was doing well: My oldest brother had gotten a promotion at the school he taught at and one of my sisters had gotten married. So for that Lunar New Year, we were able to have a celebration. My mother, sisters, and aunts cooked all day, steaming and frying. I could smell the good food with every breath I took, and I couldn't wait to eat.

In my family, before we ate, we had to honor our ancestors who'd passed away. Since Great-Uncle Zhuzhan had just died, his photo was on the family altar. So in front of his picture, we put the plates of fried dumplings, rice noodles cooked with pork and bean sprouts, a winter melon soup, and even a whole chicken with its head and feet on for extra luck.

family shrine

Each member of the family lit a stick of incense and bowed three times to the altar, with Great-Uncle Zhuzhan watching us the whole time. Then, when the incense was about one-third burned, Big Brother tossed two coins. We all leaned in to see how they landed. If either coin landed heads up, then that meant our ancestors were laughing and not finished eating yet. It also meant Big Brother would have to keep tossing the coins. Only when both coins landed tails up could we eat.

But on this day, the coins refused to land tails up. Over and over again, the coins landed — sometimes one heads up, sometimes both, but never two tails. The food was getting cold, and I was getting hungrier and hungrier! I felt as if the ancestors were laughing at us!

Everyone else in the family was getting hungry, too. And we were all puzzled. Why weren't the ancestors eating?

Then my aunt made a noise like a firecracker. "It's Zhuzhan!" she said. "He always likes things so salty!"

And she grabbed the rice noodles and rushed back into the kitchen. I watched as she threw the noodles back into her bowl-like frying pan, ladled in more soy sauce, and tossed the mixture over and over again on the stove. Then she dumped it back onto the platter and pushed it toward me to place on the altar. "Now try," she said.

Big Brother threw the coins. Up, up they flew in the air and then — cling, cling — landed on the floor. Our heads bumped into one another as we all crouched to see how they landed. Both tails! Great-Uncle Zhuzhan finally liked the food! And we could finally eat.

"So ghosts have favorite foods and flavors, just like we do," Dad said. "And for the whole month, we try to make them as happy as possible."

"Ghost Month is a whole month," I said, "and we're here for a whole month, too! Are we visiting like the ghosts are?"

"I guess so," Dad said. "Are you hungry?"

Lissy, Ki-Ki, and I looked at one another.

"Yes!" we all said at the same time.

Chapter 6

Eating Dim Sum

egg tarts

I REALLY *WAS* HUNGRY, WHICH WAS WHY I WAS GLAD TO see Uncle Flower, Aunt Bea, Grandma, Grandpa, and the cousins waiting for us at a big round table at the restaurant. It was good they had left earlier, at least good for us, because that meant we could walk past all the people waiting in line and just sit down and eat.

And we began to eat right away! For dim sum, no one ordered from a menu. Food just came to us! Women slowly pushing silver carts went from one table to the next, calling like birds. All the carts had different foods, and as they stopped one by one at our table, Aunt Bea and Uncle Flower would shake their heads or nod. If

food on carts

they shook their heads, the woman would push her cart to the next table. If they nodded, the woman would take a dish out of her cart, put it on the table, and stamp our bill.

"Ha! Dim sum is like a backward buffet," I said. "Instead of going up to the food at a buffet and choosing, the food comes to you!"

"But better than a buffet," Dad said. "See how all the dishes are small? It's so you don't get too full on one dish, so you can taste a little of everything — because there is a lot more to choose from in dim sum than at a buffet."

I looked around the restaurant. There were so many women pushing carts, it was like an endless parade. I tried to count them all, but they kept moving, and there were so many people that I gave up after thirty-eight.

"What do you want to do today?" Aunt Bea asked Mom as she nodded at a woman pushing a cart and held up two fingers. The woman stopped calling out "xia jiao, xia jiao" and placed two small plates on our table. She uncovered them, revealing in each three freshly steamed dumplings with filmy, light skins that showed

xia jiao
(shrimp dumplings)

the delicate pink of the shrimp inside, before wheeling away.

"After brunch, we have to go shopping," Mom said. "We have to buy the art supplies for their art classes tomorrow."

"Tomorrow!" Lissy said. "The classes start already?"

"Yes." Mom nodded.

Shaomai
(pork dumplings)

I was only half paying attention. I was reaching for a brown ball of meat held in a yellow silklike wrapper. *Shaomai*, the cart woman had called it. But it also looked like a dumpling and it looked good. I kept trying to use the chopsticks the "right" way, like how Lissy showed me on the plane, but the food kept slipping.

I looked around the table. No one was paying attention to me. They were all eating or talking or watching for the next cart. I changed the position of my chopsticks so that they were the wrong way, the way I had always held them before. And I grabbed a dumpling. I did it! The wrong way worked, at least for me. The chopsticks gripped the dumpling tightly until I dropped it into my mouth, the rich, savory meat tingling my tongue with flavor. *Yum.*

"What do they need?" Grandma asked. "I have a lot already."

Mom took a list out from her purse. I looked over her shoulder, but since I couldn't read the Chinese writing, I focused my attention on the food. Aunt Bea and Uncle Flower kept nodding at all the carts, and dish after dish were getting placed on the table. Some things I had eaten before—like the snow-white buns bursting with sweet, barbecued pork and the golden-fried rectangles of turnip cake. But there were things I had no idea what they were. I picked up something crispy and brown that looked a bit like a large twig from a tree. Uncle Flower had grabbed it eagerly, and Julian had one on her plate, so I thought I'd try it. It was hard to bite, and even though I was holding my chopsticks better, I ended up grabbing it with my hands and gnawing on it like a puppy with a bone.

"Lissy needs an inkstone and an ink stick. They both need rice paper, brushes…" Mom said, but then she saw me eating. "Pacy, do you like that?"

I stopped in midchew. The twig was kind of chewy and really hard to eat, but the spicy taste was okay. Mom's face looked amused, though, as if I were doing something funny. It made me suspicious. "Why?" I asked.

"It's chicken feet, did you know?" Mom said.

Chicken feet! I was eating chicken feet! *Eww!* I put it back on my plate and made a face.

chicken feet

"*Bawk-bawk!*" Lissy whispered. Mom said something in Taiwanese to the rest of the table, and the adults laughed. But Julian and Shogun gave each other a shrug. Obviously they didn't think eating chicken feet was that weird.

But I felt weird. I kept thinking about chickens scratching in the dirt with their wiry claws, and my mouth felt all rubbery.

Shogun eating at dim sum

I swallowed all the tea in my cup and reached for the teapot for more. Three drops seemed to squeeze out of it, like tears from laughing too hard.

"It's empty," Uncle Flower said, and took the teapot from me. He lifted the lid, turned it upside down, and put the teapot on the table. Almost immediately, a waiter took the teapot and replaced it with another. Uncle Flower tapped his fingers twice on the table.

"Is that a secret code?" I asked.

"What?" Uncle Flower asked.

"Tapping your fingers," I said. "Is that how you got the waiter to give us more tea?"

"No," Uncle Flower said. "Turning the lid upside down told the waiter we needed more tea."

"Then what was the tapping for?" Ki-Ki asked.

teapot with lid on it upside down

"It's a way to say thank-you," Uncle Flower said. "You know that dim sum is not from Taiwan? Like a lot of food and customs here, it is from mainland China. Taiwan has a mix of many cultures — a lot of Chinese, some Japanese, and even a tiny bit of Dutch! Tapping your fingers to say thank-you is from a story in Chinese history."

THANKING THE EMPEROR

A long time ago, the emperor decided to visit his kingdom in disguise. Discarding his brilliant yellow silk robes for the coarse, dull dress of a commoner, he and his advisers (also plainly clothed) stopped at a teahouse for rest and refreshment.

After the waiter placed the small, round teacups on the table, he lifted the teapot high in the air so that the tea flowed like a waterfall. Skillfully, with quick flicks of his wrist, he served the tea without spilling a single drop. The emperor watched with great interest, impressed by the waiter's expertise. After the waiter left, the emperor decided to try pouring the tea himself. As soon as the cups were empty, the emperor grasped the teapot and poured the tea in the same manner for his aides.

Of course, the assistants were incredibly surprised by the act of the great emperor pouring their tea! They were dumbfounded at the honor he had bestowed upon them. They wanted to jump onto their knees and bow low in gratitude, but they knew that such actions would give away the emperor's identity.

emperor (in disguise)
pouring tea

Instead, one of the assistants bowed with his

*hands. He curled his two fingers the same way his legs would
have bent if he were bowing and tapped the tips of them on the
table, in the same manner his head would have knocked on the
floor in a kowtow. The other aides quickly copied him, and they
all tapped their thanks to the emperor.*

"And that became a tradition," Uncle Flower said. "Now,
when you want to thank someone for pouring tea, you tap
on the table."

All throughout Uncle Flower's story, dishes had continued to arrive on the table and we had
continued to eat. As I slowly bit into a
sunshine-yellow egg tart, I watched a
waiter count up all our dishes to figure out the bill. The flaky crust crumbled, and the bits fluttered down to
my plate like falling snow. I put the
rest of the tart down. It was delicious,
but my tight stomach was telling me

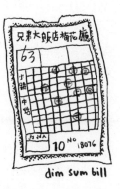

dim sum bill

I had eaten enough. If I had been the emperor's assistant, I
would have tapped on the table, too, but only because I was
too full to get up.

Chapter 7

The art Store

"forever" calligraphy
on wall

AFTER BRUNCH, EVERYONE WENT IN DIFFERENT directions. Uncle Flower and Auntie Jin went to the bookstore; Aunt Bea, Grandpa, Shogun, and Julian went to buy groceries; and Ki-Ki, Lissy, Dad, Mom, Grandma, and I went to the art store. Mom said we were going to take the subway this time because we were getting spoiled taking taxis everywhere.

As we pushed through the crowds to the subway, Ki-Ki hung on to me and I hung on to Lissy. There were so many people! We weren't used to so many people. I felt as if the crowds wanted to crush me away into nothingness.

"Ouch!" Lissy said, shaking me off. "Don't grip me so hard!"

"Sorry!" I said. My fingers were white from clutching her. No wonder it hurt. Lissy looked at me.

"Here," she said, taking a firm grasp of my arm, her annoyance gone. "I'll hold on to you instead, okay?"

Somehow we made it to the subway, Lissy dragging me and me dragging Ki-Ki through the doors. It was only then that I felt like I could finally breathe. After almost running through the hot streets, the cold air of the air-conditioned subway car made me feel as if I were going into a freezer. I was afraid the sweat on my face was going to turn into ice.

Compared with the busy city streets full of cars and black smoke, the subway felt white and shiny. Ki-Ki sat down on one of the molded plastic seats, the color of a bright blue sky, but Lissy and I stayed standing, holding on to one of the gleaming, silver poles. I watched my warped reflection in it as we swayed back and forth with the subway's movement. It was my first time on a subway. Ki-Ki and I had never ridden one before, even when we visited New York City.

me and Lissy on the subway

When we got off the subway, there were fewer people, but it felt even hotter and stickier. When we got to the art store, I felt like a panting dog. The art store was small and crowded, full of papers and shelves. A big fan stood cramped in the corner, its head swinging back and forth quickly like a man shaking his head.

Mom took out the paper from her bag again, and she and Grandma started to speak to the man behind the counter in Taiwanese. As they talked, I wandered around the store. I was looking forward to painting class. I always got an A+ in art in school, and it would be good practice for the pictures I was going to make for books. I decided I'd paint something really beautiful, like a unicorn with big blue flowers. Were there unicorns in Chinese paintings? Probably not. Maybe just a white horse, then.

I walked past piles of paper held down by round, gray-black rocks. The corners of the piles waved at me every time the wind from the fan blew by. Bamboo paintbrushes, the pointed tips looking like cattails, hung from polished wooden racks. Stacks of blue-and-white-painted bowls, dark gray slabs of stone, and ink sticks lay on the shelves with dust.

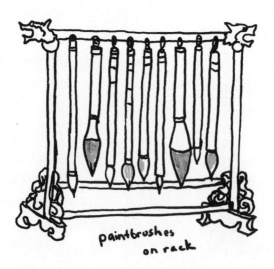

paintbrushes on rack

At the next aisle, I stopped. Hundreds of little carvings stood in neat rows on the shelf before me. Small stone figures of yawning turtles and snakes, cheerful rabbits, and laughing old men looked back at me from the shelf. I smiled as I looked closer at one figure with a carving of a lazy-looking pig.

Lissy and Ki-Ki followed me.

"Name chops!" Lissy said, taking one and rubbing it with her fingers.

"Name chops?" Ki-Ki asked.

"You know," I said to her, "haven't you seen Mom's in her desk? The ink-stamp thing that has her Chinese name on it?"

"Oh," Ki-Ki said, nodding. "So they're like rubber stamps but made of stone."

"Not exactly," Dad said, coming up from behind us. He had heard us talking. "A name chop is much more important. A name chop is someone's identity. It tells who you are. In the olden days, officials had to carry their seal with them wherever they went."

"Really?" Ki-Ki asked. "Why?"

"The chop was proof that they were the important person they said they were," Dad said. "Everyone has his or her own name chop specially carved only for him or her. It used to be when you signed an important document, you had to stamp it with your name chop as well. They still do that sometimes nowadays."

"What happens if someone steals your chop?" I asked. "Or if you lose it?"

"Ah," Dad said. "Then you are in trouble! You would have a hard time proving that you are who you say you are. Losing your chop would be like losing yourself."

I lifted the chop with the pig on it. The cloudy-gray stone was cold and hard. A shiver ran up my back as I touched the smooth bottom.

"These don't have any names or words," I said, and showed Dad the flat bottom.

"These are probably for people to buy to get their names carved into them," Dad said, picking up a caramel-colored chop with a top shaped like a lotus leaf. "Chinese words and names are an art, you know. It's not like English, where words are made of letters — A-B-C. In Chinese, everything has its own symbol."

"What?" Ki-Ki said. "I don't get it."

Dad pointed at a framed painting of a Chinese word on the wall.

"See that?" he said. "That's *yong*. It means 'forever.' In English, the word *forever* is made up of seven letters, right? In Chinese, that one character is the word *forever* — and that's it. Every object or person has its own symbol."

"So your name chop is your symbol, then?" I asked.

"Yes, in a way," Dad said. "Like I said, your name chop is your identity."

"We don't have chops," Ki-Ki said suddenly. "Does that mean we don't have identities?"

I hadn't thought about that. Did that mean we didn't exist? I didn't like that at all. I wanted an identity! "We need to get chops!" I told Dad, waving the one in my hand. "Can we get them?"

"Yeah," Lissy said, joining in. "It would be a good souvenir."

"Okay, okay," Dad said. "But only one each!"

"Why would we need more than one?" Ki-Ki said. "Unless we decide to become spies and have secret identities!"

"A lot of people have more than one," Dad said, "so they can use whichever chop suits their mood. They sometimes use a poetic phrase or word — anything that they think symbolizes who they are."

"Like what?" I asked.

"I had a teacher who had a chop that said something like 'never too tired for knowledge,'" Dad said. "And my friend had one that said 'thoughts as evergreen as a pine tree.'"

Dad looked at the chops in our hands. "Pacy and Lissy, you should switch. Lissy was born in the Year of the Pig, and Pacy was born in the Year of the Tiger."

We were all a little shocked that Dad was really going to buy the chops for us. Dad never bought us things at home. I gave Lissy the chop with the pig and took the one with the tiger. It was a warm brown, the color of wood. The small

45

tiger's mouth was wide open, showing its teeth. From one side, it looked to me like the tiger was smiling, but from the other, the tiger was scowling. I wasn't sure if I liked it and kind of wanted to pick a different one, but I was afraid that if I did, Dad might change his mind. And I really wanted a chop.

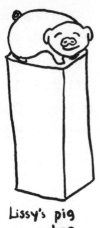

Lissy's pig chop

"And Ki-Ki needs a horse," Dad said, squinting at all the figures on the shelf. "Here's one!"

Ki-Ki grabbed the chop quickly. It was almost pure white, with pale peanut-colored streaks. The carving of her horse

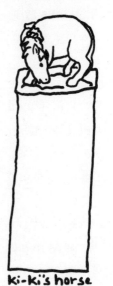

ki-ki's horse chop

looked like the white horses princesses rode in fairy tales, like the one I was planning to paint. I wished I had been born in the Year of the Horse.

We followed Dad as he walked to the counter. Mom and Grandma were still talking to the man there, but now there was a big pile next to them. Lissy, Ki-Ki, and I looked at the rolls of paper and felt, paintbrushes, tubes of paint, and black inkstones and ink stick, and then looked at one another. I wondered which of the stuff was mine.

46

Dad spoke to the man in Taiwanese, and I put my name chop on the counter with the rest of the supplies. I thought Mom and Dad were much more likely to buy it if it was mixed in with the things that they were already buying. Lissy and Ki-Ki did the same.

"We can't get your names carved on them today," Dad said. "They don't do that here. We'll have to take them someplace else. Do you still want to get them?"

"Yes!" we all said together.

"Okay," Dad said. "This way it gives you some time to think about what you want carved on it. Remember, this is your symbol! It is the mark of your identity."

Dad said this in a dramatic way that meant he was joking, but I didn't see what was so funny. Getting my name chop carved seemed really important to me. Even so, I didn't think there was that much to think over.

"I'm just going to get my name," Lissy said. "What else would I do?"

"Yeah," I said. "I'm not going to get anything like 'never too tired for knowledge'!"

"Maybe you should," Dad said. "Then maybe you would get better grades in math."

I made a face. Math was my worst subject, but I didn't do that badly. Just not as good as Lissy and Ki-Ki, who always got A's in math.

"I guess you do need something different. Maybe

47

something like 'never tired of fun,'" Dad said to me before I could say anything. "Or maybe 'never tired of TV' would be better. . . . Or . . . I've got it! It's the perfect one for you. 'Never tired of dumplings!' How's that?"

Everyone laughed at that. I looked at my name chop on the counter, and it looked like the tiger was laughing, too.

Chapter 8

The Fortune-Teller

my
hand

DAD'S NAME CHOP COULD HAVE SAID "NEVER TOO
tired for knowledge," too, because after we left the art store,
he decided to go off on his own to look for a bookstore. I
liked books, too, but since I thought all the books would be in
Chinese, I went with everyone else back to Grandma's.

From the subway to Grandma's house, we had to walk under the street—in kind of a tunnel but one just for people
walking. "These were made because the traffic above is so
crazy," Mom told us. "It's the only way to cross the street
without getting run over!"

There weren't too many people in the tunnel, so I let Mom
and Grandma walk ahead. It was a wide passageway, and on
one side, there were all these women sitting, each with a table in front of her. I stared at them as we walked by. At first I
thought maybe they were offering things for ghosts for the

Ghost Festival, like what Dad had talked about, but most of the tables were bare with just red cloths. Some had notebooks and candles, but not much more. There didn't seem to be anything a ghost or a person would be that interested in.

One of the women saw me staring and smiled. For a moment I thought it was Melody's mom, whom I hadn't seen in a long time. She had the same wavy black hair and smile.

The woman beckoned me over, as if she wanted to tell me something. What did she want? It couldn't be Melody's mom—Melody would've told me if her mom was going to  be in Taiwan. But still, I had to go over to get a better look. Her moon-shaped face was smooth except for the lines around her mouth, and she had brown freckles on her cheeks, like sprinkles of cinnamon. No, she wasn't Melody's mom. This woman's eyes were different, black and small like watermelon seeds, while Melody's mom had

fortune-teller

eyes that were wide and brown like the color of tree bark. I started to turn away, but the woman grabbed my hand and started to examine it as if she were looking for a splinter.

"Where's Pacy?" I heard Mom say, and I watched Mom and

Grandma turn around. "Aiya," Grandma said when she saw me with the woman, which I knew meant she was surprised and not pleased. I started to feel a little nervous then. What was this woman doing? Mom and Grandma both rushed back over to me, Lissy and Ki-Ki tagging behind with excitement.

The woman began to speak to me in Taiwanese. I didn't know what she was saying at all. Mom tried to nudge me away, but the woman's warm, dry fingers held on to my hand tightly. Mom said something to the woman and then Grandma said something, but the woman ignored them. Mom sighed. But since she didn't seem scared, I relaxed. I was starting to feel like I was having an adventure.

The woman traced each one of my fingers, talking the whole time. The short, black curls of her hair didn't move, even when she moved her head to squint at the tips of my fingers. She kept pointing to parts of my hand and saying things to me. She kept nodding and looking at me as if I understood, and somehow it felt rude that I didn't. So I just pretended, nodding and smiling back.

Suddenly, the woman laughed a throaty noise, kind of like a witch's laugh. I thought she might have figured out that I didn't know what she was saying. Without letting go of me, she said something to Mom, who shrugged and nodded. The woman raised her hands over my head, closed her eyes, and started to chant. I glanced over at Lissy and Ki-Ki. They shrugged, and Lissy snorted back a giggle.

She kept chanting an odd song that seemed to roll over me like ocean waves. I stole a look at Mom and Grandma. They didn't look worried or bothered by the woman anymore, just kind of bored.

Finally, the woman stopped chanting and held out her hand. Mom gave her a piece of paper money and pulled at me. The woman nodded good-bye as Mom pushed quickly through the tunnel.

Taiwan paper money

"Pacy, don't do that again! You shouldn't go off with a stranger like that," she said, shaking her head at me. She wasn't yelling, but I knew she was mad at me. "You know better than that!"

"I didn't mean to," I said. And it was true, it had just kind of happened. I thought I should try to change the subject. "Who was that, anyway?"

"She was a fortune-teller," Mom told me.

"She was?" I said. I shouldn't have been surprised, but I was. I thought fortune-tellers would look the way they were described in my books at home — long, colorful skirts; crystal balls and gold earrings; maybe even a turban. I turned my head for a quick look back. In her plain, yellow shirt, sitting in her chair, she still looked more like Melody's mom than a fortune-teller.

"Yes," Mom said. "She tricked us into having your fortune

told. By the time Grandma and I saw you with her, she had already started, so we had to let her finish."

"She did?" I said. I didn't really feel that bad about getting tricked. I was more excited about my fortune. I'd never had my fortune told before. "What was my fortune? What did she say?"

"Oh, I don't know," Mom said, trying to wave me off. "Something about how the lines on your fingers are a circle, so it means you have a special skill you'll always use."

"Really?" I said. I did a hopping step as we exited the tunnel. "What else? What else?"

"She also said the shape of your fingers means you are sensitive and creative and live in your own world," Mom said, and laughed a little. "She said because of this, you are going to get into trouble, so she wanted to give you blessings to protect you."

If your fingerprint looks like this, it means you have a special skill.

If your fingertip is this shape, it means you are creative.

"Blessings?" I asked. "Was that what her singing was?"

"Yes." Mom nodded. "She said her blessings would help you. They would help keep you safe and happy."

I thought about my fortune. I was pretty sure I knew what

the special skill was that I'd use all my life. I knew my talent was writing and illustrating books. It had taken me a while to figure that out—three years ago, I had thought about it for a whole year. But now I knew, so I wasn't too worried about that. But I was worried about the trouble the fortune-teller thought I was going to get into. What kind of trouble? How would her blessings protect me? And for how long? Would her blessings run out?

"Why does Pacy get to have her fortune told?" Lissy said. "Can I get my fortune told, too?"

"Yes!" Ki-Ki said. "Me, too! I want my fortune, too!"

"No!" Mom said, shaking her head hard and walking faster toward Grandma's building. "It's just a lot of nonsense. We don't believe any of those things. Just forget it."

Lissy looked at me jealously. She made a disappointed face, and as she passed me to go up the stairs, she whispered, "Lucky!"

Was I? The more I thought about my fortune, the more I wasn't sure.

Chapter 9

The **Garbage Truck**

Auntie Jin giving garbage
to the garbage man

THE NEXT MORNING, MOM HAD TO SHAKE US AWAKE
again.

"Wake up! Wake up!" she said. We all groaned, and Ki-Ki
tried to push her hands away.

"It's early!" I moaned.

"Not very early," Mom said, "but early enough. You have
your art classes today!"

"I don't care," Lissy mumbled, turning over. I did the same
thing.

Somehow, Mom got us all out of bed, but I felt like I was
sleepwalking. Lissy bumped my arm while we were brushing
our teeth, and I nudged her back. She elbowed me, and it
would've turned into a fight except Mom came in with Ki-Ki
to wash her face. Still, I stepped on Lissy's foot on the way
out the door. I was very grumpy.

And slow. I felt like a turtle caught in a puddle of honey. Mom had to push me to the table, and none of us smiled a morning greeting to Grandma, Grandpa, and Dad or even to Auntie Jin, who was at the stove heating something.

"Jet lag, still," Grandma, nodding, said to us.

Mom had said jet lag was when your body was confused, but I didn't feel confused at all. Instead, I felt like an irritated mosquito bite. In fact, I was certain that I was very, very grumpy.

"How many days until we go back home?" I asked, grumbling.

"We've been here for only two days!" Dad said. "You still have twenty-six days to go. Are you ready to leave so soon?"

"It's important you get to know Taiwan better," Mom said. "You'll learn about our culture. It's a part of who we are."

"I don't want to know who I am, then," I said rudely.

"Pacy!" Mom said in a shocked voice. Lissy and Ki-Ki looked at me sideways, and I shrank a little in my chair.

"Never mind, never mind," Auntie Jin said, interrupting us and coming over with a big platter. "Eat. You will feel better after you eat."

Things that looked like long, golden-fried hot-dog buns were on the platter. When Auntie Jin put one on a plate in front of me, I jabbed at it with my fingers. I didn't want to end up eating something weird again, like the chicken feet.

"What is this?" Lissy said. She was probably thinking about the chicken feet, too.

"It's called *youtiao*," Mom said. "It's kind of like a donut. You'll like it."

"Are there any Lucky Charms?" Ki-Ki asked. That was our favorite cereal at home. It had hard, sweet marshmallows in it that tasted like candy.

"We'll get some later," Mom said. "Today, eat this."

I rolled it back and forth on my plate like a rolling pin. "I'm not hungry anyway," I said.

Auntie Jin came back to the table with big cups of warm soy milk, the steam drifting from them like disappearing ghosts. "Try it with this," she said. "Dip it in the milk and eat. It'll taste good."

I watched Ki-Ki dip half a *youtiao* into a cup of soy milk and rip at it with her teeth. I picked up my piece.

Then, just when I was about to dip it in the milk, we all suddenly heard a noise outside. No, not a noise — a song! A

youtiao and
warm soy milk

chiming, jolly song was playing out on the street. Ki-Ki, Lissy, and I looked at one another in amazement. We knew that song! It was the ice-cream truck song!

"Aiya!" Auntie Jin said, and without another word, she jumped up and rushed out the door. Lissy, Ki-Ki, and I followed her. Was Auntie Jin going to get some ice cream? As we hurried, the ringing song got louder and louder, sounding like a music box with a microphone. I jumped down the stairs two at a time, and Ki-Ki kept chirping "Wait for me! Wait for me!" like a repeating bird. None of us wanted to miss the ice-cream truck. I hoped they had the chocolate-dipped ice-cream cones—the ones where the ice-cream man dipped the soft, white ice cream into a fudge sauce that hardened into a thin, delicious chocolate coating as it was handed to you. Those were my favorite. Would they have them here in Taiwan? Even so early in the morning? Maybe people in Taiwan always had ice cream at breakfast time.

my favorite
ice-cream cone

So, when we finally got to the street, it was a shock to see Auntie Jin dragging a trash bag over to a big, stinky garbage truck! There was no ice-cream truck anywhere. Auntie Jin waved to the garbageman as the garbage truck drove away, playing the jingly music that echoed through the streets. As Auntie Jin turned, we stared at her and the truck with our mouths open.

"What's wrong?" she asked us.

"Where's the ice cream?" Ki-Ki said.

"What ice cream?" Auntie Jin said, looking around, confused.

Lissy was the first one to get over our shock.

"There's no ice cream," Lissy said, and then explained to Auntie Jin, "In the United States, the ice-cream truck plays that song."

"Ice-cream truck?" Auntie Jin said. "What's that?"

"It's a truck that goes around and sells ice cream. It plays music, the same song, just like that," I said, motioning to the leaving garbage truck, "so everyone knows they can come out and buy ice cream."

"Ah," Auntie Jin said, nodding. "Here, the garbage truck plays that music so everyone knows they can come out and throw away their garbage!"

With that, Lissy, Ki-Ki, and I looked at one another. For a moment, we didn't say anything, because we were so embarrassed. But then Lissy let out a snort. "Garbage!" she said. "We came out for garbage!" And we all started to giggle. It was silly. We had run all the way for ice cream, and instead it was garbage! We laughed back up the stairs to our breakfasts, and our jet lag bad moods flew away like airplanes through the clouds.

Chapter 10

A Forest of Precious Thoughts

名字：林珮思
地址: 12 中山路
電話號碼:(02) 2941-5988

my name card

AFTER BREAKFAST, MOM GAVE US EACH A NAME CARD.

"Put this in your bag or your pocket," she told us. "I want you to carry it with you all the time, so if you get lost, you can always give that to someone who can bring you back."

I looked at it. All the writing on it was in Chinese, a mix of symbols that I couldn't understand. I knew that the first line was my name—those characters were familiar. Mom had shown me my Chinese name a long time ago. But I had never thought about it as symbols meaning something the way Dad had talked about at the art store. It was strange to think these symbols that I couldn't read were supposed to mean me.

"Lin..." I said as I drew my fingers over the characters. "Pacy."

"No," Mom said. "It says *Lin Pai-se*. See, there are three

characters, one for *lin*, one for *pai*, and one for *se*. We made *Pacy* a nickname from *Pai-se*."

木木 = LIN, my last name in Chinese

木 = tree   木木 = forest

my name in Chinese =

林　珮　思
LIN   PAI   SE
(Lin   Pacy)

"What's mine, then?" Ki-Ki asked.

"Lin Kai-se," Mom told her. "*Ki-Ki* is a nickname from *Kai-se*. The word *se* means 'thought.' *Kai* means 'victorious,' so your name, Kai-se, means 'victorious thought.' "

"What does *Pai-se* mean, then?" I asked.

"See the symbol for *Pai*? It is similar to the character for *jade*," Mom said. "So your name means 'precious' or 'treasured thought.' "

"What does Lissy's name mean?" Ki-Ki asked.

"*Lissy* is a nickname from *Li-se*, which means 'beautiful thought,' " Mom told us. I made a face. I didn't think Lissy was a beautiful thought at all. They should have called her "bossy thought" — that would've been better.

"*Lin* means 'forest,'" Mom continued. "See how *Lin* is made up of two of the same symbols? Each means 'tree.' So when you put two 'trees' together, it means 'forest.' So *Lin* means 'forest' or 'woods.'"

Pacy. Pai-se. Precious thought. Lin. Forest.

That made me feel strange. I didn't feel like a precious thought, much less a forest of them. Still, I liked the idea. I could imagine it like something out of a fairy tale where precious thoughts, glittering and glistening, grew from diamond trees. Maybe I could paint that idea with a white horse in class.

painting Class

my strange first
bamboo painting

THE BUILDING THAT AUNTIE JIN TOOK US TO DIDN'T look like a place that would have painting classes. It was just a building, almost like a hospital. We had to ride an elevator to get to the floors of our classrooms. Ki-Ki's class was in the basement, so Mom brought her there, and Auntie Jin brought me and Lissy to our classes.

We were late when we got to my classroom. Now that I was awake, I wished I hadn't taken so long to get up. Everyone stared at me as I came in, and I stared right back. All of a sudden, a heavy, hard feeling filled my stomach as if I had swallowed a stone.

It felt just like that Taiwanese-American convention. Everyone in this class was Asian, just like in the class I had taken there. At home in New Hartford, Lissy, Ki-Ki, and I were the only Asian girls. When I was in first grade, a mean bus driver asked me where I was from and got angry with me when I said I was from up the street. "No," he had said. "Where are you *really* from?" He had made me cry. I had cried at that convention, too.

But I wasn't going to cry here. *Stop it,* I told myself. *Maybe it won't be like that.*

Auntie Jin talked to the teacher, a man in a black T-shirt who was older than Dad but younger than Grandpa. Most of the back of his head was bald, but he had some hair brushed over, like thin wisps of gray smoke. When he smiled a greeting at me, I could see his teeth were yellow. I sat down in the nearest empty seat.

"Okay," the teacher said as Auntie Jin left. "Back to what I was saying. Chinese painting is not about a picture; it is about telling a message. Each object in the painting has a special meaning. So we don't look at a Chinese painting; we *read* a Chinese painting."

the painting
teacher

He spoke English slowly and with a thick accent. His English was kind of like Mom's and Auntie Jin's, but it was harder to understand him. Or maybe it was what he was talking about that was so hard for me to understand. Read a painting?

He kept talking and holding up pictures in books while I looked around the room. The other students already had their paintbrushes and paints neatly on their desks. As quietly as I could, I started to take out the art supplies from the bag Mom had given me. I wondered what the teacher's name was. I guessed I had missed the part where he introduced himself. As I shifted the thick roll of paper that was still in my bag, things rolled around the bottom like marbles. I peered in. Color paint tubes! Bright rose red, golden yellow, leaf green, and blue in small tubes, like little traveling toothpastes, just for me. I had never had paints in tubes before — at school the paint always came in shared jars or in flat colored disks you added water to. Suddenly I felt better about the class. At least I would get to paint like a real artist.

paint tubes

"Chinese artists paint flowers together that do not grow together in real life," the teacher continued. He stumbled over some of his words, sometimes repeating them. "It is more about the idea or memory of the flowers or birds or the bamboo — not what it actually looks like. We have the idea of bamboo, and we paint the idea."

I didn't know if the teacher was going to be that good. He

seemed kind of awkward and kept bumbling. I couldn't imagine him as an artist. I glanced around the room. Most of the students were looking blankly at the teacher. One boy was scratching his leg, and a girl was looking out the window. Whether or not he was a good artist, the teacher was definitely dull. No one seemed to be having any ideas about bamboo.

The girl next to me looked at me, as if studying me. Her hair touched her chin, and she had glasses with gold wire frames. She didn't seem very friendly. There was no way she could tell I was a Twinkie yet, was there? I wondered if being a Twinkie showed up in the way I walked or on my face. I quickly looked away.

On her desk was a piece of black felt with AUDREY CHIANG written in a corner in perfect white letters. That must've been her name, and I wondered how she was able to get her name to show on the black cloth. Had she used white paint? I unfolded and laid out my piece of black felt, placed my paintbrushes on the side, and took out my paper.

on Audrey's desk

Then, unexpectedly, everyone stood up. The teacher was motioning all of us to come around his desk. We watched as he squeezed drops of black ink into his small bowl, mixed the ink and the water with his paintbrush, and then, with just a few strokes and movements of his hand, painted a stalk of bamboo with blowing leaves on the paper. It looked easy. I hoped he would show us harder things, too.

"You do not erase in Chinese painting. You cannot take back anything you do," said the teacher in his hesitating way. He painted more bamboo leaves. "The only way you can change your picture is with your next stroke, your next motion. It will take a lot of practice before you will be able to do a painting for our exhibit at the end of the summer. First, we paint bamboo."

He sent us back to our desks. What was that about an exhibit? I must have missed something else, too. But now we were painting bamboo. That was disappointing. It seemed so dull and boring. And it was just black ink, no colors. I was hoping to open those tubes.

the right way to hold a Chinese paintbrush

But painting bamboo wasn't easy! The ink had a sneaky way of swelling on the paper, making careful lines into blobs. And holding the paintbrush was tricky. The teacher kept pushing my arm. "Wrist up!" he said, shaking his head when I let my hand rest on the table. He shook his head again and pointed at the painting. "Try again," he said to me before moving on. "Think about the idea of the bamboo. Only the bamboo."

I tried to think about the bamboo, but the watery ink and the paintbrush seemed to have their own ideas. Strokes spread and bent in directions I didn't want, and I couldn't erase them or cover them up. A shock went through me. I had thought my special art skill was going to make it easy and my painting would be the best in the class. But my painting didn't even look like bamboo. Instead, it looked like strange, sickly gray sausage. Where was my art talent?

I stole a look at Audrey Chiang. She was concentrating hard on her painting, flicking her wrist to make a jointed bamboo stalk. I was glad to see that her painting was even worse than mine. Her bamboo looked like dark storm clouds.

And, actually, so did her face. She saw me looking at her painting and scowled.

"Anyway, it's not like painting counts or anything," she said. She was looking at her painting, so I wasn't sure whom she was talking to.

Still, just in case, I said, "What?"

"This class is just extracurricular," she said, now looking at me. "We don't get grades, so if I don't do well, it won't go on my record."

"Oh," I said. I didn't really understand what she was talking about, but I felt surprised and relieved at the same time, as if I had caught a falling glass ornament without breaking it.

Maybe she hadn't been thinking about my being a Twinkie. She seemed to have been spending a lot of time thinking about something else. Audrey noticed my confusion.

"I know you don't get grades for the summer geometry and science classes, either," she said. "But those make sure that you get A's during the school year, and that counts."

Audrey was only making me more confused. The only summer math class I had heard of in New Hartford was if you failed something and had to make up for it. But Audrey was definitely talking about something else. A summer class so that you get A's? It must be so when you took the class again in school, it would be easier. Taking a class twice made sense if you were doing it just to get a good grade. But I thought it was kind of weird.

"I don't take summer math classes," I said to her.

"You don't?" she said. Obviously, it wasn't weird to her at all. But the way she was talking about it was making me uncomfortable. Her words were shooting over each other like fast flying bullets. It made me feel like I was being attacked. "How do you make sure you stay the best in your class, then?" she said.

"I'm not," I said. Maybe I should have lied. But it was my worst subject.

"Oh," Audrey said, and her eyebrows went up over the rims of her glasses. If she hadn't been thinking I was a Twinkie before, she was definitely thinking something like

69

that now. She looked at me like I was a dog that had been hit by a car, half-pitying and half-disgusted. Then, as if I had faded away into worthlessness, her eyebrows went back down, and she turned back to her painting. The sinking feeling came back inside me.

I squeezed more ink into my bowl and watched black drops balloon like evil genies. I wished I wasn't here. I wished we hadn't come to Taiwan. I wished I was home. How many days until I could go back home? Twenty-six days. These were going to be the longest twenty-six days of my life.

Chapter 12

The Japanese Restaurant

the masterpiece dish of
sushi and sashimi

FOR DINNER THAT NIGHT, A FRIEND OF DAD'S WAS taking us to a Japanese restaurant.

"Japanese food?" Lissy asked. There wasn't a Japanese restaurant in New Hartford, so we had never eaten Japanese food before. "Isn't that, like, sushi and raw fish? Are we going to eat raw fish?"

"I hope so!" Dad said. "You know, Taiwan has a mix of Chinese and Japanese culture, so the Japanese food is very good here."

"But raw fish!" I said. Ki-Ki and I wrinkled our noses, but Lissy's face took on a look of daring. I could tell she was thinking of bragging to her friends at home about how she ate raw fish.

"You should try it!" Dad said. "And I bet this restaurant will have the best!"

It was a fancy restaurant. I was glad I wore my nicest dress, the one with the strawberries on it. All the waiters were dressed in suits, and we could see chefs dressed in black with black hats behind a glass wall. Ki-Ki's shoes squeaked on the floor.

me in my favorite strawberry dress

Dad's friend smiled at us. "I ordered for us already," he told us. "But if you want something special, let me know."

I didn't know what there was to ask for, but I said hopefully, "Dumplings?"

"Pacy!" Lissy groaned and rolled her eyes as Mom and Dad laughed and said something in Taiwanese to Dad's friend and his wife. I shrugged. Maybe they didn't have dumplings in Japan.

"How do you like Taiwan?" Dad's friend's wife asked us.

"It's nice," Lissy said, answering for all of us. "It kind of feels like Chinatown in New York City."

"That's because we've only been in Taipei so far," Mom said, and then to Dad's friend, "Next week we're going to go to Taichung."

"Ah, Taichung!" Dad's friend said. "Better be careful traveling during Ghost Month!"

72

The Ghost Month again!

"Why?" I asked.

"Ah, don't you know?" he said, with a teasing look in his eyes. "Some ghosts want to make you into one! During Ghost Month, if you aren't careful, they can come and erase you away!"

We laughed because we knew he wasn't serious. But the idea of getting erased gave me a shiver. Mom had said that people thought hungry ghosts could make trouble, and the fortune-teller had said that my fingers had told her that I would get into trouble. Was I going to get into ghost trouble? Could I be erased?

A waiter came by with metal tongs and handed each of us a warm, moist white towel, taking my mind away from ghosts. As I rubbed my hands in it, I was embarrassed to see that my fingers left gray streaks on the snowy fabric. I quickly folded it over.

"I thought a Japanese restaurant was supposed to have those bamboo mats," Lissy said, "and make you kneel on cushions on the floor to eat."

I didn't know how Lissy knew about Japanese things, but in one of my favorite books at home, *Miss Happiness and Miss Flower*, a girl made a Japanese dollhouse with bamboo floor mats and a low wooden table. I looked around the room. Everyone had white stone tables and black leather chairs like we did. The only thing bamboo was a plant in the corner.

73

"Maybe that's only when you are in Japan," I said to Lissy. "Maybe this is a Taiwanese-style Japanese restaurant."

"I think we are getting cheated," she hissed at me behind Mom's back. I shrugged.

But we were definitely getting real Japanese food. As soon as the waiter took away the towels, he put an odd-shaped, shallow black bowl in front of each of us. A mossy-green soft mound lay nearest to me, like a lump of clay waiting to be molded. But beyond that, on top of crystals of ice, cool pink rectangles lay fanned out against one another with a squid head peeking out from behind. I didn't need anyone to tell me what they were. I knew they were the raw fish!

raw fish

Lissy's eyes took on a bold look, and she swooped into her bowl with her chopsticks and put one of the pink pieces in her mouth. Ki-Ki and I looked at each other. We couldn't let Lissy be braver than us! I took a big gulp of air, reached with my chopsticks (holding them the wrong way, of course), took a piece of raw fish, and chewed.

And it wasn't too bad. It wasn't slimy, as I'd expected it to be. The fish was cool and tender in my mouth and slipped down my throat easily. I swallowed proudly.

"Your kids can eat sashimi," Dad's friend said. "Good for them!"

"It's their first time," Dad said, looking at us, pleased.

"Try it with this," Mom said, nudging an eggcuplike bowl full of soy sauce at us.

I dipped another piece of fish into the soy sauce and took a bite. The salty soy sauce with the soft fish tasted...good! Maybe I actually liked eating raw fish?

"Is this mashed peas?" I asked, poking at the mound of green stuff. It seemed more like green mashed potatoes, though.

wasabi

"No," Dad said. "It's wasabi. You can mix it in the soy sauce. It gives the sauce a spicy flavor."

Lissy took a big chunk from her plate and dumped it into the soy sauce. She mixed it with her chopsticks, and the wasabi swirled into the soy sauce, making it the color of a dirty puddle after a rainstorm.

But I wasn't afraid. So far, eating raw fish had been easy. I plopped my third piece of fish into the muddy mixture and bit it without waiting.

Ooowww! The flavors burned up through my mouth into my nose as if I had sneezed the sun, and my eyes started to tingle with tears. I spit the fish out on my plate, not caring that it was rude. I stuck my tongue straight out of my mouth, hoping that the air would put out the fire running through my face. I grabbed my cup of tea and poured it into my mouth.

It was only after I'd swallowed the tea that I realized everyone at the table was laughing at me.

"I guess you don't like it," Dad told me. "Wasabi does have a very strong flavor."

"Pain is not a flavor!" I said hotly.

Luckily, the waiter showed up and placed new dishes in front of us, and everyone forgot about laughing at me. This new plate had a big bright-orange crab sitting on it like a majestic king, its round eyes staring at me coldly.

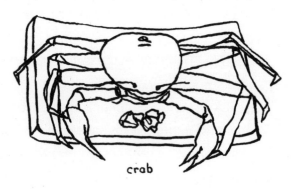

crab

"Yum!" Lissy said, attacking the crab and ripping off one of the legs savagely. She plucked the delicate snow-white meat popping from the leg shell with her chopstick and closed her eyes as she swallowed. Ki-Ki whined about not being able to eat her crab, so Mom helped her crack the shells. I liked crab, but the fiery flavor of the wasabi was still in my mouth, so I just drank tea, hoping the burning would leave.

And I kept drinking tea. Cup after cup, during the next dish — a bowl of thin-sliced meat in a souplike sauce — and when the main dish, the one Dad called "the masterpiece,"

teapot with tea

was served. It was a huge platter with a blue glass bowl of raw fish on ice, but this time pieces of fish were coral orange and reddish purple. Against a fan of brown twigs, a rainbow-glowing pillar rose from the bowl, holding two large pieces of pale pink fish (later Lissy took it out and saw there was an electric light inside). Pieces of sushi—black seaweed-rolled rice with bright patterned centers that looked like they were slices of a kaleidoscope—were arranged around the bowl on the plate so that the whole thing looked like an exotic floral arrangement. There were a lot of "oohs!" and "aahs!" when the waiter brought it out, and not just from our table.

By that time, I had drunk so much tea that I had to go to the bathroom. Everyone was so busy eating that no one noticed when I got up to go to the restroom in the back of the restaurant.

Like the restaurant, the bathroom was also very fancy. Everything was shiny and white, except for the floor—which was a soft-gray stone. It was a one-person bathroom, and as soon as I locked the door, I could make faces at myself in the big mirror that lined the whole wall.

But when it was time to flush the toilet, I was confused. There wasn't a silver lever to flush, like what I was used to.

Instead, there were all these buttons! I counted twelve of them and each one was labeled — but the labels were in Chinese! I couldn't read any of them!

I wasn't sure what to do. Why did they need so many buttons? What did all those buttons do? I was kind of scared to find out — maybe something

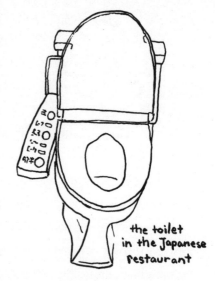

the toilet in the Japanese restaurant

really gross would happen and the water would come shooting out. Ew! But I didn't want to not flush the toilet, either.

I stared at the buttons. None of the symbols looked even a little familiar. Most of the buttons were gray circles, but there was a square yellow button and a red button. I tried to think. They would make the one that was most used the most noticeable, right? So it was probably the red or the yellow one. But which? I reached out my finger and pushed the red button.

Beep! Beeep! Beeeeep! A screeching noise like a fire engine filled the room. I covered my ears. Oh no! I had hit the wrong button!

Underneath the screaming sirens, I could hear quick footsteps coming and a shout through the door. I didn't know what to do. I was going to get in trouble! I started to hit the other buttons to try to make the alarm stop. The toilet started to vibrate and even play music! If I hadn't been so scared about the alarm, I would've thought it was funny.

Then I heard a scraping at the door. I stood frozen as the door burst open and a crowd of waiters and the receptionist stared at me.

I looked at them with big eyes. "Sorry?" I offered. The receptionist, who was in the front, shook his head and said something to everyone else. The alarm stopped, and everyone began to leave. It was only then that I saw Mom, Dad, Lissy, and Ki-Ki standing there, looking puzzled and worried. They had been in the back of the crowd.

"What happened?" Ki-Ki asked.

"I didn't know which button to push to flush the toilet," I said.

"Which one did you push?" Lissy said.

"The red one," I said, pointing.

"The red one!" Lissy said, making a face at me. "Out of all the buttons to push! Haven't we watched enough of Ki-Ki's cartoons? The red button is always the trouble one! You never push the red button!"

Mom pushed the yellow button, and the toilet flushed. "It's a Japanese toilet," she said, laughing. "And a very fancy one with all kinds of luxuries — it can even play music!"

I already knew that. Everyone else went back to the table

as I washed my hands. I thought about what a bad day it had been. The ice-cream truck had turned out to be a garbage truck this morning, Audrey Chiang had made me feel bad, I had burned my mouth with wasabi, and now I had triggered the bathroom alarm!

I still felt embarrassed when I went back to the table. People were probably looking at me and thinking about how I was the one who'd pushed the red button. My face felt about as red as that button.

But when I sat down, Dad's friend smiled.

"They almost forgot," he said as he pushed a plate in front of me. "*Gyoza*, Japanese dumplings, for you!"

Five fried dumplings sat on the plate, like nuggets of gold. I grinned and grabbed at them with my chopsticks. *Gyoza* were a little different from *jiaozi*, the Chinese fried dumplings I was used to. The dumpling skin was thinner

gyoza
(Japanese dumplings)

and crispier. But they were still delicious.

"Feel better?" Mom asked me.

I nodded, my mouth full of food. There was no day that dumplings couldn't make better.

Chapter 13

Audrey Chiang looking
at my painting

GOING TO CLASS THE NEXT MORNING WAS JUST AS
hard as it was the first time. "Come on!" Mom said to me as I
stumbled out the door. "You're going to be late again!"

And I was late again. But it didn't matter — we were still
painting gray bamboo. Even though the ink was black, we
were supposed to mix it with water so that there could be
different shades of gray. We had to paint bamboo "with vari-
ation," which to me just meant painting bamboo over and
over again.

"What's so important about bamboo?" a girl asked. I was
pretty sure her name was Eva Wong. She had long hair that
went all the way down below her waist. She could sit on her
ponytail.

"Bamboo is a symbol for long life because it never loses its
leaves, even in winter," the teacher said. "Also the Chinese

word for *bamboo* sounds like the word *wish*. So if you want to wish someone something, you paint a picture of that something along with bamboo."

That wasn't really what Eva was asking, but we all kept painting. Or at least, tried to paint. It bothered me that I couldn't erase or even cover up any of the paint strokes I made. My art skill didn't seem to be working here in Taiwan. I was used to my talent making me a good artist, but one look at my paper told me I was not. It made me feel uneasy and worried, like part of me was vanishing.

So every time I lifted the brush, I was nervous. Whatever mark I made I was stuck with. It made me feel afraid to paint. Would this stroke be okay? Would I make a mistake?

I looked around at everyone else's paintings. No one's paintings were great, but some people were getting their strokes to actually look like bamboo. Eva and the boy sitting next to her (I thought his name was Rex, but I didn't know his last name) were even painting leaves.

The teacher saw me with my brush frozen above the paper. "Relax," he said, moving my hand. "Press down, stroke, press, stroke, press."

His fingers loosened my grip on the brush and the paint glided gracefully on the paper like a figure skater on ice. *Aah*, I thought. *That's how it's supposed to look.* Too bad the teacher couldn't hold my hand while I did the whole painting. I wondered if I would ever learn his name.

I couldn't ask Audrey Chiang. I didn't know if it was because she thought I was a Twinkie, but she was not very friendly. She wasn't exactly mean, though, either. She wasn't making fun of me or whispering bad things. It was more like she looked at me as if I were a red light in a traffic jam.

I tried not to think about her. *Think bamboo*, I told myself as I painted. *Bamboo.* And slowly, as the class went on, my brush began to get the message. Even though I still made more mistake marks than good ones, my paintings were starting to get better. My bamboo stopped looking like gray hot dogs sprouting fat fingers and began to look a bit like bamboo. I let out a deep breath. Maybe my special art skill hadn't left me. But it was really hard to make it come out. At least I was getting better, though.

my bamboo
painting

Audrey's paintings were getting better, too. The lumpy

gray cotton balls she had been painting were now bamboo stalks arching across the paper. I had to admit her paintings were good. She obviously knew it, too, because her face was no longer scowling but had a look of smug contentment. She reminded me of Lissy when Mom let her choose her TV show.

Audrey's bamboo
painting

The teacher walked by and stopped between us.

"Good! Good!" he said to me. "This is a nice line here."

"Isn't that the line you helped her with?" Audrey shot out. Before I could shake my head—because it wasn't the line he had helped me with!—she said, "And everything is one shade. You said our paintings should have variations of gray."

"Ah, yes," the teacher said to me as my eyes burned at Audrey. "Remember, even though we are using only black, the painting should have shade variations. It gives the bamboo more depth. Like here."

He was pointing at parts of Audrey's paintings, and even though I was looking, I wasn't paying attention. Inside, I was seething like a teapot about to whistle. Anger was bubbling inside me, and I clamped my mouth tightly to keep it from exploding. As I watched Audrey's face settle back into self-satisfaction, all I wanted to do was slap her. Why had she done that? Why would she point out what was wrong with my painting? "How do you make sure you stay the best in your class, then?" she had asked me. This must be the way she made sure she stayed the best in the class.

I rubbed my paintbrush in the ink violently. Blackness splattered on my fingers, staining me with evil-looking freckles. All my worries and fears about my art talent dissolved with my anger. Audrey Chiang wanted to be the best? Well, I had a special art skill. I'd make it come out, and I'd be just as good as she was. No, I would be better.

I took out another sheet of paper to start a new bamboo painting. *Think bamboo*, I told myself. The teacher had said that *bamboo* means "to wish." I gripped my paintbrush. *With this bamboo*, I thought with eyes narrowing, *I wish to be better than Audrey Chiang.*

Chapter 14

Lissy sprawled on the
couch acting dramatically

LISSY WASN'T LIKING HER CLASS, EITHER. "WE SPEND
most of the time just mixing ink," Lissy said as we walked
back to our grandparents' place. She didn't use ink from a
bottle like I did; she had to use the
inkstone and ink stick — wetting
the stick with water and grinding it
into the stone to make a dark charcoal color. "It's complete misery!"

    Dad laughed when he saw our
glum faces. "It's not so bad, is it?"
he asked.

inkstone &
ink stick

    Ki-Ki laughed, too, even though
nothing was funny. Ki-Ki wasn't minding her classes. She
liked cutting paper and didn't even mind that tiny bits of
paper fell off her like snowflakes when she left class. I rolled

Ki-Ki cutting paper

my eyes at her. I liked how Lissy was miserable better. I was glad someone else felt like I did, especially when Lissy threw herself on the couch and sprawled her arms dramatically. "Yes, it is!" Lissy said, closing her eyes as if she couldn't bear to see the world. "I can't believe I'm spending my summer rubbing a stone!"

Mom and Grandma followed us into the room.

"You aren't going to be spending the whole summer mixing ink," Mom said. "In fact, Grandma has a surprise for you today that I know you'll like."

"Birthday present." Grandma nodded.

"Lissy's birthday was in June," Ki-Ki said.

"A late birthday present," Mom said. "It's something many girls do here when they are teenagers, though usually an older teenager than you. But since we're in Taiwan now, I said it was okay...."

"What is it?" Lissy interrupted. She stopped flailing on the couch and sat up, excited.

"Grandma's going to take you to get photos done," Mom said.

"Photos?" I said. "Dad could take them right here."

"No, no," Mom said. "These are special photos. They dress

87

you up like a movie star or a princess or a bride and do your hair and makeup. Girls here love it."

Lissy was starting to get excited, especially when Mom mentioned makeup. Mom never let Lissy wear makeup at home.

"So it's like a model shoot?" Lissy said. "Will I be in a magazine or something?"

"No, but we'll get you an album of your photos for you to keep," Mom said.

"Just Lissy?" I asked. I wanted to get dressed up like a princess. "Can I do it, too?"

"Me, too!" Ki-Ki said. I didn't think Ki-Ki really knew what we were talking about, but she never wanted to be left out.

"This time, just Lissy," Mom said. "It's her late birthday present from Grandma. And anyway, like I said, even Lissy is a little young for it. But you can come watch if you want. Then you can see if you want it done the next time we come to Taiwan."

The next time we come to Taiwan? I thought. So far, this first time hadn't been that much fun. I hoped the next time would be when I was much, much older.

And watching didn't sound like that much fun, either. Dad was going to go to the store, so I thought maybe I'd go with him and Ki-Ki to buy Lucky Charms instead, but Lissy said, "You're going to come with me, right, Pacy?"

"I don't know," I said. "It'll probably be boring for me."

"You should come!" she said. "It won't be bad!"

"I don't know." I shrugged.

"Please," Lissy said. "It'll be more fun if you come."

I was astonished. Lissy never wanted me to go anywhere with her in New Hartford. She was always embarrassed to be seen with me or Ki-Ki or Mom. And now she was saying it would be more fun if I went with her?

Lissy saw my amazement, came up close to me, and said in a low voice, "I don't want to go by myself."

Suddenly, I understood. Lissy felt like I did! She didn't say it, exactly, but I knew she meant that the crushing crowds, the flying Taiwanese words, and the depressing painting classes made her feel uneasy and nervous, too. A warm feeling wrapped around me, and I felt like reaching toward her with a hug. Instead, I nodded.

"Okay," I said. "I'll come."

Lissy looked relieved. And I felt good. One of my teachers in New Hartford had taught me the saying "Misery loves company," and I realized that was true of a lot of things, not just misery. Sometimes, sisters loved company, too — at least they liked it in Taiwan.

Chapter 15

Lissy's Photo Shoot

makeup
at the photographer's
studio

THE PHOTO STUDIO WAS ON THE TENTH FLOOR OF AN old building. It wasn't so old that it didn't have an elevator, but the elevator felt rickety. I was glad when we got to the right floor. But as we went through the glass doors, I saw that everything was shiny and new and polished like it had all just come out of a magazine.

"Ni hao, Ni hao," a woman at the desk said. That meant "hello"—I knew enough Chinese to know that. Grandma spoke to her for a little while and then pointed at Lissy. The woman smiled and then beckoned Lissy to follow her to another room. Lissy followed the woman, and then we followed Lissy, like a parade.

In the other room were a counter and a whole wall lined with mirrors. The counter was covered with all kinds of makeup—little tubes of pink and red lipstick, black and gray pencils, beige powders, and tubs of shimmery brown and blue eye shadow. It was as if someone had bought everything in the cosmetics aisle in our local pharmacy. Bright lightbulbs framed the mirror, and another wall was hidden by racks of hanging clothes, silky and colorful. It was just like a dressing room for a movie star. Lissy's face lit up as brightly as the lightbulbs.

The woman said something to Lissy, who looked at Mom to translate. "She said you should pick your clothes first," Mom told Lissy. "You can choose three different dresses."

That was fun. We all started looking at the dresses, pushing through them as if we were trying to make waves in water. There were hundreds of pretty dresses, but Lissy was picky. "How about this one?" Mom would say. "This one?" Grandma would say. "No," Lissy would always reply, shaking her head.

Finally, Lissy chose two dresses and had only one more left to decide on. I thought Lissy had horrible taste in clothes. One dress was black with

Lissy and me looking at dresses

91

sequins sewn in the shape of a bow around the waist. The black skirt looked like it was made out of layers of nets and stuck out like an upside-down dandelion. Her other dress was red with rows of lace that made her look like a cross between a fire engine and a cake. I would've chosen one of the flowing chiffon dresses that had little diamonds sewn into it or at least the pink silk one with birds embroidered all over the top.

Lissy picks a dress

"Let Grandma choose your last dress," Mom said. "She's the one who's giving this to you."

Lissy nodded, and Grandma chose a Chinese dress the color of a blue butterfly. It was long and shiny and had a golden feathery pattern all over it. I could tell Lissy was disappointed, but she tried to hide it.

Now that Lissy was done choosing her dresses, another woman came in and had Lissy sit in the chair in front of the mirror. The woman looked at Lissy's dresses, took Lissy's chin in her hand, and then said something in Taiwanese to Grandma. Mom answered.

"What?" Lissy asked.

"She just wanted to know what kind of makeup you wanted," Mom said. "I told her the natural look."

Mom might have said the natural look, but what the woman was doing to Lissy was not looking that natural. The woman was brushing a beige color all over Lissy's face like she was painting a wall. Another woman appeared and began brushing and pulling and twisting at Lissy's hair. Lissy loved it. Ever since Lissy turned thirteen a year ago and said that she was officially a teenager because *teen* was at the end of her age, she rarely smiled. I guess she thought she was too old to show that she was happy. But now the corners of her mouth kept creeping up, and her cheeks, the parts that hadn't been painted beige, were blushing pink.

One of the women motioned for Lissy to close her eyes, and I was expecting her to put some eye shadow or something like that on Lissy, but she didn't. Instead, she measured Lissy's eyes with her fingers and then cut tiny slices out of a piece of clear sticker paper. Then she peeled the backing from her tiny shapes and carefully stuck them on Lissy's eyelids. What were those for?

Then the woman started smearing brown powder that looked like hot-cocoa mix on Lissy's eyelids, covering the stickers. She layered on more and more powder, some silvery, some charcoal gray, all the way up to Lissy's eyebrows. Those she plucked into clean arches, which made Lissy give

93

a little squeal with each pull. Ouch! Now I was glad I wasn't getting my photos done, too.

"Okay," she said to Lissy. She wasn't finished, but she meant that Lissy could open her eyes now.

"Eye folds!" Lissy said when she looked at herself. I was mesmerized. Our eyes were one of the biggest differences between us and our classmates in New Hartford. My friends Becky and Charlotte both had creases on their eyelids that made their eyes look round and big. My eyelids were smooth and heavy, which made my eyes look small. And slanted — the way they looked when the boys at school used to pull the corners of their eyes to make fun of me for being Asian. "Can you even see out of your eyes?" a boy once asked me.

But now Lissy's eyes looked big and round, almost like Becky's — though coated with a lot of makeup. I guess the woman needed to put that much on to hide the stickers. It was strange to see Lissy like that. With one woman dabbing pink onto Lissy's lips and another adding fake curls to the top of Lissy's head, Lissy wasn't looking much like Lissy anymore.

When Lissy came out of the dressing room in her black dress, her face looked like a mask of paint, and her hair was like a curled poodle on her head. She was smiling, though.

"I feel like a movie star!" Lissy said.

"You look like a movie star," Grandma said to her, and Lissy glowed like Christmas lights. But I didn't think she looked that good.

"They put too much makeup on you," I told her.

"In photograph, will look natural," the woman said. I guess she understood some English. I felt a little bad then. I didn't want her to think that I thought she did a bad job.

A man with a camera as large as a shoe box came into the room then to take Lissy to another room, where all the sets were.

"Better alone," he said to me in his broken English when I moved to follow them. "Person nervous when other people and bad photo. Alone, more relax."

That meant Mom, Grandma, and I stayed in the dressing room while Lissy got her photos done. That was boring. We could hear the clicking and snapping of the camera and the man's instructions. "Just small smile," he kept saying to her. "No big smile." I thought that should've been easy for her, but I guess this whole thing was making Lissy happy in a way that was unusual.

As Mom and Grandma talked, I looked at all the tubs of makeup and brushes and bottles that the women had used on Lissy. You needed a lot of stuff to look like a movie star. Some of the tubs on the counter reminded me of my ink and brushes in painting class. I wondered if Audrey Chiang thought she looked like a movie star. Probably not — she was full of herself, but she wasn't stupid.

I looked at myself in the mirror. I didn't really know if I was pretty. I knew I didn't look like a movie star, but

I did hope I was pretty. I didn't put my hair in barrettes anymore — I was too old for that. And Mom was letting me grow my hair long, and it was already a little past my shoulders. I wondered if I should grow it as long as Eva, that girl in my painting class, had grown hers. Her hair looked nice, though it probably took forever to comb. But even if I had really long hair like Eva's, I knew I'd never be really pretty, like my friend Charlotte in New Hartford was. Charlotte had wavy golden hair and blue eyes. Last year at my birthday party, Charlotte had said I wouldn't make a cute couple with Sam Mercer, the boy I liked in school. He had brown eyes and sand-colored hair. She had said I didn't match him, because I was Chinese. "It's hard to match you in a cute couple," she had said. "You don't fit anyone else."

I pulled up my eyelids to make my eyes bigger. If I had eye folds, would I be easier to match with Sam Mercer? In the fairy tale, Snow White had black hair, but she wasn't Chinese. Was it just my eyes that made me Asian? Being here in Taiwan, where I didn't know what the foods were, where I couldn't read the signs or even ask questions — I didn't feel Asian at all. Maybe eye folds would help me match who I was on the inside.

Chapter 16

Going to Taichung

Dad and his
new camera

LISSY WOULD HAVE TO WAIT TWO WEEKS BEFORE SHE could see her photos and then a week after that before she would get the album to keep.

"That's so long!" she said. I agreed. We'd be getting her album right before we left, and that was a long time from now, even though the days were passing a little faster.

But at least for now we were going to get a break from our classes. We were going to visit Taichung, where Dad's family lived, for about a week and stay with Big Uncle, Dad's oldest brother. Taichung was in the middle of Taiwan. It even *meant* "middle of Taiwan." "*Zhong* means 'middle,'" Dad said, "and *bei* means 'north' — *bei* is where the *pei* of *Taipei* comes from. *Zhong* is where the *chung* of *Taichung* comes from. So *Taipei* means 'north of Taiwan' and *Taichung* means 'middle of Taiwan.'"

Dad said we were taking the special bullet train that would get us there faster than the regular train. "They didn't have that when I was young," he said. I wondered if it was called a bullet train because it went faster than a speeding bullet — like Superman!

The train station was a huge building that I couldn't really look at because there were so many people. Ghost Month

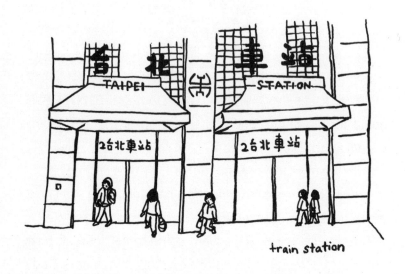

train station

wasn't scaring many people from traveling, either, no matter what Dad's friend had said. Mom said we weren't going for very long, but she, Lissy, and Dad had rolling suitcases and Ki-Ki and I had heavy backpacks. Mom also carried a big shopping bag full of presents and her purse, and Lissy had another bag of gifts.

Around Dad's neck was what we thought was the worst

piece of extra luggage—a brand-new camera that he'd bought at a store down the street from our grandparents' place. It was supposed to take especially good photos, but, to us, it just took an especially long time to use. "Let me take a picture," Dad would say in the middle of whatever we were doing, and we would have to stand there forever while he figured out which buttons to press. Sometimes my face would get sore from holding the smile as he stood there trying to hit the right button for the right setting. I wondered if the camera was Japanese, like that toilet was.

Dad found out where we were supposed to be, and after more elbowing and squeezing, we found ourselves waiting on a platform. Lots of other people were waiting, too. I let my backpack drop to the ground, and Lissy sat on the suitcase she had been rolling behind her.

"I have to go to the bathroom!" Ki-Ki said.

"Really? Now?" Mom sighed.

Dad looked at the big clock. "There's time," he said. "You can go."

"Me, too!" I said. I didn't really have to go, but I thought it would be better to go with Mom to the bathroom than to try to go by myself later. I didn't want to push the wrong button again.

So Ki-Ki, Mom, and I shoved through the crowds again (it was a little easier this time without all our luggage) to the bathroom. It smelled bad.

"Here," Mom said, and she opened her purse and took out a blue change purse with gold embroidery. She handed it to me, brought me close, and whispered, "These are tissues. They don't have toilet paper in public bathrooms. Use this. Don't throw it down the toilet. There should be a garbage can in the corner, throw it there."

I nodded as Ki-Ki and Mom vanished into a stall. I went into the stall next to them but stopped. There was no toilet in there! There was a porcelain-covered hole in the floor. That was strange. It was kind of like a urinal but in the ground.

toilet at train station

I didn't look that closely. Instead I went to the next stall and then the next. Same thing! Were we in the boys' bathroom? Or maybe someone had stolen the real toilets? And they couldn't afford to put a whole toilet in, so they just put in those? That didn't make sense. Why wouldn't they just have fewer stalls and put a whole toilet in each one?

By then, Ki-Ki had finished and I still hadn't found a toilet. As Mom and Ki-Ki left the stall, I saw there was a toilet in there, so I used that. That was the only toilet in the whole bathroom!

"Are we in the boys' bathroom?" I whispered to Mom as I washed my hands.

"What? No," Mom said. "Why?"

I nodded over at the stalls, and Mom laughed. "Those are a different kind of toilet. You're supposed to just squat over them."

It took me a little while to picture it, but once I did, I said, "Ew!"

Mom laughed again as I shook the water from my hands. "Those kinds of toilets were here before the ones you're used to. And most people like those better. See how there is only one Western toilet in the whole bathroom?"

"Why?" Ki-Ki asked.

"Well, people think they are cleaner," Mom said, motioning to a sign on the wall that I had missed before. It showed how to use (and not use) the bathroom.

sign on how to use (and not use) the squat toilet

101

"They're not cleaner," I said. "Those toilets are in the ground!"

"They're cleaner for people using them," Mom said. She was laughing as she pushed us out the door. "Think about it. With these toilets, you don't have to worry about other people's butts."

We laughed, too, mainly because Mom said the word *butt*. And it felt better to think about that and laugh than to think about what she was saying. All this toilet talk was making me feel gross, and I was glad to leave it back with the bathroom.

Chapter 17

Hungry on the Train

apple candy

ALMOST IMMEDIATELY AFTER WE GOT BACK FROM THE bathroom, there was a thundering roar and the train came rushing in. As it screeched to a stop in front of us, the crowds buzzed and swarmed. Then the train doors slid open, and there was a great shove as people rushed through the doors like grains of salt through a funnel.

But as soon as we sat down and the train left the station, all was still. Not that the train wasn't moving—it was going fast. I watched out the window as the buildings passed faster and faster. But inside the train, everyone seemed like silent, sitting statues.

Dad fell asleep almost immediately. I guess he still had jet lag. Every once in a while, he would snore and we would all laugh.

Dad
sleeping on
train

"How do you say 'I can't speak Chinese' in Chinese?" Lissy asked Mom.

"*Wo bu hui shuo Hanyu*," Mom said.

"Woo boo huwaay..." We all tried to repeat it, and the words tangled into a jumble. Ki-Ki and I giggled. Lissy shook her head.

"Too hard," she said. "I think one word at a time is better. What's the word for *bathroom*?"

"*Xishoujian*," Mom said. "But in Taiwanese, it's *ben-so*."

"Wait," I said. "There's a big difference? Chinese, Taiwanese — it seems the same to me!"

"You know," Lissy said, "Taiwanese is like slang."

"Not exactly," Mom said. "I guess Taiwanese is considered a dialect and Chinese the official language."

"What's a dialect?" Ki-Ki asked. This time, I was glad Ki-Ki was asking questions because I didn't know what a dialect was, either.

"Hmm..." Mom thought hard before she spoke. "If every state in the United States had its own language in addition to English, that language would be a dialect. In China, some areas have their own languages—their own dialects—but Mandarin Chinese is the official language everyone knows. When the Chinese took over Taiwan, they made Chinese the official language. But people still speak Taiwanese at home."

That was really confusing.

"So do people speak Chinese or Taiwanese here?" I asked.

"Well, Chinese is what people speak at work or at formal events," Mom said. "Chinese is more universal—the language that more of the world knows. But Taiwanese is what most people here speak at home with their friends or family. So we use both."

That meant all this time in Taiwan, people could've been speaking Chinese or Taiwanese to me and I would never have known. I sighed. It seemed hard to me, but Lissy wasn't discouraged.

"You'd better teach us Chinese, then," she said. "Then we can use it outside of Taiwan, too."

"Okay," Mom said. "In Chinese, the word for *bathroom* is *xishoujian*."

"*Xishoujian*," we all said together.

"What's the word for *please*?" Lissy asked.

"*Qing*," Mom said.

"How about *sorry*?"

"*Duibuqi*."

"*American*?"

"*Meiguoren*."

A woman with a cart of snacks came by, and I was glad. My stomach had been rumbling the whole time. Mom 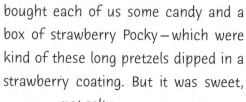 bought each of us some candy and a box of strawberry Pocky — which were kind of these long pretzels dipped in a strawberry coating. But it was sweet, not salty.

strawberry Pocky

Mom wanted to teach us more Chinese words, but now we were more interested in our Pocky. I ate each pretzel one by one, scraping the pink strawberry layer with my teeth before crunching it, looking out the window the whole time.

After I finished my box of Pocky, I opened the bag of apple candy. It was good, but I was still hungry even after I ate the whole pack. I played with the wrapper, crinkling the Chinese words as I rolled it around in my hands. I wondered if the label just said *apple candy* or if the candy had a special name that meant something, like how *Pacy* meant "precious thought."

Thinking about my name reminded me of the name chops we were going to get carved. I still didn't feel much like a precious thought, so I wasn't sure if I wanted my name on it. I liked how some of Dad's friends had different things on their name chops. I didn't want "never too tired for knowledge," but "thoughts as evergreen as a pine tree" sounded kind of pretty. Like a piece of a poem. But the only poem I knew was the one that was on Valentine's Day cards: "Roses are red, violets are blue, sugar is sweet, and so are you."

burning money for
Ghost Month

And I wasn't going to put that on my name chop!

Outside the window, barrels burning bright flames for Ghost Month blurred by, and I thought about the ghosts visiting the living world. Maybe the ghosts felt the same way I did in visiting Taiwan. Here, everyone had conversations that flew through me, like I was steam from freshly cooked rice. Sometimes I felt as if no one even saw me, and that made me hollow and empty.

But maybe I just needed something to eat.

Chapter 18

Cousin Clifford

lady on
bicycle

WHEN WE GOT TO THE STATION, BIG UNCLE WASN'T there. Instead, beaming at us was Cousin Clifford!

"Surprise!" he said as he came up to us. "Are you happy to see me?"

We were. Ki-Ki and I ran over and jumped up and down, and Mom and Dad gave him a big hug. Even Lissy smiled. The last time we saw Clifford was when he got married in Boston, Massachusetts. Ki-Ki had been a flower girl, and I had jumped on his bed for good luck. He looked fatter and softer, but his grin was exactly the same. Seeing him made all my grumpiness from being hungry fall away like rain being shaken from a wet umbrella.

"We heard you were in Taiwan!" Mom said, even though she hadn't told us that. "Where's Lian?" Lian was Clifford's wife.

"She's at work," he said, grabbing one of the suitcases.

"Our company is probably going to keep us here for another year. Then we'll go back to the States."

"How long have you been here?" Dad asked.

"Since May," Clifford said. He put the suitcase down for a moment and started counting on his fingers. "So before this, I lived in Taiwan for two years. Now it's a total of two years and three months that I've lived here. But Lian says I still speak Taiwanese like a seven-year-old."

"What's wrong with that?" Ki-Ki asked, offended.

We followed Clifford out of the train station, and he spoke to us fast without a break. He said he was excited to speak in English to "native speakers" again. I kind of knew how he felt. Except for when I spoke with Lissy or Ki-Ki, speaking English here in Taiwan felt like work and made me feel impatient sometimes. In class, whenever the teacher spoke, it always took me a couple of seconds to understand what he was saying, as if I had to wait for an echo. Here, speaking English to almost everyone—Grandma, Grandpa, Aunt Bea, Uncle Flower, even Mom and Dad—was slower and clumsy.

"Sorry, you guys will have to take a taxi. Hope you don't mind," Clifford said. "I came on this."

"This" was a silver-gray motor scooter. It was a mix of a motorcycle and a bicycle—there was an engine and everything, but parts were covered by plastic, and there was a basket in the back. I liked it!

"Can I ride on it?" Lissy asked.

"Me, too! Me, too!" Ki-Ki and I echoed excitedly.

Mom shook her head at us. "I don't think it's safe for you," she said.

"It probably isn't." Clifford laughed, took a helmet out from the little carrier in the back, and began to strap it on his head. "People say they can tell that I'm from America because I use this helmet. Most people don't wear one. But I think that's crazy! The joke here is that traffic lights are not rules, just suggestions."

Clifford on a
motor scooter

We saw what he meant as the taxi drove us to Big Uncle's place. It stopped and jerked and swayed, leaving angry honks behind us. Everything seemed confused, and the streets were small. One old lady was bicycling with boxes piled so high behind her that she looked like a moving mountain that took up a lot of room on the street. The taxi just squeezed past her, and as I worried that we might hit her, I saw a turtle's head stick out of one of the boxes. Most people were on motor scooters like Clifford's that swerved and sped around us like miniature rockets. There were a lot of motor scooters that had two, even three, kids clinging on to the driver.

Now I was kind of glad Mom hadn't let me ride on the motor scooter. In New York City and in Taipei, traffic had been really busy, but here in Taichung, it was a busy, fast-moving mess. In school, one of my vocabulary words was *chaos*, and for the first time, I felt as if I understood what that word meant. Even in the taxi, I didn't feel that safe.

chaos in
Taichung

"It's different here," I said. "I mean, different from Grandma's place."

"Yes, it'll be more…" Dad paused and then said, "I'm not sure how to say it in English. It will be more real Taiwan."

Real Taiwan? Weren't we already in real Taiwan? It was strange to hear Dad say that. How could it be more real? Was it like those dumplings that could tell if you were a real

Chinese person? Thinking about dumplings made me hungry. I didn't know if we were in real Taiwan, but I did know I was really hungry!

"There'll still be dumplings here, though, right?" I asked.

"Yes," Dad said in a voice that pretended to be annoyed, but I knew he was just joking. "There will still be dumplings! Don't worry! There will never *not* be dumplings anywhere in Taiwan."

I grinned.

niu rou mien
(beef noodles)

BIG UNCLE WASN'T BIG. HE WASN'T SHORT OR SMALL,
but because everyone called him Big Uncle, I thought he was
going to be really tall and strong. Instead, he was just a little
taller and wider than Dad and had a red face with droop-
ing, tired-looking eyes. But he did have a big smile, which
welcomes us as we got out
of the taxi.

He, Aunt Ami, and
Clifford had been waiting
for us, and almost before
we were all out of the taxi,
Clifford had unloaded our
luggage. He took it inside
up to Big Uncle's apartment
and came back out.

Big Uncle

"What do you want for dinner?" Clifford asked as he led us down the street.

"Pacy wants dumplings!" Lissy and Ki-Ki said together. I was a little embarrassed, but everyone laughed.

"I know a good place close by that does beef noodles," Clifford said. "It probably has dumplings, too."

We followed Clifford across the street. Crossing the street was hard. I realized that if traffic lights were just suggestions for cars, then they were also just suggestions for people walking in the streets, too. I squinted my eyes shut and walked close to Clifford as cars honked and motor scooters swerved around us, but he and Big Uncle just walked without concern. They must've been used to all the confusion.

Clifford led us through a door to a small restaurant. The place was very plain with old but clean white tiles on the floor and five rough wooden rectangular tables with benches on either side. In the back was a small kitchen with a man standing over a huge steaming pot, like in the pictures of witches stirring their brew.

"*Ni hao, ni hao*," Clifford said to the man, who stuck his head out of the kitchen. Except for *ni hao*, I didn't understand the words Clifford said or what the man said back. But Mom and Dad looked pleased and ordered food with big smiles.

"What did he say?" I asked as we all sat down at one of the tables.

"They make *niu rou mien* here," Dad said, "special beef noodles—they are thicker than normal noodles and hand-pulled. They're very good! I haven't had real ones in a long time."

"What do you mean, 'real ones'?" I asked.

"The real good noodles are the ones that people make by hand. Come over here, and maybe you can see him make some," Dad said, motioning me over to his side of the table. Lissy, Ki-Ki, and I crowded beside him and stared.

The man was quickly rolling a big mound of dough. When it looked like a perfectly round white log, he took it and stretched it wide, as far as his arms could reach. Then, so fast that we could barely see what he was doing, he began to wave his arms back and forth, twisting and slapping the dough onto the counter in front of him. He seemed to whirl and whip the dough around like he was casting some sort of spell or enchantment. And maybe he was, because Lissy, Ki-Ki, and I didn't even notice that we'd walked closer to get a better look.

And it was magic, or close enough. Because, suddenly, in his hands were hundreds and hundreds of noodles. He had somehow stretched and pulled that roll of dough into long, perfect noodles—each one looking exactly the same. We were amazed.

He didn't think he had done anything that wonderful, though. He calmly took a pair of big scissors and cut the

116

noodles into the waiting, steaming pot. As he stirred, he smiled at us, and we felt a little silly for staring at him with our mouths open. We went back to the table.

man making noodles

"He made noodles with his hands!" Ki-Ki said.

"Yes, I told you," Dad said. "Hand-pulled noodles. They're the best."

I wasn't sure if they were the best, but they looked pretty good. The bowls had big chunks of beef sticking up like mountains in a sea of savory brown soup filled with pale yellow noodles. The steam wafted, and my mouth watered as a bowl was put in front of everyone. Everyone except me, that is.

"Hey, where's mine?" I asked.

"Yours is coming," Mom said. "Have some of mine while you are waiting."

The hand-pulled noodles were good. Very good. Spicy and rich, the soup began to melt away the hungry ache in my stomach. But I wanted my own bowl. Where was mine?

"Here you go!" Clifford said as a different bowl was put in front of me. "We got this special for you."

I looked into the bowl. "Dumplings!" I said. "Wonton soup!"

"Not exactly," Clifford said. "You know, in America, what they call wontons is from a word in Cantonese, the dialect in Southern China."

"Really?" I said, but I wasn't that interested in what Clifford was saying. I was too busy eating.

"And if you translate the Cantonese word *wantan*, which *wonton* comes from," Clifford said, "it means 'swallowing clouds.' So you can consider eating a wonton like swallowing a cloud."

"Why?" Ki-Ki asked.

"Maybe because the wonton feels smooth when you swallow it," Clifford said. "Or maybe because of the shape — like clouds, no two wontons are exactly the same. Anyway, these dumplings aren't wontons. You can tell because they are in the shape of ears."

"Ears!" I said. I stopped eating for a moment. "What?"

STORY OF DUMPLING SOUP

Once there was a famous doctor, Zhang Zhongjing, who lived by the river in a cold part of China. He treated and cured many things, but in the winter, the things he treated the most were people's ears! That sounds strange, I know, but where he lived in China, the winters were particularly cold. The icy wind whipped and burned any exposed skin.

It was so cold that when a villager joked that his breath froze into pieces of ice in the air, all believed him because even if the cold did not freeze one's breath, it really did freeze people's ears. The doctor was kept busy during the winters treating frostbitten ears. He knew that people with frostbite needed warmth to heal, so he began to make a remedy that would warm people's insides as well as their outsides. He cooked meat with warming herbs and finely chopped it. Then he wrapped it in thinly rolled dough and boiled the pieces in soup with more herbs. When the mixture was finished, he called it "soup that takes away the cold," or "qu han jiao er tang." He then served it to his frostbitten patients, who not only healed quickly, but enjoyed the soup so much that they continued to eat it.

qu han jiao er tang
(Chinese dumpling soup)

People made the soup at home,

usually eating it in the winter. They say the dumpling is the shape that it is because it is made to resemble an ear, in honor of Dr. Zhongjing's treatment of people's frostbitten ears. The name of the soup, qu han jiao er tang, was shortened to jiao er tang, and the dumplings were eventually called jiaozi.

"*Jiaozi!*" I said. "I know that word! Dumplings! But we usually have them fried."

"Well, these are *jiaozi*, too." Clifford laughed and pointed at my bowl. "And they exist all because of frostbitten ears."

"How do you know all this?" I asked Clifford. I was impressed he was so smart.

"School, of course," he said as he began eating again.

"Did you go to cooking school?" Ki-Ki asked.

"No." He grinned between bites. "It was a Chinese culture appreciation course. But I really paid attention during the parts about the food."

Chapter 20

The Market

bag of frogs

WHEN WE CAME BACK FROM DINNER, LIAN WAS HOME from work, and there was more hugging and talking. More adults showed up—some were relatives and some were old friends. They all sat at the round table in Big Uncle's apartment, talking and talking in Taiwanese while Lissy, Ki-Ki, and I sat there bored and unimportant. At home, Mom was always so picky about when we went to sleep, but here she didn't say anything, even when the sky became as black as burnt incense. When I went to bed, everyone was still laughing around the table. I sighed. Mom had stopped noticing me, too.

And when I woke up the next morning, Aunt Ami, Mom, Dad, Big Uncle, Lian, and Clifford were still laughing and talking around the table. I knew they must have gone to sleep and woken up, because they were all wearing different clothes, but it felt as if nothing had changed.

"What are we doing today?" I asked.

"I'm not sure," Mom said, and handed me a bowl of rice porridge before turning back to the kitchen. "Dad thought we might go to the cemetery to see his parents' graves, but we're not sure yet."

I hoped Dad changed his mind. Going to a cemetery definitely did not seem like fun. Dad's parents died a long time ago; I never knew them. The only thing I did know of them was that two big black-and-white photos of them hung on the wall in the back corner of our living room. I tried not to look at them much, because they were serious, unsmiling portraits with grim eyes that seemed to look at me disapprovingly. Once, a long time ago, Lissy took down the photo of Dad's father, held it over her face, and chased me with it. She got in a lot of trouble.

"Aunt Ami doesn't want us to go to the cemetery," Clifford said.

"Why not?" Ki-Ki asked.

"Because it's Ghost Month," Clifford said, "and she thinks the only ones that would be at a cemetery now are hungry ghosts. Aunt Ami is very superstitious, you know. She won't even hang her laundry out to dry in the evenings."

"Why not?" Ki-Ki asked.

"Because ghosts might move into them!" Clifford said. We all laughed.

Our parents must have listened to Aunt Ami, because we didn't go to the cemetery. Instead, we went to the market. Going to the market was even harder than going to the noodle restaurant. We had to cross a couple of streets, and each time I felt like a car almost hit us. The streets seemed to get narrower and narrower and fuller, with more and more people. I had to step over planks of wood on the ground that covered holes in the road, garbage, and sleeping dogs. When I looked up, all I saw were layers of bright signs with Chinese words I couldn't read.

I wasn't sure when the street stopped being a street and turned into a market, but somewhere in the noisy, sticky

market in Taichung

crowd it had. Big umbrellas shaded the crates of fruit on display, and faded red paper lanterns lined the sky. Mom, Dad, Lian, Aunt Ami, and Big Uncle began to stop at different stalls and buy things.

"Clifford," Lian said, pointing at a display of some rosy, bell-shaped fruits, "your favorite!"

"Oh boy!" Clifford said, grinning. "Wax apples!"

Clifford began to fill a bag. "He can eat a whole bag in one day," Lian told us. "He is the super wax-apple eater."

wax apples

"You can't blame me! They're so good," he said, handing me, Lissy, and Ki-Ki one each. "And you can't get them in the States. Try it."

I took a bite, and the juice dripped down my chin. The fruit was crispy and sweet and so juicy! It was kind of like an apple, but not exactly. It was lighter and fresher — like an apple crossed with a bubble. I could see why Clifford loved them.

pot of eels

As I crunched, I almost walked into a big aluminum pot on the ground. Good thing I didn't! The silver pot was full of water and long black ropes. No, not ropes — eels! There was another pot next to it full of dark fish wavering in the water like captured shadows. Another pot had turtles, their small eyes looking at us like black stones, and next to all the pots was a mesh bag full of croaking frogs.

But I couldn't look at everything, because the person in charge of the stand said something in Chinese to me in an irritated tone. She seemed upset with me, probably because I almost stepped into her eels. I shook my head at her, and she said something louder. The skin of her round face was so tan that it was almost the same color as her eyes, which were flashing at me. I felt a little scared. A burning rushed through me. How did I say I couldn't speak Chinese, again? I couldn't remember. What were those words Mom had taught us on the train?

"*Meiguoren! Meiguoren!*" I said. That was the only word I could remember. *American.* She had the same look in her eyes as that mean bus driver in New Hartford from so long ago. "Where are you from?" he had asked me. My answer didn't satisfy her, either. She said something else to me, louder and louder, and all I could do was stare at her red-printed flowers on her apron, too frightened to look at her face. I knew she was angry, but I didn't know why. My cheeks burned red as if her words were slapping my face. "*Meiguoren! Meiguoren!*" I said again, stupidly — like a parrot. I didn't know what else to say. I felt like crying.

"What's up?" Clifford said, grabbing my arm. The woman

yelled something at him. "*Duibuqi, duibuqi,*" he said as he waved her away, and nudged me toward the road. "Sorry, sorry." I saw her shake her head in disapproval and disgust as Clifford dragged me away.

"She was mad at me!" I said to Clifford.

"She wasn't mad, exactly," he said. "She just didn't understand why you couldn't speak Chinese."

A heavy feeling fell upon me, like a crushing boulder. "Twinkie!" those girls at the Taiwanese-American convention had called me. "You lost your culture! Twinkie!" But I stuck my chin out.

"We don't speak Chinese in New Hartford," I said sullenly.

"I know," Clifford said. "Your parents wanted you guys to fit in there, so that's why they never taught you. But that woman didn't know that."

"I told her I was American," I insisted. "I said '*Meiguoren, Meiguoren*' over and over."

"She probably didn't know what you meant," Clifford said. "Here, people like us are called *Huaren* — 'overseas Chinese.'"

"She knew what I meant," I said stubbornly. "They just don't like people to be Americans."

"That's not true," Clifford said. "You know the Chinese word for *American*, but do you know what it really means? The word *ren* means 'people,' *guo* means 'country,' and the word *mei* means 'beautiful.' So *Meiguoren* means 'people of a beautiful country.' It's actually a compliment."

But even so, I still felt as if I were a twisted knot. I was angry at all of them—the bus driver, the convention girls, the market lady. I wanted to yell "I'm American!" but they wouldn't have believed me. Inside, I felt hard and stubborn, like a fist clutching a stolen pearl. I didn't want to learn Chinese, I didn't want to paint bamboo, and I didn't want to be here in Taiwan. Here, people either despised me or acted like I wasn't there, looking through me like a ghost.

Clifford walked with me, pointing out other things and making jokes, so I tried to brush away my hurt feelings. But it was hard. Every time the convention girls' mocking laughter, the market lady's angry voice, or even Audrey Chiang's condescending stare began to fade away, they seemed to come right back to haunt me.

Chapter 21

Temple in Lugang

ghost money

THE NEXT DAY, DAD DECIDED THAT SINCE WE WEREN'T going to go to the cemetery, we should go to Lugang. Aunt Ami and Big Uncle and his friends said it would be a fun place to visit. "It's one of the oldest towns in Taiwan," Dad said. "Also, there's lots of good food there."

The first place we saw when we got there was a famous temple, though it seemed more like a fair than a temple. There was a welcome gate, like the one in Chinatown, but this was much more elaborate and colorful. It was gold and green with detailed carvings of flowers and dragons.

old gate in Lugang

"This gate is very old," Dad said.

"Older than Grandma?" Ki-Ki asked.

"Older than Grandma's grandma," Dad said. "It's one of the oldest things in Taiwan."

Across two of the columns, underneath painted carvings and gold Chinese writing, there was a long screen flashing words in Chinese in electric lights.

"Is that as old as Grandma's grandma, too?" I asked, pointing.

"Well, no," Dad said. "But it's as old as Grandma's granddaughter. It's a gate that crosses all generations!"

Through the gate to the temple, there was a rainbow plastic awning, lines of golden lanterns, and calling vendors with smoking food stalls on either side.

temple in Lugang

In the courtyard of the temple, there were tables of food on rough wooden tables. I think the food must have been for ghosts, because no one touched it. There were wax apples and other fruits, but there were also packaged foods, like boxes of tea. There were even packages of Oreo cookies! That was a little unexpected. But I guess there was no reason why ghosts wouldn't like junk food.

package of Oreos

There was also a large stage set up with two people acting out some sort of play. They wore bright costumes of pink and blue and yellow and strange makeup. Their faces were thickly painted white with brilliant pink cheeks and black eyebrows. Not very natural-looking! In fact, it was the opposite of natural. They looked like aliens. If Mom hadn't told the makeup woman at Lissy's photo shoot to give her a "natural look," I wondered, would Lissy have ended up looking like that? Lissy would have looked awful! But I would've laughed.

opera singer

No one was laughing at these people; instead, there was a big audience watching. The only empty chairs were the ones in the front row, and there were lots of people standing in the back. I wondered why they didn't sit down in the empty seats.

"See that?" Dad pointed. "That's a Chinese opera they are doing."

"Why are they doing opera at a temple?" Lissy asked.

"It's to entertain the ghosts, to show them a good time while they are visiting. And that row?" Dad said, pointing at the empty chairs I had just been wondering about. "No one sits there because those are reserved for the ghosts!"

Everything was a mix of old and new. The temple building was ancient and elegant with intricate carvings and watching lions. It made me feel like I should be quiet and respectful. But the plastic canopy, the brashly colored stage and acting, the loud peddlers, and the junk food made me want to run and yell. Not that I could yell, because there was so much smoke! Everyone seemed to be burning something — incense, ghost money, paper clothes. I watched people buying paper objects from a booth. There were paper dresses and suits wrapped in shirt boxes as if they were from a department store. In other boxes, there were fake teeth, gold watches, perfume, and even computers. I saw packets of ghost money, too, and next to those was a pile of fake American money.

ghost money that looked
like American money

"Those are U.S. bills!" I said, pointing. "Why do they have fake American money?"

"To burn, of course." Dad laughed. "Nowadays, U.S. money is worth more than most other countries' money. People always say American dollars are better, so they think they must be better for the ghosts, too."

We laughed. Through the smoke, I saw Clifford disappearing into the temple and followed him.

"Where are you going?" I asked him.

"I haven't been here in a long time," he said. "The last time was when I was still in high school. I want to see if my green onions are still there."

"What?" I asked as we entered a small room. Clifford went straight to a shrine that had a fancy red and gold case. In the case was a statue of a bearded man with a gold robe and a round belly. There was a stone table in front of it covered with papers, garlic, radishes, celery, and green onions!

"Is he a gardening god or something?" I asked.

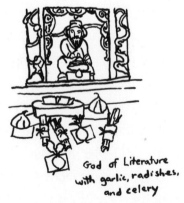
God of Literature
with garlic, radishes,
and celery

"No," Clifford said, and laughed. "He's the God of Literature."

"You gave him onions?" I asked. "Why does he need onions?"

CLIFFORD OFFERS GREEN ONIONS

Like I said, the last time I was here was before I went to college. I visited the summer before I was going to be a senior in high school, the summer before I was going to take the SATs.

It's way too early for you to worry about it, but the SAT is a really important test. If you get a bad score, it can keep you out of the college you want to go to. The better your score, the better school you can get into. I was really nervous about it.

When I told Aunt Ami about the SATs, she told me I should make a prayer to the God of Literature. "Students in Taiwan take many exams," she told me. "And they all make offerings to him for help."

What did I have to lose? I was willing to take any help I could get. Aunt Ami helped me prepare. "What kind of test is it?" she asked. "If you need talent, we'll get a radish. If your test is very detailed and long, you'll need some celery. Or if it is an intelligence test, we'll get green onions."

"What?" I said. "Why do I need those vegetables?"

"They are offerings," Aunt Ami said. "The word for clever in Chinese is 'congming' and the word for onion is 'cong.' See how

133

they sound alike? So by giving the God of Literature an onion, you are asking for intelligence."

"So the word for radish sounds like talent?" I asked.

"Yes," Aunt Ami said. "And celery sounds like the word diligence — you know, hard-working. Oh, is it a math test? We could bring garlic, too — garlic sounds like the word for count."

I couldn't decide which of them to bring. Really, I felt like I needed all of them. But the SATs are supposed to be some sort of intelligence test, so I decided on the green onions.

When we got here, I watched other students make their offerings. They would place a paper on the table, then their vegetable of choice on top. Then, gravely, they would bow to the God of Literature with a smoking piece of incense. Some wrapped their celery with their papers and tied them, like little presents.

"What are the papers?" I asked.

"Those are their test permits," Aunt Ami said, "so the God of Literature will know which student they're for."

That made sense. There were probably thousands and thousands of students taking tests. But I didn't have a test permit. What was I going to do?

"Just write your name on a piece of paper," Aunt Ami said.

But that didn't seem enough to me. There were probably a lot of Clifford Lins in the world. In fact, there was another Clifford Lin right in my school. How would the God of Literature know which one to help out? I thought hard. Well, how did the government know which Clifford I was? My Social Security number! That was it!

So, on a piece of paper, I wrote my name and Social Security number. I rolled the paper around the onions and tied it with a red string. I placed it on the table and took a piece of incense. As I bowed, I thought, Mr. God of Literature, please help me out on my SATs. I really need a good score. I'm all the way in the United States, so you might have to travel a bit, but you should be able to find my test using my Social Security number. Thanks.

And then I almost started to laugh. But I held it in until we left the temple. It seemed so silly, and I felt a bit foolish. I didn't tell anyone what I had done. I was a little embarrassed.

"Did it work?" I asked. Maybe I should ask the God of Literature to help me paint better than Audrey Chiang. I wondered if she knew about him. If she did, she probably brought a whole wheelbarrow of vegetables every day. "How did you do on your SATs?"

"You know, I did pretty well," Clifford said. "And I even got into the college I wanted to, too. So maybe it did work. That's why I wanted to see the God of Literature again."

With that, Clifford took a piece of incense and bowed. "Thanks, God of Literature," he said. "You're a good guy!"

And we both burst into laughter.

Chapter 22

The **Four Pleasures** of **Life**

dragon fountain

AFTER THAT, I WANDERED THE TEMPLE. IT WAS BIG, WITH different rooms. One room was filled with brilliant gold statues; there was so much bright gold that it hurt my eyes. At home, I had read a story about King Midas, who was granted the wish of turning everything he touched into gold. I imagined that room to be like his home after he touched it.

But most of the temple was filled with the heavy smell of incense and smoke. The ancient, elaborate carvings on the walls and ceiling were the same color as the dark smoke. People were bowing and crowding around a black statue of a round-faced woman, and I knew there was probably a lot to see, but the smoke made me cough at every turn.

So when I saw Ki-Ki at the fountain in the back courtyard, I joined her. There were a lot of kids at the fountain, kneeling on the ledge and leaning against the railing. In the jade-green water, an ancient stone dragon seemed to be climbing out to yell to the sky. The water spurted white against its green moss-covered body and orange-and-white carp swam around it like dancing jewels. The whole thing looked like a painting.

Lissy and Clifford came up next to us. "Too busy in the temple," she said. "Too much smoke and too much noise."

"Yeah, it's different from a church, isn't it?" Clifford said.

That was true. Churches at home were always clean and quiet with people speaking in whispers. Here, it was dirty from smoke and incense, and loud with people talking and kids screaming across the courtyard.

"Churches are more serious," I said.

"I don't know if they are more serious—a lot of people here believe deeply," Clifford said. "But there is definitely more of a sense of humor. Did you see the four little statues on the gate over there?"

We shook our heads.

"They are supposed to represent the best pleasures in life," he said, "which are—yawning, picking your ears, scratching your back, and picking your nose!"

"No!" we all said in unison, giggling. "Gross!"

"It's true!" Clifford said. "I'll show you the sign on the way out."

"Those aren't the best pleasures, though," Lissy said. "What fun is picking your ears or your nose?"

the statue for the pleasure of yawning

"Well," Clifford asked, "what do you think the best pleasures are, then?"

"Shopping," Lissy said. "Or maybe watching TV."

"Eating candy!" Ki-Ki said.

"No! Eating dumplings!" I said.

"We could just say eating," Clifford

the statue for the pleasure of picking your ears

said. "All right, I choose laughing. That's my greatest pleasure. Pick the last one, Pacy."

I thought hard. Greatest pleasure...what did I like to do the most?

the statue for the pleasure of scratching your back

I wanted to say making art, but I thought about my class and painting next to Audrey Chiang. That wasn't a pleasure at all. I liked writing, too, but it wasn't the writing that gave me the

the statue for the pleasure of picking your nose

greatest pleasure. I liked it best when people read my writing and liked it. That's what made me happiest.

"Reading!" I said.

"Reading?" Lissy said, wrinkling her nose. She was disappointed, probably because she didn't like books so much. "You and books. Boring!"

"Hey, I think reading is a good one!" Clifford said before I could make any remarks about shopping being boring. "I think just being able to read is really one of the greatest pleasures in life, and not just reading books."

"What do you mean?" Ki-Ki asked.

"Well, when I first came to Taiwan, I could barely read anything," Clifford said. "And I remember the first time I went into a store and I could read the signs. I felt so happy. It was truly a great pleasure!"

We laughed. I sort of saw what he meant. In some ways, not being able to read the papers or signs or menus was worse than not being able to speak. All the unreadable words felt like a secret that everyone knew except me.

"You know, the longer I've been here," Clifford said, "the more I realize how hard it must've been for our parents, moving to the United States. It's all the little things, like not being able to read signs or understand directions, that make things so hard."

Mom and Dad had told us about how they had moved to the United States, but I hadn't thought about their not understanding TV commercials, not being able to order food, being ignored because you didn't speak the language — all the things I found hard here in Taiwan. Maybe when Mom

139

and Dad were first in America, everything was just as strange and confusing to them as Taiwan was to me now. It was surprising to think about.

"Good! I'm glad!" Ki-Ki said loudly, shocking us all.

"Glad about what?" Lissy asked.

"That reading is a pleasure," Ki-Ki said. "Because I know how. I can read chapter books all by myself now."

"That is good," Clifford said, laughing. "And think of the even greater pleasures in your future!"

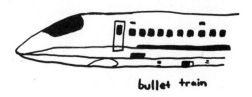

bullet train

EVEN THOUGH IT WAS TWO DAYS LATER, IT SEEMED LIKE almost as soon as we got back from Lugang, we were saying good-bye to Clifford, Lian, Big Uncle, and Aunt Ami and getting on a train back to Taipei. Aunt Ami didn't want us to go. "It's because you'll be traveling into the night," Clifford told us. "She's afraid of ghosts!"

I had laughed then, but as I sat on the train watching the sky get darker and darker, I did feel a tiny bit worried.

"Do they really say if you travel at night, ghosts will come?" I asked.

"Oh, yes," Dad said. "And there are even more superstitions. If you whistle at night, you're inviting ghosts."

"They say the same thing about cutting your fingernails," Mom said. "If you cut them at night, you are inviting ghosts, too."

That just seemed silly! We all laughed at that.

"But we don't really believe in any of those things," Mom said.

"Some people do," I said, thinking of Aunt Ami.

"Yes, that's true," Mom said. "But Grandma and Grandpa always discouraged our family from all that. Some traditions were fine to practice, but they said you also had to use your common sense."

"What do you mean?" Lissy asked.

"Like when my aunt Suying was married," Mom said.

GRANDMA BREAKS TRADITION

When Aunt Suying was to be married, her parents consulted a fortune-teller for a favorable wedding day. This was a custom back then, to ensure a lucky and long marriage, and her parents took this very seriously. The fortune-teller, an old and wrinkled woman, took all the details of the birthdates of both the bride and the groom. Not just the date — the time they were born, too. With that information, she calculated the day and time they should be married.

"September ninth is good," she told them. "But the marriage must take place during the mao period."

Suying's parents were surprised. Each Chinese day was divided into twelve periods, each period two hours long. The mao period was early in the morning, 5 AM to 7 AM! Still, that was

142

Branch	Time
子 zǐ	2300-0100 hrs
丑 chǒu	0100-0300 hrs
寅 Yín	0300-0500 hrs
卯 Mǎo	0500-0700 hrs
辰 Chén	0700-0900 hrs
巳 sì	0900-1100 hrs
午 wǔ	1100-1300 hrs
未 wèi	1300-1500 hrs
申 shēn	1500-1700 hrs
酉 Yǒu	1700-1900 hrs
戌 Xū	1900-2100 hrs
亥 Hài	2100-2300 hrs

day calendar for
Chinese fortune-telling

the luckiest time, so they made the preparations accordingly.

The night before the wedding, Suying had a sleepover bridal shower. All her friends from school, cousins, and sisters came. Grandma went, too. It was a fun time with all the girls laughing and talking. They didn't go to bed until very late.

It ended so late that everyone had a hard time waking up in the morning. And they were supposed to wake up early! When Suying finally woke up, it was already time to go.

What a panic it was! Aunt Pinmei was there to do Suying's hair. She was the "good-luck woman." According to tradition, the bride's hair must be arranged by a married woman with many children and a good husband, so that the good luck would be passed on to her. The good-luck woman was supposed to speak auspicious words while she combed the bride's hair and placed on the headdress.

But Suying was already so late that everyone was frantic. Aunt Pinmei could only quickly stammer a couple of lucky phrases as she coiled Suying's hair and stabbed in the bridal comb.

"It's crooked!" Suying wailed as she looked at herself in the mirror. The comb with its red tassels perched awkwardly on her head, with one tassel hung over one ear and the other tassel below her other ear. She reached to fix it.

143

Aunt Suying on her wedding day

"No!" Aunt Pinmei said, pushing her hands away. "You can't redo it! It would be bad luck. You can only do it one time. It's like marriage — once it is done, you have to keep it!"

Suying would have argued, but she was too busy getting pushed out the door to the wedding. She made it just in time, and they were married before the mao period ended. Grandma said no one really remembers the ceremony because they had to do it so fast.

After the ceremony, Suying and her husband were sent to the wedding chamber. Relatives, aunts, and uncles were positioned outside the room — sometimes with teases and jokes, sometimes with food. But there was always someone there, guarding the door, because according to tradition, brides were not supposed to leave the wedding room until the morning after the ceremony.

Now this was fine most of the time, but Suying had been rushed in there at seven in the morning, and there was no bathroom in the bedroom!

By the middle of the afternoon, she, of course, had to use the bathroom. But every time she poked her head out, someone was there, stopping her from leaving the room. Her aunts and mother shook their heads at her. "Hold it," they told her. "It will be bad luck if you leave. You'll have a bad marriage."

Finally, it was Grandma's turn to watch the door. Everyone else had gone downstairs as Suying poked her head out again. "I really need to go!" she whispered urgently. "Pleeaaaase!"

Grandma looked at Suying's begging face. To her, this was not the way a bride should spend her wedding day. A crooked hairstyle, a prisoner in a bedroom — how could any of this ensure a happy marriage? This was just a lot of silliness! At the very least, a woman should be allowed to use the bathroom.

Grandma checked to make sure no one else was around. "Quickly," she said, and motioned Suying out of the room. Suying ran to the bathroom and back without anyone else knowing.

"Thank you!" Suying whispered, and she was so grateful. Grandma was the only one willing to break the tradition and overlook the superstition. Suying was very thankful and remembered it always.

"In fact," Mom said, "she still thanks Grandma for it, even now."

"How was her marriage?" Lissy asked. "Was it still lucky?"

"Yes," Mom said. "She and Uncle Wu have a big house in Fresno now and two sons. One is a doctor, and the other is a computer programmer, and everyone is very happy. So as you can see, all those superstitions aren't really true."

That story made me feel a little better. I also hoped that when I got married, there would be a bathroom in my room.

the sculpture in front of the
tower that was supposed to
symbolize coins with the holes making
the numbers 101

RETURNING TO TAIPEI ALSO MEANT COMING BACK TO
Chinese painting class. Audrey Chiang hadn't changed at
all. If anything, she was worse. The class had stopped painting bamboo and had moved on to flowers, but I couldn't
even get excited about using my color paints, because I was
too busy trying to get my art talent working. It would show
up only once in a while, and I didn't understand why. The
fortune-teller had said my special skill would be used all my
life. Why did it keep disappearing? It made me hollow and
fragile, like an empty eggshell. Compared with Audrey's pre-
cise, clean flowers, mine looked like pink gum balls melted
into one another. I hated it when Audrey would glance over
with one of her disdainful looks. And she couldn't hide her
satisfaction when the teacher stopped me from painting the
sky blue.

"But my plum blossom branch is outside," I said. "A blue sky will make it look more real."

"Remember," the teacher said, "in Chinese painting, we are painting the idea of how things look, not how they look for real."

His words reminded me of how Dad had said Taichung was more "real Taiwan." And that was still puzzling to me as well. Even after being there, I didn't know what was more real about it.

"I was wrong," Dad said when I asked him later. "Taipei, Taichung — it's all real Taiwan. Because Taiwan is both old and new, modern and traditional. You're right."

I wasn't sure what I was right about. But I guessed that Taipei was the "modern" Dad meant. Because it was only when we got back that I noticed how large and clean the sidewalks were. So far, to me, "modern" meant it was a lot easier to walk around.

But all that was forgotten because Dad was starting to pack his suitcases. He was leaving, going back home tomorrow. That meant thirteen days until we went back home.

"Don't you want to stay for Grandma's birthday party?" Ki-Ki asked him.

"Of course I want to," Dad said. "But I can't. These were the only days I could get off from the hospital. Anyway, there will be so many people at the party, no one will even notice I'm not there."

"But you're going to miss everything!" Ki-Ki said.

"I will be missing some things," Dad said. "But not everything. Before I go, we'll go see Taipei 101!"

"What's that?" Lissy asked.

"It's Taiwan's most famous building!" Dad said. "I'm sure you've seen it from a distance. It's the tallest building. In fact, it's the tallest in the world!"

"Second-tallest," Mom said. "There is one in Dubai that is taller."

"Still," Dad said, "it is Taiwan's shining modern icon! We'll all go before I have to go back."

As the taxi drove us there, I did recognize it. Taipei 101 had always been in the landscape. It was made of blue-green glass that matched the deepest part of the sky and looked like stacked boxes reaching high above all the other buildings.

"Is the address 101?" I asked as we got out of the taxi. "Is that why it's called Taipei 101?"

Taipei 101 building

"No," Mom said. "It's because it has 101 floors."

"Why?" Ki-Ki asked.

"It's symbolic," Dad said. "It was built for the new century plus all the new years after. So that is why it's one hundred plus one. One hundred years, one hundred floors, and one symbolic extra for the extra years to come."

I stared up at the building. It was very, very tall! The glass sparkled in the sun, and I got dizzy trying to see the top of the building.

"See that?" Dad said, pointing at what I had thought was just a sculpture of three huge stone circles. "Those are to symbolize ancient Chinese coins. Back then, coins had holes in them. See how the holes make the numbers 101?"

Lissy had also been staring up at the building. "Is that round thing on the side of the building a coin, too?" she asked, squinting.

"Yes," Mom said. "Coins are good-luck symbols."

"Why?" Ki-Ki asked.

"Because they are money!" Mom laughed. "So they mean wealth — which is lucky!"

"Let's go in!" Lissy said. "I don't want to just look at the building all day."

"Okay, okay," Dad said as we went inside. "Should we eat or look first?"

I was going to say eat, but Mom said, "Let's look first. Going up the elevator might upset our stomachs."

We went to the fifth floor and got our tickets. The word OBSERVATORY was above the counter.

"It's in English!" I said, pointing, as we waited in line.

"A lot of things will be in English here," Mom said. "This is a famous tourist place, so things will be in a lot of languages. People from all over come here."

Mom was right. As we crowded onto the big elevator, two people I guessed were Americans got on the elevator after us. They were a couple. The woman's light skin was so blotchy red from sunburn, she was like the colors of strawberries and cream. Her husband was tall and bearded, with sandy hair. They stuck out among everyone else in the elevator, like sunflowers in a daisy patch. Looking at them made me see how we must look in New Hartford. I wondered how they felt.

As the elevator doors closed, a pretty Taiwanese lady in a black uniform began to welcome us. First she spoke in Taiwanese, then Chinese, then Japanese, and then English! A lot of languages really were used here.

"This is one of the fastest elevators in the world," the uniformed lady said in her accented English. "It travels 1,010 meters in one minute. So to take us from the fifth floor to the eighty-ninth floor, it will take thirty-seven seconds."

"That's fast," the American lady said.

"Yeah," her husband said. "Fastest elevator I've ever been in!"

As they spoke to each other, I realized they probably thought that we were Taiwanese or Japanese and couldn't understand them. It gave me a strange feeling. I wanted to say something to tell them we were American, too. But I

151

didn't want them to think I was listening to their conversation, either, so I kept quiet.

The elevator began to move, and the lights dimmed. Above, on the ceiling, twinkled hundreds of tiny lights, arranged just like the night sky. I stared with my mouth open. On the wall, an oval screen lit up with an image of the building and numbers next to it with floor, height, speed, and time on it. The numbers flashed as we passed floors. The elevator was fast! So fast! Tenth floor! Thirty-seventh floor! Two hundred and fifty meters! Three hundred and forty meters! The numbers that told the speed of the elevator went so fast that they blurred, and I couldn't read them. Faster and faster we went. I thought I would feel dizzy or my ears would plug up like they did on the airplane, but neither happened. It was a really modern elevator!

The doors opened, and we emptied out onto a floor that was completely walled in by glass. Past the stalls selling souvenirs and postcards, the world stretched below—buildings, trees, cars, streets, people, all smaller than dollhouse miniatures. I felt as if I were standing on a cloud looking at the earth below. I hadn't realized Taipei was so big. It always looked so small when I saw it on a map. There were so many buildings, but there were also green mountains around everything, too. The mountains layered upon one another in softer and softer colors until they matched the color of the sky and melted away.

I walked aimlessly, looking through the glass at the city below all around. At every corner, there was a plaque with the history of the building and other information. I found Lissy reading one of them. Mom was helping Ki-Ki see through one of the tall standing binocular machines.

"It says this building is shaped to look like bamboo," Lissy said.

"It is?" I said, surprised. I thought about the bamboo I had painted in class. I could see that the segments that joined together to make a stalk of bamboo were kind of like the stacked glass shapes of the building.

"And there are eight sections," Lissy said, "because eight is a lucky number. It sounds like the Chinese word for *prosperity*."

highest
mailboxes in
the world
(I think)

"You don't have to tell me," I said, standing closer to the sign. "I can read, too."

But past the sign, I saw a post office. No, not exactly a post office, but a mailing area. There was a big sign that said MAILBOX AIRMAIL with round mailboxes underneath playfully labeled. One box said FAMILY on a colored striped background, another said FRIEND in blue and white, and the last one said

LOVER on a big red heart.
Behind the mailboxes
was a counter where
people could write their
messages on postcards.
I watched as the Ameri-

place we could write postcards

can couple from the elevator dropped their postcards into
the box that said FAMILY.

"They're the highest mailboxes in the world!" Lissy said.
I didn't know if she read that or thought of it herself, but I
was excited.

"Let's mail something!" I said, and immediately thought of
Melody. It gave me a little shock that I hadn't thought about
her in such a long time. It wasn't that I had forgotten about
her, exactly, but at home I had been used to her being with
me, so I missed her a lot. Here, I wasn't expecting her to be
with me, so I didn't feel lonesome. But she was still the person
I wanted to send a postcard to the most.

Lissy and I both rushed over to Mom to get her to buy us
postage stamps and postcards. Of course, then Ki-Ki wanted
to buy them, too, even though she had no one to send postcards to.

"We can buy this ten-pack of postcards," Mom said, "and
you can share."

I didn't like that, because the postcards in the ten-pack
were all of the Taipei 101 building at nighttime and with

fireworks. And we were in the building during the day. I
didn't want Melody to think I had seen the building when
there were fireworks. It would have been kind of like lying.
And I would've rather picked the special wood postcards that
were on display—cards that were made of paper-thin wood
with pictures that looked like they had been burned onto it.
But when I showed them to Mom, she just looked at the price
and wrinkled her nose. "The ten-pack is a much better deal,"
she said, and I knew that was what we were getting.

We split up the cards (Mom took one for herself so that
they would be divided evenly among the three of us) and
went to the counter near the mailboxes. I put my postcard
to Melody in the FRIENDS mailbox. I chose the card with the

Dear Melody,
    I'm sending this
to you from the
highest mailbox in
the world (I think)! I
am in Taiwan in the
famous building that's
on the front of the postcard.
It is hot here. I ate raw
fish! And chicken feet (by mistake).
    More later because I'm running out of room. ♡ Pacy

POSTCARD

Melody Ling
2328 Palm Ave.
Diamond Bar,
CA
92168

sunset behind the building. That was the most like what I actually saw here in Taiwan. I felt I should send postcards to my friends Becky and Charlotte, too, but I couldn't remember their addresses. I could picture their houses and the streets they lived on, but I had never had to mail anything to them before, so their addresses were just a big blank. Oh well. Mom said the postcards wouldn't get there for two weeks anyway. Maybe I'd just mail them from home and pretend I sent them from Taiwan, though I guess the stamp would give that away.

I looked at the other mailboxes — there was also a mailbox for FAMILY, but Lissy and Ki-Ki and Grandma and Grandpa were here in Taiwan, and I'd never sent anything to any other family before, so it'd seem weird to do it now. The last box had a big red heart on it that said LOVER. I definitely didn't have a card to put in that box, either. The only boy I liked in school was Sam Mercer, and I wasn't going to send him a postcard from Taiwan. Then he would know I liked him!

At the counter, there were also stamps and red ink pads. When I stamped one onto my postcard, it showed a little picture of the building and said TAIPEI 101 at the bottom.

"I'm done," Lissy said. "I'm going to put mine in the mailbox."

"What did you write?" I asked, looking over her shoulder.

"Hey!" Lissy said, hiding her card. "That's private!"

"It's a postcard!" I said. "It can't be that private. Did you write secrets or something?"

"No," Lissy said. "Just the normal things, like 'I'm in Taiwan, having a great time, blah, blah, blah.'"

"Are you having a great time?" I said. "You don't seem like it."

"Sure," she said. "I don't like class, but the rest is okay. Most of the time, the food is good, it's nice to see Grandma and everyone, and it's kind of interesting to see all the different Taiwan stuff."

That was true. "But I don't like how everyone here in Taiwan acts like we're dumb because we don't speak Chinese," I said.

"Yeah," Lissy agreed. "That's no fun. Now that I'm here, I wish I knew Chinese. Maybe I can learn it later and come back. That would make it better."

"Maybe," I said. I wouldn't mind knowing Chinese, but learning it seemed kind of hard. And it was also hard to think about coming back for another trip. This one wasn't even finished yet.

"But it is annoying now," Lissy continued. "Everyone gives us that stupid, shocked look like we just swallowed a cow or something when they find out we don't know Chinese. Then they ignore us."

"Yeah!" I said, nodding hard. I hadn't realized how much Lissy felt like I did. I knew she didn't like class, but knowing she felt invisible sometimes, too, was comforting.

"Not speaking Chinese is probably the worst thing so far,"

157

Lissy said. "That and class...and the toilets are gross, too. People don't flush their toilet paper; they throw it out in the basket. It's so disgusting."

"Yeah!" I said again. We laughed. I was surprised. Sometimes, when she forgot she was a teenager, Lissy was actually nice to talk to.

"But the rest of it," Lissy said, "is not bad, don't you think?"

Before I could answer, Ki-Ki announced, "I'm done!" She slapped her pen down with a decisive *clack!* and held her postcard in her hands triumphantly, as if it were a prize.

"What did you write, Ki-Ki?" Lissy asked. Ki-Ki, unlike me and Lissy, had liked her class from the start and still did. She didn't worry about whether her paper cuts were good, and she was making lots of friends. "Everyone wants to sit next to me," she had said, "so I can teach them English words."

"Things," she said vaguely but proudly. I couldn't imagine it being that interesting. Ki-Ki marched over to the mailboxes. Slowly but deliberately, she took her postcard and pushed it through the slot of the box that said LOVER! Lissy and I stared open-mouthed.

"Ki-Ki has a boyfriend!" Lissy said as Ki-Ki walked back toward us. "Ki-Ki, who's your boyfriend?"

"No one!" Ki-Ki said, scowling at our giggles. "I don't have a boyfriend!"

"Well, then who did you mail your postcard to?" I asked.

"Who else would you mail a postcard to from the LOVER box?"

"I mailed it to myself," Ki-Ki said, sticking her chin up. "I didn't have anyone to send a postcard to except myself. And I love myself, so I put my postcard in there."

Lissy and I burst out into loud laughter, and Ki-Ki joined in. So silly! And I realized that maybe Lissy was right. Even though I didn't love being in Taiwan as much as Ki-Ki loved herself, maybe it wasn't so bad after all.

Chapter 25

McDonald's rice burger

"THE FIRST FIVE FLOORS OF THIS BUILDING ARE A MALL," Dad said, "and in the basement is the food court."

"Let's go there!" I said. "I'm hungry!"

Back in New Hartford, at the Sangertown Square Mall, there was a food court with about a dozen fast-food restaurants. It was kind of dark, with brown plastic tables and chairs and fake plants and flower arrangements that looked kind of dusty. I was expecting the food court here, especially since Dad said it was in the basement, to look the same.

But it didn't at all. The food court was shiny and white, the floor so clean that it sparkled. And there was so much food! There was a bakery with cakes of bread wrapped in plastic and frosted pink donuts that looked like baby rattles. There were restaurants with glass cases displaying plates of shiny plastic food and others that had huge mountains of fried rice and noodles on the counters. One restaurant had pale chickens hanging in its case, their heads still on. I had seen that in Chinatown but never in a mall!

And the best thing was that a lot of places had Chinese *and* English. I could read almost everything! Premier Beef Noodle had noodles with clear soup and soy soup. Sergeant Chicken Rice had a chicken rice bowl and chicken liver (yuck!).

That's also when I noticed that there were all kinds of foods at the food court. There was a French pastry place and an Indian place. There was an Italian place called Benito

the Italian fast-food restaurant at the food court

and a Japanese restaurant called Karen. There were so many places, I didn't know what to choose.

Until Ki-Ki shouted, "Look! McDonald's!"

Lissy and I rushed over to where Ki-Ki was pointing. There really was a McDonald's. There was the big, glowing yellow M, just like the McDonald's we had at home. Suddenly, I missed New Hartford. I missed our white house with green shutters, the big green lawn and trees. I missed talking to Melody on the phone, my friends in my class, the orange brick library, and even my box-shaped school. Seeing McDonald's here was like seeing something from home. It made me excited, like finding a lost shoe.

"Let's eat there!" I said.

"Really?" Dad said. "You want McDonald's?"

"Yes!" Lissy, Ki-Ki, and I said in unison.

"Okay." Dad shrugged. "*Mai Dang Lao.*"

"*Mai Dang Lao?*" I asked. "Is that what they call McDonald's here?"

"Yes." Dad nodded and laughed. "When there are Western words that there are no Chinese words for, they just put together Chinese words that sound like English."

"Really?" I said. "What else?"

"Um..." Dad thought hard. "Like hamburger. We pronounce it 'hanbao'!"

"And chocolate," Mom said, "is pronounced like 'chokoli.'"

We laughed. It was funny how it sounded the same but different. I wished all Chinese words were like that. It would've been a lot easier for me to learn Chinese that way.

Well, not only was McDonald's not called exactly the same thing in Taiwan, but it also didn't look exactly the same, either. This McDonald's was a lot cleaner and brighter, with white floors and walls and wood tables. It wasn't anything like the plastic red and yellow tables we had in New Hartford.

And the food was different, too. As we stood in line and looked at the glowing menus overhead, I was confused. Only some words were in English, like EXTRA VALUE MEAL, but the rest were in Chinese. There were photos of food, but some of them were pictures I had never seen in a McDonald's before. On a banner, there was a photo of round fried balls next to a bowl of corn soup. Corn soup? At McDonald's? Also, in some of the photos, there were fried chicken and weird-looking hamburgers with buns that looked like thick, sesame-sprinkled rice crackers.

"What are those?" I asked, pointing.

Mom looked at the photos. "Rice burgers," she said. "Do you want one?"

I shook my head. "I want chicken nuggets," I said.

Ki-Ki and I got the chicken nuggets, and Lissy got fried chicken. Mom ordered for us. We had gotten used to Mom and Dad doing all the ordering and talking, but I never really got used to the questioning looks the clerks gave us when Mom spoke to us in English.

"It comes with a side order," Mom said, "of french fries or corn. Which do you want?"

"Corn?" I asked, and I noticed another customer's order to our side. There was a small cup of corn kernels on his tray. Weird! "French fries!" I said. Lissy and Ki-Ki ordered the same. Mom and Dad got the rice burgers and a bowl of corn soup each.

cup of corn

The rice burger came in a green cardboard container, kind of the same as how a large order of fries was packaged back home, except with a lid. It was strange to see the yellow M logo with Chinese writing. Dad lifted the lid of his container, took out his rice burger, and unwrapped it from the wax paper so we could see it. The bun wasn't a rice cake or a rice cracker, like I had thought it'd be. It was rice tightly packed and toasted to make a bun shape. Instead of a meat patty and pickles, there was pork with slices of lettuce.

"Want to try?" Dad said, offering it to us.

I hesitated, but Lissy took a big bite. She chewed slowly. "Hmm," she said.

"Is it good?" I asked.

"It's not bad," she said slowly. "But it's not a hamburger."

Well, I had to try it then. I took a bite, and the rice bun crumbled and began to fall apart. But it was moist and soft, and the pork was covered with a sweet sauce. It tasted like a Chinese pork dish Mom made at home, but it was shaped like a hamburger.

"I think you are supposed to eat it with the paper wrapper around it," Mom said, "so that the rice doesn't make such a mess."

But I had had enough of bizarre McDonald's food. I wanted the real stuff. I dipped my chicken nuggets in honey and chewed away. *Ahh! Just like home.*

"What's for dessert?" I asked when we finished.

"Let's look around," Dad said as he threw out our tray. "You know, this is the first meal we've had that Pacy hasn't eaten dumplings."

That wasn't exactly true, but it was the first time we had eaten that I hadn't thought about dumplings. I frowned. I felt like I was losing some kind of bet.

Dad stopped us in front of a display case of hundreds of pretty round balls dusted with sugar like little snowballs. Some were pale pink, others a soft gray-green, and there were even light yellow ones, the color of buttercups.

"Are they chocolate?" Lissy asked. "Chocolate truffles?"

"No," Dad said. "*Mochi.* We'll get some of these. You should try it."

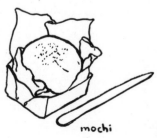

mochi

I took one of the pale pink ones, the same color as the peonies Mom grew at home. The

16

fine sugar dust sprinkled down my shirt as I bit into it. The *mochi* had a smooth skin, soft and chewy. A strawberry-flavored, creamy filling oozed into my mouth, with a smell even sweeter than the taste. The whole thing blended together and seemed to melt in my mouth. It was delicious.

"Like it?" Dad asked us.

We nodded and reached for more.

"You know what *mochi* really is?" I asked.

"What?" Dad said.

"It's a dessert dumpling!" I said.

"Oh, is it?" Dad said, laughing. "Does this mean you have eaten dumplings every day since you've been in Taiwan?"

"Almost!" I said, and grinned.

Chapter 26

Painting Class, again

the teacher's fancy
chops

"THIS IS OUR LAST WEEK OF CLASS," THE TEACHER SAID
to us the next morning. "So in the next few days, you must
choose which painting you want to show in our exhibit."

Exhibit! I remembered he had said something about that
on the first day of class, but I hadn't remembered it until now.
Audrey Chiang waved her hand in the air as if it were a flag.

"Is there going to be a prize at the exhibit?" she asked.
"For the best painting?"

"Yes," the teacher said, and smiled. "The teachers usually
honor the painting they like best with a ribbon."

"Only one?" Audrey asked. "Only for the best?"

"Well, one for each class. You know there are other classes
here, right? For Chinese writing and other things," he said,
and then repeated himself as he often did. "So one in this
class."

Audrey sat up straight, as if she had already won. She wasn't really doing anything — yet I still wanted to slap her.

"But before anyone can be awarded a ribbon, you must learn how to make a painting," he said.

That was confusing. Hadn't we been making paintings all this time?

"Up to now, I have been just teaching you elements," he said, as if reading my mind. "Bamboo, flowers, birds — it is how you put them together that makes a painting. Most students spend years just painting bamboo, but this course is just to give you a taste of how to paint. So today, I will show you how to make a painting, and then you can try your own."

I still didn't really understand all that he was saying, a little bit because of his accent and his stuttering. He motioned for all of us to stand around him like we did the first day. As he lay a piece of snow-white rice paper down on the table in front of him, using his carved paperweights to hold it down, I found myself standing next to Audrey Chiang. I tried not to look at her. The teacher fingered his bamboo paintbrushes lovingly, finally choosing one and swirling it in the water and ink. And then, just like he did the first day of class, he made just a few strokes, and a bamboo stalk grew on the paper. He added more leaves and crimson flowers.

the teacher's paintbrushes

"For painting," he said, "it is about composition and balance. You don't want everything to be busy. You need an area of focus, but also the other areas to balance it."

His hands lingered over his brushes, as if deciding. Then his hand swooped down, quickly seizing one. His fingers reminded me of chopsticks picking the best pieces of meat from a dish. Then he seized another brush and circled it in the pink paint he had just used to paint plum blossoms, and he painted a bird flying on the bare side of the page.

After struggling to paint a bamboo leaf right, I felt awed. Each stroke was strong and certain and his hands quick and controlled, blotting and brushing in a graceful dance. His eyes darkened in concentration, and every one of us watched, mesmerized. He took his name chop and pressed a red mark into the painting.

the teacher's painting

"Everything in the painting must be balanced," he said. "Even your mark has to be placed carefully; it's part of the painting. The red color has to be balanced — it can't be too

169

close or too far from elements. Never put your mark on top of a bird or in the middle of your bamboo."

"What does the stamp say?" Eva, the girl with the long hair, asked.

"Li Mengshan," the teacher said. "My name!"

I was glad I finally learned his name. It was kind of funny that it was only today, during this last week of class, that I learned what it was. But in a strange way, it was kind of fitting, too. Because after watching him paint, I felt like I was meeting him for the first time. I remembered on that first day, I just supposed he wasn't a good artist, because he couldn't speak well. He spoke English so hesitantly, bumbling and stumbling over words, I had thought that was the kind of person he was. And he wasn't. I realized that was probably how people saw me here because I couldn't speak Chinese. They thought because I couldn't speak the language, I didn't have anything important to say.

"I don't have a name chop," Eva said.

"It's okay," the teacher said. "I have some you can use."

"But then our paintings will have *your* name on it!" Audrey sputtered.

"No, you won't use this chop, the one with my name," the teacher said. "I have others."

And he reached over and untied a small roll of cloth. Inside lay three more chops. The figures on top were beautiful, bigger, and more intricately carved than my tiger. One chop was made out of red stone with gray flecks in it, and the top had a carving of two fish swimming on a wave of water. Another was a creamy ivory color with a bamboo carving, and the one with the lotus flower was gray with muted orange and brown shining through.

"These are my chops for different moods," he said. "Sometimes I add another mark with my name to add to the mood of the painting. I have some at home I will bring for you to choose from. You can borrow them for your painting if you don't have your own. In the future, maybe you can add your own to it."

"What do these say?" I asked. These must be chops like the one Dad's friend had that said "never too tired for knowledge." It reminded me that we hadn't gotten ours carved yet. I'd have to remind Mom.

"This one," the teacher said, stroking the red stone seal with the carved fish, "says 'this moment will last in my memory.' The gray one says 'spring opens the heart to happiness,' and the bamboo says 'fulfilling wish.' The ones you can borrow, which I will bring, will be more simple, better for you."

"What will those, the ones we can use, say?" a square-headed boy asked—for some reason I thought his name was Alex, but I wasn't sure.

" 'Joy,' 'love,' 'harmony,' " he said, "that kind of thing. Simple, but it will still look very nice. But when you choose, make

171

sure it matches the mood of your painting. Every detail in your painting is important."

We all went back to our desks. I guessed the simple chops would be okay. Lots of people had nodded when Eva said she didn't have a chop, so most of the class was probably going to use the teacher's chops. But I'd rather have my own. I wondered if I could get mine carved in time for the exhibit. But what would I have carved? It was driving me crazy that I couldn't decide.

Or maybe it was Audrey Chiang who was driving me crazy. I'm sure she would get something like "forever the best" carved on her name chop with plans to decorate it with the winning class ribbon. As she took out her paper, I watched her as she carefully looked around the room at each of the students. There were lots of good painters in our class, but there was no one who I could say was the best. Eva painted bamboo really well and that boy Rex could paint nice flying birds. And I was pretty good, too.

But I could almost see Audrey calculating how to be the best. I was calculating, too. How was I going to beat her? I was not going to let Audrey Chiang win the ribbon in our class. I had a special art talent, and it was not going to let her win. At least, I hoped not.

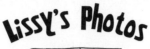

Chapter 27

Lissy's photo

DAYS WERE MELTING AWAY. DAD HAD LEFT, AND NOW
we had only ten days left in Taiwan. Today we were going
to the photography studio so Lissy could choose her photos
for the album, and tomorrow I had to choose which painting I wanted for the exhibit. Mom had said I had to use the
teacher's chop because she didn't have time to get our
chops carved. "Later," she'd promised. "I'll get your chops
carved later."

Maybe there wasn't any time because everyone was planning for Grandma's birthday party. Aunt Bea had already
chosen the restaurant for the party, and Auntie Jin had sent
out the invitations before we even arrived in Taiwan. And
Uncle Flower, Shogun, Julian, and their father had been and
were still practicing "a secret!" Uncle Flower had said.

"What has Grandpa done for the party?" I asked.

"He's too busy working to do anything for the party," Auntie Jin said, laughing. "He's paying for it!"

Mom felt bad that everyone else had done so much work for the party already, so she said she would order the cakes. "We can stop by the bakery on the way back from the photo studio," she said.

Lissy was eager to see her photos. She tried to hide it, but I could tell by the way she tapped her foot on the subway. I was curious, too.

We were kind of taken aback when the woman and the photographer pushed Lissy in front of a computer. But we quickly figured out what was going on. Lissy was supposed to click a little box on the screen if that was a photo she wanted in her album. We all peered at the monitor.

looking at Lissy's photos

"Who's that?" Ki-Ki asked.

"Me!" Lissy said, giving Ki-Ki a don't-be-dumb look.

"No, it's not!" Ki-Ki said. "They mixed your photos up with someone else's. We've got the wrong set."

"No, we don't," Lissy said, sighing in annoyance. "They're my pictures."

I didn't blame Ki-Ki for thinking they weren't Lissy's photos. The girl onscreen had luminous eyes and glowing skin that looked as soft as a freshly laundered bedsheet. Her hair was glossy and smooth like black embroidery floss, and her pink lips formed a delicate doll smile. The girl in the photo was glowing and plastic-looking, like an actress or a movie star. She did not look like Lissy.

And even when we knew it was Lissy, it was still hard to believe. When I looked closely, I could see a small resemblance — the nose, the teeth, the way she held the fan. But it felt like we were looking at a stranger.

"I think they made you taller on the computer," I told her. I couldn't exactly tell what they did, but she sure looked different. "Or something."

Lissy didn't seem to be bothered. She swung her legs as she clicked and scrolled and asked us over and over again which picture we liked better.

"This one with the umbrella?" she'd ask us. "Or the close-up in the rainbow room?"

"I like them both the same," I said. Which was true, because I didn't like either of them.

"Okay, both, then," Lissy said happily. "Mom, there's a little box I can click if I want a poster made. Can I get a poster made?"

A poster! I didn't know if I wanted to see a big-size version of these photos, but Mom said, "Okay, but only one."

I shrugged.

Soon, Ki-Ki and I got bored of watching Lissy go through

14

her pictures. We left her and Mom at the computer and sat in the waiting area, flipping through magazines. They were

Taiwanese fashion magazines

all in Chinese, so I couldn't understand them.

"Look," Ki-Ki said, stopping at a page. "This is the same dress Lissy is wearing in her photos."

It wasn't exactly the same dress, but it was close. But what was weird was how much the model in the magazine looked like Lissy did in her photos. I looked at Lissy at the computer, squinting into the screen with her hair tangled at the ends and her dirty feet in flip-flops. There was no way she looked like a movie star or a model in real life. But if I didn't know her, her photos might have made me think so. If they could make Lissy look like a hairspray model, they could make anyone look like one. I started to flip through the pages of the magazine again and realized — they were all fake! All these fashion models were probably photographed like Lissy, lots of makeup, fake eyes, and lighting and computer changes. It was all a big lie.

I went back over to Lissy. She was almost done.

"You know you don't really look like those photos," I said to her.

"I know," Lissy said. "But it's fun. Like a story or a movie. You don't have to be mean about it."

"No," I said. "I meant you don't look like those photos, and it's good. I think you look a lot better in real life."

"Oh," Lissy said. She didn't say anything else, but a little pleased smile curved on her lips. I'd never really said nice things to Lissy before, but for some reason I felt like this was important. Because it was true. I did think she looked better in real life. She didn't look like someone fake. In real life, she looked like Lissy — someone who was sometimes nice, sometimes mean, but always my sister. Just being herself was much better looking than one of those models pretending in the magazine.

But that meant Lissy kind of was a beautiful thought, then, I realized in surprise. Her Chinese name was right about her. I would never have believed it.

Chapter 28

The **Bakery**

pineapple
cake

AFTER THE PHOTO STUDIO, WE WENT TO THE BAKERY so Mom could order the cakes for Grandma's birthday party. As soon as we entered, a warm, buttery smell filled our noses. We kept taking deep breaths with our eyes closed, trying to eat the smell.

But maybe we didn't need to try to eat the smell, because it looked like there were free samples all over the bakery for us to taste. There were rows of trays full of all kinds of cakes and breads and cookies. A lot of things I had never seen before, but everything looked good. Crowded together were round yellow buns with sandy sugar tops, sunshine-colored egg tarts like the ones we had eaten at dim sum, and even bread in the shape of pig heads!

One row was filled with small rectangle cakes — the shape of toy wooden blocks. Each one was wrapped in plastic and

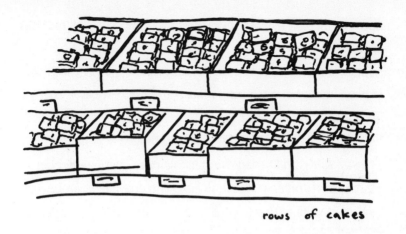

rows of cakes

was a golden, toasted color. I thought they were all exactly the same until I noticed that the sample plates in front of them showed different colored fillings. Mom's eyes lit up when she saw them.

"Pineapple cakes!" she said. "I love these!"

"Are they all pineapple?" I asked.

Mom looked down the aisle. "They make them in many different flavors now," she said. She went to the stack of empty boxes at the side and handed one to each of us. "You can each fill a box with them to bring home."

That was exciting. Lissy, Ki-Ki, and I rushed over to try the samples. But as Lissy reached for a chunk of cake with a nut-colored filling, I suddenly got worried.

"They are samples, right?" I said,

pineapple cakes in a box

179

tugging at her arm. "They aren't food left out for ghosts, are they?"

Lissy's arm froze with her hand hovering over the plate, and we looked at each other. But then a teenage boy passed us, casually took one of the cake pieces, and popped it into his mouth. We grinned. They were samples!

Lissy, Ki-Ki, and I tried every single one. There were cherry, walnut, pineapple, lychee, and egg. The egg-flavored one was kind of peculiar. There were also a couple of cakes that we couldn't tell what the flavors were. There was one with a darkish purple filling and another with an orange filling that didn't taste like orange at all. We agreed that the pineapple ones were the best, with their thin, buttery crust and sweet, firm pineapple filling. I guess that's why they were the original ones.

We could put fourteen cakes in each box, so filling it was a hard decision for me. Lissy put every flavor in her box, even the weird egg one. Ki-Ki just put in all pineapple. I decided to put in mostly pineapple but a couple of the cherry- and walnut-flavored ones, too.

It took us so long to choose our cakes that Mom was waiting for us by the time we had finished. She had talked to the woman at the counter for a while, ordering cakes for the party.

"Did you get pineapple cakes for Grandma's party, too?" Lissy asked as we left. The big bakery bag that held our cakes knocked against her knees.

"No," Mom said. "I ordered special cakes for the party.

Peach buns—remember, like the ones we had with soup dumplings? And turtle cakes."

"Turtle cakes? Not made of turtles, right?" I asked. I didn't think so, but I had to make sure.

"No, it's just a cake that looks like a turtle shell," Mom said. "Turtles mean longevity, too, just like the peaches. It's because turtles are known for living such a long time."

We rode the subway home. It was crowded but not as busy as the first time we rode it. This time Mom let us each scan in our subway token as we went in. The tokens were round, purple, plastic discs that reminded me of toy money. When we got off the subway, we were supposed to drop them into a machine.

The subway car came, and Lissy and I squeezed onto a seat with the bakery bag in our laps. Mom held Ki-Ki's hand with one hand and a silver pole with the other, her bag on her shoulder. Crowds of people pressed into one another, and I watched a

Subway tokens

group of girls giggling and a man trying to read a book as the train swayed. I was getting used to not knowing what people were saying. But not being able to understand Chinese meant that all I did was look at things. And eat—I did that, too.

I remembered the samples I had eaten at the bakery and how I had wondered if they had been for hungry ghosts. I knew they hadn't been, but a small part of me still worried. What if I had eaten food meant for a hungry ghost?

As I sat silently with all the passengers casually ignoring me, I realized that I was like a ghost myself. Everything here — the crowds of people who tried to walk through me, the signs I couldn't read, the words I couldn't say, and even the art I couldn't paint — made me feel like I was invisible. Sometimes I felt like I was disappearing. Just like a ghost.

man pretending to read on subway

The subway lurched, and the doors opened. Mom and Ki-Ki pushed against me as people rushed out. As the man with the book staggered past us, I saw his thin hand reach into Mom's bag! Faster than my mouth could open, a blue change purse from Mom's bag vanished behind his book.

"Mom!" I said, pointing. Lissy saw it, too. "Mom! Mom! Your purse!"

But it was too late. The crowd of people had already thrust him out of the subway, and he was gone.

"He stole something from your bag!" Lissy said, her words running into each other.

Mom's eyes and mouth opened, each making round circles of panic. She quickly opened her bag and started to look through it.

"It was a little blue purse," I said, "in the front pocket."

"My blue purse?" Mom said, and she was still for a moment. Then she started to laugh.

"What's so funny?" we all asked. It didn't seem funny to us at all. Mom had just been robbed!

"That purse had tissues in it!" she said, laughing harder. "Tissues for the bathroom! He stole tissues!"

We all started to laugh then. We laughed so hard that everyone in the subway car looked at us. But we couldn't help it; it was so funny! I wondered what the thief would do when he opened Mom's change purse and just found tissues.

Mom's change purse with tissues in it

The subway car started moving again, and Mom and Ki-Ki tilted forward. When they swayed back, Mom had stopped laughing.

"I always thought they only pickpocketed tourists," Mom said, more to herself than to us. "I guess they can tell that I am not from here anymore."

Mom's face looked kind of sad. I hadn't thought about Mom not being from Taiwan anymore. It was probably weird coming back to Taiwan, the place that used to be her home but wasn't anymore. She was really from America now, just like us. And we were all just like visiting ghosts.

Chapter 29

The Last Painting Class

the teacher's chops that we
could use

IT WAS FRIDAY. WE HAD NINE DAYS LEFT IN TAIWAN. IT was the last day of painting class and the day I had to choose which painting I wanted in the exhibit. The actual exhibit wasn't until next week, but we had to hand them in so they could be mounted.

"Does it have to be mounted?" Rex, the boy who sat next to Eva, asked.

"Yes," the teacher said, almost astonished that someone would ask that. "It's very important. Do you see how when your paint dries, your paper is wrinkled?"

We nodded. I had noticed that. It was a pain. I was always trying to smooth out my finished pictures.

"When we glue it onto silk, when we mount it in our special way," he said, "the painting becomes flat again and the silk makes a border. A painting is not considered finished unless there is a border around it."

"Our paintings will be mounted on silk?" I asked. That sounded really fancy!

"Yes," the teacher said again. "Mounting a painting is important. The Chinese word for the mounting silk is *ming zhi* — that means 'life paper.' Mounting your painting brings it to life. That is how a painting is finished."

I was used to the way the teacher spoke now. I didn't mind so much that he repeated himself or didn't really answer the questions we asked. Ever since he had shown us how to make a painting, I respected him a lot. He was a real artist.

I was an artist, too, at least sometimes, when my talent decided to work. But even then, I wasn't as good as he was. So far I had a couple of paintings that I thought were okay, but I kept hoping I'd paint an even better one. I wondered which one of her paintings Audrey was going to choose. She had one with red flowers growing out of old, weathered branches that looked almost like the teacher had done it. I didn't paint flowers as well, I think, because I missed those classes when we went to Taichung.

But I could paint nice birds. I mixed up some carmine-red paint with some white and it made a brilliant pink. It was the same color as those awful pink dresses Mom had made us wear on the plane to Taiwan. I remembered how I had

185

imagined Lissy, Ki-Ki, and I had been bright pink birds and how grumpy I was that we had to come. It seemed such a long time ago. And we would be flying back home soon.

I started to paint three pink birds. One for me, one for Lissy, and one for Ki-Ki. Not bad, but the birds were just floating in the air. They'd be better on a branch or something. Oops, I should have painted a branch first. I took out another sheet of paper. I sighed. It was annoying that I couldn't erase or cover my marks.

I painted an arching bamboo. Was there enough room for the birds? Well, Ki-Ki was small. I felt like I was squeezing both Ki-Ki the bird and my art talent at the same time. C'mon! There! Three birds on a bamboo. A warm, happy feeling filled me, like I had swallowed a bowl of delicious soup.

I leaned back to get a better look at my painting. Yes, this was my best one. I was sure of it. My art talent had been stubborn, but it had appeared this time. I looked over at Audrey, who was looking at my painting fiercely, as if I had written insults on it. Ha! That meant it was good.

I walked up to the teacher's desk. He had brought in the chops for the class to use. They were all simple, without any elaborate carvings, but the smooth stone felt nice in my hand. The teacher knew most of us couldn't read Chinese, so he placed each chop on a piece of paper with the meaning in English written on it. There were a lot of chops, maybe a dozen to choose from. He probably wanted to make sure there were enough choices to match our paintings. Some were the ones he had mentioned earlier — "love," "harmony," "happiness," and "spring." There were also some that I thought were kind of odd for paintings, like "forever," "mercy," and "profundity." I didn't even know what *profundity* meant. I'd have to look it up in the dictionary when I got home.

So which chop matched the mood of my painting? Since the three birds were supposed to be me, Lissy, and Ki-Ki, I wasn't sure which chop to pick. "Harmony" or "peace" wouldn't be true — we always fought about things. "Spring"? Was it spring in my painting? I hadn't really thought about it. The birds were on a bamboo, so it could be any time of year. The teacher had said painting a bamboo meant to wish something. Hmm, what were we wishing for? Not love. That would look stupid.

But I had to decide fast. Class was ending, and the teacher was calling on everyone to give him their paintings. Everyone was frantically sorting through their papers, and there was a mad rush as people clamored around the table to get one of the chops to stamp their paintings. *Which one?* I thought. I grabbed the chop on the paper marked "happiness." I wasn't sure if that was exactly right, but it kind of fit. Lissy, Ki-Ki, and I always wished to be happy, right?

I brought the chop and the red ink over to my desk and quickly but carefully stamped my painting. I made sure to leave plenty of room below the stamp to put my own name chop, whenever we got those.

my painting

Audrey's painting

Maybe that's what the three birds were wishing for, for their name chops to be carved!

I lined up behind Audrey to give the teacher my painting. Over her shoulder, I saw she had chosen the red flower painting. It was really good. Was it better than mine? I looked at my birds. I couldn't really tell. I guess we'd find out at the exhibit.

woman at night market
making cakes that looked
like hockey pucks

THAT NIGHT UNCLE SHIN ARRIVED. HE HAD COME ALL the way from Philadelphia to Taiwan for Grandma's party, and everyone was happy to see him. When he laughed, everyone else laughed, too. And he laughed a lot. Uncle Shin was always jolly. Mom said he was a playboy, which I thought was true because he always likes to play and have fun. And instead of eating at a restaurant for dinner, Uncle Shin wanted to go to the night market.

"What's that?" Lissy asked.

"You haven't taken them to the night market!" He looked at Mom and shook his head. "It's what Taipei is famous for—the night markets."

"But what is it?" I asked. "Is it just a market at night?"

"Yes," Uncle Shin said, "but not just shopping, like a flea market. There's lots of food! My favorite food is always at the night market. It's a lot of fun. You have to see it!"

"Well, they'll see it now." Mom laughed. Aunt Bea called her home to get our cousins Julian and Shogun to meet us there, and we all rushed to leave.

Outside, the sky was the color of ink. When Julian, Shogun, and their father met us, the streetlights shone down and I stared at my long shadow in front of me. Taxis streaked by, their headlights looking like staring eyes in the dark. I remembered how Aunt Ami didn't want us traveling at night during Ghost Month and looked quickly at everyone else. No one seemed worried. In fact, everyone was quite cheerful.

"This way!" Uncle Flower said, leading us down the street. We all followed Uncle Flower like we were in a parade. The noises of the street got louder and louder, and more and more people began to pack around us. A strong, hot smell filled the air, a mix of frying oil and smoke. Glowing signs lit the streets as bright as the sun, making it easy to see the peddlers crowded with their stands of frying foods. It was like a carnival or a fair. It reminded me of being at the temple in Lugang, except it was at night, busier, and, as I soon found out, much bigger.

"Is this the night market?" I asked Uncle Shin. I had to say it loud so he could hear me over all the sounds and clattering of the crowd.

"It's the beginning of it!" he said to me. "There's a lot more!"

I followed him deeper into the masses of people. It felt like everyone in Taiwan was at the night market, too. Everyone was coming and going, pushing and crowding. It was hard to keep my eyes on Uncle Shin when there were so many things to look at. One peddler had piles and piles of meat on sticks laid out on trays in front of a grill. At another stand, a woman was frying six big omelets on a round stove that looked like a metal barrel. Another stand had a steaming hot metal form with circles molded in it, like a line of cups. As the peddler poured in batter, round cakes — the shape of hockey pucks — baked golden brown. I was starting to get hungry.

the night market

"Can we eat?" I yelled to the back of Uncle Shin's shoulder. He nodded and pointed to a cart nearby. When we got there, I saw there was a long line.

"We'll start with this!" he said.

191

"What is it?" Lissy asked. She, Mom, and Ki-Ki had been right behind me the whole time.

"Chicken cutlets!" Uncle Shin said. "One of the famous foods of the night market. I'll take you to all the famous foods tonight, okay?"

Chicken cutlet

As we waited in line, Ki-Ki tugged on my arm. "Look!" she said.

At the cart next to us, there were fat hot dogs on a stick. But not any hot dogs. These were baked in bread that looked like waffled cones. Some sticks had a wavy line of something that imitated ketchup or mustard on it, but I think it was really frosting. A couple of them had candied eyes on them, and one even had a bow tie!

"Waffle dogs!" I said. "They should make one that looks like a dog!"

We looked at the rows of waffle dogs waiting for buyers. There was one made to look like a baby, with a pink bow, but no dogs. We were a little disappointed.

waffle dogs

Uncle Shin handed each of us a huge chicken cutlet wrapped in paper. It was flat and round and so big that it had to be folded in half for our hands to hold it. It was like a super-extra-large piece of fried dough at a carnival, except it was meat. I didn't think I could finish all of mine, but it was so good! The meat was tender and juicy, and the fried batter was salty and crispy. It was like the best chicken nugget I could imagine — as well as the largest.

We were just taking our second and third bites in the chicken cutlets when Aunt Bea, Shogun, and Julian came up to us. Shogun and Julian were sharing something that looked like a sauce-covered baseball from a carton.

"Everyone else is down there," Aunt Bea said. "They wanted *chou doufu.*"

"*Chou doufu!*" Uncle Shin said. "We'll get that next. That's famous, too."

We pushed our way down the street. This was the most crowded place I had ever been. It was busier than the subway, the train station, and the temple in Lugang. The heavy smoke smell of grilled foods and charcoal hung like a fog, and the mixture of all the people talking, bells from nearby games, and music blaring from stores was just a loud, confusing noise. There was a pink booth filled with hanging toys and a row of small, desk-sized pinball machines actually made with real pins and had marbles for balls. One woman laid out clothes on a large cloth in the middle of the road, and we had to squeeze on either side of her display. We even passed a booth selling wigs!

But mostly the night market was full of food. So much!

Little golden cakes in the shape of cute pigs and ducks. Colorful fruits looking like a rainbow on ice. Shiny, egg-shaped sausages. Some things were just weird, like little tomatoes skewered on a stick with a candy coating on them. It was like candy apples—but tomatoes! We had no idea what other things were. "What's that?" we kept asking and pointing. "What's that?"

"Quail eggs," Mom said about some small batter-fried balls with a brown sauce.

"Pig's blood cake," Aunt Bea said about dark, almost black mounds on a silver tray.

"Duck tongues," Uncle Shin said about some deep-fried things that looked like insects. "Want to try some?"

We shook our heads hard, and I started to think maybe we should stop asking. But Lissy pointed at a sign with a drawing of a frog on it, and among all the Chinese writing, there were three English words written exactly like this: WOW FRog egGs.

"Frog eggs!" Lissy said. "Is that a mistake? Did they mean frog legs?"

Either way, I hoped we wouldn't eat there.

Mom looked at the sign and laughed. "No," she said. "They really mean frog eggs. But it's not what you think."

"It's a drink," Uncle Shin said. "Let's get some."

We followed, cautiously, as Uncle Shin bounded over. At the stall a woman was wearing a white apron with the same frog on it as the one on the sign. It didn't say "WOW FRog egGs" on her shirt, though. She was stirring a big silver bowl full of tea-colored water and what looked like clear Jell-O. Behind the bowl were two deep vats we couldn't see inside of.

frog-eggs drink stand

Uncle Shin nodded, ordered, and then passed us each a plastic cup with a straw as wide as my thumb sticking out of it like a flagpole. The cups were full of golden-colored water and ice, but at the bottom, floating around like tadpoles without tails, were round balls.

"What are those?" I asked. "Are those the frog eggs?"

"Those are tapioca," Mom said. "They just call it frog eggs because they think that's how the tapioca looks."

I looked again at my cup. They really did look like what I imagined frog eggs would look like. I took a sip. Kind of lemon-tasting but not lemonade. It was cool and sweet. A tapioca pearl rose up the straw and into my mouth. It was smooth and slippery as I chewed and swallowed it. Fun! It was like eating a drink. I was glad they weren't real frog eggs. "You can get this in the States now. They serve it in all different flavors of drinks and teas," Uncle Shin told us. "But it's called bubble tea or black pearl tea. 'Frog eggs' didn't sound appealing to Americans!"

We laughed, even though I thought it was a good name change. Frog eggs didn't sound appealing to me at all. I was American that way, too.

As we walked farther down, Uncle Shin said, "Ah! *Chou doufu!* Can you smell it?"

I sniffed the air. The only thing new that I smelled was an unpleasant odor that reminded me of the bathroom at the train station. Ki-Ki looked at me and pinched her nose, so I knew she smelled it, too. But we kept following Uncle Shin.

It was only when we met Grandpa, Grandma, Auntie Jin, and Uncle Flower in front of a food cart did I realize the smell was coming from there! I looked at the cart — nothing looked horrible. Silver trays full of golden fried squares of what I guessed was tofu. A woman, completely uncon-cerned by us, painted a brown sauce over them. Was it the food that smelled like that? I stood closer and sniffed . . . and then covered my nose and mouth! Yes, it was the food that smelled!

"What is that?" Lissy said, pinching her nose, too.

"*Chou doufu!*" Uncle Shin said. "Stinky tofu! It's famous!"

"Famous for smelling bad?" Lissy choked out.

"Yes," he laughed, "and for tasting delicious. You want one?"

"No way!" I said. "It smells like throw-up!"

chou doufu
(stinky tofu)

Everyone laughed. Grandpa, Grandma, Auntie Jin, and Uncle Flower stood to the side, all of them already eating from plates full of it. They seemed to really like it. And it looked like a lot of people did because as we stood there, person after person came up to the stall and bought some. None of them seemed disgusted.

"Here, try some of mine," Mom offered, holding up a piece of the tofu in her chopsticks.

Ki-Ki shook her head and clamped her lips tight. Lissy and I stared. It looked just like the fried tofu we'd had many times before. How could something that looked so harmless smell so bad?

"You try it," Lissy said to me.

"I don't want to try it!" I said. "You try it!"

"It's really good!" Aunt Bea said. "It's a Taiwan specialty. You shouldn't leave Taiwan without even trying it."

"I'll try it if you try it," Lissy said.

I hesitated. I had eaten raw fish and chicken feet. I should be able to eat some tofu, even if it did smell bad. "Okay," I said finally. "But you go first."

Lissy plugged her nose with her fingers again and reached for Mom's chopsticks. She took a deep breath, made a face like a squished lemon, and dropped the tofu into her mouth. And then swallowed. Everyone clapped and cheered as if she had just won a contest.

"Good for you!" Uncle Shin said. "See, pretty good, right? Now, Pacy, you try it!"

Lissy whispered to me, "I didn't really taste anything. I just swallowed it as fast as I could."

But now it was my turn. I pinched my nose like Lissy did, closed my eyes, carefully put the tofu in my mouth, and chewed. The tofu was soft with kind of a tangy taste that wasn't bad.... But I could still smell it! And in my mouth, it seemed to smell even stronger. I quickly swallowed.

"What did you think? Delicious, right?" Uncle Shin said as he ate his last piece. "I'm going to get some more. Do you want me to get you some?"

Lissy and I both shook our heads. I hoped no one else wanted more. I wanted to get away from the stinky tofu as soon as possible.

Chapter 31

Trouble

fortune-teller
at night market

EVERYONE FINALLY FINISHED EATING THE STINKY tofu, and we continued walking down the street. I was still hungry, but there was no food in the next part of the street. Instead, a row of red booths appeared. I watched as one of the peddlers tapped a gold disc that looked like a metal pancake with a chopstick. *Tap-tap-tap-tap!* The peddler hit it quickly, looking at a sheet of paper at the same time. Were they some sort of drum musicians? If they were, their music wasn't very good.

"Who are they?" I asked, rudely pointing.

"Fortune-tellers," Mom said, pushing my finger down.

More fortune-tellers! I was still surprised when I saw them. I kept thinking fortune-tellers would look more spooky or bizarre. These ones looked the same as Aunt Bea or Uncle Shin, wearing sweatshirts and glasses. I remembered the fortune-teller who had told my fortune, who had also looked so normal. She was the one who said I had a special skill that would stay with me. But my art talent had kept leaving in painting class, so she had been wrong about that. She also said I was going to get into trouble. Maybe she was wrong about that, too.

We passed the fortune-tellers, and then I saw lots of kids crowding around something in the middle of the street. Ki-Ki, Lissy, and I went over to see what was so interesting.

It was a big red plastic tub full of water. In the water, hundreds of goldfish swam and shimmered like shiny pennies.

"What are they for?" I asked.

"It's a game," Aunt Bea said. "You get a net and if you catch a goldfish, you can keep it."

the goldfish
game

"That's it?" Lissy said. "Some game!"

But the game was harder than it sounded. I watched as a pigtailed girl all dressed in red tried to catch a goldfish. She chased an orange fish with her net, trying over and over again to scoop it up. By the time she caught it, the net had crumbled and the fish easily escaped. It was only when she held up her tattered net and wailed did I realize that the nets were made out of paper.

"Can I try?" I asked.

No one answered me. I looked up and Mom, Lissy, Ki-Ki, Shogun, Uncle Shin — everyone — weren't there!

I was alone.

Chapter 32

Lost

photograph of
Dad's mother

I JUMPED UP. MAYBE I JUST HAD TO CATCH UP WITH them. But which way did they go? I couldn't remember which way we had walked from.

I followed the movement of the crowd. There were so many people, but none of them were Mom or Uncle Shin or Grandma or Grandpa. The night market was endless. Food, shopping, and games kept going and going. I kept walking aimlessly, wandering and looking.

Where were they? The longer I walked, the louder the noises grew in my ears. Where were they? Words I couldn't understand tripped and ran into each other over and on top of me. The smoke and smells flooded the air, and the neon signs glared with their garish colors. Where were they? The black sky seemed to come alive, and I felt like I was getting pressed into the mouth of a giant monster. The bright demon-colored red of the fortune-tellers' booths reappeared and the *tap-tap-tapping* of the sticks echoed my heartbeat. Where were they? Where were they? Where were they? I started walking faster and faster. And suddenly, like a stabbing knife, fear cut into me. Where was I?

I was lost. That first fortune-teller had been right. I was in trouble, big trouble.

People swarmed and shoved, walking as if they didn't see me. As if I were invisible to them. The burning air filled my lungs, and I gasped to breathe. I was the tree that no one saw, that didn't exist. I was erased; somehow a ghost had gotten me, and now I was a ghost, too. A hungry ghost, desperate and scared, that no one could see and no one cared about. A sick, nauseous feeling formed at the bottom of my throat. I didn't belong here! This place with the meaningless words and the harsh lights was fading me away. Soon, I'd be gone, evaporating into nothingness. I was going to disappear.

All of the sudden, someone grabbed my arm. I almost screamed, but then I saw it was Shogun.

"Pacy?" he said, and then he said a lot of words in Chinese I didn't understand. But I didn't care. I was so glad to see him! Tears started to pour out of my eyes, and my breath

Shogun when he found me

started to hiccup. Shogun tightened his hand on my arm and pulled me down the street.

Then I saw Mom and Auntie Jin and Aunt Bea, Lissy and Ki-Ki. Seeing all of them again, their familiar faces after being so scared—I cried even harder. Mom hugged me tight and Auntie Jin and Aunt Bea joined in, too. Even Lissy and Ki-Ki were relieved.

"Where were you?" Lissy said. "Everyone is looking for you!"

"You're supposed to stay in one place when you get lost," Aunt Bea said, "so people can find you!"

"Grandma and Grandpa went home, just in case you gave your name card to someone and they brought you there," Auntie Jin said, her words streaming over Aunt Bea's.

I tried to stop crying, but I couldn't. I knew I was too old to cry like this, but the tears flooded from my eyes like an overflowing pot. I hadn't thought about staying in one place or my name card. I had been so scared, I hadn't thought about anything and I still couldn't. All I knew was that I didn't want to be there anymore. I didn't want to be in Taiwan. I wanted to be back in New Hartford, back where I knew where everything was and understood everything and I wasn't a ghost. "I want to go home!" I sobbed.

Mom looked over me at Aunt Bea. "I'll take her back," Mom said. "The rest of you can stay."

Mom held my hand tightly through the crowds, even though it was all wet and slobbery. When we got to the main street out

mom holding my hand as we left the night market

of the night market, instead of going toward the subway, she raised her arm for a taxi. As we got in, she took out a new change purse, green this time, and handed me some tissues.

Seeing Mom's new change purse reminded me about how she was a visiting ghost, too. Her home was New Hartford, just like mine. But this used to be her home. She and Dad chose to become ghosts. In a way, they made us ghosts.

"Why did you and Dad move to America?" I said after blowing my nose.

Mom was quiet for a moment, and I thought she didn't hear me. But suddenly she said, "When we left, things weren't good in Taiwan. There was martial law then."

"What's martial law?" I asked.

"It's when the government is scared and so mistrustful that they are very strict and suspicious with the people," Mom said. "Sometimes they are so strict that they are cruel. We wanted to get away from that."

"What do you mean?" I asked.

"Remember Big Uncle?" Mom said. "The government was cruel to him."

WHEN BIG UNCLE WAS ARRESTED

When Dad was a young boy, Dad's oldest brother — Big Uncle — was the one who supported the whole family. Big Uncle wasn't much older than a boy himself, but he was smart and hardworking; the five brothers, two sisters, the parents, and the grandparents all survived mostly on Big Uncle's salary as a schoolteacher.

But late one night, there was a loud bang on the door, like the sound of arriving thunder. It was the military police! They had some questions they wanted to ask Big Uncle, they said, and they put him in a jeep and disappeared.

The family didn't know what to do. They didn't know where he was, what happened, or why. But they knew the military police were always secretive and always serious. The next day, Dad's mother gathered all the jewelry and money in the house and went from one official to the next, bribing them for information about Big Uncle.

It was a hard time. As the news was whispered that Big Uncle had been taken for political reasons, everyone was afraid. Friends and relatives stayed away. It was almost like Dad's family had become poison. No one wanted to be connected to Dad's family because then they, too, might be arrested. And without Big Uncle's salary, the family was so poor. They even had to beg for scraps to feed their pig. Days and months passed, and you can't even imagine how poor they became. They had to make horrible choices. Sad choices. When Dad's mother had a new baby girl, her mother-in-law forced her to give up the baby to be adopted.

Then, almost two years later, there was another late-night noise at the door. This time it was a single soft knock, tired and resigned. Only Dad heard it, and when he opened the door — there was Big Uncle!

He was in rags and looked like a starving beggar. But it was only then that they found out why he had been arrested. A vice principal at Big Uncle's school had a scholar friend who had been caught with a book on Communism. Because of that, any friends of the scholar and anyone associated with those friends had been arrested. Luckily for Big Uncle, some of those people had connections with the government and were able to get the charges for the whole group overturned, which was why Big Uncle could finally come home.

But even after Big Uncle came home, things weren't easy. He had been cleared of the charges, but people were still afraid *to be connected to him. His reputation was damaged. People looked at Big Uncle as if he were a dangerous bomb. He couldn't teach at his school — or any school — anymore. It was hard to find a job. It was hard to find friends.*

"That's why," Mom continued, "when Dad got the opportunity to go work in America, his family said, 'Go! Go!' They knew it would take him far away, but they wanted him to be in a place where things that happened to Big Uncle could not happen to him."

"I didn't know Dad had a younger sister," I said.

"They try not to talk about her," Mom said. "They were ashamed they couldn't keep her, and I remember if she ever came up in conversation, Dad's mom would cry."

I realized the baby girl was my aunt, an aunt I would never know. I remembered the photo of Dad's mom on our wall back home, her serious eyes staring out. Those were the hungry ghosts, I thought. Sad memories and bad memories were those ghosts that haunted. When Dad's mom was getting her photo taken, there had been ghosts around her. Dad and Big Uncle had ghosts around them, too. Everyone did. Even I had ghosts, not as bad as Big Uncle's, but smaller ones like the mean bus driver and the horrible girls who called me Twinkie and the angry woman at the market in Taichung. Those were the ghosts that always came back, no matter what you did to try to keep them away.

But I thought about Big Uncle and how even though his face looked tired, it still wrinkled into a big smile and his laugh was deep and hearty. I thought about Dad being a young boy, poor and hungry, and then how now he could eat. "The best!" he had said with his eyes sparkling. Those ghosts hadn't stopped them from being alive and happy. They had learned to live with their ghosts. And I could, too.

Chapter 33

Found

dinner back home

GRANDMA AND GRANDPA WERE WAITING, JUST LIKE Auntie Jin said they would be. When they heard our steps climbing the stairs, they threw open the door and sighed as if they hadn't breathed all day. When we reached them, they both hugged me tight, and a few more tears crept down my face. It was just so nice to be there, in the kitchen with the round table I ate at in the morning and sofa that I sat on. When I had said I wanted to go home, I had meant New Hartford, but being here felt good. I realized that being here felt like home, too.

Mom gave me a warm cloth to wash my face, and Grandpa poured me a glass of sugarcane juice. I had just finished my second cup and was feeling better when we heard the familiar pounding up the stairs. As the door opened, everyone came in, looked at me, and smiled broad grins.

"Better?" Auntie Jin and Aunt Bea asked as they patted my shoulders. "Good," Uncle Shin said, giving me a hug. Uncle Flower rubbed me on the head. "Pacy, glad we found you. Glad you are okay."

"I thought you'd stay a lot longer at the night market," Mom said. "We've only been back a little while."

"We did stay for a bit," Uncle Shin said. "But we didn't think it was as much fun without you there, so we decided to come back."

"I won a goldfish!" Ki-Ki said, thrusting a plastic bag full of water and a googly-eyed orange fish at me. "We can share if you want."

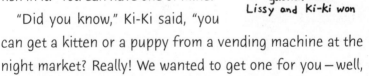

goldfish that
Lissy and Ki-ki won

"No, I won two," Lissy said, dangling her bag with a silver and a black fish in it. "You can have one of mine."

"Did you know," Ki-Ki said, "you can get a kitten or a puppy from a vending machine at the night market? Really! We wanted to get one for you — well, really, for all of us — but Uncle Shin wouldn't let us."

"Good!" Mom said.

"But we brought home a lot of food," Aunt Bea said. "Just in case you didn't get enough."

All the fear I had at the night market was melting away, like ice in front of a warm fire. I felt embarrassed about crying so much and being such a baby about getting lost, but I kind of liked how everyone was being so nice to me. Auntie

Jin got a bowl for our goldfish, and we dropped them in. Lissy said I could choose which fish I wanted, but I knew she wanted the black one and was just being nice. So, to be nice back, I took the silver one.

Aunt Bea and Mom unpacked the food. There was a lot of it — deep-fried golden cubes, pancake-looking bread with green onions, copper-colored rolls of something, meat in brown sauce on rice, a carton of green vegetables cooked with garlic, and fat-fried chicken wings. "These are special," Uncle Shin said as he displayed the wings. "There are no bones in these. They take out the bones and then stuff the wings with fried rice and egg yolks."

chicken wings stuffed with rice and egg

"This isn't all for me, is it?" I asked, looking at all the food. "I'm not that hungry!"

"We didn't know what you would like," Uncle Flower said. "So we let Lissy and Ki-Ki pick a little bit from every stall, too."

"You're lucky we chose," Lissy said, "or else you'd be stuck with more stinky tofu. They make it grilled and fried, and Uncle Shin thought you might want to try both."

Everyone laughed at that, but I was grateful. Just the smell of that tofu would have ruined the rest of the food.

"Well," Mom said, "I don't think Pacy can eat everything, so why don't we all have a second dinner?"

"We should do this every night!" Uncle Shin said, and then

he stopped and gave a wry smile. "I meant the second dinner every night. Not Pacy getting lost."

"Yes, not that," Uncle Flower said, and looked at me. "That was terrible, not knowing where you were. We thought you had disappeared."

I shivered. I had thought I had disappeared, too. But I hadn't. I was still here, and I was glad.

"Hey," Ki-Ki said. "Where's the big one?"

"Oh, the special one!" Auntie Jin said. She looked around and then picked up a plastic bag Shogun had left on the chair. She took out a big carton and opened it on the table. A warm, savory smell drifted out, and I knew right away what they were.

"Dumplings!" I said.

jiaozi
(dumplings)

Everyone laughed, and I joined in. But sitting at the table, I remembered how I had sat there on the first day of painting class and said to Mom, "I don't want to know who I am, then!" That wasn't true. I did want to know who I was. I had thought of myself as a lot of different things here in Taiwan— a Twinkie, a ghost, an artist—and I hadn't felt that my Chinese name fit. But as I looked around the table at everyone, with their faces smiling at me, I felt safe and treasured. I guessed I was a precious thought, after all.

213

Chapter 34

The **Exhibit**

Ki-Ki's paper cut

FOUR DAYS LATER, LISSY, KI-KI, AND I WERE GETTING ready for the exhibit. Grandma said we should look nice, since we were the artists. At first I thought that meant I had to wear my special Chinese dress, but Mom said to save that for Grandma's party. So I just wore my strawberry dress again.

Grandma, Aunt Bea, Auntie Jin, and Uncle Shin came, too. Grandpa wanted to come, but he had to work. The exhibit was in the same building we had our classes in, but on a different floor. It was new to have so many people in the elevator with us. It felt unfamiliar pressing the number five instead of the other three numbers we were used to, and when the elevator doors opened, the floor was really different, too.

Instead of a hall of classrooms, there was a glass wall on one side with clean Chinese writing on it. I think it probably said GALLERY on it, because I could see it was like a museum inside.

Pictures hung on the wall under spotlights, little sculptures stood on blocks, and the floor was shiny and polished. I felt a little awed and unsure if we should enter. But I thought I saw Alex and Eva from my class in the gallery, so we went in.

Everything looked so good, like real artists had done it. One wall had all the work from Lissy's class. About twenty scrolls hung next to each other, each painting mounted on red silk with a dragon pattern on it.

"Which one is yours?" Mom asked Lissy.

Lissy walked down the length of the room. "Here it is," she said, stopping in the middle.

To me, it looked just like everyone else's but with different characters. Well, the brush strokes were thicker. Lissy's painting had only one character, so the marks were thick. The scroll to the right of hers had a whole line of characters that looked like a map of dance directions.

"What does it say?" I asked her.

"'Happiness,'" she said. I looked closer. I had stamped "happiness" on my painting using my teacher's chop, but I didn't remember the character looking like that. Maybe I was remembering wrong.

"Mine is over here!" Ki-Ki said, pulling at us.

Lissy's "happiness" calligraphy

215

The paper cuts in Ki-Ki's class weren't mounted on scrolls but were instead framed under glass. If the teacher hadn't given us the talk about mounting the paintings, I would've thought it was kind of cheap that we didn't get ours framed, too. Anyway, the paper cuts were a lot smaller, so they were probably cheaper to frame.

Ki-Ki pointed at a red paper cut on the wall. It was like a snowflake, but it had intricate flowers and leaves radiating out of a center star. I was really impressed.

"Did you really do that?" Lissy asked. She was impressed, too.

Ki-Ki nodded. We all crowded around it.

"So good, Ki-Ki!" Uncle Shin said. "Was it hard to do?"

"No," Ki-Ki said, shaking her head. "But it took a lot of time. Especially cutting the little pieces."

I was feeling a little jealous. Where was my painting? The work from my class had to be somewhere. I looked around and saw a row of olive-green scrolls on the wall in the other room. Those must be ours.

I left everyone with Ki-Ki's paper cut and walked over to the scrolls. Yes, they were my class's. Mounting the paintings did make them look finished. The brownish-green silk had a subtle, small leaf pattern all over it. I was glad it wasn't red, like Lissy's, because I didn't think red would look good with my pink birds. And there they were! Right at the end, next to Audrey Chiang's painting.

I felt proud when I saw my painting. Somehow, the mounting had made the colors more delicate-looking, and the sheen of the silk seemed to make my painting glow, too. I glanced over at Audrey's. Hers looked better, too. I worked hard not to glare at it.

Lissy came over to me, holding something in a napkin.

"There are refreshments!" she told me. "Just soda and different kinds of cookies, though."

She stopped in front of the paintings. "Which one's yours?" she asked, cocking her head. I pointed. I didn't tell her that the three birds were supposed to me, her, and Ki-Ki. She might think that was stupid and laugh.

"Huh," she said. Then she squinted close. "What does the chop say?"

"'Happiness,'" I told her.

"No, it doesn't!" she said. "I should know. I had to paint that character a hundred times."

"*Happiness* is what the paper said," I insisted. "Maybe it's just another Chinese word for 'happiness.'"

Uncle Shin, Mom, and Ki-Ki came over. Uncle Shin and Mom had cookies in their hands, and Ki-Ki had cookie on her face.

"This one is yours?" Mom asked. "Very good!" Uncle Shin nodded in agreement.

"But that doesn't say *happiness*, does it?" Lissy said, pointing at my chop mark.

"Hmm," Uncle Shin peered close so that his nose almost

touched the paper. "No. It says, um, how do you say it... 'unchangeable', 'permanent.'"

"'Unchangeable'?" I said. I didn't even remember that being a choice.

"More like 'lasting,'" Mom said. "'Forever.'"

Forever? Oh no, someone must have mixed the teacher's chops up, and I had used the *forever* one. That made no sense with my painting! Why would three birds wish for forever? Why would Lissy, Ki-Ki, and I wish for that?

"forever" stamp

Then I saw Audrey Chiang. She was wearing a dark purple dress with black buttons. She was walking to her painting, which meant toward us, with a tall, thin lady with short hair. I guessed she was her mother.

Audrey nodded at me, and the woman said something in Chinese, probably asking if Audrey knew us. Audrey nodded again, and the woman smiled at us.

"*Ni hao, ni hao,*" she said, and then she said something to me in Chinese. I tried to guess what she was saying. Either she was asking if I was in Audrey's class or which painting was mine. Or maybe she was asking if I liked painting. I had no idea. So I just shook my head.

"*Bu hui shuo Hanyu,*" Mom jumped in. I could figure out what Mom said there! *She can't speak Chinese.*

"*Bu hui shuo!*" the woman said. I knew that, too. *Can't speak Chinese!* Her eyes widened as if Mom had said

meeting Audrey's
mother

something horrible, and she looked at me as if I had suddenly turned into a purple worm. She was definitely Audrey's mother.

The woman said some more words in Chinese to Mom. I couldn't figure those out, but Mom looked embarrassed and shook her head. Again! I wanted to let out a big sigh. The same heavy, discouraged feeling draped over me, like it always did when this happened. I glanced at Audrey, expecting to see a mirror of her mother's scorn.

But when I looked up, Audrey looked... sorry? She looked

uncomfortable, as if she thought her mother's words were rude. Her eyes met mine, and she gave me a small, rueful smile.

I was confused. Maybe Audrey wasn't that bad? I wasn't sure, but suddenly I didn't hate her completely. I still wanted my painting to beat hers, though. Then Mom and Audrey's mother stopped talking, and Audrey and her mother walked away.

"What did she say?" I asked.

"Oh, nothing important, hello and where do you live," Mom said. "Those kind of things."

"No, the part where you were talking about me," I said.

"She was surprised that you didn't know Chinese and couldn't believe I didn't teach you," Mom said. "Is her daughter your friend?"

"Not really," I said. Audrey was more like my enemy. But now I was more interested in what Audrey's mother had said. It sounded like she thought it was Mom's fault I didn't know Chinese. I wonder if Mom felt as bad as I did when people thought I was a Twinkie.

"Do you wish you taught us Chinese?" I asked Mom.

Mom stopped and thought seriously. "Yes," Mom said. "Sometimes, I regret I didn't teach all of you when you were younger. But I can't change that now. And just because you don't know the language doesn't mean you are not Taiwanese."

"But I'm not Taiwanese," I said. "I'm American."

"You're Taiwanese-American," Mom said. "And, no matter what, that's what you'll always be."

Forever, I thought. I'd always be Taiwanese-American, no matter if I spoke Chinese, made my eyes bigger, or was called a Twinkie. Even if I didn't like it. Being Taiwanese-American was like making a brush stroke. The mark couldn't be erased, and the ink and the paper could never be separated. They were joined forever.

"Mom!" I said, grabbing her arm before she walked away. "For my name chop, can I have my name carved in Chinese and English? Can they do that?"

"Yes." Mom nodded, a little surprised. "I'm sure they can. I'll order them today."

"Good," I said, and I felt as if I had just taken off a winter coat after discovering it was summer. I was glad I had found my identity.

Chapter 35

Being the Best

Eva Wong happy
after winning

I WAS SO HAPPY ABOUT FIGURING OUT MY NAME CHOP that I almost forgot about the ribbons for the best class painting. Audrey Chiang hadn't forgotten, though. As I stood by the refreshment table, trying to decide between an almond cookie and a buttery, lacy-looking one, she came by and hissed, "They're giving the prizes now!"

"They" were all the teachers, five of them together in a group. I recognized my teacher — he had a clipboard in his hand. An older lady with a yellow rose pinned to her bright orange shirt carried the prize ribbons in her hands. They were blue, and, against her shirt, they seemed to glow.

They were walking to each wall, looking at the list on the clipboard, and then pinning a ribbon next to the winning art. Everyone began to follow them. It felt like a circus parade. When a teacher in a green dress pinned a ribbon onto a rose embroidery, everyone clapped and shouted.

Lissy's class was next, and the blue ribbon went to one that had two columns of words up and down the paper. Lissy didn't seem that disappointed. She just smiled and clapped, and we kept following the teachers. They were heading over to the paper cuts. One of the younger teachers walked over with a blue ribbon and pinned it onto Ki-Ki's paper cut! Ki-Ki had won a ribbon!

Uncle Shin, Lissy, and I whooped, and Mom and Aunt Bea clapped so hard that I could see their hands turning red. Ki-Ki beamed a thousand smiles. I quickly scanned the rest of the paper cuts. Hers was the best. She deserved it. I felt proud.

But I couldn't pay any more attention, because now they were walking over to my class's paintings. We were the last group, I guess because our work was on the farthest wall. Audrey Chiang watched, unsmiling, just staring at the group as if trying to hypnotize them. My hands went cold, and the cookie I had eaten seemed to be stuck in my throat.

The lady in orange handed my teacher the last blue ribbon. He looked around at all of us and smiled. He checked his clipboard and walked down toward Audrey's painting and mine. Which one would it be? Would I beat Audrey?

No. The teacher walked by both mine and Audrey's and pinned the ribbon on a painting of two birds flying under a flowering branch. I hadn't painted that. Neither had Audrey. A squeal of happiness came from the audience, and I saw Eva jump up and down in happiness. I hadn't won. Each one of Eva's hops seemed to flatten me, like a teddy bear losing its stuffing. My eyes stung with disappointment, but I was able to blink it away and clap politely. At least Audrey hadn't beaten me.

Eva's winning painting

I looked at her. She was clapping politely, too, but the smile on her face looked more like she was clenching her teeth. She looked like a cat ready to attack.

The crowd began to spread out, and I walked over to Lissy, Aunt Bea, and Uncle Shin. Grandma, Auntie Jin, and Mom were taking photos of Ki-Ki by her winning paper cut. I felt better seeing Ki-Ki grin. It made sense that Ki-Ki would win. Her name meant "victorious thought." Besides, Lissy hadn't won, either.

Grandma & Mom
taking a photo of Ki-ki

"I just want to know what I could've done to make my painting better." Audrey's voice carried over to us, and we all looked over. Audrey was questioning our teacher like he was a spy. Her mother was standing behind her, nodding.

"That girl is weird," Lissy said. Then she pretended she was talking to Audrey. "Your painting wasn't the best. Get over it already."

"Maybe she just wants to know how she can improve," Aunt Bea said. "That's always good."

"No." I shook my head. "She just wanted to win."

"I know people like that. Some people are only happy when they are first or the best," Uncle Shin said, and then he looked at us with a playful grin. "But, for me, that's no fun."

"Pacy," Grandma said. "Let's take a photo of you by your painting."

"But I didn't win!" I said.

"I still love it," Grandma said. "I think it's beautiful."

"Yes! Your painting is still good anyway!" Auntie Jin said. "Go stand by it!"

"And smile!" Mom said.

I followed their orders. Grandma, Mom, and Auntie Jin clicked away at their cameras and then pushed Lissy toward her painting. As I turned around, I saw Eva by her painting.

"Congratulations," I said. I was still a little jealous, but I tried not to let it show. I looked at her painting. The brown birds were soft and graceful, and the flowers had fine, delicate heart-shaped petals. It was a really good painting. I still kind of liked mine better, but I could see why hers had won a ribbon. I wondered why I had never really paid that much attention to Eva or her paintings before. I guessed it was because I was so busy watching Audrey.

"Thanks!" Eva said. She was bubbling over with happiness. "I just loved painting class! I can't believe it's over. I'm going to miss it. The class was so much fun, don't you think?"

I smiled at her, but I was surprised. Painting class, fun? I thought.about all the days I spent there, gritting my teeth at Audrey and trying to force my art talent to paint better. It hadn't been fun for me.

And then I realized I was more like Uncle Shin than I was like Audrey. If my painting had won tonight, I would've been really happy. But when Clifford had us pick the four best pleasures in life, being the best hadn't even come to my mind. Maybe it wasn't that Audrey was so horrible; maybe it was just that trying to be better than everyone else was what she thought was fun, the only thing that made her happy. But it wasn't for me. Winning was fun, but it wasn't the only thing that made me happy.

"I really liked your painting," Eva said. "I thought all your paintings in class were nice."

"Thanks," I said. Eva's big smile reminded me of Melody's. "What chop did you use?"

"Well, I meant to use the chop that said 'profundity,' because it sounded good, even though I don't know what it means," Eva said. "But my mom told me that the stamp says 'spring'!"

"That happened to me, too!" I said. "I thought I was stamping 'happiness,' but I got 'forever'!"

"Someone must have mixed up all the stamps," she said.

"What does *profundity* mean, anyway?" I asked.

"I still don't know," Eva said. We looked at each other, and we both burst out laughing. Why had I been so caught up with Audrey? I should've talked to Eva before.

"Eva! We have to go!" a woman, probably Eva's mom, called.

"I better go," she said. "Good-bye."

"Good-bye," I said, and I felt sad. Why had I wasted all those days of class, making myself unhappy, trying to beat Audrey? Instead, I could've become friends with Eva, and it would've been fun. Instead of dreading painting class, I could've loved it just like Eva did. And maybe Eva and I could've become really good friends like me and Melody. But now it was too late. I probably wouldn't see Eva again.

"In Chinese painting," the teacher had said, "you can't take back anything you do." I guessed that was true in real life, too. But I wished it wasn't.

Chapter 36

Four Days Left

Grandma's corsage

ALL THE DAYS WERE RUSHING BY. LIKE A TRAIN, TIME WAS moving faster and faster. There were only six days left here in Taiwan, then five, and now four. The crowds, busyness, and dirtiness of the city didn't bother me so much anymore. I didn't feel scared about how everything was so different than in New Hartford. Of course, I still didn't like it when shopkeepers looked at me strangely because I didn't speak Chinese — though, when I thought about it, sometimes the shopkeepers in New Hartford gave me the same strange look.

But I had gotten used to eating big meals and laughing even when I didn't know what was funny. I liked going to the street market and choosing wax apples and munching them on the way home. It was those everyday things that happened over and over again that I couldn't imagine ending. But they would, once we left Taiwan. Our time here was running out.

eating a wax
apple & walking

Tomorrow was Grandma's party, and we would be leaving two days later. I was excited about Grandma's party, but it was odd to think we would be leaving so soon. Aunt Yoko, Uncle Sam, baby Sylvia, and Auntie Kim were in Taiwan now, too, and everyone was busy doing things—talking on the phone, ordering things, and getting special dresses dry-cleaned. Uncle Flower, Julian, Shogun, and their father were always hiding someplace to practice their "secret." I really wanted to know what the surprise was. Lissy said she thought they were going to put on a play or sing a song. But I didn't know why that would have to be a secret.

The main room in Grandpa's place felt like a flower shop, full of colors and sweet smells. Bouquets of flowers had been delivered, big pink flowers with feathery ferns. A wreath made of flowers came, too. We weren't sure if they were gifts or things ordered for the party.

The only thing we were sure of for the party was a clear plastic box that held a regal purple orchid decorated with a sheer lavender ribbon and ferns. "Grandma's corsage," Mom said, and she put it in the refrigerator. It was funny to see it next to the eggs and juice.

"I hope when I turn sixty, people have a big party for me," Lissy said.

"Me, too," I said. But I couldn't really imagine turning sixty years old. It seemed so far away and unreal and...old! "You really deserve a party when you're sixty."

"Uh-huh." Ki-Ki nodded. "Because you're so old then!"

Uncle Flower was on his way out to go practice "the secret" but stopped when he heard us. "Is sixty so old?" he said, laughing.

We nodded.

"Well, an old emperor agreed with you," he said. "It's another reason why we celebrate a person's sixtieth birthday."

THE VALUE OF ELDERS

Once, there was a young emperor who didn't believe his elders held much wisdom. In fact, he felt as soon as they reached the age of sixty, they became useless and were simply a burden to the state and family. Convinced of this, he made a decree that once a person reached the age of sixty, he or she would be executed.

The emperor had an adviser who not only did not agree with this, but also had a father (to whom he went to for all advice) who was about to turn sixty years old. "I can't let my father be executed!" he said to himself. But what to do? Finally he decided to hide his father in a mountain cave, bringing him food every day.

The adviser soon had other worries, as well. A neighboring state

constantly clashed with the emperor's kingdom, and a war seemed inevitable. So it was a great surprise when one day an emissary from the state arrived seeking an audience with the emperor. At his visit, the emissary brought out two pieces of rough wood. They looked exactly alike and were the same shape and thickness.

"These pieces of wood are from the same tree. One is from the branch and the other from the root," the emissary said. "If you can tell me which is from the root and which is from the branch, our state will cede our authority to you."

The emperor could not tell the difference. Neither could any of the court officials or advisers. The emperor offered a reward throughout his kingdom, yet no one stepped forward. The neighboring state began to grow restless, and war loomed closer and closer.

When the adviser brought his hidden father food that day, the

emissary with two pieces of wood

father couldn't help noticing his son's worried face.

"What is it?" he asked.

The adviser told his father about the emissary's visit. "How can one tell the difference between wood from a branch and wood from a root?" he said.

His father laughed. "Ho, ho, quite easily," he said. "Put them both in water. The root will sink, and the branch will float."

The adviser hurried away and did as his father told him. It was true! The emperor solved the state's riddle, and both sides put down their arms. War was averted! There was great rejoicing.

"You are a brilliant man! I will reward you well!" the emperor said to his adviser. "How did you find the solution?"

The adviser kowtowed low. "I did not find the solution myself. It was my father and his wisdom and experience that told me. For my reward, I ask that you spare him execution for his age."

The emperor was astounded. "Your father?" he said, and then after much thought, "I have thought that the old are useless and foolish. However, it was only an elder's wisdom and experience that prevented war. I was wrong."

The next day, the emperor took back his decree of execution for all elders. The adviser brought his father back from the mountains, and the emperor held a grand celebration in the old man's honor. Coincidentally, it was also his sixtieth birthday.

"And that became a tradition," Uncle Flower said. "That's why we are making Grandma's birthday party so big, with all the flowers, food —"

"And your secret?" I interrupted.

"Yes!" Uncle Flower said, smiling. "We want to make sure this is a big and special celebration. The emperor, so long ago, honored the sixtieth birthday, so we try to do the same."

"Yeah," I said. "Because it's so old."

Uncle Flower sighed.

Chapter 37

Gift for Grandma

GRACE PACY

mark that
my name chop
made

WHEN UNCLE FLOWER LEFT, I LOOKED AT LISSY AND
Ki-Ki. "We're the only ones not doing anything for Grandma's party," I said.

"Well, it's not like we can help with anything," Lissy said.
"We can't speak Chinese, and we don't know where anything is."

That was true.

"We should give Grandma a birthday present!" Ki-Ki said.
"You have to give a present at a birthday!"

"I don't think we have time to go shopping for a birthday present," Mom told us. "Today, we have to pick up your
art from the exhibit, your name chops, and Lissy's photos. If
there is time afterward, we can try."

But there wasn't any time afterward. On the subway,
even as Lissy enjoyed the glory of her album, I fingered the

my finished
name chop

smooth stone of my carved name chop, and Ki-Ki clutched her blue ribbon, we felt ashamed. We had been in Taiwan for twenty-four days and had known about Grandma's party the whole time, yet we didn't have a single birthday gift. That was pretty bad.

"Grandma won't care if you don't give her anything," Mom said. "But if you really want to give her something, she wouldn't want a gift from the store anyway. You should make her some-thing or give her something that is really from you."

I thought hard as the subway screeched to a stop and we all walked back home. The sun was set-ting, and the sky looked as if bright

feeling ashamed on subway

pink and orange paint had been spilled on it. We were go-ing to be flying home in that sky soon. I wished I could slow down time.

After we got inside, I ran for some scrap paper. I was eager to try out my chop. I plied open the shallow, round tin of ink that we had bought for the chops. The ink was vivid red and sticky like paste. With a firm grip, I rubbed my chop in the tin, making sure the whole surface was covered with ink. Then, as hard as I dared, I stamped the paper. *Clunk!* Carefully, I lifted it, gently holding down the paper as it tried to stick. There it was.

I looked at it with satisfaction. It seemed to look back at me cheerfully. The crisp red square, the Chinese characters, and GRACE PACY in block letters. Should I have gotten *Grace Pacy Lin*, since that was my whole name in English? Hmm. Well, some of the Chinese characters meant *Lin*, but none meant *Grace*. So maybe it was okay. Maybe it made things kind of equal. *Grace* was the part of me that was all American, *Lin* was the part that was all Asian, but *Pacy* was both. Besides, *Grace Pacy Lin* probably wouldn't have fit. *Grace Pacy* looked a little squished to me already.

I gently rubbed it with my finger. The ink had dried already, not a line smeared. Anyway, on the paper, my mark, my identity, was forever.

I took out my painting from the exhibit. I rolled it out, the heavy, stiff silk felt rich against my fingers. The pink birds looked happy sitting on their bamboo, their colors delicate and vivid at the same time. I was kind of surprised that I still liked it. Because it hadn't won the ribbon, I thought maybe it wasn't any good. But I had thought it was good before Eva won the ribbon and the painting hadn't changed at all. Just because it hadn't won, why should I think any different about it now? And even if Audrey had been a better painter than me sometimes, I was still an artist. My talent was forever, too. I had thought it had kept disappearing, but it was still there. I just hadn't been looking at it the right way.

The pink birds were on bamboo. When you painted bamboo, that meant you were wishing something, I remembered. What were the birds wishing? I had never figured that out. If the birds were me, Lissy, and Ki-Ki, then maybe we were wishing Grandma a happy birthday. Grandma had said she loved my painting. I decided I'd give it to her.

But it wasn't finished yet. I rubbed my chop in the red paste again, over and over again, double the number of times I did before. I wanted this chop mark to be perfect. I took a deep breath and carefully centered my hand where I wanted the mark to be. *Clunk!* I stamped.

my finished painting

I was almost afraid to lift the chop to see the mark. What if I had ruined the whole painting? But I carefully lifted it. Perfect!

237

I sat back and looked at the whole painting. The three birds, the "forever" mark, and my name. The tiger on my chop grinned at me. The painting was perfect. It was the perfect gift for Grandma. Now Grandma's birthday party could come!

Chapter 38

Grandma's Party

Grandma
all dressed up
for the party

WHEN WE WOKE UP THE NEXT MORNING, IT SEEMED like the day was already at full speed. I had said that Lissy, Ki-Ki, and I had nothing to do for Grandma's party, but even we were rushing and running around. It was like we were trying to catch Grandma's party in a chase.

"If you have a gift for Grandma, put it in this bag," Aunt Bea said. She and Auntie Jin were leaving before us to get the restaurant ready. "We'll bring it for the gift table."

I put my rolled-up painting in the bag, and Mom pushed me to get ready. We had to get all dressed up in our fancy Chinese dresses. I remembered that when we packed them, I had thought we would be wearing them all the time, since they were our only Chinese clothes. But this was the first time we were wearing them all summer. Part of all the busyness and hurrying around had been to get our clothes to fit. Mom had made us try them on in the morning, and they had all been too tight. In mine, I had felt like a bulging caterpillar trapped in a cocoon, and Lissy's dress wouldn't even zip up.

Mom was going to run out and buy us new ones, but Grandma had shook her head. Instead, Grandma turned all he dresses inside out and took out stitches and resewed them. Now my silk dress wasn't tight anywhere, except for at the collar. But it had always

Grandma fixing my dress

been tight there; that was just the way Chinese dresses were.

I was really disappointed that we didn't get new dresses. I had never liked my dress, anyway. I was still wearing the frog-green one that Lissy outgrew. As I buttoned the smooth silk collar, I saw there were small Chinese symbols embroidered on it. I had never paid attention to them before, but now I saw one was a character I had seen before. Which one was it?

"What does this mean again?" I asked Mom, pointing at the symbol. "Is it 'forever'?"

"No," Mom said, "This one is 'happiness,' remember? They usually put the word for 'happiness' on clothes for kids and 'long life' on clothes for adults."

Happiness. Like Lissy's painting. "Long life" must have been the symbol that was on Grandma's dress, then. Grandma wore a dress the rich color of the fine, polished, red-stained wood-carving and a green jade bracelet and button-shaped earrings. Mom pinned the large purple orchid near Grandma's collar. I wondered if it was still cold from being in the refrigerator.

me in my
fancy Chinese dress

At the restaurant, there were already people waiting. Grandma's party was in a private room in the back, and when she and Grandpa entered, a great cheer went up. But I didn't really hear it, because I was looking at everything. No wonder Aunt Bea and Auntie Jin had left early. They had had a lot to do. At every dinner table, there was a vase of flowers, and on each of the chairs was a box holding a decorated rice bowl. The bowls were deep pink with a design of curlicue flowers surrounding the Chinese long-life symbol (which I now knew). Mom said they were party favors for the guests.

On the side, there was a gift table that was covered with presents. I didn't see my painting there, but maybe it was underneath. There were so many gifts! Some of them weren't wrapped, and we could see that they were gold Chinese symbols mounted on red velvet or silk and framed. I saw a long-life symbol in the pile. All the gifts looked expensive. I wondered if the symbols were made of real gold.

A table with a bright red silk cloth was right by the door with some black markers.

Uncle Shin
signing the red fabric

"Here, sign your name," Uncle Shin told us.
"Why?" I asked.

"It's kind of a guest book," he told us, "but Chinese style."

The cloth was already marked with black signatures and Chinese symbols. I thought it ruined the cloth, which was smooth, shiny silk. It could've been made into a beautiful dress or shirt if it hadn't been messed up by all the markers. But since it was already spoiled, I wrote my name in the corner. I wrote it in English and Chinese, just like my chop, though I wasn't completely sure if I got all my Chinese name right.

Aunt Bea came up to Uncle Shin and talked to him in Taiwanese.

"Time for me to be the master!" he joked at us before he strode away to the middle of the room. "Master of the ceremony, I mean."

And after clinking his wineglass with a fork, Uncle Shin began to make a speech to everyone in the room. It was in Taiwanese, of course, so I didn't know what he was saying. But Grandma and Grandpa looked happy and proud standing next to him. People laughed and clapped at different times until finally Uncle Shin said something very loudly. This made everyone clap even louder, and then people started to move. Mom pushed us toward the dinner tables. It was time to eat!

Chapter 39

Lots of Gifts

red envelope
with money

FOOD WAS PLACED ON THE TABLE IN A RUSH. AS SOON as we sat down, the waiters almost threw down a big bowl of thick, silvery soup; a platter of shrimp with nuts that looked as if they were candy-coated; a golden roasted chicken already sliced into bite-size pieces; a dark brown duck with snowy steamed buns surrounding it; and shiny jade-green vegetables with black mushrooms. There were also little barbecued birds, one for each person at the table.

"Are these baby chickens?" I asked.

"Quail," Uncle Shin said.

By now, I was no longer shocked by anything we ate. Compared with all the other foods I had eaten, quails were pretty ordinary.

"You notice how there are a lot of birds for dinner?" Uncle Flower said. "The quails, chicken, and duck? They are to symbolize the phoenix, which is the mythical bird that represents the empress. Having all these birds is a way to honor Grandma."

"Really?" I asked.

"I should know," Uncle Flower said. "I listened to your Auntie Jin talk about the menu for months and months."

In the center of the table, on a big plate that matched the design of the rice bowl gifts, there was a mountain of yellow noodles stir-fried with meat and slices of green onions.

"And you have to have this," Uncle Flower said, putting a big scoop of noodles on my plate. He had to lift his arms high in the air to make sure the long noodles didn't touch the tablecloth.

"Why?" Ki-Ki asked.

"Because they are long-life noodles," Uncle Flower said. "It's a tradition for birthdays."

"Why?" she asked again.

"They say there was a man who lived to be eight hundred years old," Uncle Flower said. "He had a very, very long face. *Mianchang* is the word for 'long noodles,'

platter of long-life noodles

and it sounds like the word for 'long face,' too. So, by eating these noodles we hope we will live as long as the long-faced man."

245

"He really lived to be eight hundred years old?" I said.

"Who knows?" Uncle Flower said. "But people have been eating noodles for even longer than that."

So far, Grandma's birthday party was a lot like Clifford's wedding, which we went to last year. Everything was in Chinese and Taiwanese, and there was a lot of food and a lot of people — mainly adults, too.

Then suddenly, the lights began to flicker. *BANG-ba-ba-ba-BANG! BANG!* A deafening, rhythmic banging thundered through the room and made us all jump. I covered my ears with my hands. The sound seemed to push people away, and we could see a drummer standing at the front of the room hitting a large drum as tall as his waist. *BANG-ba-ba-ba-BANG! BANG!* It was so loud! I saw the muscles in the drummer's arms with each strike.

"What's going on?" Ki-Ki said, clinging to Mom. But Mom didn't have a chance to answer, because two huge Chinese lions came springing into the room!

I had never seen the Chinese lion dance before in person. I had seen photos of it and parts of it on TV, but never right in front of me. I knew they were people in costume, but they really did look like strange, wild beasts. There were two bright yellow lions, the color of sunflowers, with patterns of sparkling sequins and wavy hair. Their giant, fur-trimmed eyes made up most of their oversize heads. Designs of shiny gold, red, and black were painted all over. Pom-poms like fuzzy cherries bounced over their noses and round horns grew out of the tops of their heads. But it was their large, grinning mouths full of painted teeth that made you feel like you couldn't trust them.

lion dance

The lions jumped and darted back and forth, sometimes in unison, sometimes at each other. You couldn't tell if they were playing or attacking or if their mouths were laughing or snarling. Every movement was to the loud BANG-ba-ba-ba-BANG! BANG! of the drum, until it seemed like they were just flashes of gold and red.

"I don't like it!" Ki-Ki said loudly. Her voice filled the gaps of sound in between the drumming.

"Shhh!" I hissed at her, and Lissy nudged her, too. "Stop! That's rude!"

Ki-Ki didn't care. She scrunched her eyes and covered her ears tightly. She didn't scream, but I could tell that most of the guests had seen her by the amused smiles on their faces. My face burned with embarrassment. I heard someone ask Uncle Shin a question in Chinese.

"*Meiguo*," Uncle Shin replied.

"Ah." The person nodded. "*Meiguo hua qiao.*"

American. Again. Now Ki-Ki had made us look like we were a bunch of babies and almost ruined the show. Somehow we were always doing something wrong.

But the booming drum made any kind of talking impossible, and the bright colors of the leaping and swaying lions were hypnotizing. With a final *BANG-ba-ba-ba-BANG! BANG! BANG! BANG!* the two lions fell to the floor at Grandma's feet. As the silence soaked through the room, it was replaced by loud clapping and cheering. The lions stood up, shook off their bodies, and took off their heads. Underneath, grinning, were Uncle Flower, Shogun, Julian, and their father! This was what they had been practicing all the time! This was the secret! I was a little jealous.

Everyone clapped even louder, and Grandma and Grandpa jumped to their feet to hug them. People started getting up and walking around. The waiters began to put new dishes on the table and serve tea. We followed Uncle Shin to the front of the room.

"You were really good!" I said to Julian. She was younger than me, but she was just as tall. The small hairs that had escaped her braid were moist from her sweat. She was still a little out of breath, but she gave us a shy smile and her eyes lit up so that they looked like the inside of a poppy flower.

"Thank you," she said.

"Everyone liked it!" I said. It was hard to think of what to say that she would understand. "Well, except Ki-Ki. I think she was scared."

"Ki-Ki, lion," she said. "Not used."

"Yes," I said. "She wasn't used to the Chinese lions."

"Not used," Julian said. "No like."

"Yeah, you don't like things you aren't used to," I said, and then I stopped. That wasn't really true. I hadn't been used to sushi, but now I kind of liked it. And I hadn't been used to wax apples or the subway or the markets or sugarcane juice, and those were some of my favorite things. I hadn't been used to Taiwan, but now I liked it, too.

Uncle Flower said something to Julian in Chinese, and the waiters began serving the peach buns and the turtle cakes. Julian and Shogun went to change out of their costumes, and Lissy and I went back to the table. Ki-Ki was already sitting there, completely happy now that the lions were gone. The peach buns looked prettier than I remembered them, pink and white and soft. The turtle cakes didn't look as much like a turtle as I thought they would. Since the peach buns looked so realistic, I was expecting the turtle cakes to be green with a head and a tail. But the turtle cakes were flattish ovals and shiny red and sticky-looking, as if they were made of Jell-O.

The molded turtle pattern on top of the cakes made them look like oversize plastic jewels from Ki-Ki's Barbie doll.

Mom cut one of the turtle cakes into pieces, and I saw it

turtle cakes

was filled with red-bean paste, just like the peach buns. But before I could take a bite, Uncle Shin was at the front of the room again making a speech, with Grandma and Grandpa standing behind him. He was speaking in Taiwanese, and he called Aunt Bea, Auntie Jin, Uncle Flower, Shogun, Julian, and their father to stand next to him. It was probably to praise them for doing such a good lion dance. Everyone was clapping, and I felt a little jealous again, as well as a little ashamed. All the uncles and aunts and cousins had done great things for this party, and we hadn't done anything—except for Ki-Ki to be scared of the lions. We were from *Meiguo*, and I felt like we had made America look bad.

But then I heard Uncle Shin say, "Lissy, Pacy, and Ki-Ki!"

Mom walked forward, motioning us to follow. But before we moved, Auntie Jin shoved a bag at Lissy. "Give Grandma her gifts now," she whispered. I had forgotten about my painting. There it was, rolled up in the bag with another cylinder and a small flat board. Those must be Lissy's and Ki-Ki's gifts. I wondered what they were.

We all gave both Grandpa and Grandma hugs, and then

Lissy stepped forward and took out the paper cylinder from the bag and gave it to Grandma. "Happy birthday," Lissy said. Grandma unrolled it. It was a poster of Lissy! It was from her photo shoot! She was in that blue Chinese dress, holding an oiled umbrella, and smiling flirtatiously at the audience. The real Lissy turned bright pink, but everyone clapped and Grandpa said "So beautiful!" while Grandma hugged her.

Lissy handed me the bag, and I took out my painting. Grandma didn't even unroll it before she hugged me. Her face wrinkled into a hundred smiles. Someone said something to her in Chinese, urging Grandma to show everyone my painting. When she did, a flattering cry of "ohh!" went all across the room before another round of applause. I knew the painting was good. The pink birds and the bamboo all seemed to glow together.

I gave the bag to Ki-Ki, who took out her flat board. It was covered with gold paint and sparkles. It was very shiny. Ki-Ki had written in big letters #1 GRANDMA. I laughed. Ki-Ki had made Grandma an award! She probably got the idea from winning her ribbon.

After hugging Ki-Ki, Grandma held up the award for everyone to see. She lifted it over her head, like a prize-winning boxer, and laughter thundered through the room as people clapped at the same time.

"I didn't know that we'd be giving the gifts in front of

everyone," Lissy said. "I wouldn't have given Grandma the poster if I knew that."

"Why?" I said. "Grandma liked it. The poster was a good idea."

"You think so?" Lissy said, looking relieved.

I nodded. Giving Grandma the poster meant I wouldn't have to see a huge version of a weird-looking Lissy hanging at home. To me, it was a great idea.

"*Gau! Gau!*" a guest said to Mom, nodding toward us. Mom beamed. She looked just like Ki-Ki after she had won the blue ribbon.

"What did he say?" I asked Mom. "What does *gau* mean?"

"It means 'talented,'" Mom said. "He said you all are very good."

I smiled. Inside, I felt cozy and warm as if I were a soup dumpling myself. In fact, I felt like I was going to burst with happiness, I felt so glad. We were good. Even though we were Americans and we didn't speak Chinese, people in Taiwan still liked us.

And, I realized, that was what the three birds on the bamboo had been wishing for. Lissy, Ki-Ki, and I had been wishing to like Taiwan and for Taiwan to like us. The wish had come true. Some parts of Taiwan, like Grandma and Grandpa, even loved us.

But I couldn't think anymore, because Grandpa was motioning me, Lissy, Ki-Ki, and the cousins toward him and Grandma. Now what? As we came forward, Grandma reached into her purse and gave us each a bright red envelope, the color of the last roses of summer. "*Hong bao*," Mom said. "Lucky money. It's a gift."

We got gifts on Grandma's birthday? That seemed backward, but no one else thought it was odd. Lissy, Ki-Ki, and I grinned at one another. We had never gotten birthday presents at someone else's birthday party before, but we liked it. I knew we weren't supposed to open gifts in front of people, but I couldn't help sneaking a peek inside the envelope. Grandma had given us American money, and I counted three twenty-dollar bills! That was sixty dollars! *Wow!* She must have given us sixty dollars because she was sixty years old. We each rushed up to Grandma and Grandpa to thank them.

"I hope we come to your birthday every year!" I said to Grandma.

She gave me a big hug. "Me, too," she said.

Chapter 40

Good-bye!

suitcase with things from Taiwan

AND THEN IT WAS THE LAST DAY. INSTEAD OF DOING anything fun, all we did was pack. It was very hectic packing all our things. I hadn't thought we had bought that much new stuff, but not everything fit in our suitcases, and Mom ran out to get another bag. And we had filled the extra suitcase we had used to bring gifts from the U.S., too.

There *was* a lot of new stuff. Every time we put something in, I kept thinking, *It's the last day. It's the last day.* We didn't want to forget anything. Everyone's projects from class, our name chops, our lucky money. Mom kept jamming in extra packs of seaweed and rice crackers. We all kept grabbing and packing food that we knew we couldn't get in New Hartford. Lissy bought ten tins of sour plum candy, and Ki-Ki took bags of white melon

tin of plum candy

candy. I didn't bring candy, but I did ask
Mom if we could go back to the bakery
for more pineapple cakes. She said yes,
and we rushed all the way there to get
them.

melon candy

Of course, there were lots of things we couldn't bring.
We couldn't pack our three goldfish. Those would have

goldfish looking

to stay behind, and they seemed to know
it. Whenever we passed the bowl, the
fish looked at us with big, reproachful
eyes.

And we couldn't bring back Aunt Bea
or Auntie Jin or Grandma or Grandpa, either. Somehow, going home made me feel sad. I was glad to be going back to
where everyone spoke English, where I could call Melody on
the phone, see Becky and Charlotte, and peek at Sam Mercer. And New Hartford had our comfortable white house
with the green shutters, clean wind, and trees that grew as
if they could hug the sky. But I'd also miss the stories Uncle
Flower told us, the hugs from Grandma and Grandpa, and
Auntie Jin's morning smile. I'd miss Taiwan's rich, thick air
full of food smells and the window we looked out of at night
to see the city lights brighten the sky like stars. New Hartford and the United States was still my homeland. But I had
gotten to feel at home in Taiwan.

I wondered if the ghosts felt that way, too. "Ghost Month

is ending," Auntie Jin said that night. "So soon there'll be no more burning things on the streets. The ghosts are going home."

Like us, I thought.

And then the next morning, Lissy, Ki-Ki, and I were wearing our pink over-all dresses again. They didn't fit that well. Lissy's was so short that she wore plaid shorts underneath. I felt like a too-full water balloon in mine, and Ki-Ki's had a button that kept popping open.

Lissy
wearing shorts
under her dress

Our suitcases closed, surprisingly, and stood behind us like a castle wall. We had to call for a special, extra-large

Grandma hugs
Mom good-bye

taxi. It was really a van, not a taxi. As it arrived, Grandma and Grandpa hugged and kissed us good-bye—a small silver tear, the size of the head of a pin, silently dropped from the corner of Grandma's eye onto Mom's shoulder. Aunt Bea, Auntie Jin, Aunt Yoko, Auntie Kim, Shogun, and Julian waved as the taxi pulled away, and we kept waving, turn-

ing around in our seats to see them through the back window.

"So are you happy to be going back?" Uncle Shin asked us. He and Uncle Flower were going to the airport with us.

"Yes and no," Lissy said.

"It's forever like that," Uncle Shin said. "For me, as soon as I am in Taiwan, I miss the United States. When I am in the U.S., I miss Taiwan."

"It's because we're both," I said, thinking about my name chop. America and Taiwan. English and Chinese. "We're mixed up."

"Uh-huh," Uncle Shin said. "But I wouldn't want it any other way. Would you?"

Would I want it any other way? Would I want to live in New Hartford and not know that peaches meant long life or the taste of a soup dumpling? Or to live in Taiwan and not know about Thanksgiving turkeys or what a real McDonald's hamburger was like?

"No," I said. "I'm happy this way."

The taxi arrived at the airport, and we pushed and pulled our luggage out and through the terminal. When we got to the part of the airport where Uncle Shin and Uncle Flower couldn't follow, there were good-byes all over again. This was the last good-bye. Mom sighed before she gave Uncle Shin and Uncle Flower a hug, and I thought I saw a tear, like a dropping pearl, fall from her eye. It was just like Grandma's when we said good-bye. Ghost Month was over, but I had learned that some ghosts never leave.

plastic bag

Uncle Flower shoved a tightly tied plastic bag at me. "Here," he said. "Don't open it until you are on the plane."

"What is it?" I asked.

"A good-bye present," he said. "Your Auntie Jin told me to give it to you."

Then he smiled, and he and Uncle Shin pushed us forward. As we walked away, we waved using our whole arms, as if we were saying good-bye to all of Taiwan, not just them. We turned the corner, and they disappeared from our sight. It was time to go.

On the airplane, Mom let me have the seat closest to the window first. "Since you asked first," Mom said. "But you have to share. In the middle of the flight, you and Lissy can switch."

"We're going to be flying forever! Ugh!" Lissy grumbled. "I don't mind being home or being in Taiwan—it's getting there that I don't like."

Uncle Flower and Uncle Shin waving good-bye

258

The flight attendant began to give the talk on airplane safety. We all watched in silence, even though it was in Chinese. She gave it again in English, and we still said nothing. I felt that all of us, even Ki-Ki, were thinking about how our month in Taiwan was now ending.

The airplane began to move. Faster and faster, the landscape blurred. Then, as if the airplane were taking a deep breath, we were up in the air.

"Are you sad?" I asked Mom.

"No," she said. "Well, a little."

I was, too. I wished I could think of something to say. I pulled at my bright pink dress and thought about how we were pink birds again, this time flying home. What had Dad said about traveling, so long ago? "You take something with you, you leave something behind, and you are forever changed," he had said. "That is a good trip."

Our trip to Taiwan had been a good trip, then. We were taking a whole extra suitcase of things with us, and we had left our gifts to Grandma and our goldfish behind. But was I forever changed? In my painting, there were pink birds on bamboo with a chop mark that said "forever." I was one of the pink birds, and I had wished on the bamboo to like Taiwan. It had happened. My changed feelings for Taiwan would be forever.

I thought about the fortune-teller who had given me her blessing. She had said her blessing would help me and make me happy. Mom had said it was a lot of nonsense, but I was

259

glad she had blessed me. Maybe it was her blessing that helped me live with my ghosts and find my identity. Maybe it was her blessing that helped me like Taiwan and Taiwan like me. I kicked at the bags at my feet.

"What's that bag?" Mom said, pointing at the tightly wrapped plastic bag.

"I don't know," I said. "Uncle Flower gave it to me. He said it was a good-bye gift and not to open it until I was on the plane."

"Well, open it!" Lissy said.

I untied the plastic bag and took out a large Chinese food container with a pair of chopsticks taped to it. The container was still warm, and the heat spread to my lap. I took off the chopsticks and opened the flaps, and inside were . . .

DUMPLINGS!

We all laughed.

"The summer, all those days in Taiwan — it was fun, wasn't it?" Mom asked.

"Yes," I said, nodding. This time, Mom's idea of fun was exactly the same as mine. "It was."

all the different dumplings I had in Taiwan

xiaolongbao
(soup dumplings)

xia jiao
(shrimp dumplings)

shaomai
(pork dumplings)

gyoza
(Japanese dumplings)

qu han jiao er tang
(Chinese dumpling
soup)

jiaozi
(Chinese
dumplings)

mochi
(Japanese dessert
dumplings)

261